WELCOME TO THE JUNGLE

BAEN BOOKS by JOHN RINGO

SHADOW'S PATH
Not That Kind of Good Guy
Welcome to the Jungle (with Casey Moores)

TRANSDIMENSIONAL HUNTER (with Lydia Sherrer)
Into the Real • *Through the Storm* • *Behind the Veil*
Beyond the Rift (forthcoming)

PEGASUS LANDING (with James Aidee)
Beyond the Ranges

BLACK TIDE RISING
Under a Graveyard Sky • *To Sail a Darkling Sea* • *Islands of Rage and Hope*
Strands of Sorrow • *The Valley of Shadows* (with Mike Massa)
Black Tide Rising (edited with Gary Poole)
Voices of the Fall (edited with Gary Poole)
River of Night (with Mike Massa • *We Shall Rise* (edited with Gary Poole)
United We Stand (edited with Gary Poole)

TROY RISING
Live Free or Die • *Citadel* • *The Hot Gate*

LEGACY OF THE ALDENATA
A Hymn Before Battle • *Gust Front* • *When the Devil Dances*
Hell's Faire • *The Hero* (with Michael Z. Williamson)
Cally's War (with Julie Cochrane)
Watch on the Rhine (with Tom Kratman)
Sister Time (with Julie Cochrane) • *Yellow Eyes* (with Tom Kratman)
Honor of the Clan (with Julie Cochrane) • *Eye of the Storm*

COUNCIL WARS
There Will Be Dragons • *Emerald Sea*
Against the Tide • *East of the Sun, West of the Moon*

INTO THE LOOKING GLASS
Into the Looking Glass • *Vorpal Blade* (with Travis S. Taylor)
Manxome Foe (with Travis S. Taylor) • *Claws that Catch* (with Travis S. Taylor)

EMPIRE OF MAN (with David Weber)
March Upcountry • *March to the Sea* • *March to the Stars* • *We Few*

SPECIAL CIRCUMSTANCES
Princess of Wands • *Queen of Wands*

PALADIN OF SHADOWS
Ghost • *Kildar* • *Choosers of the Slain* • *Unto the Breach*
A Deeper Blue • *Tiger by the Tail* (with Ryan Sear)

STANDALONE TITLES
The Last Centurion • *Citizens* (edited with Brian M. Thomsen)

To purchase any of these titles in e-book form, please go to www.baen.com

WELCOME TO THE JUNGLE

JOHN RINGO

with CASEY MOORES

A Baen Books Original

Baen Publishing Enterprises
P.O. Box 1403
Riverdale, NY 10471
www.baen.com

ISBN: 978-1-6680-7289-9

Cover art by Sam R. Kennedy

First printing, October 2025

Distributed by Simon & Schuster
1230 Avenue of the Americas
New York, NY 10020

Library of Congress Cataloging-in-Publication Data

Names: Ringo, John, 1963- author
Title: Welcome to the jungle / John Ringo.
Description: Riverdale, NY : Baen Publishing Enterprises, 2025. | Series:
  Shadow's path ; 2
Identifiers: LCCN 2025035080 (print) | LCCN 2025035081 (ebook) | ISBN
  9781668072899 hardcover | ISBN 9781964856377 ebook
Subjects: BISAC: FICTION / Science Fiction / Action & Adventure | FICTION
/
  Science Fiction / Crime & Mystery | LCGFT: Science fiction | Fantasy
  fiction | Superhero fiction | Novels | Fiction
Classification: LCC PS3568.I577 W45 2025 (print) | LCC PS3568.I577
  (ebook)
LC record available at https://lccn.loc.gov/2025035080
LC ebook record available at https://lccn.loc.gov/2025035081

Printed in the United States of America

10 9 8 7 6 5 4 3 2 1

As always
For Captain Tamara Long, USAF
Born: May 12, 1979
Died: March 23, 2003, Afghanistan
You fly with the angels now.

CHAPTER 1

"Welcome to the Jungle" —Guns N' Roses

"Hi," Mike said. The six-foot-tall—as of a recent growth spurt—brown-haired, light-blue-eyed thirteen-year-old held up his Common Access Card, or "CAC." "Michael James Truesdale. I need a temporary visitor badge for my counsel, Derrick Sterrenhunt."

He'd had a lot of different names in his time, and still did depending on the setting, but his most public name was courtesy of the US Marshals.

The lobby of the Jacob K. Javits Federal Building was, as usual, bustling with activity. There was a long line out front of people waiting to get in to see ICE. When Mike had contacted Super Corps, Tony DiAngelo told him to just use the front entrance.

The building's two-story foyer was expansive compared to the constrictive, claustrophobic feel he now got in most of the city. Of course, *that* was a feeling he'd never really experienced in New York before. But that already felt like a lifetime ago.

Even though he hadn't been away all that long in the grand scheme, there was still a tremendous culture shock returning to darkest New York City after his time in Montana Big Country. Mere days prior, he'd been camping in the open. By "camping," he meant learning Lakota-style survival from his father. It had been as far from civilization as one could get, and now he was back in what some might call the paragon city of western civilization.

"Sternoot?" the access manager said, looking at her screen. She was in a heavy-duty bulletproof glass enclosure. "I see a visit from a Michael Truesdale to Super Corps, but the designated adult is S-T-E—"

"It's pronounced Stern-hoont," Mike said while looking at the big man beside him and nodding toward the counter. "It's spelled weird."

Counselor Sterrenhunt produced his Montana driver's license, which was duly scanned.

Derrick Sterrenhunt was still a little taller than Mike but with much broader shoulders, black hair cut short and graying a bit, blue eyes, high cheekbones and forehead, and an erect carriage that screamed former military. More about his look and moves, a robotic walk that at the same time was graceful like a panther, screamed former operator. Which he was.

Nicknamed "Hunter," he'd spent his military career in the Combat Activities Group and ended it as a command sergeant major in Joint Special Operations Command.

Beyond all that, he was Mike's biological father. Though Mike had feared the man might just as soon have told him to pound sand, he'd taken Mike at his word—but verified it with a DNA test. Their relationship proven, Derrick hadn't hesitated to welcome Mike into the family. And it was quite the ginormous family for one to spontaneously join.

"Okay," the receptionist said, her eyes still narrowed as if annoyed. "Counselor. Temporary visitor's badge. You have to have an escort."

"I don't count?" Mike asked.

"No," the receptionist said curtly. "It should be just a moment."

Mike led Derrick back into the lobby and gestured around.

"My digs," he said.

"You own the whole thing?" Derrick said. Whether his father was joking, curious, or indifferent, Mike had no idea. His father was far more difficult to read than the average boulder. Of course, as an Earther, Mike had gotten particularly adept at reading your average boulder—especially after his time spent at Pirate Bill's Rock Emporium off US 2 outside of Kalispell, Montana.

"I do, as a matter of fact," Mike said. "This is *my* building."

He was checking it out under his longer-range Earth Sight. Pretty much the same as the last time he'd been here. He could see all the way to Super Corps headquarters and recognized their "escort." He couldn't help but smile.

When Mike's originally assigned Super Corps handler—for lack of a better term—walked through the security doors, he grinned and raised his hands dramatically.

"Alexander of Alexandria!" Mike boomed in his fruitiest voice. "I *greet* thee!"

Alexander couldn't help but laugh. They shook hands and back-slapped.

Alexander Thompson was a six-foot-four slender black man in his twenties, and was turned out as always in dress slacks, neatly cropped hair, and a Super Corps polo shirt.

During his previous tenure in New York, Mike had found out that the guy was nice but *so* indoctrinated into what Mike knew were Society memetics. He also had found out Alexander was a comic book nerd who was super into the Corps in general and the costumes in particular. Mike was surprised to find out, from others, that he'd gone to Duke on a basketball scholarship, which said words about his skill with hoops.

"The Prodigal returns," Mike said, smiling. "I hope that the fatted calf has been slaughtered in my honor. I told you I'd be back! I told you!"

"You did," Alexander said, nodding and looking at Counselor Sterrenhunt.

"Alexander of Alexandria, may I present the right honorable Derrick of the Sterrenhunt clan? Father, Alexander. Alexander, Counselor Sterrenhunt."

"Counselor," Alexander said, shaking hands. "Alexander Thompson, deputy administration officer. Honored to meet you. Welcome."

"Thank you," Derrick said.

"So . . ." Alexander said, looking back and forth. "Wow. Mike, you've . . . changed a *lot*. I hardly recognize you. Same scar. Weird."

"I think this is what I'm supposed to look like," Mike said, waving at his face. He'd hardly noticed his face slowly morphing until he pulled out his old ID and compared it in the mirror. His cheekbones were higher and his chin sharper than it had been.

Much of his face had been reconstructed after a particularly bad beatdown when he was eight. Since the doctors didn't know what he was supposed to look like, they did their best job. Regenerative healing was morphing his face to what it *should* be, which turned out to be a lot like his father's.

"Well, don't want to keep Mr. DiAngelo waiting," Alexander said, gesturing to the door. "This way."

"Mine still work?" Mike asked, waving his card.

"No," Alexander said. "We locked you out when you took off. Nothing against you, just protocol."

"I can't believe you left me out in the cold," Mike said, sniffing theatrically. "Left me to the fate of this cruel, cruel world."

"While we had half the DOJ and DHS looking for you," Alexander said as they walked in the secure area. "And marshals. The marshals were sort of put out they couldn't find you."

"Don't go anywhere they expect you to go," Mike said. Truth be told, Mike could only consider himself extremely lucky to receive the reception he'd gotten—seeing as he'd disappeared without word to take care of some "business" before tracking down his father.

They proceeded to the elevator, then up to sixteen. Mike showed his badge to the marshal door gargoyle and received a nod.

"Miri!" Mike said as they entered the lobby.

"Mike," Mr. DiAngelo's fortysomething brunette executive assistant said from her desk on the other side of the lobby. "Welcome back."

The lobby of the Super Corps New York office was a little nicer than most such government buildings. Two stories in height, it was about four thousand square feet with decorative marble pillars, a marble floor with the Super Corps emblem on it, wood-paneled walls, and potted plants in selective corners. Directly opposite the entrance was the "flyer exit," a sliding glass door that led to a small runway for flyers to take off on their patrols.

Pretty much the entire sixteenth floor of the Javits Building was devoted to the Corps despite the fact there were only about a hundred total supers who worked there, and most were out on patrols.

The federal government did not stint when it came to convincing their Supers that they wanted to be part of the team.

"Does the prodigal get a hug?" Mike asked.

"The prodigal does, yes," Miri said, hugging him. "Despite all the furor. The reason for the prodigality is a valid excuse. Counselor," she added, nodding at Derrick.

"Ms. Jones," Derrick said, nodding.

"You have a last name?" Mike said, his eyes wide. "I thought you just had one name!"

"Mr. DiAngelo is waiting," Miri said, smiling and gesturing at the door. The nameplate beside it read ANTHONY DI ANGELO, CHIEF OF SUPER CORPS, NEW YORK OFFICE. Absent was his other title, Italian Falcon.

"I'll wait to show you around," Alexander said. "Kevin insists on seeing you."

"And I insist on seeing Kevin," Mike said as the door unlocked. There was a muffled "Come on!" from the other side.

"Falcone!" Mike said, holding his arms up again. "I told you I'd be back!"

"So you did, kid," Italian Falcon said, shaking his head in comically feigned disgust and waving at the chairs. Falcon was five foot eight with broad shoulders, a burly look, brown hair and eyes. He had retained a thick Staten Island accent. "Mr. Sterrenhunt, I'd shake your hand, but you probably want to keep it."

He looked the two of them over and shook his head.

"You've changed your look," he said to Mike, frowning.

"Told you most of this was reconstructed," Mike said, circling a finger around his face.

"You two even have the same scar," Falcon said, nodding. He shrugged and turned his attention to Derrick. "So, Counselor Sterrenhunt, welcome to Super Corps. I'm Anthony DiAngelo, Italian Falcon, invulnerable flyer and office chief for New York Super Corps."

"Yes, sir," Derrick said. He settled into his characteristic expressionless stone face, though his eyes still took in everything—always scanning, assessing, calculating, and judging. Even Mike, a kid genius with superpowers, couldn't help but wonder what his father thought of him.

Tony motioned to the guest chairs and took a seat at his desk. Mike casually took in the office's impressive view of Tribeca. Looking out across the city, he realized he hadn't really developed *claustrophobia* in New York City, it was just that his innate paranoia had returned. This city had eyes everywhere, many of them attached to nefarious people. His deeply ingrained anxiety, his apprehension and distrust in everyone around him had relaxed—for the first time in his life—substantially in Montana. Not only had there been far fewer people and a distinct lack of gangs, criminals, and Society members who wished him dead, but he'd spent most of the time among family.

He'd gone from exactly zero family—after Miss Cherise had been murdered—to a huge family: grandparents, aunts, uncles, cousins... several gorgeous and brilliant cousins, in fact. Stepping into the strange new world of a large family had been far more disorienting than Acquiring superpowers.

"I will say officially and formally I'm glad this kid is somebody *else's* problem," Tony said, snapping Mike back into the room. Tony grinned to relieve the offense. "Half the time I didn't know whether to strangle him or try to adopt him. But you've got a good kid there. He's got a good heart. Crazy. But a good heart. So, how are you settling in?"

"We're not precisely settling," Derrick said, sitting ramrod straight. "I wanted to discuss that with you personally."

"Oh?" Tony said, leaning back. "Not...settling in? I heard you hadn't taken the moving package."

"Mike will be completing his mandatory community service," Derrick said, "as well as additional time. However..."

"They're making me go to college," Mike said, his face long. "I got my GED when I was in Montana."

"Oh," Tony said, perking up. "Congratulations on convincing him."

"It wasn't as hard as you'd think," Derrick said. "My entire family homeschools, and early entry is sort of normal. Also, he probably won't be going to college in New York."

"Oh?" Tony said. He gestured at the window. "We've got some great colleges here in the city."

"And as Mike Truesdale I'm not canceled," Mike said, tugging his ear. "But...I'd feel more at home at a different college. A bunch of my family and their friends have gone to Osseo in Michigan. It sort of caters to homeschoolers."

"I've heard of it," Tony said, his brow furrowing. "I didn't realize you were that..."

"Conservative?" Mike said shrugging. "I'm not. It's just I think Osseo will be a better fit than Columbia. Anyway, I'll be here through the mandatory time plus into the summer. We plan on going back to Montana for a good bit of that. I'm also required to study traditional culture and techniques. I learned to build a fire with two sticks!"

"You did, huh?" Tony said, smiling.

"I went easy on him," Derrick said.

"I tried to get your military service record," Tony said. "They told me to take a hike. What I *did* get was mostly redacted and that was enough. Jeez, Sergeant Major! *Fourteen* Bronze Stars? Fourteen."

"They exaggerate," Derrick said with the slightest tilt of his head.

"Riiight," Falcon said slowly. The two men stared at each other for a few uncomfortable seconds.

"There's a couple more points we need to hit," Mike said. "There's something I need to talk to you about, out of school, if you agree. The Secretary can be read in but that's it."

"Okay," Falcon said, his brow furrowing again.

"I also was able to establish who my biological mother was," Mike said. "She is deceased."

"Sorry to hear that, Mike," Falcon said with genuine sympathy. After a moment, he frowned. "How'd you find them at all? We did look on DNA stuff."

"Yeah," Mike said, nodding. "And I appreciate that. You remember when youse guys got Mama's phone from the marshals to pass to me?"

Whenever Mike was talking with someone, he tended to take on their accent. When he talked with Falcon, he'd slowly start to sound like he was "bridges and tunnels" in the local lingo.

"Yeah," Tony said.

"My friend at Baltimore PD said that the one thing the street ladies would say is she wanted me to have her phone when she died," Mike said. "Which was sort of weird and didn't make any sense. But then when I looked through it, 'cause I had the open code, it was mostly all the same stuff. Lots of selfies of Mama..."

He paused at that point, but not for dramatic effect. Miss Cherise had been the closest person he'd had to a real mother growing up and it still hurt. He distracted himself by stretching his Sight out and around to somewhat lazily check on the goings-on elsewhere in the building. The first time he'd been in this office, he'd academically known Sight was possible but hadn't any concept of how it worked.

He visually scanned down to look through the windows of the gym across the street, where Mike had once strained to search for the beautifully athletic bodies of spandex-clad young women working out. However, now he instinctively examined their bone structure with Sight rather than drinking in their curves. He really had changed more than he realized.

"I'm sorry she, uh, didn't get buried," Tony said, frowning. "We were looking at, uh . . ."

"Oh, I got her buried," Mike said, waving his hand. "I got some people to contribute. Sort of a crowdfund thing. What with MS-13 not liking me very much, I didn't attend the service. But she got buried."

"Glad to hear that," Tony said, nodding. "I know she was important to you."

"Yeah," Mike said then perked up. "But I've got, like, forty relatives now, so . . . Moving on. There was one photo that stood out on Mama's phone. It was completely different than the rest. Can I use your plasma?"

"Sure," Tony said. He hit a couple of buttons, and a wooden panel retracted to reveal a large flat-screen TV.

Derrick had questioned the wisdom of sharing the information with Tony or even discussing their plans regarding the inheritance this soon, but Mike had vouched for Tony's trustworthiness. It said a lot that Derrick already trusted Mike's judgment. Mike had spent most of his life with almost no one to trust, but now he seemed to have an abundance. It was an even stranger feeling than suddenly having a family.

Mike linked in and brought up the photo. It was of a couple sitting at a table at what was obviously a formal event. A younger Counselor Sterrenhunt was wearing a dinner jacket seated next to a petite blonde in a low-cut dress with a sweater on her shoulders.

"This was what I had," Mike said. "And I had to wonder who those people were. It was out of place with the other photos. The photo had a metatag on it that listed it as 'Master Sergeant Sterrenhunt and plus-one Anna.' You recognize the woman?"

"No," Tony said, shaking his head. "Pretty. That your bio mom?"

"Yes," Mike said.

"At this point, proven by DNA," Counselor Sterrenhunt said.

"Okay," Tony said.

"It was about a one-day news item," Mike said, bringing up a cropped version of the photo. "When it hit the news, I was here in New York and saw this photo. So, when I saw the full photo, I recognized her right away."

He pulled up a banner headline from the *New York Post* with the same photo in it.

REMAINS OF DEAD HEIRESS MISSING!

"Oh, shit," Tony said, putting his hand over his mouth. "I remember this story. *That's* your bio mom?"

"Yes," Mike said.

"She's worth, like, a billion dollars!" Tony said, looking at them.

"Yes," Mike replied. "I don't think I got left in an alleyway. No way Mama had that photo on her phone if she didn't know who my mother was."

"That makes sense," Tony said, frowning. "And that's the one where the chief of security ended up in the East River."

"Yes," Mike said.

"There's a lot hinky about those guys," Tony said. "Follett, right?"

"Yes," Mike said.

"And you're going to try to get a piece of it."

"Yes."

"Yeah," Tony said, thoughtfully then chuckled. "Sorry for laughing, but I was starting to think 'This kid might be in a little danger.' Then I remembered."

"Right," Mike said, also chuckling.

Derrick gave a barely audible grunt and shifted.

"I sincerely doubt the Follett Trust would take direct action in the case of my son," Counselor Sterrenhunt said. "They'll probably try to just brand him a kook. Character assassination versus actual assassination. But I did drag my feet a touch on bringing Mike to New York. I made the excuse that there were personal matters to clean up in Montana—which was true. The personal matter, though, was establishing his claim by DNA testing.

"When Mike made the decision that he would like to bring suit to inherit, the issue was evidentiary DNA. With the remains in Philadelphia missing, that was an issue. We managed to find an old sample that had been kept from a juvenile arrest. It has been tested by a forensic lab I'd worked with before. Mike is, unquestionably, the son and sole living heir of Annabelle Follett—who, I might add, was the only person I slept with during the time when he would have been conceived."

"Right," Tony said, nodding.

"That photo," Mike said, gesturing at it. "It was taken by the Fort Myer Officers Club official photographer and is still up on Annabelle

Follett's Facebook memorial page. That one doesn't have the metatags. FB strips them as part of compressing the file. And that photo, cropped admittedly, showing Annabelle in the company of the person proven to be my biological father, is pretty hard evidence in itself. But I'm sure the Trust isn't just going to roll over."

Tony shrugged in agreement but also squinted one eye as the wheels visibly turned in his head.

"My life, my problem," Mike said, shrugging. "But that's going to be going on."

"Hopefully that's not going to cause too many problems," Tony said. "But it's your life."

"Secretary should be informed," Mike said. "There will be quiet questions from senators when Mike Truesdale, aka Stone Tactical, goes after a billion-dollar inheritance. I do not want to sideswipe her on that. Cannibale, yes. This, no."

"Thank you for that," Tony said. He took in the view and sat silent. After a moment, he turned back and brightened a little. "How was Montana?"

"Mountainous," Mike said, smiling. He sighed while looking out the window again. "I told Dr. Swanson that what I really needed was somewhere to heal. Somewhere where people weren't beating on me, psychologically or physically. Kalispell was a good place to heal. I'm in better shape, psychologically, than I think I've ever been in my life. Though it's incredibly *quiet*! No sirens! No traffic noise! It's weird. That took some getting used to."

"So, you're not going to be here permanently," Tony said.

"We anticipate being here most of the next six months," Derrick replied. "After that, decisions will have to be made."

"And while I may not be full time with the Corps," Mike said, "I do intend to be at the very least Corps Reserve. So, I'm not breaking with the Corps even over the suit. About which . . ."

"We need to not say nothing," Tony said, waving his hand dismissively. "And I almost broke that omerta."

"We've got a meeting with the attorneys handling the suit tomorrow," Derrick said with a glance at Mike.

"Where you at?" Tony said. "Where are you staying?"

"Rental condo in SoHo," Derrick said.

"Nice digs," Tony said.

"Fortunately, the reward money for Cannibale came through," Mike said. "'Cause otherwise that would have been tough. *Anywhere* in New York would have been tough for temporary housing."

"If we can get Mike into college, I'll probably be heading back to Montana," Derrick said. "I was recruited after I retired for various law firms with offices in New York and Washington. If I wanted to be in New York, I'd be in New York."

"Some people won't live anywhere else," Tony said, shrugging. "That's me. Some people think it's hell."

"Oh, I've lived in hell," Derrick said. "It's not hell. Just not my style."

Alexander led Mike and Derrick down the wide hallway leading to Kevin's expansive fitting room. Displayed on both sides were some of Kevin's proudest creations—the iconic California Girl outfit, Tony's original Italian Falcon costume, the matching outfits of power super couple Summer Storm and Bonfire, and more. Notably absent were the outfits of Electrobolt, currently incarcerated pending trial for sexual assault on both Jorge Camejo—Hombre de Poder—and Mike, aka Stone Tactical. The other more notable absence was the costume of Lieutenant Colonel James King, aka Major Freedom. But then, one wouldn't display the outfit of the man who'd become the Nebraska Killer.

The double doors at the end of the hallway flew open with a flourish.

"Kevin, dahling!" Mike said, holding out his arms for a hug.

The Designer clasped his hands to his face.

"My little Michelangelo's *David* is back!" Kevin squealed.

Kevin Winchard was about five foot six, with a sandy blond coif— the only word to use—that cascaded to his shoulders, and a well-preserved fifty or so courtesy of extensive but well-done plastic surgery. He was trailed by his invariably silent, gender-uncertain assistant, Maureen.

They hugged and did the side-kissy thing, and Kevin held him at arm's length.

"You've *grown*," Kevin said, professionally. "*And* your face has changed."

He stood back and looked at father and son.

"Yes, you're *definitely* becoming the little Native American brave,"

Kevin said, clasping his chest. "So handsome!" he added, looking at Derrick. "I *love* the erect carriage."

"Twenty-three years in the Army will do that," Derrick said.

"Even the same scar," Kevin said, waving at the left side of his face.

"Yes," Mike said. "If I may formally introduce: Counselor Derrick Sterrenhunt, The Designer, Kevin Winchard. Kevin, Counselor Sterrenhunt."

"Pleasure to meet you, sir," Kevin said, extending one languid hand.

"Likewise," Derrick said, shaking his hand. "Mike talked about you."

"All lies and vile calumnies, I'm sure," Kevin said, primly.

"Actually, he said you were the nicest guy he'd ever met," Derrick said. "Also, something about his first costume."

"We all have our little moments," Kevin said, wincing.

"I kept a copy," Mike said. "I showed it to him."

"You didn't!" Kevin said, grimacing. "In retrospect..."

"Every genius has that moment, Kevin," Mike said. "Have you ever seen Fabergé's spider brooch? It's *hideous*."

"So, I don't know anything about you, sir," Kevin said, turning to Derrick. "Just that Mike had found his biological father in *Montana* of all places! And that he was an attorney. No one mentioned military."

"Twenty-three years Army special operations," Derrick said.

"Delta Force," Mike whispered from behind his hand.

"Oh, my!" Kevin said with dramatically wary eyes and chin tucked to the side. "Well, *that* explains a few things! Michael, we're going to have to refit you for your formal costume. I'd barely gotten the first one done when you *disappeared* on me! You shameless, *naughty* boy!"

"I was looking for my father," Mike said with a shrug. "And I'm not sure when I'd wear it."

"I was *hoping* you'd be wearing it for the press conference for capturing Cannibale," Kevin said. "But they didn't even trot you out. There will be a time. But we do need to get you remeasured. You had a growth spurt."

"I did, yes," Mike said.

"So, we'll have to schedule it," Kevin said. "No time today."

"My schedule hasn't been fixed, yet," Mike said. "I took the GED when I was in Montana, so I'm done with primary schooling. And I've been convinced to go to college but probably not 'til next fall."

"Oh, excellent," Kevin said. "Columbia?"

"Probably not," Mike said. "It'll probably be out of New York. But I'll be back from time to time to do Juniors. Just . . . there are things. Right now, we've got some scheduled meetings. But it'll be easier to fit it in the schedule without having to arrange around school. And I'm done with that."

CHAPTER 2

"Lions" —Skillet

"Good to see you again, Derrick," the counselor said, shaking Derrick's hand as they were dropped off at his office by a secretary. "Long time."

Counselor Wilder Perrin Kennedy was six foot one and probably about 160 pounds, with soft brown eyes and flaming red hair. He was dressed in a striped dress shirt with his sleeves rolled up and there was a nice suitcoat hanging on a rack.

The offices of Adams, Walker, Brauer, Bergman and Bhatt were tucked away in a late 1800s six-story stone commercial building off Remsen Street in Brooklyn. It was flanked on either side by much larger, taller, and newer business buildings. Wilder's fairly small office had a charming view of the building across Remsen Street, another older commercial building that was being renovated.

"And you must be the putative heir," Wilder said. "Call me Wilder. Grab a chair."

Mike gauged there was a good deal of nervous energy hidden behind Wilder's casual demeanor. That was easily explained by the crazy stupid amount of money involved as well as the forces arrayed against them. In the end, Mike had to give the counselor credit for maintaining a relaxed, confident façade.

"Can I get you anything?" a bright-eyed, boy-faced assistant asked. "Water, coffee, anything?"

Both Mike and Derrick shook their heads, and Wilder politely waved him off. Using Sight, however, Mike knew the assistant took up a position a few feet outside the door, no doubt to rush in if anyone suddenly needed anything.

"So," he continued when the three of them were situated. "Based on what you sent me, Derrick, this *should* be an open-and-shut case. We've got a positive evidentiary DNA match, your statement as an officer of the court that Annabelle Follett was the only woman with whom you had sexual relations during that time frame, your proven DNA familial relationship to the plaintiff, which has already been accepted by the State of New York for paternity, *and* a photo of you with Annabelle Follett, taken by a professional military photographer during the time frame that Mike would have been conceived.

"The only argument is that there is *too* much weight of evidence," Wilder said. "So, it should be open and shut. Should."

"Should," Mike said. The Society was guaranteed to use every dirty trick conceived by man to eliminate that "should." Mike was well aware of the difficulties they'd face in wrangling his inheritance from the large and powerful claws of the Society, but he was curious to hear the counselor's thoughts on the legal aspects.

"After you contacted me about this, I did some research," Wilder said, "including speaking to one of the name partners about it. All I said was that I had a potential client who was looking at suing the Follett Trust. For privilege reasons couldn't get into why. I will say that Mr. Brauer was enthusiastic about a suit. He's tied in much more tightly than I am with the general ebb and flow of the complex power dynamics in this town. He referred to the Follett Trust in scatological terms I will not repeat."

Wilder pursed his lips, narrowed his eyes, and looked to the side in a moment of contemplation.

"Then there's the matter of the missing remains," Wilder said, drily. "And I'm not sure if you've kept up with this, but the chief of security of the Trust was found in the East River not too long back."

"I was here when that happened," Mike said. "I do recall, yes."

I do recall helping to beat the rapist, murdering son of a whore to death.

"All in all, we're dealing with some very squirrelly individuals," Counselor Kennedy said. "Which shouldn't matter in court, but it may. The Trust is tightly connected to New York politics and has been for quite some time, so I'm expecting headwinds on this one."

"I'm expecting the roof to fall in and the towers to crumble," Mike said. "These guys are beyond squirrelly. From the point that we file, there is no such thing as privilege. There is no such thing as private. Expect every dirty trick that you've ever heard of and then some. They'll try to bug your home. They'll try to bug these offices. They'll be trying to pay off your staff for inside intel. Don't be surprised if they come at you or your family. They'll try to buy me off with a settlement of some sort. A harassment payout. Not going to happen."

He didn't mention that he'd already tried to hack the law firm's servers and found them remarkably well defended. Not so defended he couldn't get through, but the Society's hackers weren't as good as Gondola trained. Gondola, led by the mysterious "Faerie Queen," was the secretive network of hackers who ran counter to the Society's sinister global plotting. The Faerie Queen had recruited Mike at age eight after he'd semi-accidentally accessed one of their minor servers.

Mike did a quick scan through the building's goings-on in Sight, trying to gauge the overall culture and professionalism of the office through any available indicators. Outside of the assistant outside hitting on a female clerk across the way, there wasn't any of the outright sex or drug use as he could generally find in abundance in just about every single building in New York. So that was a plus.

"Do you have some information about the Trust I might not have?" Wilder said, curiously.

Mike looked over at Derrick and sighed. His father, for the most part, remained as still as a statue during the discussion outside of his cold, calculating eyes taking everything in.

"I growed up on the street," Mike said, his accent changing slightly. "Talked to a fella one time about a life of crime. I'd planned on being a career professional thief at one point. Wanted to know the dos and don'ts."

"He told me first thing was, you get popped don't tell the poh-leese shit," Mike said, smiling. "Fifth Amendment the one right nobody can take away. All it takes is keep your mouth shut 'til you can get advice of counsel."

"Good advice," Wilder said.

"Second thing he told me," Mike said. "You get in with your attorney, you tell him absolutely everything. Don't hold nothin' back. And be honest—the truth, the whole truth, and nothing but the truth."

"Also good advice," Wilder said, though he narrowed a calculating eye as he waited for the "but."

"In this case, let's say that I'm reading the same tea leaves you are," Mike said. "Anything I know other than what is publicly available... we'll just set to the side 'cause why would a kid know more?

"But I'll warn you, definitively," Mike said, "this is not going to be easy. It's a billion dollars. That right there says it's not going to be easy. But it's going to be worse than that. Expect the judge to be biased. Might as well say bought. Expect them to throw every high-priced lawyer in New York at it. They'll be investigating us. They'll be investigating you. They'll be investigating this firm. They'll try to find some way to buy you. Suborn you. Blackmail if you've got anything they can blackmail you with. They'll go to disbarment if they can find an edge. They're going to try like hell to bury you and bury this suit. Guaranteed."

Mike gestured at the surroundings and frowned slightly. One thing he had determined about the building was that it really was as old as it was purported to be. While the foundation was still surprisingly robust and there had definitely been more than a few remodels, there were some sections of stone here and there that were going to cause problems within the next decade.

"I do not want this to come across as an insult, sir..." Mike said, cautiously.

Wilder grinned.

"I know what you're going to say," the attorney said, smiling. "Are we a firm that can handle this? Don't judge on the basis of the building. This firm has been in business for a *very* long time. The reason we're in this building was the firm *built* it in 1886. The firm has been in business since 1860 and its lineage traces back further. We're one of those very quiet, very powerful firms here in the City.

"As to the blackmail and disbarment," Wilder said, shrugging and looking around. "I'm one of those straight-arrow lawyers. I honestly cannot figure out any way that someone could do that to me."

"Then stay that way," Mike said. "If we're in the middle of this and some pretty lady starts chatting you up somewhere, don't think it's due to your rugged good looks."

"I doubt they're going to go that far," Wilder said, smiling.

"Don't doubt it," Derrick said. "I agree with everything Mike said. Expect honey traps. That goes for anyone in your firm. Expect attacks from odd angles. Expect blackmail and even direct action. This is *not* going to be easy. But when it's over, you'll have a new billion-dollar client."

"Which would be nice," Wilder said, nodding. "Okay, I'll keep that firmly in mind. I will," he added, nodding at Derrick. "You chose not to use the law firm that is handling the sexual harassment suit?"

"They're too close to Fieldstone Holdings, which is, in turn, too close to the Trust," Mike said. "Also, they're dragging the negotiations intentionally. The Corps has more or less accepted fault. Not legally. They'll never do that. But they've accepted they're going to have to pay out. The question is how much."

On the other side of the door, the assistant slumped and moved back to the door. At a guess, he'd run out of clever things to say and thought he'd struck out. However, the woman's open posture with a tilted head and shoulders back ("tits out") actually indicated she was still interested.

"That firm took it on a light contingency," Mike continued. "Ten percent of whatever we get plus they're going for usual and customary fees against the government. The longer they draw it out, the more meetings they have, the more motions they file, the more usual and customary they get at the end.

"I know that's a tactic and that it's considered a legitimate one by most law firms. But it pisses me off a bit. As long as that suit is ongoing, I'm in an ambiguous position with the Corps. And I'd rather be in a friendly position for long-term reasons. I'm the primary named plaintiff. I haven't even hinted that I'm annoyed, but I'm annoyed. That's another reason.

"I didn't mean any insult questioning the firm," Mike said, looking around again and furrowing his brow quizzically. "We didn't come here just because my father knew you. Your firm came highly recommended."

"Good to hear," Wilder said, nodding. "We're better than we look. That's in part deliberate; we are very quiet. And if it makes you feel any better, the only reason I took you on as a client was I knew your father and Mr. Brauer supported it. I had to unload some work to take it on.

"But I'm looking forward to this suit and I'm looking forward to having you as a client long term. But we do need to discuss the matter of fees."

"I got a million dollars for El Cannibale," Mike said. "Half of that had to go into an escrow account. Gary Coleman law. The other half is for support here in New York and the suit. And I've got the suit with the Corps. I'm the superior named plaintiff. I can accept where the Corps is at any time if I need more."

"True," Wilder said. "That's a good thing. Because despite the look of the building, we are *not* cheap . . ."

"So, our newest hopefully billionaire client," Brauer said, looking Mike over carefully.

Ahuvit Brauer was small, barely five foot five, and wiry with olive skin, blue eyes, and curly black hair gone almost entirely white. His office on the top floor of the building wasn't much nicer than Wilder's, though the leather furniture was nicer. The suit coat hanging in the corner was, if anything, a tad shabby. Certainly old and worn.

"You're an interesting character," Brauer added.

Brauer, Wilder, and Mike sat around a coffee table rather than Brauer's shiny mahogany desk. Mike had his suspicions as to why one of the senior partners wanted to meet him without his father present, but he kept those to himself. The senior partner was laid back and relaxed into his dark brown leather chesterfield chair. Meanwhile, Wilder was a little more wide-eyed and deferential than he'd been downstairs, and keeping a respectful upright posture.

"So are you," Mike said. He'd been examining him under Sight and the elderly lawyer's bones were worn in the same patterns as his father's. He'd jumped out of more than one airplane. And in the faint trace of earth in the soft tissues, Ahuvit looked to have nearly as many scars.

"God is building an army," the lawyer said.

Mike got a buzz on his phone at that moment.

"Pardon me," Mike said, pulling it out.

Ahuvit held up his hand to forestall Wilder as Mike checked his phone.

TA: B is Level One ally. Cleared for almost everything. Knows about Eisenberg. Was backup attorney if you got caught. W is cleared for general Society and Omega. Not cleared Eisenberg.

⊕ ⊕ ⊕

Mike put his phone away and nodded. Butch Eisenberg had been the owner of the *Gotham Herald* until he'd died of "natural causes." He'd also been a Dark Hand of the Society and high up on Gondola's list for elimination. Thus, when a need developed to distract the public from the Electrobolt sexual assault court case, they'd sent Mike in to deliver some "natural causes." The papers spent weeks mourning the death of such a "truly great man," and all but the most militant of trans protesters immediately forgot about the Electrobolt case.

As to Omega, it was the slightly more public name for Gondola. Contacts, for example, would interact with "Omega," while members knew they worked for "Gondola."

"God has an army," Mike said. "Israeli para. Shin Bet?"

"Mossad," Brauer said, nodding. "Good guess."

"One or the other," Mike said.

"How are our servers?" Brauer asked.

"Could be better," Mike said. "But my professional estimation is that the Society cannot penetrate them. Your guy is good. It would take one of the major nation-states or, well, us."

"Did you use the network's systems?" Brauer asked.

"No," Mike said. "My own. But it would take Omega training to penetrate. Or very high-level other. Every time the Society gets someone that good and they come to our attention, we just direct them to the Society's dirt files and they go 'Oh. I'm on the wrong side!' and flip. They've never kept anyone very good past that point."

"Interesting way to flip people," Brauer said.

"The Society sorts very carefully for people to be read in at high level," Mike said, "if for no other reason than people get sickened at what they see. Yes, you can get paralegals and attorneys and general staff, but even then they have to be very careful. I have no clue how many people like that have gotten the choppy-chop simply because they saw something above their level.

"If you show someone who is working for them the truth, and they are in a position to see enough information to know it's the truth, they generally flip in an instant."

While Mike was in the private meeting, he could tell Derrick was wandering through the building under the guise of looking for a restroom while actually gauging the building's physical security. Mike had done the same under Sight and judged it to be decent enough, but he had to grant that his former Delta father would probably pick up on a lot more deficiencies than he had.

"But unquestionably they're going to be going after your staff," Mike said. "You need to be careful about that. They need the Trust to stay in operation as is."

"Details?" Brauer asked. "If you're cleared to discuss. Wilder, this is above normal privilege if so."

"Yes, sir," Wilder said.

"Bit confused?" Brauer asked.

"Yes, sir." Mike could tell his anxiety level had also spiked, though he was doing a good job of settling himself.

"Stay that way. Is there a specific reason they want to keep the Trust in operation? Other than the obvious greed."

Mike thought about where to start and what to leave in and what to leave out.

"The Society mostly pays for buying elections and officials through black funds," Mike said. "Various other carrots. Notably the selection of the Trustees is an example. They're all connected to politicians."

"Right," Brauer said.

"But the straightforward illegal cash comes from their black accounts," Mike said. "They can only divert so much from white accounts into that. There are investors and audits, and embezzling enough to matter is tough. Most of the money comes from profits on their international child-trafficking arm."

"Right," Brauer said.

"Wait, wait..." Wilder said, a little exasperated. "Child what?"

Brauer and Mike both looked at him and he subsided.

"The Trust is a nice little piggy bank," Mike said. "There's no one except authorities they control to audit it. There's no beneficiary. And while their holdings of Fieldstone are public knowledge, there have been dividend payments going on for years with no increase in purchase of *any* public stock. Fieldstone, that's it, and they haven't bought any of *that* in five years. It's more than is necessary to support three houses even in New York. That's about five million a year, maximum, and there's been far more than that returned in dividends."

Someone had sent Wilder's assistant to track down Derrick, who was now entertaining himself by avoiding said young man and continuing his unescorted tour of the building. Mike had to fight to suppress a grin as it would be horribly out of place in the current discussion.

"There's two million one hundred and twenty-eight thousand shares of Fieldstone," Mike said. "Two hundred and twenty-three million, more or less in dividends. Eight years at five million per year for the properties including upkeep and taxes is forty million dollars. There's no indication that money has been reinvested. Where'd the other approximately one hundred and eighty million go?"

"Into the black accounts?" Brauer said.

"Bingo," Mike replied. "That, it turns out, is where *most* of it is going. That and into the pockets of the senior trustees.

"A few years ago, we had a head-to-head clash with the Society," Mike said. "Wasn't just a bump or a rub or a needle. We banged horns hard. Three years as of last Christmas. They stole a bunch of our money, then put it in their black accounts. We traced it and stole it all. Ours *and* theirs. It was *a lot* of money, and it was their black money that they use for buying politicians and elections.

"We've also been cutting into their child trafficking through rescues, which has reduced their margins."

Wilder's anxiety visibly transitioned to anger. One hand clenched into a fist, and he straightened as his muscles tensed.

"They'll need *at least* fifty-five billion dollars to buy the next Presidential election," Mike said. "Twenty-twenty's was fifty-two. With inflation it's probably going to be at least sixty. And *all* their candidates suck. It could go well into the sixties. They desperately need every dime they can scrounge up. Thus, they *cannot* afford to lose the money from the Trust.

"Then there's the fact that the Trust is so closely tied to that black money," Mike said. "They are *not* good at laundering, lemme tell ya. Not as good as they think. Once it becomes obvious the Trust has been robbed, good forensic accountants are going to be following it. At some point the FBI will probably take over, just to keep me from searching. But they can only sustain a cover-up investigation so long. At some point, I'll be hunting my money again.

"That could potentially lead right to the door of some of their skullduggery. Especially since Omega is going to be out on point feeding back what they've found. We generally stay out of sight and don't come into the light any more than the Society. But if I've got a suit and discovery going that's turning over rocks, hey, that's just some kid trying to regain his inheritance! And it will all be right out there in a court of law. And, at first glance, I'd prefer to *not* file suit here in New York. Too much Society influence. I'd like to wait until I'm unquestionably a resident of some less Society state with less influence on the federal courts."

Wilder leaned back at this in mild confusion. Ahuvit narrowed his eyes and pursed his lips but waited for Mike to continue.

"But this is where the fight is, and they're guaranteed to get overconfident fighting on what they think is their own turf. We'll just have to stay ahead of them."

Derrick had finally looped fully around to the break room where he'd started. He sat at a table drinking coffee as if he'd never left when the exasperated aide popped his head in.

"So, it's going to be all out there in the open every time there's a hearing or a filing. If they've been as stupid as it looks like they have, it's going to be hard for the authorities to ignore. And I'll be pumping every revelation to every media who will pay attention.

"The DOJ is mostly dirty but there's enough clean in there that at some point there potentially could be a *legitimate* grand jury investigation. An attempt to figure out what the hell is going on as opposed to a cover-up. The Society only succeeds by being in the dark. *That* would be *way* more sunlight than they'd like."

Ahuvit hadn't budged during Mike's diatribe. Wilder kept a strong poker face and looked relatively calm on the outside, but his minute nervous fidgeting was clear as day to someone who could literally see his bones. The junior counselor was finally starting to understand the proceedings really were sure to play out well beyond the courtroom.

"So, they are going to fight tooth and nail on this suit. They *need* the money and if there's a suit about the embezzlement, it could turn over *way* too many rocks. *That's* why it's going to get *very* strange."

"Pretty much the same brief I got," Brauer said. "I was sitting here thinking about how they could bump you off... Then I remembered."

"I'm a super," Mike said. "Pretty hard to kill. And I'm paranoid. When I eat or drink anything that isn't sealed or I've prepared I always test it. I also have a filed will leaving everything to my father and if we co-decease it all goes to the various large clan. No point to lethal action. But if Wilder's going to be in a hearing, we need to make sure his coffee isn't spiked with LSD. This is the Society we're talking about. MK Ultra is alive and well."

Wilder's fidgeting picked up another notch. His knee was twitching, and he was now grinding his teeth as well.

"True," Brauer said, nodding. "And we'll do everything possible to make sure Wilder is okay as well as the staff."

"The other problem is the judge," Mike said. "For a variety of reasons, the Society owns most of the judges on the Supreme Court of New York."

The Supreme Court in New York was not the highest authority court. It was the New York term for what in most states was called a circuit court.

"The sole clean judge is Judge Eizenstat," Mike said. "If we bring it directly to Judge Eizenstat, he'll have a perfectly natural heart attack or die by self-inflicted gunshot wound."

"They'll go that far?" Brauer said, his tone impassive rather than surprised.

"They'll go that far," Mike said. "Definitely. Since we don't want to get the good judge killed over this, we'll need to hand carry it to another judge, lest it get randomly passed to Eizenstat. The preferred judge is Mickelson."

"I wouldn't trust Judge Mickelson as far as I could throw this building," Brauer said.

"Neither would I," Mike said. "Work with me. Have Mr. Wilder take it to Judge Mickelson."

"Can I have more than 'work with me'?" Brauer said.

"We've got *kompromat* on *all* the judges," Mike said. "But we've got the strongest on Mickelson. So does the Society, don't get me wrong. But at a certain point I *will* end up inheriting. 'What could I do, it was an open-and-shut case!' Shortly after that he'll retire. Or, possibly, suffer a fatal heart attack if they get angry enough about it. Or if they find out he threw the case. But he'll go along."

"I'm not hearing any of this," Wilder said, shrugging and shaking his head. "What part of 'I'm a straight-arrow guy' was unclear?"

"Welcome to the bigs, kid," Brauer said, waving his hand as if raising a glass. "When you're working in a town this bent, sometimes the arrow has to fly around corners."

"Going to need a good accounting firm at some point," Mike said. "It's going to be serious forensics."

"I know people," Brauer said, drily. "Israeli. Very good at that sort of thing."

"Oh, *those* guys?" Mike said. "I know nothing."

"I've heard you're pretty good at finance as well," Brauer said.

"I can hum the tune," Mike replied.

"Well, this has been fun," Mr. Brauer said, clapping his hands. "What's life without challenges, eh? We need to do dinner some time. Do you golf?"

"I do," Mike said. "But I generally let my father do my golfing for me. I'm lazy that way."

CHAPTER 3

"When You're Evil" —Aurelio Voltaire

"You never call me with good news, Dion," Wesley Conn said. He was tall, handsome, and still remarkably fit for a fifty-year-old man. In the small video in the corner of his screen, he noticed there were a few new strands of gray in his otherwise thick black hair.

On the other side of the video call, Dion Bafundo was five foot nine and a chubby 220 pounds. He had denim-blue eyes, thinning blond hair, and a baby face that was entirely lacking in guile. As the corporate counsel for the Follett Trust, Conn knew he was fully aware of the depths of corruption associated with it and happily participated.

The office in Dion's background was simpler, more modern, and more utilitarian than Conn's. Wesley had a wealthier, more classic-looking office filled with pictures, memorabilia, and what were essentially trophies from his greater successes in business and "elsewhere."

"Oh, this is about as bad as it gets, Wesley," Bafundo said, smiling broadly. "Why's it always Friday afternoon when I'm headed out the door when I get these emails?"

"Then why are you smiling?" Conn said.

"Because it's that or jump out the window," Dion said. "We have an heir!"

"Bullshit," Conn said, shaking his head and smugly leaning back. "If you're talking about Annabelle, she had an abortion. If you're talking about Dela . . . unlikely. And if you're talking about Lukessi, he knows better than to try."

"The abortion apparently didn't take," Dion said. "I have the filing with the court right here in my hand. Just delivered, practically after working hours. One Michael Truesdale, formerly a resident of Schenectady. Raised in foster care. Mr. Truesdale recently reunited with his biological father—proven by DNA—one Counselor Derrick Sterrenhunt of Kalispell, Montana. All sorts of things about his father's heroic military record included—"

"Heroic military record?" Conn said.

"I'm thinking this guy was Delta," Dion said, shrugging. "Lots of fruit salad mentioned and he retired as command sergeant major of Joint Special Operations Command."

"I know as little about the military as possible," Conn said. There wasn't much reason to know anything about the idiot pawns who went out to die on behalf of the Society's global interests. "Go on. Why does that make the kid the heir?"

"This is a picture of the counselor," Dion said, putting up the picture of Derrick from the event at Fort Myer. "Look familiar?"

"Vaguely?" Conn said.

Dion put up the picture including Annabelle.

"How about now?" Dion said. "The counselor has sworn, as an officer of the court, that the woman pictured who has previously been *widely* identified as Annabelle Follett was the only woman with whom he had relations during the time frame Michael Truesdale would have been conceived. Further, that he was in an ongoing relationship with her during the *entire* period in which such conception might have occurred. And he has other witnesses he can summon who were aware of the relationship."

"Okay," Conn said with a dismissive shrug. He looked out his windows to take in the city below. His wasn't quite the highest office in Manhattan, but he was still able to look down on most of it. "So, some lawyer from Montana turns up with his brat claiming a billion dollars. You can beat, that I assume?"

"It gets worse," Dion said. "They somehow found evidentiary DNA of Annabelle . . ."

"Impossible," Conn snapped, locking his eyes back onto the screen.

"We got rid of her autopsy sample, she was cremated, and we even had her room scrubbed."

"You missed something," Dion said. "I'm not from back when she was around, and I don't know who was doing the full cleanup. But they missed that there was a blood sample from a juvie bust in Kennebunk. The Kennebunk police still had it. It's already been tested by a lab in Washington State and it's a positive match. *And* they put it on CODIS."

"Oh, shit," Conn said, his eyes blinking rapidly. His mind exploded with a million panicked thoughts.

"You thinking about all the stuff we have to cover up before he inherits?" Dion said. "Because I can hold this up for a while, but this is a done deal, Wesley. This would be closed in a week under normal circumstances. I don't think we can get it dismissed."

"Who's the judge?" Conn asked.

"That's the one bright spot," Dion said. "Mickelson. Your friends have him, right?"

"Right," Conn said. "You'll need to meet with some people. Pass this on. We'll try to buy him off. If that doesn't work . . . *I'll* need to meet with some people as well."

"I'm advising you as corporate counsel and as someone who's in this," Dion said. "Don't kill the kid. With what happened with Bear, questions are going to be asked. Do we know, yet, what happened with Bear?"

"No," Conn said. He looked out the window again, but this time his thoughts were racing too much for him to really see anything. "We'll do what we have to do. Right now, it would be a really bad time to let go of the Trust. Extremely bad. We need to play this carefully. Narrative: While we, of course, need to ensure that everything is in order, we are very interested and would love to continue providing excellent financial services if the suit is successful. I've been with the Folletts since his great-grandfather's time. Et cetera. Don't start off banging the table."

"Got it," Dion said.

"In the meantime, we'll do everything we can to get this to go away in the background," Conn said, thoughtfully.

"But with Bear just being in the news, the kid is probably going to be big news," Dion said. "He's a foundling, foster care, just reunited with his bio dad, and suddenly he's Oliver Twist. Right now, it's a John Doe submission. The other stuff is in stuff that's to be sealed by the court. But . . . probably a bad idea for the kid to disappear. His dad's an attorney. For sure there's a will."

"Interesting that he shows up so soon after Bear," Conn said. "Was he in the New York area?"

"Just says he was raised in Schenectady," Dion said.

"We need to know more about this Michael Truesdale," Conn said. "We're going to be having meetings all weekend. Clear your schedule."

He drew in a calming breath. He'd dealt with far worse than a snotty little kid. There was work to be done, but nothing to really worry about.

"One more piece of good news," Dion said. "They put out a press release and are having a presser Monday morning. This is going to make the papers on Sunday."

"I'll take care of that . . ."

"*Mi amigo!*" said Jorge Carnejo, aka Hombre de Poder, as he came into the expansive and largely empty lobby. The diminutive but bulky Hispanic male threw out his arms to give Mike a hug. Considering he was an invulnerable Ground—"hulk" was the impolite term—his hugs were capable of crushing a regular human.

"Whoa there, Tonto," Mike said, holding up three fingers in front of him.

"So *triste*," Jorge said, putting out a finger and gently touching his friend's. "*Mi amigo!*"

"How's your mom's restaurant doing?" Mike asked.

"It's just getting started," Jorge said. "But business is pretty good. She makes shrimp tacos . . ."

"I'm planning on heading up there as soon as I can," Mike said, dramatically licking his lips.

"He's back!" said Josh Ford, aka Metalstorm, as he walked in the front doors. The tall blond young man wearing a polo shirt was about as close as one could get to a caricature of a preppy white male. "How are you doing, back in the big city?"

As the doors were closing, Mike caught sight of a man in a T-shirt and sunglasses trying to get a peek inside. Tourists were known to loiter outside the Javits Building in the hopes of catching a glimpse of supers. Technically, their identities were classified, but it wasn't all that hard for amateur internet sleuths to put the pieces together.

Since anonymity wasn't guaranteed, security was quick to disperse crowds of more than a few people. However, something about this man's demeanor told Mike this wasn't a tourist. Mike made a mental note to track the man's skeleton.

"Doing pretty well," Mike said. He wasn't looking forward to breaking the news to Josh. "Busy busy."

"What crimes have you been committing?" Josh asked. The Junior Super Corps team leader seemed a little standoffish, but then Mike had run off without any warning.

"I'm totally legit these days!" Mike exclaimed.

Except for, you know, the whole international hacker thing and the assassinations . . .

"That'll be the day."

"Wheeee!" Laura said, running over and throwing her arms around him. "He's back! He's really back!"

"I thought you didn't like me," Mike said, leaning in happily. Laura, aka Fresh Breeze, was a bimbo, but she was a very squeezable bimbo. The seventeen-year-old was five foot two with brown hair and very nice . . . *features.*

"What made you think that?" Laura said.

"I dunno," Mike said. "Maybe all the times you said you hated me?"

"I was just venting," Laura said.

"Like a steam locomotive," Mike said as Sasha came in. Laura was pretty hot, as all supers were very good-looking. Sasha Nikula, aka Ivory Wing, however, was an outright goddess, with emerald-green eyes, long, jet-black hair, and the type of face poets had struggled to describe for eons. Mike had only barely progressed to the point where he was capable of coherent speech in her presence.

"Hey, Stone," Sasha said. He'd been desperately hoping for a Sasha hug, but she simply gave a casual wave as she walked up. She seemed muted, perhaps distracted. "Welcome back."

"Thank you, Miss Ivory," Mike said, nodding to her. "So, since we're all here, I have information to impart . . ."

"Can it wait?" the muscular, redheaded Bonfire said, as he walked over. The thermal super (because "pyro" was considered offensive) had taken over as Junior Corps mentor after the Electrobolt "incident." He also happened to be the husband of the platinum-blonde beauty Summer Storm. "Briefing time."

"I'd prefer right now, if that's okay," Mike said respectfully. "This is going to take some discussion, and I'd really like to get it out of the way."

"Okay," Bonfire said, furrowing his brow.

"Ahem," Mike said. "Josh, let me say in preamble that I think your dad is great and that even though I went with another law firm, it has nothing to do with the representation we've received from his firm."

"Okay?" Josh said, narrowing his eyes and frowning.

"My dad had a friend from law school at a firm here in Brooklyn, so we went with that firm," Mike said. "My dad, his choice. Ahem. Without further preamble: I'm an heir."

"An Air? Like a Tinkerbell?" Jorge said. "I'm pretty sure you're an Earther, *hermano.* For one thing, Airs are always women, and I don't care what anybody says, you can't just say you're a woman and become an Air. It doesn't work like that."

"Jorge, a person can choose their gender," Laura said, primly. "Gender is an artificial construct of the patriarchy."

While they argued, the man loitering outside received a phone call. It only lasted a few seconds and, as soon as he hung up, he walked away.

"You think so?" Jorge argued. "Then how come none of these so-called women ever become Airs or Waters, huh?"

"Not that kind of heir!" Mike said, cutting off the ongoing argument.

"What other kind of Air is there?" Jorge said. "Is there some new superpower? Or is this one of those weird English things? Your language makes *no* sense at all, you know that? Why doesn't everyone just speak Spanish?"

"It's one of those weird English things," Mike said. "H-E-I-R. As in one who inherits."

There was a collective sigh of sympathy and sorrowful expressions all around.

"Oh!" Jorge said, his eyes wide. "An *heir*! Why didn't you just *say* so?"

"What kind of heir?" Laura asked.

"The kind that inherits from his deceased biological mother," Mike said.

"I'm sorry, Mike," Sasha said.

"She died years ago," Mike said, shrugging. "About six months after

I was born. But she made the news a little while ago. Her name was Annabelle Follett. Recognize it?"

"I remember hearing it..." Laura said, frowning in deep thought.

"The billionaire runaway?" Sasha said, her eyes wide. "The one that got killed by a serial killer? Are you *serious*?"

"Yes," Mike said. He'd already pulled out his phone and pulled up the picture. "That's the picture that the news showed about Annabelle Follett. They'd cropped out my biological dad. That's him on the right."

"Oh, my God!" Laura said, snatching the phone and looking at it. "Does that make you a billionaire?"

"Eventually," Mike said. "And there's already been a DNA test. It was confirmed."

"Oh, my God!" Laura repeated, sidling up to him. "So, you got a girlfriend back in Montana?"

"No," Mike said, laughing. "Buncha cousins."

It didn't seem the time to mention the Allen girls—three gorgeous, honey-blonde sisters who homeschooled with his cousins. Though he couldn't suppress a vision of all three in red dresses and white bonnets.

"Does that cover it?" Bonfire asked.

"It does, sir, yes," Mike said. "Thank you for allowing me the time."

"Rest of it you can cover in the locker room and on patrol," Bonfire said, clapping his hands and rubbing them together. "Briefing time..."

"So, you went with your dad's friend, huh?" Josh said. "My dad's going to be very unhappy about that."

They'd had a quick, mostly pointless brief with Bonfire that centered entirely on conflict avoidance. Bonfire was a good guy, but his marching orders were clearly to keep the Junior Super Corps out of the spotlight at all cost. Now the team was in their swank, NFL-level locker room. It was still a co-ed locker room with guys at one end and girls at the other, despite the fact that arrangement had been codified by Bonfire's pedophiliac predecessor.

"Nothing against him or his law firm," Mike lied. He pulled off his shirt and pants and tossed them in the locker. He was carefully trying not to use Sight to watch the girls get undressed. There really wasn't a point. It was just a misty outline around skeletons—though there was the occasional hip wiggle or arched back to get his blood pumping.

"My dad just had a friend. You know how that goes. And it's a top firm. Quiet and smaller than your dad's but still a top firm."

"Are you going to stay with them past the suit?" Josh said. He set his gold-and-black full-face mask with winglike protrusions to the side and dug further into his locker.

"Probably," Mike said as he pulled on his tactical pants. He'd soundly defeated Kevin in the fight between a fully tactical outfit versus the Village People's rhinestone fantasy getup Kevin had designed.

"So, you said you might not be coming back to New York full time?" Laura said.

"My dad and aunts and uncles and grandparents are all dead set on me going to college," Mike said. "Most of my cousins graduated high school early and the majority are going to college or planning on it. So, yeah, I'm headed off to college next September, probably. If I can get into the college of my choice."

"Which one?" Sasha asked.

Mike hesitated at that.

"Can't decide?" Josh asked. "I think going in when you're fourteen you'll have your pick."

"Yeah," Mike said. "I mean, as Mike Truesdale I haven't pissed off anyone. Yet. But . . . don't judge me, okay? There's reasons. Osseo."

"What?" Laura asked. He could tell she was squeezing into her skintight green-and-yellow bodysuit that Mike had internally nicknamed the "Instant Cameltoe Device." It really could use at least a skirt or something. "Why would I judge you for that? Never heard of it."

"Because you've never heard of it," Josh said. "You're serious. *Osseo?*"

"Josh, I got canceled when I was eleven by the progressive left," Mike said. "I'm not any of the things that they say I am. But they canceled an eleven-year-old and had a riot and burned down half of Baltimore, just because an eleven-year-old kid didn't want to be a statistic. That's every kind of wrong, unless it's not obvious. Then when the Electrobolt thing came down, who did they blame? Did they blame the thirtysomething pedophile or the thirteen-year-old victim?

"I'm not the things people say I am," Mike said. "But it doesn't matter. I'm nuanced on all those subjects except the pedophile part.

But you're not allowed to have nuance. You're required to march in lockstep."

"That's not really true, Mike," Josh said.

"You haven't even taken college courses, Josh," Mike said. "And you're a fish that swims in water. In a lot of ways, my rural cousins are more educated than you are, private schools or no. They're more broadly educated, that's for sure. And more trained in actual history."

"I bet they aren't," Laura said. As her costume was the skimpiest by far, she was already done dressing and was now touching up her makeup in her locker mirror. Even though she'd cover her face with an opera-style mask, she still spent a whole lot of time getting her eyes just right. "It's probably all a whitewash! Do they even cover slavery or the slaughter of the Native Americans in your homeschool?!"

"Laura," Mike said, shaking his head and just gave up. "Never mind."

"Laura," Sasha said as she secured her heavy chest piece. Counter to Laura's tight little next-to-nothing, Ivory Wing's outfit was built for the extreme pressures of supersonic travel. "Mike is literally Native American? Or did you forget?"

"Sure, but what about those homeschoolers?" Laura asked, angrily. "They never cover slavery or the repression of the Native Peoples!"

"Oh, my God," Mike groaned as he put on his armor. "Let it stoppp."

"Laura?" Sasha said, then shook her head. "Never mind."

"What?" Laura said. Mike had never really thought about it, but she and Sasha never really helped each other with hair and makeup like cheerleaders or dancers might. Then again, Sasha never spent too much time on either.

"I got to choose my Native American name while I was there," Mike said. "I chose the Cat Who Walks the Mountains of the Star Hunter sept. Or, in other words, my Native American name is Mountain Lion Star Hunter. My cousins already had their Native American names."

"So, you just get to *choose* a native American name?" Laura said. "Can I have one? I'm thinking Wind of the Early Spring."

"You do if you're, you know, *Native American*," Sasha said, putting on her helmet gently.

"You forget he's Sioux, *chica*?" Jorge asked. "And I would guess so are his cousins."

Jorge had finished dressing shortly after Laura, as Hombre de Poder wore a simple blue muscle shirt with red accents, red wrestling shorts with blue accents, and a red-and-blue Mexican wrestler-style mask.

"My dad was Mr. Sioux Nation," Mike said. "One of my cousins was third runner-up. Mr. Sioux Nation isn't a beauty contest. Neither is Miss Sioux Nation. It's about traditional skills including stuff like how to make your way through a wilderness. How Rob could have been third runner-up I have no idea. The guy knows approximately *everything* about the outdoors. And, yes, all my cousins are more legally Sioux than I am. They're all registered with the Nation."

"Are you?" Sasha asked.

"I haven't yet," Mike said. "Noodling it. There are issues with being registered. The law is complicated and not worth discussing. But for one thing the Nation considers that it sort of owns your kids. And I'm not entirely comfortable with that."

"Homeschooling is just indoctrination," Laura said, stoutly.

"Said the indoctrinated," Sasha replied.

Glad I didn't have to say it. Wait. That sounds like Sasha isn't indoctrinated. What the hell?

Mike had been trying to get a read on Sasha since they first met and never really could. He knew it was in part due to her extreme beauty just shutting down his brain. Also, since she was a flyer, she rarely patrolled with them. But he'd gotten hints that she wasn't quite as far to the left as most of the rest of the junior supers and he knew she had a dry sense of humor.

"We sort of got off of Osseo," Josh said. "You sure?"

"They're not into cancel culture," Mike said. "That's reason one. You don't know how much of a relief it is to be able to just say some things and not have to worry about backlash."

"Like what?" Laura asked.

"Like nothing I'm going to discuss here," Mike said. "People don't realize how much they self-censor until they get out of a censorship regime. And you are, trust me, in a censorship regime. And the average age is younger. Osseo caters to homeschoolers. It's the top destination for them. The question is, can I get in? It's late to apply. If I can't, I'll just remote study. See if I can get in next year."

"It's not a highly regarded school, Mike," Josh said, trying to explain to the younger super. "You could get into *Harvard*. They don't have to know your other name, right?"

"If I chose a school like that, I'd choose Stanford over Harvard," Mike said. "Among other things, I'll be applying as a Montana resident. That trends you west coast. But I'm not applying to Stanford, either. I already got an automated letter of interest from them when I passed the GED at thirteen."

"You got a GED?" Laura said.

"That's what you get when you matriculate in home school," Mike said. "Some states there's a state test that's a High School Equivalency but most you just take the GED. And smart schools see the early GED and don't care about an HSE. Took the SAT and ACT in Montana as well. We're still waiting on those scores. Nice thing about Osseo: though it likes things like an essay on 'Why Osseo' and things like volunteering, it mostly chooses on academic merit instead of, you know, 'holistic.'"

They were dropped off at Fifth Avenue and East Ninety-seventh. The throngs of fans and reporters were waiting in the East Meadow. It still greatly disturbed Mike that absolutely everyone knew exactly where they'd start their patrols. The number of fans was slightly above the norm, but the reporters were out in force. It wasn't quite the reception they'd gotten after the Electrobolt incident, but close. On that occasion, the media had been militantly displeased with a belligerent white kid who'd assaulted a poor, helpless adult trans... super. The flaws in their logic had been legion, and Mike had done his part to point that out with limited success, but adapting a narrative to fit new data wasn't exactly a media virtue.

"Stone Tactical, is it true that you recently went *rogue* and risked violating the terms of your service to the Junior Corps?"

"Excuse me, *Rogue*—sorry, I mean *Stone* Tactical, care to comment on the appalling incarceration conditions of the defendant in your ongoing suit? Were you aware that, by all accounts, their access to gender-affirming care has been limited in their current situation?"

"Can you confirm reports that your *rogue* operation to capture El Cannibale—which was rumored to have been largely your plan— greatly endangered countless lives in the surrounding neighborhood? Has there been any action on behalf of the Super Department to restrict your ability to lead such rogue operations in the future?"

"You've been described in many circles as a *rogue* agent or a loose cannon, care to comment?"

Mike begrudgingly stepped forward, but Josh grabbed his arm to hold Mike back.

"I got this, Stone," Josh said before he stepped forward.

"As has been said before, no member of the Junior Super Corps will make any comments, official or otherwise, regarding ongoing litigation or criminal cases to which we may be parties. Please direct any queries or official correspondence to the Secretary of Super Affairs."

More questions erupted before he'd finished, and Josh waved dismissively and continued with noncommittal, pre-canned official statements that basically repeated what he'd already said.

"Hey, Stone, over here," Jorge said. "Metalstorm's supposed to be the leader, right, so let's let him lead this time."

Mike nodded and followed Jorge away, more than happy to give someone else the spotlight.

"So you say you got a big family now, huh?" Jorge asked. "How's that feel?"

"Don't you have a big family?" Mike retorted.

"Well, yeah, but I've always had one, you know what I mean?"

Mike shrugged and then reluctantly nodded. "I get you. I mean, before I went to Montana, believe it or not, you guys were the closest thing I ever really had to some kind of tribe. But to your point, it's both amazing and freaky as hell to have a real-life—just like I've only seen on TV—kind of family. And it's an *actual* tribe to boot. Wonderful and weird, all at once."

"I know what you mean, *mi amigo*, but I gotta say, I'm happy for you, man." He clapped Mike on the shoulder with a warm, genuine smile.

"*Muchas gracias*, Jorge. That means a lot."

Of course, Mike considered Gondola tribe, though he couldn't say that to Jorge. Even so, everything was always so clinical and mission-focused with Gondola. Plus, he'd never met any of them in person, which meant it was possible, however unlikely, that they were all the same person, or AIs like AutokId or ... *anything or anyone*, really. At the very least, his only knowledge of who anyone actually was had come from rumors circulating amongst themselves.

"There he is!" Laura practically screeched and knocked Mike out of his reverie. "Get over here, you!"

She rushed up, gently but firmly took Mike's hand, and led him toward the horde of fans.

"Come on, Stone, let's give them some pictures of Earth and Air, side by side."

She dragged Mike to the front, wrapped an arm around his waist, and smiled and waved at the crowd.

You mean let them start generating rumors about the two of us and a possible relationship? You do realize you're almost four years older, right? In less than a year you're legally an adult and I'll still be a minor...

But Mike kept his mouth shut and did his level best to pose. While holding her own smile and poses, Laura gave him a flurry of instructions: "Chin up, don't look so menacing, relax your arms/don't cross them, turn to the side a little, a slight profile is almost always better than straight on, here let's do a back-to-back pic," et cetera. Mike acquiesced without any pushback as it was still in his best interests to stay on the team's good side.

He briefly wondered what Sasha was up to. She and Patrick "Iron Eagle" Thesz usually went on an aerial patrol when the weather allowed. The range of Mike's Sight had increased considerably since the last time he'd been on patrol with them, but it still wasn't far enough to track flyers more than a few hundred feet up.

The reporters quickly dispersed under the counter onslaught of Josh's official jargon, and the photo shoot transitioned to autograph signing. Mike started to back away at that part, but then he caught a familiar face.

"Hey, Davon, how's things?" Mike said to a nine-year-old black kid with a book full of super autographs.

"I'll tell you how he's doing," his small but powerful mother said as she edged her way next to Davon. "He's doing great in school, and he tells me it's all because he 'can't let Stone Tactical down.' My little baby boy is doing great and he says it's all because of you. So I had to come up within him today to say thank you, Mr. Stone Tactical. Thank you for helping my baby boy do what I know he can do."

It was a good thing Mike had a helmet covering his eyes, so he didn't have to hide the water buildup.

"I'm sure I didn't tell him anything you haven't said," Mike said and turned to face the boy. "Did I, Davon? So listen to her, okay? But it's great to hear you're doing well, Davon, it really is. Especially hearing that you're doing it for me. But from here on out, don't do it for me, do it for yourself and do it for your mom here, okay? But I still want updates, cool? Can you do that?"

"Yeah, man, that's cool."

Mom gushed some more, and Mike graciously smiled and nodded. As they were moving away, his ghetto-ingrained paranoia picked up on a trio of kids glowering under a tree about fifty yards away. Mike had spotted more than a few miscreants who were watching him and the other junior supers, but these were clearly fixated on Davon for some reason.

One kid elbowed another and pointed when Davon and his mom moved away. All three shot to their feet and shuffled after the pair. They half-heartedly tried to look casual but miserably failed as they were nervously looking every which way to see if they were noticed. Mike had zero doubt they had ill intent for Stone Tactical's biggest fan. The how or why was wholly unimportant.

While continuing to shake hands and sign autographs, Mike reached out and grabbed one of the kid's ankles with Earth Move. It only took a gentle tug to make Wannabe Thug Two sweep a foot out and trip Wannabe Thug One. As WT1 fell, Mike had WT3 elbow WT2 in the ribs. That's all it took to get all three into a full-on bloody, bare-knuckle brawl.

It wasn't long before they'd gained the attention of the cops who were there to monitor the Junior Super fan and press crowd. Mike recognized two approaching cops as Officers Gill and Clevenstine— with whom he'd spoken on previous patrols. WT1 was surprised to find his fist flying at Gill's nose. WT3 threw a lazy kick, and Mike didn't even have to encourage WT2 as he joined in on the assumption that was just what they were doing now. All three quickly found their faces in the dirt and their hands cuffed behind their backs.

"Alright, team, crowds are dying down," Josh said with an admirable level of authority Mike hadn't heard before. It seemed he'd gained a little confidence since taking down El Cannibale. "Let's head out and grab some food."

"This one's on me, Stone," Jorge said with a clap on his back. "And it's not to butter you up 'cause you're about to be super rich. It's mostly to apologize for not realizing you were strapped on those first couple patrols."

Mike shook his head and frowned. "Thanks, but not necessary. No way you could've known that."

"We all should've known," Josh cut in as he walked up. "We're teammates, but we weren't acting like it back then, before, you know . . . But I more than anyone should've paid attention to what's going on. So this one's on me, and you're not saying no, got it? Hombre de Poder, you can get the next one."

"Yes, sir," Mike and Jorge said almost simultaneously, and only a little bit sarcastically.

"They can get your lunches," Laura said with a smile and a gentle, friendly elbow. "I'll get you dinner sometime."

"Oh, good!" Mike said. "There's a good steakhouse I've been dying to try."

Laura's face screwed into an angry frown, and she shifted away a sharply. "Deal's off. Meat is still murder."

"Tasty, tasty murder," Mike said.

Since there were no shrimp tacos to be found, the tasty lunch murder came in the form of gyros from a food truck named It's All Greek to Me. Vasilios, the guy running it, did look authentically Greek, bone structure and all, but had a heavy Staten Island accent. Josh, Jorge, and Mike all got thick pita stuffed with deliciousness, while Laura got a vegan power bowl from another truck.

Using Sight, Mike picked up on a few lookouts who were clearly keeping tabs on the junior patrol, but none struck him as particularly malevolent. They were probably just there to alert others if the juniors decided to go drug dealer or rapist hunting as they had on Mike's first patrol with the group.

"So, Mike," Jorge said between bites, "first time we met, you were talking about the Storm. Said you hoped it was like *A Quiet Place*."

"Which I still don't get, that movie was freaky," Laura said with a sad face. "And so depressing, with the toddler and the dad . . ."

"Well, yeah, but my point was that just plain old monsters—whether they're keyed in on sound or whatever—would be a breeze as far as attempted apocalypses are concerned. Especially here in the good ol' US of A where there's a gun behind every blade of grass."

"Which we really need to do something about!" Laura scoffed. "They're so dangerous."

"I'm letting that one go," Mike said, wiping tzatziki off the corner of his mouth. "But the point is, lots of guns to shoot at those what need shooting. In so-called gun-free zones, cities, and what have you, maybe everyone but the gangs and the cops would be getting eaten, sure. But in most of this country, it'd be open season with no limits and 'how do they taste on a po' boy?' They'd hardly need us supers if that's what the Storm is."

He took another big bite and rolled his eyes in satisfaction.

Josh took a slurp of soda, suppressed a small burp, and then cleared his throat. "Okay, well, what about zombies? Movies and TV show it spreading like a pandemic faster than the government can react."

Mike swallowed and took a sip to wash it down. "First off, I'm going to say just about everything happens faster than the government can react. They're usually too busy figuring out what's politically viable in terms of reelection to actually get around to anything resembling a proper response, but that's beside the point. You asked about zombies." He took another drink to better wet his whistle.

"Slow-moving zombies, piece of cake. Easier than just about every monster, even if it's all part of a pandemic. I mean, even in the original black-and-white *Night of the Living Dead*, zombies are only a serious problem for a small group of trapped people for a single night before good ol' boy Sheriff Chubby Redneck and his posse sweep through with hunting rifles and clear the area. Worst-case, slow-moving zombie pandemic kills more than any pandemic that came before, but it'd settle down and I think civilization would more or less survive just fine—and that's with or without us."

"Okay, but fast running zombies, like *28 Days Later*?" Jorge asked. Then he stuffed in his last bite and crumpled up the paper it was served in.

"Those'd be a much bigger problem, sure, assuming they were engineered in a way to keep them from simply dying off on their own within a few weeks. That's a whole discussion that largely boils down to they're better off naked. But fast zombies would be a civilization killer whether or not they'd die off. Especially since people are stupid, would ignore all the signs for weeks and, hell, would probably still be having huge concerts here in Central Park right up until the moment the shit truly hit the fan. In such a scenario, we'd be useful, but not necessarily any more useful than lots of seventeen-year-olds with lots of machine guns. Other than our far superior immune systems, that is."

With that, Mike scarfed down the last bite of his gyro and washed it down with the last of his soda. The three boys were done, and they all looked at Laura, who was still picking lightly at her bowl of rabbit food. She caught them all staring and shrugged her shoulders in mild embarrassment.

"Please, don't rush on our account," Josh said.

"I'm not really hungry, but I don't want it to go to waste. Anyone want some? Lots of good nutrition in here. They don't call it a power bowl for nothing."

All three stared at the bowl for a second without answering.

A few minutes later, she tossed the rest of her bowl, and they resumed their "patrol." Josh had suggested they go looking for more drugs or scare more would-be rapists out of bushes like they had the first time they'd been on patrol with Mike. Mike humored them and they went exploring, but he knew they weren't going to find anything.

By now it was abundantly clear the local criminals had organized an informal network to track them and pass around word of the junior supers' route. The problem was, Mike knew this because he could See the skeletons of the watchers—the more nefarious types—scattering as he and the others approached, but he couldn't tell the others on the team. It wouldn't be a big deal for them to learn he had Sight, but it would be a big deal for them to learn just how far and how well he could See. He was becoming powerful, and the Corps considered that a major problem for a very specific reason.

"What about aliens?" Josh asked, leading the way more than he had on previous patrols. "Storm could just as well be aliens, right?"

"And what, we're going to assume any aliens are bad?" Laura said. Her arms were crossed for warmth as it was just a little chilly that afternoon and her outfit was barely more than tissue paper.

"Correct me if I'm wrong," Mike said, "but we all have the impression the Storm is bad, right? Like Apocalypse-Ragnarok-Armageddon bad?"

Everyone nodded in agreement, even Laura though with some reluctance.

"So *if* the Storm is aliens, it follows they're bad—for humans, at the very least. But that possibility carries with it something we haven't discussed yet."

"Who gave us these powers," Jorge said, a statement rather than a question.

Mike smiled and nodded emphatically. "Exactly. If it's monsters or zombies or something supernatural, demons even, maybe it's something supernatural giving us these powers. I don't know, and those possibilities are endless. Angels, a coven of hot witches—"

"Why do they have to be hot?" Laura asked with narrowing eyes.

"Because this is my conjecturing, I'm a thirteen-year-old boy, and in a thirteen-year-old boy's conjecturing, the witches are hot. Hulké, can I get some backup?" Mike looked at Jorge.

Hombre de Poder made an "oh yeah" expression. "The witches are definitely hot, busty, and wearing lacy, mostly see-through dresses."

Laura groaned.

"Guys," Josh said as a half-hearted warning.

"Anyway, like I said, those possibilities are endless," Mike continued. "On the other hand, if it's aliens, it is extremely likely these powers come from *other* aliens. Maybe a splinter faction, a competitor race, rebels, but other aliens no matter how you slice it. If the Storm is aliens and these powers didn't come from other aliens, then we're mixing genres and that just gets super confusing and, to be honest, it'd be horrible fiction if you saw it in a movie."

"Can we move on from aliens already?" Laura asked. "And hot witches, and Bible-thumping stuff like angels and demons? What else could the Storm be?"

"It's probably not robots, right?" Josh asked. "Like Terminators or anything?"

"That is fairly unlikely," Mike said, "and comes out on the same level as aliens. If the Storm is an AI, the powers probably come from a counter AI. But considering how long ago Colonel King got his powers, I seriously doubt it's that—unless it's alien AI, which brings us back to aliens."

Silence. Laura shivered, and Jorge gave Mike a nervous, almost frightened glance. Mike had broken Supers Rule One: Though Shalt Not Mention the True Name of the Nebraska Killer.

But Mike had done it on purpose.

"Mike . . ." Josh started to say.

"I know," Mike said. "We don't talk about Colonel James King, or Major Freedom as he was called. But we need to remember that he started out just like us, and he was given his powers for the same reason we were. The fact that we don't know that reason doesn't change anything. Whatever the Storm is, *something* wants us ready for it. Odds are the powers we've been given are very specifically meant to counter whatever the Storm is. We don't train our powers because of what happened to Colonel King, to the Nebraska Killer, but if the Storm really is coming, training our powers is precisely what we need to be doing."

Laura shuddered again, and all three studiously avoided looking at Mike. They spent the rest of the patrol in silence, alone with their thoughts.

Sunday headlines:
New York Post: MISSING HEIR FOUND?
Gotham Herald: EARLY DAFFODILS MEAN GLOBAL WARMING

CHAPTER 4

"Thank you for taking my call, sir," Mike said over the video link. He hadn't set up a proper video call spot in their rental apartment yet, so he was sitting at the kitchen table against a wall with a New York night cityscape picture behind him.

"We don't get many calls from thirteen-year-olds who stand to inherit a billion dollars," Dr. Brian Walker, president of Osseo College, replied. He was in his private office in front of a wall of bookshelves.

"I know that there are a lot of kids who want to go to Osseo," Mike said. "And I'm aware that I filed after the deadline. I'm hoping that you can handle fifteen hundred and one in September."

"And I certainly would prefer to do that," Walker said. "But, silly as most college presidents would find this to say, we cannot accept you for the September semester, Mr. Truesdale. I'm sorry."

"No, I got my application in late," Mike said, shrugging. "I get it."

"That is the entire reason," Walker said with a sigh. "You would be a tremendous student. Just your published papers put you in the top of the category we would like to see as students here at Osseo. I'm more interested in that than the billionaire part."

Mike had gotten his Harvard paper "The Three Goat Problem" published in *The Octagonal*, a leading journal of intersectionality, under the pseudonym Adrian Kornbluth, a nine-year-old pansexual goatherd from a polyamorous commune in Vermont. At age ten and under the pseudonym Thomas Phillips, he'd written "The Effects of Hawking Radiation on Nucleosynthesis" for a class he'd audited at

Stanford. It was subsequently published in the *American Journal of Astrophysics*. Finally, under the name Phillip Crawford III, he'd been lead author of "International Trafficking of Minors: An Economic Model" for the London School of Economics, which had been published in *The Economist*. However, the world had eventually learned all three were published by one Michael Edwards, his previous legal name, and Michael Edwards had been canceled once the world learned he'd refused to be murdered by poor, disadvantaged minorities.

"But in the category you'd fall into, notably fourteen-year-old freshmen, all of the slots were filled by the time we received your application. And all the incoming class has already been informed that they were accepted."

"I can understand that," Mike said. "That's just fair. It's being honest, which is something I find refreshing."

"I do hope you'll consider applying for next year," Walker said. "We might even have slots for next winter-spring semester. We do experience a few dropouts."

"What about if I do some of the basics remote in the interim?" Mike said. "Try to apply as a sophomore or junior?"

"That should be doable," Walker said. "We really would like to see you here as a student."

"Just ain't room," Mike said, smiling. "Get that. Everyone with any sense wants to go to Osseo to get an education not an indoctrination."

"That is part of the problem, yes," Walker admitted. "We have to turn away more students than Harvard these days."

"Problem is there aren't enough Osseos," Mike said. "Wonder if a *billionaire* could do something about that . . ."

"What do you have for us, Mr. Kindred?" Conn asked. He, Dion Bafundo, and the mysterious Mr. Kindred were in a small, lower-level hotel conference room the Society kept eternally reserved for just this sort of discreet meeting.

He'd never dealt with Mr. Kindred—*if* that was his real name. But he'd heard of him. He was the Mr. Fix-It for serious problems with the Society in the US. So at least they were taking this heir business seriously.

"Mostly an update on who you're really facing," Mr. Kindred said. He had a quiet, grim demeanor and gaunt, pale appearance. In short, he looked the way Conn had always imagined Death would look if you ever met him in person. "First of all, the proclaimed heir. Michael Truesdale was born Mike Edwards in Baltimore, Maryland, on July fifth, 2011."

"So, he's using a fake name?" Dion asked, making a note. Counter to Kindred's potential lack of a pulse, Dion had an annoying nervous energy. "That's falsification of court documents."

"As far as we can determine, it is a legal name change," Mr. Kindred said. "And I would appreciate if you would wait for me to finish, Mr. Bafundo."

He paused and considered the attorney with dark eyes for a moment.

"Mike Edwards was raised in foster care in East Baltimore," Kindred continued. "Do either of you recognize the name?"

"No," Conn said, relaxing back in his chair.

Dion shook his head.

"Severely abused," Kindred said. "We have his social services file and there's a think tank of psychologists going over it right now to pick out his weaknesses. According to his therapist notes, he was reading at two, doing calculus and advanced programming by six, definitely started auditing college courses through an online university when he was eight. Published his first paper in the field of queer and transgender theory when he was nine, astrophysics at ten, economics just last year. He has an untestable IQ, ADHD, PTSD, and probably OCD."

"Published papers?" Conn said. "In economics?"

"Team paper at the London School of Economics," Kindred said. "Cover paper in *The Economist*. 'International Trafficking of Minors: An Economic Model.'"

"I thought *we* had that one done," Conn said with a slight frown.

"One of our assets was *on* the team," Kindred said. "Mike Truesdale, aka Phillip Crawford the Third, was the lead author."

Dion shot Conn a nervous, concerned glance, but Conn dismissively waved him off. So the kid was smart. It still wasn't any cause for concern.

"Was recruited to top schools and turned them down," Kindred said. "Starting from at least ten when he was recruited to Stanford for the Astrophysics paper. Canceled when he was eleven. He was attacked by a drug gang, defended himself and survived. We . . . had some things we didn't want to turn up in the news so BLM got involved. There was a riot, then it sort of fizzled out when they realized the white supremacist was an eleven-year-old child. But it got a little issue off the front page.

"Attacked again when he was thirteen, this time by MS-13. Which was when he Acquired Earther superpowers, killing his last three attackers with them."

Now *that* got Conn's attention. He sat up a little.

"He's a super?" Dion said, leaning so far forward he was almost up on the table.

"That would tend to be the meaning of what I just said, Mr. Bafundo," Kindred said. "Which was when, as far as we can determine, the US Marshals changed his name. Which makes it quite legal.

"Thus, Michael Truesdale is Mike Edwards, aka Thomas Phillips, aka Phillip Crawford III, aka Adrian Kornbluth, aka Boogie Knight, aka Stone Tactical, and who knows how many other aka's."

"Boogie Knight?" Conn asked.

"One of his street names," Kindred said. "Any serious questions at this time?"

"So, we can't use the fake-name thing," Dion said.

"Not unless you want to also piss off the US Marshals," Kindred said. "Because you've never *heard* that name and know *none* of this."

There was a pause in the conversation as Dion gave Conn a glance that seemed to ask, *Just who in the hell is this kid?* With a low growl, Conn settled himself.

"What else do you have?" Conn asked.

"Then we get to the issue of his father, Counselor Derrick Sterrenhunt," Kindred said. "Also known as Hunter. Fortunately, only one known aka.

"Career operator in Combat Activities Group—you would know that as Delta Force. Multiple languages. Should have noted that about the son as well. Took his bachelor's in International Affairs, University of Maryland extension service, in two years while serving as a junior enlisted in the 10th Mountain Division. Made sergeant in about the same time. Passed Ranger School as a Distinguished Honor Graduate. Also, two tours in-country, Iraq and Afghanistan, picking up his first Bronze Star on his second tour."

Conn almost interrupted with "Blah blah blah war hero," but refrained. It was probably best that he listened to everything Kindred had to say.

"After reenlisting, went through full Special Forces qualification as a special operations engineer. That's . . . hard to explain precisely but among other things it's a world-class expert at explosives. As part of Special Forces training attended Defense Language Institute to learn Dari. Was switched to Arabic shortly after joining. Graduated qualified fluent in written and spoken Dari, Arabic, Spanish, and German. Later picked up multiple other languages either at subsequent visits to DLI or from just picking them up in-country.

"Was assigned to his unit and went to the next scheduled Combat Activities Group qualification phase. Passed. Passed OCT with the closest you can get to a perfect score and became an operator in CAG. Quickly rose to master sergeant. Along the way he attended Georgetown Law and passed it in a year. Was if not the youngest group sergeant major, then very close. Group sergeant major, squadron sergeant major, and retired as command sergeant major of Joint Special Operations Command.

"IQ of one fifty-two, speaks twenty-two languages, fourteen Bronze Stars, two Silver Stars, Distinguished Service Cross, and has killed more people than you've had hot breakfasts."

Conn had to admit that was worth knowing. So, the score was now one baby superhero and one aging super soldier. It still wasn't that much of a threat next to the endless resources of the Society, but it couldn't be so easily discounted.

"You will, of course, insist on a DNA test taking place here in New York," Kindred said. "The FBI will pick up the DNA before it can be shipped here. It's important to the ongoing investigation of Annabelle Follett. And it will be lost in evidence."

"Good," Conn said, nodding. "That's the sort of thing we're looking for."

"And do you assume that that will end it?" Kindred asked. "That the problem just goes away? The agents who are picking it up won't know who they're really working for. It's just an errand. We cannot, therefore, insist that the FBI ensure that the *entire* sample is gone. There's no reason for such an order. It's a vial of blood and you need less than a drop to establish DNA.

"Counselor Sterrenhunt has previously worked with the establishment in Washington. If you don't think he's anticipated the DNA disappearing, think again. He will have a backup plan and a backup plan for that plan.

"One thing to keep firmly in mind about Delta," Mr. Kindred said. "Delta is *not* SEALs. SEALs train in HUMINT—human intelligence. What you'd call spying. Delta comes from the Special Forces background. They are half soldier, half spy, and *very* good at both. You're going to be dealing with a person who not only has killed more people than you've had hot breakfasts but is the sort of person you only normally see in an action movie. He has a unique skill set."

This was the first time Mr. Kindred had gotten excited in any noticeable way. Try as he might, Conn didn't really have it in him to be impressed. The Society had some truly scary people in its ranks, and many of them were at Conn's disposal. Still, there didn't seem any point to interrupting the man's diatribe.

"Deltas tend to be invisible. They *like* to be invisible. They are the silent warriors. They don't go around hunting movie options. Counselor Sterrenhunt's LinkedIn notes that he was career Army Special Operations. Though being a former Delta would be a cachet and possibly get him more work, it isn't on his public profile because *he does not want anyone to know.*

"You cannot conceive of someone not promoting themselves to the utmost degree. Because you do not understand the silent-warrior ethos.

"You're going to be sitting across the table from someone who has more brains than you do, vastly more experience of the world, and who probably knows more about you than you'd imagine he could. Someone who can read you like a book. Another part of their training. And who will appear on the surface as just some yokel lawyer from Podunk. Because he is the silent warrior.

"My people have prepared dossiers on both of them and it is probably pointless. As I have told others, you are going to be sitting across from both of them, totally outclassed and unable to comprehend that. How could some former soldier and small-town lawyer be smarter and more capable than a person who sits in a corner office in Manhattan? You will also totally dismiss the actual heir because he's just some kid. Another mistake I guarantee you make.

"While there are perks to working with this organization, dealing with people such as yourself, Mr. Conn, is why I wonder if the money's really worth it."

CHAPTER 5

"Lawyers, Guns, and Money" —Warren Zevon

"They're going to come in here with about a hundred people," Mr. Brauer said to Mike, "Don't let that intimidate you."

The first meeting between the two parties had been scheduled for Tuesday morning at the law offices of Bruck, Kadish, Packard and Ulmer, opposing counsel.

The room was well lit and fairly spartan, mostly filled with a very long table. There were chairs at the table as well as along the walls. Mike, Derrick, Brauer, Kennedy, and a female counselor had gotten there first and lined part of one side of the table.

"I'm just gonna be sittin' here playin' on my phone the whole time, Mr. Ahuvit," Mike said. "You gots this. 'Sides, I don't know nothin' 'bout no law stuff!"

He assumed the room was bugged. *He'd* have bugged it. In fact, thanks to a brush pass from Gondola he'd bugged it when they were walking in.

Sure enough, a couple of minutes later a file of people started entering the room. They were split about four-fifths obvious male/female with the other fifth being various unsure gender. About half took seats at the table. The rest stood behind them ostentatiously holding notepads.

Time slowed nearly to a stop as Wesley Conn entered with the group. Until this very moment, Mike had only seen pictures of the man who'd serially raped his mother before having her hunted and killed. Even though Mike had faced down and captured an MS-13 leader literally named *El Cannibale*, Conn now ranked as the most evil man Mike had ever met in person.

With a simple thought, Mike could snap the man's neck and be done with him. In fact, he had dozens of options and none of them would even be traceable.

Patience.

Conn took a seat across from Mike, who looked up and gave him a friendly wave and a smile and went back to looking at his phone. He had earbuds in and was apparently rocking to whatever he was listening to. Conn similarly seemed bored, indifferent, like he didn't have a care in the world and was wondering why he had to bother meeting with a mere kid.

You are going to suffer for what you did to my mother. He kept his face bland and appeared to be totally engrossed with whatever was on his phone. *Just like your SEAL buddy suffered. But worse.*

"Alright," one of the men on the other side said. "Let's get to some introductions. I am Larry Packard, name partner here at Bruck, Kadish, Packard and Ulmer. Ahuvit, good to see you here! Why don't you start with your side?"

"Thank you, Larry," Ahuvit Brauer said, nodding. "For those who don't know me, I am Ahuvit Brauer, name partner at Adams, Walker, Brauer, Bergman and Bhatt. On my right is Wilder Perrin Kennedy, partner at Adams, Walker, Brauer, Bergman and Bhatt and the lead counsel on this case. To my left is our lucky heir, Michael James Truesdale, then his father, Counselor Derrick Sterrenhunt. To the counselor's left is one of our associates, Ms. Diane Fisher."

Fisher was brunette and brown eyed. Five foot nine and about 150 pounds, though she'd probably argue for 120.

"That's all of our people. Larry? Care to introduce *some* of your people? Preferably not all."

"Of course, Ahuvit," Mr. Packard said, smiling. "To my right is the chief managing trustee of the Follett Trust, Mr. Wesley Conn. To his right is the chief counsel for the Follett Trust, Counselor Dion Bafundo. To my left is Rich Lowe, primary counsel for this matter. I think we can leave off the various other legal professionals."

Lowe was a wispy little weasel of a man. Mike imagined a villain origin story where Lowe had gotten beaten up a lot as kid and became a lawyer to get revenge.

"Alright," Ahuvit said, clasping his hands together and looking to his right. "Let's get to it. Plaintiff normally starts. Counselor Kennedy?"

Wilder gave a respectful nod and swept his gaze across the opposing side.

"My client wishes me to thank the Follett Trust on his behalf for its excellent work over the years in managing his funds," Wilder said. "But given Counselor Sterrenhunt's written and sworn statement that the only woman he had sexual relations with during the time frame where Mr. Truesdale could have been conceived is Annabelle Follett, along with the positive DNA test, this meeting really should be a discussion of how we are going to manage handover of the assets. Should we just begin there?"

"That's *distinctly* premature, Counselor," Rich Lowe snapped. "Right now, we've got some DNA that was supposedly tested in a questionable lab that has association with the plaintiff's father and, no offense to the Honorable Counsel, but we're talking about a billion dollars here. We're not going to just hand it over on his say-so . . ."

The arguments went back and forth and remained precisely the same. The Trust should just turn over the dooley and Mike and his father should crawl back under what rock they'd come out from under. They never directly insulted Counselor Sterrenhunt or accused him of just making it all up. But they came close several times. Conn was particularly supercilious. Though doing his best to hide it, Mike could tell he was sweating.

Mike wrote off everyone on Conn's side as lap dogs except for Conn himself, Packard, and one unnamed female associate. She never spoke, but she took in everything with cold, calculating eyes.

"So, what do you think of all this, young man?" Packard said at a point when it had gotten heated. Every time Conn or Bafundo got involved it got heated.

"Man, I don't gots no idea 'bouts law," Mike said in his best ghetto slang. "It a billion dollas! That more money ye gots! Where I's come from, folk kill you for a dolla! A billion dollas? Gonna needs a billion bodyguards!"

Then he'd studiously gone back to playing on his phone and trying very hard not to give anything away.

His father had given a master class in appearing to be the hick from the sticks. They knew that the Trust knew who they were. That his father was, in fact, quite smart. But every time he spoke, he took on precise legal diction but talked very . . . slowly . . . to the point that Mike really had to tune him out. People who talked that slowly drove him nuts. He also used a slight speech impediment that made him sound just a little like Gomer Pyle or Forrest Gump.

Mike could tell that *intellectually* the other side knew he wasn't a moron. But he was giving such a convincing imitation of someone who never should have been able to pass the bar that they were increasingly dismissing him.

After four hours, they came to the conclusion that there was no conclusion. The Trust had offered a small cash settlement to get him to go away. It had been rejected. Finally, both parties agreed to bring the sample to New York and have it tested in a to-be-determined, mutually accepted fashion. The army of associates and paralegals filed out of the room.

"So, Ahuvit," Larry said as the main parties were leaving. "See you at the club this weekend?"

"Should be," Ahuvit said.

"Looking forward to it!" Larry said. "Until then."

"This is what your American special operations call 'feet wet,'" Ahuvit said when they'd entered the limousine.

It was roomy enough for everyone to stretch out a little. Mike and Derrick sat along the rear seat, with Ahuvit in the middle and Wilder and Fisher near the front. Wilder passed bottles of ice-cold water around.

"Are we sure?" Derrick said, holding up his phone.

"That's covered," Mike said, still concentrating on his. "Can't vouch for anything else."

Though still looking with his eyes at the phone, he stretched his Sight out to watch for tails or, worse, physical threats. Seeing at cars was difficult as he couldn't see metal, but there were plenty of other elements to track as well as the drivers themselves.

"Edgar?" Ahuvit said.

"No one got in the car, sir," the driver said. "And it was swept this morning. I've had my eye on it the whole time."

"You gave a master class in the country bumpkin, Counselor," Ahuvit said.

Fisher rolled her eyes and gasped in exasperation.

"If I had to wait for one more long pause . . ." Wilder said, chuckling.

"Oh, it was going right up Conn's nose every single time," Mike said. "Mine as well, to be honest. God, *how* do you *do* that? I was getting ready to strangle you. *Just finish the sentence!*"

"Years of practice in patience," Counselor Sterrenhunt said. "It even drives *me* a bit nuts."

"And everyone in the room winced every time it was your turn to speak," Ahuvit said with a chuckle.

"Based on microexpressions," Mike said, "they started off seeing us as a serious threat and by the time we were done pretty much *everyone* was sure we were just a couple of morons from the sticks. Except unnamed senior associate number four to the left from Conn. She saw right through it."

"How were you reading microexpressions?" Diane said. "You never looked up from your phone."

"Peripheral vision," Derrick said. "I noticed her, too. She wasn't falling for it."

"She also wasn't particularly well regarded by them," Mike said. "There was no real interaction with the principals. And that's a tell, since there was some subtle body language with some of the other associates. But on the way in and out the non-principals around her were dismissive. She's not a fair-haired girl in the firm. But she is very bright."

"You could tell all that from peripheral vision?" Diane asked.

"Yes," Mike said.

"Concur," Derrick said. "I'm going out on a limb that she'd make a good pickup for you after this is over."

Mike nodded absently and Derrick gave him a brief, questioning look. Mike had identified a small sedan that had remained roughly behind them through their first major turn. A tail was fine, just so long as it wasn't ensuring they followed a route into an ambush. The driver was under orders to take a long, circuitous route to Brauer's office, but that didn't mean a planned hit couldn't adjust—especially if they had eyes on. He kept his attention divided behind possible tails behind them and possible traps ahead of them.

"What did *you* notice, Diane?" Ahuvit asked.

"They know Mike's the heir," Diane said, shifting in her seat. "And is Truesdale your real name?"

"You caught that," Ahuvit said. "Bafundo kept starting to refer to him as Edwards."

"Which means they know I'm from Baltimore," Mike said. "And about Stone Tactical and about all the accusations. The judge has put a gag order on this but next week, probably, the *Herald* will start talking about it. They're ignoring it for now. It's harder to decide which narrative to craft these days. It's a committee instead of Eisenberg making the rules."

The tail car turned away at an intersection, so Mike looked around to check for possible hand-off vehicles.

"So, they'll have anonymous sources close to the discussions bring up that they're not sure that Mike Truesdale is a real person. Or have a reporter investigate Michael Truesdale of Schenectady and determine that he does not exist. They may not reveal my name just yet. But it *will* be revealed. And there will be questions about my identity implying that I'm some sort of a con artist same for my father.

"The defense will call for an emergency hearing. The judge will want to know what my real name is. How do we handle that?"

"Give him your real name?" Wilder suggested.

"My real name is Michael Truesdale," Mike said. "The name I was born with doesn't *exist* anymore. There isn't a *birth certificate* by that name. There is no Social Security number tied to it. It is history, biology. It's gone.

"And if we use that name, even with a justification, it gives the judge another reason to be biased. In addition, it means that the defense now officially knows that name and will leak it to the press. My recommendation is don't give an inch. 'Michael Truesdale is his legal name, Your Honor.' Which it is."

Though he Saw a couple potential tails, none were obvious and none lasted long. Either the tails knew what they were doing, or there weren't any. Prudence dictated it was the former, so he stayed sharp.

"If His Honor presses, suggest he take it up with the US Marshals.

The defense will still know my real name but if they leak it, there's no secondary source. That name is gone except as news articles. And my face has changed enough that's hard to connect. Let His Honor try to prise things out of the marshals. What do we do when the DNA sample disappears?"

"You really think it will," Wilder said in more of a statement than question.

"Let's say it's a ninety percent probability it's already gone," Mike said. "What then?"

"How would it disappear?" Diane asked.

"It will," Mike said. "What then?"

"We'll have to look at that when the time comes," Ahuvit said.

"Roger," Mike said.

"You ever considered studying law?" Wilder said.

"I used to be eligible for the bar, but I lost my eligibility," Mike said, his face long.

"How?" Diane asked.

"I found out who my father was."

The legal proceedings, as expected, progressed slower than most glaciers, leaving Mike with a great deal of free time. He was up in the geologically diverse Inwood Hill Park checking out Inwood Marble traces when his phone pinged. Wilder was calling him on video.

"Hello, Mr. Kennedy," Mike said. "To what do I owe the honor of a call?"

"I really hate you," Wilder said with a sigh that overloaded the phone's speaker. His disgruntled expression said he might not be joking.

"That's a common refrain," Mike said. "Many people have tried to kill me over that very fact. What am I hated for this time?"

"The FBI picked up the sample in Washington state," Wilder said. "That's not actually disappeared but it's close."

"Did they have a reason?" Mike said. He casually glanced around but studiously avoided looking in two specific directions. Instead, he watched some of the wonderfully fit women in tight, skimpy clothes with excellent running form. "Or did they just steal it for shits and giggles?"

"It's important to the ongoing Annabelle Follett investigation,"

Wilder said, clearly skeptical. "I'm starting to believe some of the crazier aspects of this case."

"Believe," Mike said. "The Truth is Out There. It will disappear from evidence. But go ahead and get a subpoena for a sample. There's no reason they have to have every last drop. If the judge will give you one."

"What do we do if it *has* disappeared?" Wilder said. "I know you've got a backup."

"That's not something to discuss over this link," Mike said. "I take it you've told my dad?"

"I have," Wilder said.

"Just subpoena a sample from the FBI," Mike said. "I'd like to get them on record as having lost it. Then we'll proceed to the next phase. I won't even say next plan. We're still on Plan A.

"First, send a request to the judge. Despite this setback we still consider me to be the legitimate heir, slug all the reasons, and staying in New York is expensive. We'd like to be able to use one of the properties as lodging. Either the townhome or the apartment."

"I doubt he'll go for that," Wilder said.

"Keeps them on their toes," Mike said. "And I want to see what their response is. At the very least a tour and meet the help."

"I'll enter the motion," Wilder said.

Two young mothers pushed baby strollers past while chatting up a storm. He couldn't help but stare at the strollers. As far as he knew, he'd never been in a stroller, and had definitely never been pushed around a park if he had.

"Second, subpoena a DNA test from my maternal grandfather, Carmen Lukessi," Mike said. "Dela Follett was not cremated. If we get her disinterred and a DNA sample and I'm the grandson of Lukessi and the grandson of Dela, game, set, match. In the meantime, I'm going to keep studying geology. Anything else?"

"Didn't you mention telling your attorney everything?" Wilder said.

"We'll set up a meeting in a secure location," Mike said. "Talk to my dad about that."

"Will do."

"Out here."

Mike continued to study the metamorphosed limestone while using Sight to keep a check on his surroundings as he always did.

The tail was still there. Tails. Two of them—one male, one female—both armed, he'd marked as Society. The third was a Gondola asset. He'd warned Gondola about the others so as not to have the asset burned by the Society.

He'd gotten used to lookouts in Central Park and assorted watchers keeping tabs on him and the others, but this was the first time he'd been actively followed. So, he led them on a merry chase as he wandered around New York City from rock formation to rock formation.

It was something to pass the time until the assassins showed up. Then it would get fun.

"Thank you for your time, Under Commandant," the distorted voice said.

"Always good to hear from you, Omega."

Jeremy Kackley was the deputy director of the US Marshals Service. As such he was the primary point of contact for Omega. Given how many tips they'd gotten to affect child rescues and felony warrants from the volunteer force, he was always willing to pick up the phone.

"We need a favor this time," Omega said.

"I think we owe you *all* the favors," Kackley said. "What's the favor?"

"We need a sample of DNA moved from Washington state to New York City and held under the marshals' protection. And we even have a reason for you to do so . . ."

CHAPTER 6

"James Bond Theme" —Monty Norman

The entrance to Super Corps Headquarters that was normally used by the supers was not an easy route. First, you went to 291 Broadway. Use the third elevator and insert your CAC card to summon it. It would only work for people with the right clearance and there was an undercover US marshal to keep people from following the super, either because they were lost or because they were following them.

Mike decided it would be fun to play with his food, so he got on the subway and headed for 291.

It was the usual ruck of human vermin in the damned thing. Plenty of good people, yes, but the beasts were becoming increasingly common. When you didn't manage the monsters, they bred.

The male hopped onto the subway car ahead of his and the female got into the one behind his.

Most of the way was what Mike thought of as the "blue line." At the Fiftieth Street station, a group of eight "youths" boarded the train wearing hoodies and COVID masks. That would be how the *Herald* reported them. Youths. Not a bunch of punks looking for trouble. He could just make out that most of their weapons were shivs and small knives. The leader, though, was sporting a small-caliber handgun.

Mike was strap-hanging despite the train being lightly used but he'd noticed the pretty Latina without really looking. She was about fifteen at a guess. It was a school day and midday, so he wasn't quite sure why she was on the train at all. Of course, the same could be said for him. And the "youths."

The leader of the group gestured toward the girl, and they surrounded her. It was far enough away that Mike couldn't quite pick up what they were saying but he was sure it was the usual.

Why couldn't people just be decent to each other?

When the leader of the group grabbed the girl's breast, Mike sighed, pulled out his earbuds, put on a COVID mask, pulled up his hoodie, and put everything breakable like his phone into his backpack.

"Excuse me, ma'am," Mike said to an elderly lady sitting on the left. "Would you mind keeping an eye on this? I have something I need to do."

"Um . . ." the woman said.

"Just give me a moment, if you please," Mike said.

"Well . . ."

There were people filming. With any luck they hadn't caught his face. He wasn't close to the "incident."

He set the bag down by her, casually walked over behind one of the "youths," and started by punching him as hard as he could, full super-strength, in the kidneys. He followed that up with an elbow to the back of the head that took that one out of the fight.

Then it really got started.

When supers Acquired, they didn't just get superpowers. Even non-invulnerables like Mike got higher strength, speed and agility along with regenerative healing. When they reached around eighteen, they hardened and got skin that was resistant to knives and bullets. They were all on the order of Captain America in terms of physicality.

Mike had been raised in a hard school and unlike most of his ghetto companions, he didn't disdain martial arts. At least if they were fighting arts and not dojo dancing. So, he'd studied videos of things like Brazilian jiu-jitsu and Krav Maga growing up and practiced them. Since the latter was just advanced and specialized street-fighting, Mike particularly enjoyed it.

Brazilian jiu-jitsu was useful for dislocating joints which definitely took someone out of the fight.

The gun was easy enough to get rid of. He'd disarmed a prepared assassin when he was eleven. The leader wasn't all that. It was hubristic but Mike actually did the thing you only saw in movies. He grabbed the automatic and held the slide back so it couldn't operate.

The motion was decidedly easier when one could subtly control the gunman's hand with Earth powers.

Then he punched the guy so hard it broke his jaw and teeth went flying.

The "youths" got in a few licks, but what with Mike having been beaten on repeatedly growing up and having regenerative healing, it didn't really matter. Compared to what he'd suffered as a kid they were love taps.

When it was over, he nodded to the young lady. The demeanor of his tails changed dramatically. Where before their postures had been casual and confident, they were now hesitant and cautious. On the one hand, he'd just confirmed they were definitely tailing the right person; on the other, they'd just learned *who* they were tailing.

"*De nada.*"

Then he walked over, picked up his backpack, and stepped off the train as it reached the Chambers Street Station.

When he reached 291, he walked in and waved at the undercover marshal on duty while half singing the *Captain America* theme song.

"Hey, there's a dude following me," Mike said. "Don't look, male subject examining the tenants list. He's armed. Don't know if he's permitted. I'm going to hop the elevator. Mind at least giving him some hassle, try to get an ID? Be advised, though—handgun."

"I can do that," the marshal said, frowning.

"I'll explain later," Mike said. He walked to the third elevator, inserted his ID card, and summoned it. The doors opened immediately, and he stepped in.

As he did, he could see in Sight that the tail walked in and over to the elevator. Since you needed a CAC to summon it, he wasn't getting it to return.

Mike proceeded to the underground lobby, still watching in Sight. The female tail was outside the building, texting. The Gondola asset was across the street, having been warned to stay away.

The marshal got up from his security desk and approached the male subject. There was discussion. The undercover marshal was openly armed. Discussions proceeded. The male subject was getting visibly distressed. The marshal was calm.

Suddenly, the male subject reached for his gun.

The marshal was prepared and had alerted the response team. The marshal wrestled the gun away from himself as the response marshals flooded the room. In seconds, the guy was on the ground and cuffed.

Mike was prepared to use powers to prevent harm to the marshal, but it wasn't necessary. Good, he could continue to pretend he was just a nobody kid. With superpowers.

With NYPD arriving and all the commotion, the female subject broke contact.

Mike took the steam tunnels to an alternate entrance and followed his erstwhile tail as she made her way to the City Hall subway station. He couldn't follow her there; she'd make him in an instant if they were on the same platform.

He thought about it for a few seconds and grimaced.

He put on his COVID mask again and waited for her to get on the R line going uptown. Then, as the train left the station, he took off flying. Early on, he'd flown by lifting a rock in a tightly secured backpack, but now he'd grown capable enough to confidently lift his skeleton.

The outfit he was wearing was not the best for flying. His hoodie top kept flapping in the breeze and he was having to keep up with the subway. He couldn't let it get ahead of him too far because he had to keep an eye on the tail. He still was only up to a few hundred meters range. He just tucked the hoodie under his backpack and kept it there to the best of his ability. He also got very watery eyes from the wind. He finally just closed his eyes and used his Sight to fly. It was a bit nerve-racking, but it worked. He didn't hit anything. So far, so good.

She changed trains twice, possibly to avoid being tracked, and got off in Washington Heights. To minimize the odds of being seen, he worked to avoid flying outside large windows or directly past open balconies or terraces.

He landed on a roof and continued to trail her, moving from rooftop to rooftop using flight as necessary until she entered a six-floor walk-up on the corner of West 159th Street and Amsterdam Avenue. It was the heart of the Heights, so he wasn't too sure why the hell she'd be there.

The answer arrived when she went into an apartment on the fifth floor. A man met her at the door and delayed letting her in until he'd checked the hallway and interrogated her for a bit. Mike couldn't tell what was being said, of course, but safely assumed he was ensuring she wasn't being followed. They sat and chatted for a bit, then she left. Neither seemed particularly agitated.

Mike waited for the man to leave as well. The woman was a disposable asset. The new mark pulled out a burner phone, sent a text, then got up and left, leaving the burner behind.

This time it was a car. That was, honestly, easier to track than the subway. Rush hour had started, and the car wasn't going anywhere very fast. And it was headed downtown.

Mike was scanning around as he flew, keeping up and to the side so as not to be noted by the driver. But when the trip led to the East Side of Manhattan and he got into skyscrapers, he had to fly directly over the car.

Which was when he discovered a super racing up behind him. He could tell it was a flyer because, for one, they were flying, but also because of their picturesque horizontal posture with arms extended. Though there was some aerodynamic advantage, they mostly flew that way for the image. When Mike flew, he levitated upright because he was simply carrying his skeleton with Earth Move.

"Stone Tactical?" Iron Eagle blurted. He looked a little awkward as he pulled up next to Mike, as if he wasn't used to going so slow and didn't know which dashing superhero pose was most appropriate.

"Hey, Patrick!" Mike said. "I'm trailing a suspect!"

"A suspect in what?" Patrick asked. His head panned all around as he searched for Mike's target.

"Long story!" Mike shouted as the car pulled out. "I'll catch you up later! I don't want to lose this car!"

Mike dropped and then shot forward in a burst of speed. Patrick lagged for half a heartbeat before catching back up. The car pulled into a garage on East Seventy-ninth, so Mike slowed to a hover out of view while the car eased into a parking spot. The male subject got out and headed for the street. Patrick lowered between levels to get a better look inside the structure.

"Come on," Mike said, pulling on Patrick. "Don't let him see you!"

"Let *who* see me?" Patrick asked but he nonetheless followed Mike off to the side.

Mike pulled them back over the building the guy had parked in and waved at the street.

He gave Patrick a brief rundown of the trail.

"The boss parked the car in the garage and is walking. I want to see who he meets."

"We can't even see the *street* from here, Mike," Patrick said, reasonably.

"I'm following him with Earth Sight," Mike said. "Can we keep that between us?"

"You've got *Sight*?" Patrick said. "Since when do you have Sight?"

"I got it right away," Mike lied. Sight was the sort of thing supers got from training with their powers—as Mike actually had. Training with their powers was a no-no. "But most people don't seem to get it. Dunno why. He's headed to the street. I want to see where he goes."

"Okay," Patrick said. "Is this Corps business?"

"The girl's partner followed me into Two-ninety-one," Mike said with a shrug. "Dunno. Ask the marshals."

The man crossed the street at the light, then went up East Seventy-ninth to a 1970s frosted-glass office building.

Mike realized they were potentially in view of the offices in the building. That wasn't good.

"Come on," Mike said, pulling on Patrick. "We need to move."

Mike flew down to Second Avenue, across to the other side of the street, then up to over the building and landed.

"Why did we just do that?" Patrick asked. Where he'd seemed a little awkward flying slow, Patrick looked positively confused trying not to be seen. Flyer patrols were largely symbolic, and the primary goal was to let the populace see them flying around, giving the appearance of safety under the watchful eyes of the supers. Sure, they could be stealthy when needed for an actual mission, but Patrick didn't seem to have made that mental transition yet.

"So if there was someone in one of the offices in this building, they wouldn't see us," Mike said, distantly. He'd had to reacquire the subject who, fortunately, was just getting on an elevator when they got there. The subject had broken a leg at some time in the past and various other injuries, so he was recognizable under Earth Sight. But it took a lot of focus to identify one particular bone on one particular man at a significant distance while flying. "I lost the guy for a minute and had to reacquire."

The man went up to the ninth floor and proceeded to an office that was, fortunately, on the back side of the building. There were various people in the offices, but he went to the back to an office, knocked on the door, paused, then entered.

The man he was meeting with was also someone with rough background and definitely had been in the military from the wearing on the padding in the knees. Multiple broken bones in the past.

"What are you doing?" Patrick asked. He finally looked graceful while they hovered, though he had his hands slightly out to the sides and one leg bent. Again, it was always about the image.

"The guy I trailed from Washington Heights is meeting with his boss," Mike said, distantly. "Can't figure out what they're talking about, obviously, but he's reporting what happened. This is the guy who had someone tail me into Two-ninety-one. Was it about supers? Or was it about the inheritance? I dunno. But it's totally legal for me to surveil people."

"I'm not sure about the Sight thing," Patrick said. "I'm getting a call."

"I've got this," Mike said. "Not going to confront anyone. Just curious. And please don't bring in the Corps on my Sight. You know they'll want to use me as a guinea pig."

"Right," Patrick said, looking down and grimacing. "We *all* hate that. Don't get yourself in trouble." He switched to superhero voice to say, "Iron Eagle, responding." Then he shot into the sky.

The guy finished his verbal report and left. Mike waited on the rooftop, but the office boss didn't seem to be going anywhere. Over the next half hour, other people came in, reported, and left. Calls came in on the phone. Mike found a good angle to see there were also reports coming in on the computer.

He could've surveilled the new mark until he left for the day, if he ever did, but it didn't seem worth it. Mike could find out some other time and way what the company was. He might as well head home.

This time the normal way.

⊕ ⊕ ⊕

"How was your day?" Derrick asked when he walked in the condo. His father sat at his desk in front of his laptop and stretched as if he hadn't stood in a while. There was an empty coffee mug and half a glass of water beside him.

The loft they'd rented in SoHo was, easily, the nicest home Mike had ever lived in. It was described as "bright" in the listing and it was, mostly because of the large windows and brilliant white paint of the walls. It was sometimes *too* bright. There were three bedrooms, one for each of them and the third for a home office for Derrick. They'd cleared just enough space in the third bedroom that Derrick could also use it for working out.

Incongruously, two of the rooms had cribs. Mike wasn't sure what was up with that.

"Great," Mike said. "I wandered all around New York looking at various rock formations and training my powers. Then I beat up some assholes who were hassling a cute girl on the subway, then lured one of my two tails into the marshals. I'm sure they'll be asking him some hard questions and I'm just as sure he won't answer. But I trailed the other one to her boss, then trailed him to *his* boss and found a secret Society lair on East Seventy-ninth. Also, had an *amazing* calzone for lunch. You?"

"Back up," Derrick said. "What was that middle part?"

"Grandpa's Brick Pizza Oven," Mike said, rubbing his stomach. "*Fantastic* pizza! Oh, my God! And the crust is just . . . scrumptious!"

"The *other* middle part . . ." his father said.

"You just like playing with your food, don't you?" Derrick asked. His eyes were very slightly narrowed in an expression that could either be disappointment or concern. The two were hard to tell apart with Derrick.

"I do, yes," Mike said. "Patrick nearly blew my stakeout, the idiot."

"Someone in Corps now knows you have Sight," Derrick pointed out.

"I think he'll be cool," Mike said. "What I'm wondering is what the company is that the guy reported to the boss. I'm going to go with a Society Dirty Tricks Department. The guy in charge was former military. Can't really tell for sure special operations but I'm going to go out on a limb. Thing about it is . . . something weird about his bone structure. You can't tell nationality with bone structure but something weird. Lots of facial reconstruction surgery, that's for sure. Not sure what the guy originally looked like. I'm going to turn in a report to Gondola, see if they have anything."

"Right," Derrick said.

"Also, just riding around on the subway is fantastic Earth training and I get to beat up assholes," Mike said. "I might just spend my time riding that filthy, pestilential trash-heap. Though tomorrow I'm going to try to get a lunch date with Sasha."

"The love interest," Derrick said.

"I'm not sure if I should be as interested as I am," Mike said. "But she's right around the corner from here and she does tutoring to have more time for modeling. She'll be free for lunch. And she can get into the building and find out what the company is. Then I'll do some research on them."

"Are you sure you're not a little too into this Encyclopedia Brown Detective Agency thing?" Derrick said.

"I have no idea what that is," Mike said, "but I can infer from context. I'm pretty sure I'm one: not going to get arrested; two, interfere with any of the lawsuits; or three, get killed. Because one: Super. We get protected by the Feds for all sorts of stuff. Two: This shouldn't interfere except to take away one of their assets. Three: Super. We're very hard to kill. And since I missed the beginning of the semester, I can't take any courses right now. So, it's train my powers, investigate the Society, and generally just be a junior superhero."

"Right," Derrick said.

"I've gotta see if I can get ahold of Sasha," Mike said. "What's for dinner? I'm thinking Thai."

"Hey, Sash!" Mike said, opening his arms for a hug. "Gently!"

They had agreed to meet outside SoHo Park, a trendy burger place. It had been closed down for a while but recently reopened after a remodel. Sasha was looking as radiant as ever and was, thankfully, unaccompanied.

"Hey," Sasha said, giving him a careful hug. "Why are you wearing a mask? We don't catch stuff."

"I care about others," Mike said, pulling one out for her. "Do you mind? There's a reason, I promise."

"Okay," Sasha said, shrugging. She put on the simple surgical mask. "We can't eat in these, you realize."

"Let's get a table," Mike said. "It's a nice day. Want to sit outside?"

When they were seated and the waitress had gotten their drink order, Mike sighed.

"The reason for the mask, which we'll be taking off in a bit, is that it's nearly impossible to lip-read someone wearing one," Mike said. He didn't think he had any uninvited guests watching him this time, but it never hurt to be cautious.

"Is that a thing?" Sasha asked. "As in, someone is going to lip-read us?"

"Possibly," Mike said. "And much as my brain goes to mush at your eyes, the real reason I asked you for this little tête-à-tête is that I need a favor."

"Does this involve MS-13 again?" Sasha asked. She straightened a little and there was a flash of excitement in her eyes.

"I'm pretty sure they are sick of me," Mike said. "No. Yesterday, someone followed me into Two-ninety-one."

"I heard Two-ninety-one might have been compromised," Sasha said. "Got a text."

"Right," Mike said. "But it wasn't about the Corps. It was the inheritance thing."

She drew in a breath, tucked her chin, and relaxed a little. "So, you're really going to be a billionaire?"

"Really and truly," Mike said. "There's not much that they can do to prevent it eventually. And it's about to become news. All the right channels will be against the little upstart from Montana or Schenectady or somewhere unimportant. How dare he claim a fortune that is old money and proper people? So much fun."

He then succinctly summarized events of the previous day for her. She listened intently, tensing back up as she did.

"I need to find out what company is in that set of offices. *I* can't go in the building. I might be spotted by security, and they'll know I'm onto them. But *you* are just a famous teenage supermodel. No big deal if you wander in there and get off at the wrong floor and go to the wrong office and just look at the name of the company."

"So, you want me to do your dirty work for you?" Sasha said playfully.

"Look, if you wanna marry a billionaire there's things you gotta do, honey," Mike said. "It never comes easy when you're diggin' for gold."

"Oh, you son of a—"

"Oh, come on, Sasha!" Mike said. "It's literally just going up the elevator of a building on Seventy-ninth! You want us to get our billion dollars so we can afford all those kids or not?"

"Us?" Sasha said. "Mike, there is no us."

"Come *on*," Mike said. "What else do you have to do? Some photo shoots? Flying off to Fiji to loll around in the surf half naked? Covered in saaand and oillll . . . ?" He trailed off.

"You have a very active fantasy life, Mike," Sasha said, chuckling and shaking her head.

"Do you have the basic concept of the mission?" Mike said, recovering. "'Cause if you do, we can take off these masks. But you do not mention the mission. Roger? Just decide while we talk about cabbages and kings."

"Okay," Sasha said, taking off the mask. "But someone's probably going to recognize me."

"That's part of this," Mike said as he took off his own. "There will probably be pictures. You're all over Instagram. Some passersby will tag you and probably geolocate you as well. Bastards. People will ask, 'What in the *world* is Sasha Nikula doing with that admittedly handsome, well-dressed, and debonair young man?'

"And when it turns out that that well-dressed, handsome, and debonair young man is a billon-hair, the question will be answered. The real question being how Sasha Nikula knew him before his name became public."

"Will it become public?"

"You went right past the billion-hair?" Mike said. "I thought that was rather clever."

"Yes."

"You and my father," Mike said. "You've both had your sense of humor surgically removed. But eventually, yes. The judge will eventually make my identity public. And when Sasha Nikula is asked how she knew *Mike Truesdale*, she will answer, honestly, from an after-school volunteer program she's in."

She narrowed her eyes and pursed her lips.

"Everyone in the know will know what that volunteer program is.

And everyone will assume it's about the money, which is fine. At least on my side. If you're really upset by it just tell the truth. That we're just friends. And I'm fine with being just friends, Sasha... *liar*... No really, I'm good with being just friends wi... *liar*... with Sasha! *Liar! You shouldn't be a lying liar!*"

"Oh, my God, Mike," Sasha said, chuckling.

"There," he said. "Get 'em to laugh and you're halfway there."

"Halfway where?" Sasha asked.

"Probably severe bodily harm."

"Would you two like to order?"

CHAPTER 7

"Ocean Avenue" —Yellowcard

Sasha took a picture of her food, then tapped on her phone. Her public demeanor was far more cheerful and commanding than he was used to. It reminded him of the time she'd publicly accepted the Junior Super Corps' award for finding drugs in Central Park when she'd had no part in doing so.

"Having lunch with a friend from a volunteer program," Sasha said into the phone, then hit SEND. Several of the other patrons—notably a table of twentysomething women—definitely noticed her taking pictures. Of one the women jabbed a thumb toward Sasha and whispered something. A guy on a lunch date was trying and failing miserably not to undress Sasha with his eyes, and his date was well aware.

"I hope that wasn't geotagged," Mike said.

"It's not," Sasha replied, tapping at the phone. "And there's a team that goes over my social media and anyone that geotags my location they get it pulled down."

"Your food's getting cold," Mike said, cutting into the enormous burger.

"It's a salad," Sasha said. "Can I take your photo?"

"Sure," Mike said, holding up the enormous burger in front of his face. "Go for it."

"Seriously," Sasha said.

"Okay," Mike replied, setting the burger down and raising a thumb. Now the table of women were glancing at him and gossiping quietly.

She checked the photo and raised an eyebrow.

"Have you ever considered modeling?" she asked.

"You're joking, right?" Mike said.

"Mike is the friend of mine from the after-school volunteer program," Sasha dictated. "He's homeschooled so we could get free for lunch."

Sasha's social media voice was eloquent and well practiced.

"I passed my GED," Mike pointed out.

"You don't do social media at all?" she said, still glued to her phone.

"No," Mike said.

"Why not?" Sasha asked.

"Social media is like . . ." Mike said, then paused and thought how to explain. "Back in the Victorian era, carts would go through the streets filled with gin. People would buy it for very cheap in pint glasses and drink it straight."

"Seriously?" Sasha asked.

"Seriously," Mike said. "The Royal Navy had a grog ration. Every afternoon around dinner they'd dole out the rum ration with a squeeze of lime in it. The lime was to prevent scurvy, which was smart. But the rum ration was a *pint* of a hundred and fifty-one-proof rum."

"Oh, my God," Sasha said. "That's pretty powerful, isn't it?"

"Very rarely sold anymore," Mike said. "But it used to be a standard proof. As a society for a very long time, alcoholism was just *common*. It wasn't even considered alcoholism. It was just how you lived. People who *weren't* alcoholics were considered weird."

He took it as a minor miracle that she actually still looked interested. He'd expected to lose her at "Victorian era."

"John Adams was the first secretary of the Navy and when he stated that US Navy ships were to be alcohol free everyone in the world assumed they'd never be able to operate. 'Who would serve on ships without a grog ration?' It's still standard in certain fields. Politicians are mostly functional alcoholics, which explains most Acts of Congress."

She genuinely smiled at the joke. Some of the women at the neighboring table were actively eavesdropping. It was so strange to keep someone's attention during these diatribes, much less gain more attention.

"Back in the ooold days," Mike said, "water was a pretty questionable substance. Good, pure water was rare in cities. With aqueducts having become a lost art, most of it came from contaminated wells. You were better off drinking beer or wine. It was less likely to kill you. People got used to that.

"Then came distilled alcohol and they just went *nuts*.

"Serious and endemic alcoholism existed right up to Prohibition. That's really the only thing that killed it in the US and then slowly elsewhere. Lots of areas it's still common. Russians?"

Still smiling, Sasha shrugged. "Okay, great history lesson, but where are you going with this?"

"I view social media that way," Mike said. "It's an addictive substance that has most of the *world* paralyzed. The world's addiction is just considered *normal*. 'What do you mean you're not constantly on social media?' is like 'What do you mean you don't consume at least a quart of hard alcohol an hour? How can you survive *without* being drunk all the time?' We're not programmed with defenses for the endorphin hits we get. We are not well suited to this world. So, I'm like one of the early Temperance League. I'm a Quaker. I just foreswear social media."

"Okay," Sasha said.

"You've sort of got it under control," Mike said, taking a bite of burger. "But look at poor Laura. Women are particularly susceptible to it. It's about building social capital and women have *always* been more about social capital than economic capital. But it's an addiction, a disease."

"I get that you don't like it," Sasha said, "but you've got a bunch of likes already."

"*Really?*" Mike said, trying to look around her phone, then chuckling. "Whatever. There is one benefit to it, though, and that is that it's reduced gatekeeping on information. Reduced it, not eliminated it."

There was a momemt of silence as both ate a few bites of their food and retreated into contemplation. Their audience got bored and returned to their own conversations.

"What are you going to do about the Electrobolt thing?" Sasha asked softly, keeping one eye on the phone as she ate. "There were some really nasty things said about you that were objectively untrue."

Mike thought about whether to answer the question.

"Essentially, I'm dealing with one thing at a time to the best of my ability," Mike said. "Right now, I've got the suit against the Corps as well as the inheritance suit. That's enough on my plate."

"Why did you switch law firms?" Sasha said. "Really. I get that he's your dad's friend but Josh is pretty put out. Or do we need to put the masks back on?"

"The majority of the inheritance is Fieldstone stock," Mike said. "Just announcing that there was a potential heir caused the stock to drop. There was more than a billion dollars cut off of the value of the company in a few hours. It may recover but it was a hit. Just inheriting means that I'll have to sell about half of it to pay taxes. Maybe more. Financial companies don't like big sells and analysts know that it will have to be sold if I inherit. So, there's a lot of pressure for me not to inherit. You get that?"

"Yes," Sasha said.

"Guess who the number one client of O'Connor, Causey, Early and Bruck is," Mike said.

"Fieldstone?" Sasha said.

"Got it in one," Mike said. "They're a good firm. And they would insist that that's not a conflict of interest. Pull the other one; it's got bells on it."

"I get that," Sasha said with a sigh. "Why the hell are teenagers having to worry about all this?"

Mike shrugged and casually glanced at the table of women. One had been gawking at him and quickly looked away.

"You know one of my favorite songs?"

"So far I'm going for 'Because the Night,' the Cascada version, or 'Memory' from *Cats*," Sasha said.

"Both good," Mike said. "But, no: 'Ocean Avenue,' by Yellowcard. Do you know it?"

"*The one about how they were sixteen and stayed up all night talking?*" Sasha said. "That one?"

"Yep." Mike half sang the first few lines. "That's the life I'd *prefer* to live. Just...being sixteen. Thirteen still, in my case. If I even could *comprehend* that life. But what really gets me is that that particular life is gone."

"What do you mean 'gone'?" Sasha asked.

"The song's set in LA," Mike said. "If you're sitting in a place on Ocean Avenue hanging out late at night, you're probably going to be pestered constantly by street people looking for some money to get a fix. Attacked. Hassled by somebody who wants you to denounce transphobia or white supremacy or that dogs are better than cats. Don't go walking on the beaches barefoot, either: needles."

"It's not that bad," Sasha said. "Not in parts, anyway. I've been to LA."

"But down near the beach?" Mike asked.

"It's . . . pretty bad," Sasha admitted.

"Ever been to Fiji?" Mike said.

"Are you picturing me part naked?" Sasha asked.

"No . . . ?" Mike said.

"Are you picturing me *all* naked?" Sasha asked with a menacing glare.

"I don't have to *picture* you naked, Sasha," Mike pointed out. "I've seen it and it's *very* nice. Seriously. Ever been to Fiji?"

"No," Sasha said, looking mildly confused. "Why?"

"Want to go?" Mike said. "We've both got some free time. We can get married on the beach."

She laughed again and smiled that beautiful smile of hers. "You just don't stop, do you?"

"Joking," Mike said. *Liar!* "It's on my bucket list. I want to learn to scuba dive. I want to go see a tropical reef. Growing up in the ghetto, I wasn't sure I'd make it out *alive*. There were things I decided I was going to do if I ever made it out. I'm out. I want to start *doing* them. I didn't learn to ski or snowboard in Montana, though I *did* get lots of practice on a snowmobile."

"You went snowmobiling?" Sasha said.

"A tale I shall tell thee, O Light of the East: My grandfather is a character with a capital Errr . . ."

"This has been fun, but I've got to get going," Sasha said a little over an hour later.

It *had* been fun. He'd gotten her to laugh at least four times. They would have many children who would be both smart and beautiful.

"What do you think about what I was talking about when we first got here?" Mike said.

"I'll check it out," Sasha said. "But where—"

Mike held up his hand and pulled out a slip of paper. Then he put on his mask and gestured for her to do the same.

"There," Mike said. "Fly at least part of the trip."

"I was just planning on walking in," Sasha said, muffled.

"If you fly, you'll break any tails," Mike said. "Just wear normal clothes and fly a couple of blocks. That way they'll lose you. If you're tailed. You shouldn't be but the mask thing is sort of obvious."

"That will sort of tell the people tailing me that I'm a super," Sasha pointed out. "As well as, well, everyone around me."

"Wear a mask for when you take off and land," Mike said. "Don't land right by the building. Just to break the tail. The people tailing you will know anyway."

"I'll think about it," Sasha said.

"I've got the tab," Mike said, picking up the bill. "Holy smokes! What was that Wagyu beef?"

Two days later, Mike opened the door to his apartment and waved Sasha inside. She was wearing a delightful halter top and tight jean shorts.

"Hey," Sasha said, looking around the condo. "Nice."

"Thanks," Mike said. "Probably not as nice as yours but it's the nicest place *I've* ever lived. This is my father, Derrick Sterrenhunt."

"Mr. Sterrenhunt," Sasha said, nodding.

Derrick had hurried into the room when Mike had opened the door. He was covered in a light sheen of seat from a workout.

"I hear you don't shake hands much," Derrick said.

"I can but it's . . ." She waggled her head. "When I'm around people who insist I just make my hand like a handshake and don't actually clasp. I can do it if I'm really careful."

"That must be difficult," Derrick said. He glared at Mike. "Anyway, I didn't realize we were having company. If you'll excuse me, I need to go clean up."

"So, can we talk?" Sasha asked. "I checked what you were asking about."

"Dad's read in," Mike said. "But we probably should go to the office. It's a bedroom but it's where we've got the office. Is that okay?"

"Are you going to get handsy?" she asked.

"I like my face the way it is," Mike said. "But you've got to leave your phone . . ."

⊕ ⊕ ⊕

"You get the bed," Mike said, sitting down at the computer. The bedroom was a windowless interior. "And I'm not going to get fresh. You're about to meet professional Mike."

"Professional Mike exists?" Sasha asked.

"What did you find out?" Mike asked. "Give me the whole thing."

"I can't believe I actually flew in regular clothes," Sasha said, shaking back and forth slightly. "But I wore my mask out from the house. I'm right around the corner from here. Did you know that?"

"My dad picked the condo," Mike said dismissively. *Though I might've suggested the neighborhood.* "Did you complete the mission?"

"Yes," Sasha said. "Wooten Security."

Mike turned to the computer and brought up a search engine.

"Spell that," Mike said.

"Wooten Security," Mike said. "President, Jared Kindred. They provide a variety of professional support to the modern executive apparently."

"What's that mean?" Sasha said, looking over his shoulder.

"I'm going out on a limb and say they *aren't* about cards and keys," Mike said, going through the website. "I'm going to guess dirty-tricks group. This is a mass of corporate double speak. It essentially tells you nothing."

"So..." Sasha said.

"So..." Mike said. "This is going to take a while. You wanna stick around?"

"I wanna find out what's going on, yeah," Sasha said.

"You might want to hang downstairs, then," Mike said. "I'm going to be a while."

"Okay, got it," Mike said, walking into the living room while looking at his pad.

"You have *got* to be kidding me!" Sasha said, laughing. She was relaxed on the couch with a glass of water and snacks laid out on the coffee table. Derrick was in the adjacent chair.

"I've got a very good relationship with Cecelia and Sir Ian," Derrick said, shrugging.

"Mike, your dad is fantastic!" Sasha said. "He's actually got *funny* golf stories! I usually *hate* golf stories."

"I have noted that," Mike replied. "Where are we on electronics?"

"We're clear," Derrick replied. "What did you get?"

"Wooten Security is a Delaware LLC that was incorporated nine years ago," Mike said, looking at his notes. "But here's the thing: it didn't begin *functioning* until *three* months ago. Before that it was just a shell. They moved into that office two months ago. And Jared Kindred does not exist."

"So, who is he?" Sasha asked.

"Jost Alnes," Mike said.

"You're joking," Derrick said. "Here?"

"Yes," Mike said. "Over on East Seventy-ninth Street. In New York terms, we're practically neighbors."

"Who is . . . Jost Alnes?" Sasha asked.

"Former Norwegian Navy Ranger officer," Derrick said. "What we would call SEALs. He was accused and convicted of stealing and selling state secrets. Escaped custody. Disappeared."

"Another large-reward guy," Mike said. "Interpol Red Notice. FBI most wanted. Some of those state secrets were *ours*. Notably things like our Navy's Baltic Plan in the event we had to take on the Ruskies as well as communications, codes, et cetera.

"Since then, he has been selling the secrets, and his capabilities, to the highest bidder. How he got into the US is a good question. He's on *every* most-wanted list. May be a normal but he's a *much* more dangerous guy than Cannibale or Death Strong."

"Then we report it to the Corps," Sasha said.

"There's a problem with that," Mike said, looking over at Derrick.

"What's the problem?" Sasha said, looking somewhere between agitated and confused. "Mike, we sort of came out okay going all Junior Super Corps one time. We're *not* going to if we do it again."

"The problem is, the people he is working for have the FBI penetrated," Derrick said. "If you report it to the Corps, they get a warrant from the FBI. The instant his name goes on the database, he disappears."

"*That's* the problem," Mike said. "And, yes, this would get us in *serious* trouble. Just wait . . ."

He thought about it for a moment and shrugged.

"Does it make any sense at all that Electrobolt was in charge of us?" Mike said.

"It never did," Sasha said. "What's that got to do with an international criminal?"

"The same people who were pulling the Secretary's strings on that are connected to this," Mike said. "And you're going to have to take my word on that. But I'm serious. This isn't just about the billion dollars. This is about things much larger. The best thing to do is just to grab him out of his office. Fly up and grab him."

"I can do that but..."

"It will seriously piss off the people who pull the Secretary's strings," Mike said.

"You're assuming the Secretary has her strings being pulled," Sasha said. Her expression said his might have touched a nerve. She'd probably spent her young life admiring California Girl.

"How else do you explain Electrobolt?" Mike asked.

"He was popular with senators?" Sasha said, a little defensively.

"Who do you think he's talking about?" Derrick replied. "You probably haven't looked at the board of the Trust. Senator Drennen's brother-in-law is on it. He gets paid five thousand dollars a month just to turn up from time to time and approve the management trustee's decisions."

"And if you think the honorable senator isn't getting a cut of that, think again," Mike said. "Then there are the charities that she and other senators and congressmen are associated with—meaning siphon off cash—that the Trust contributes to. Right now, my inheritance is a slop fund, and all the little piggies have their noses in it."

"We don't have to move on it immediately," Derrick said. "We know what's going on and we know where they are. We can run them for a while and see what comes up."

"But we don't know how long they'll stay," Mike said. "If they pull up stakes they'll vanish without a trace. Alnes has been *very* hard to pin down. I wasn't expecting Alnes. When you went there, what exactly did you do?"

"Um," Sasha said. "I checked the directory for what was on the ninth floor, then went up there. But then I sort of made like I was lost and went up to the tenth. There's a modeling agency up there and I sort of talked with them a little, gave the impression I maybe wasn't totally satisfied with my current agency. Then I left."

"So, you had a cover," Mike said.

"Good job," Derrick said.

"Thanks," Sasha said. "Just seemed like the thing to do. So, what are we going to do?"

Mike sighed as his phone buzzed.

TA: **Bag him. Need him off the table. Operations order TBD.**

"We're going to bag him," Mike said, putting his phone away.

"Isn't this the sort of thing we're not supposed to talk about around electronics?" Sasha said. "'Cause you made me put my phone up."

"Yours isn't secure," Mike said. "Mine is secure except to certain people. Who want to bag him. Would you mind not getting the reward this time?"

"I'm fine with that," Sasha said. "I'm doing okay money wise."

"Good," Mike said, looking at Derrick, then back at Sasha. "Can I ask you a personal question?"

"Maybe," Sasha said.

"You're from Missouri," Mike said. "What are your politics?"

"I'd rather go to Osseo as well," Sasha said. "You're a lot more right-wing than you try to let on, aren't you?"

"I'm not entirely comfortable with either side," Mike said. "I'm an old-fashioned liberal, which these days makes me to the right of Attila the Hun. And to the right these days that makes you just another liberal. My cousins can't get that I'm okay with trans in general. The left can't handle it when I point out that if you've got a Y chromosome, you're not a woman—shouldn't, e.g., be in women's sports. Which puts me out in the nowhere. But at least I can talk about it with people on the right. You can't with progressives."

"They're way too close-minded," Sasha said. "Yeah, I'm pretty much the same."

"Okay," Mike said. "And virtually no selfies on your Instagram."

"I don't like selfies," Sasha said.

"Do you happen to know Daryl Haubenstricker?" Mike asked.

"Not all famous people know all famous people, Mike," Sasha said.

"Okay," Mike said, frowning.

"But, yes, I do," Sasha said. "He's a nice guy. Is he tied up in this?"

"He is a nice guy," Mike said. "You know he runs a program to find children who are being trafficked?"

"Yes," Sasha said, curiously. "I've contributed to it. Please don't tell me it's some kind of evil front."

"Oh, it's not," Mike said. "It's the real deal."

"And you know this how?" Sasha said.

"OPSEC," Mike replied.

"What?" Sasha asked.

"It means I'm getting to the point that I have to stop talking," Mike said. "But the point is, the reward money will be going to a *very* good cause. I don't think we're going to be directly involved. Though . . . we might. *You* might, anyway. Hmmm . . ."

"What are you thinking?" Derrick asked.

"We still owe that FBI guy," Mike said. "This would be an even *better* collar."

"What FBI guy?" Sasha asked.

"I'm not even sure," Mike said. "But to take Alnes it would be safest to use a super. And if that was when *you* were patrolling with Patrick . . ."

"I'd sort of get credit for the collar, but I wouldn't get the reward," Sasha said.

"The problem is we've got to prove to a reasonable level that it *is* Alnes," Mike said. "And that is going to require some finesse. He's probably using temporary prints or had them wiped. Which means DNA."

"Which means you're going to have to set up surveillance," Derrick said. "Or someone is. And the moment you put his DNA on CODIS, he's gone."

"Then we don't put it on CODIS," Mike said. "We get a sample, and we get it tested offline. Then we do a visual comparison from CODIS."

"Where do we get the sample?" Sasha asked.

"Well, we could do an elaborate surveillance," Mike said. "Or we could just do it the easy way."

"What's the easy way?" Derrick asked.

"Black bag his office," Mike said. "His office chair will be *covered* in DNA."

"Black bag?" Sasha said.

"Break in," Derrick said. "It's literally a security company, Mike."

"And what do you want to bet that his *ninth-floor* office window is not alarmed?"

CHAPTER 8

"Danger Zone" —Kenny Loggins

"You keep getting me into these situations," Sasha whispered. She floated with her arms and feet casually crossed. Credit where credit was due, Sasha was able to casually hover without having to strike a superhero pose.

She and Mike were hovering nine floors over East Seventy-ninth Street at three A.M. Sasha's parents didn't even care she was out in the middle of the night. Mike still wasn't clear on whether her parents were even in the country.

"Nobody is going to hear us up here," Mike said. "Just don't shout."

"What happens if somebody *sees* us?" Sasha asked.

Cars and pedestrians on the street below were sparse. There were still more office and apartment lights on than one might expect at that hour, but few of those were actually occupied and none of those occupants were looking outside. As always, none of that gave them an excuse to ditch caution.

"That is why we are wearing fashionable dark clothing," Mike said.

He'd gotten a glob of random flecks of silica onto the latch of the window but was being very careful opening it. It was fortunate that the building was pre-air-conditioning. It had been retrofitted but the windows still opened. As predicted, there was no alarm. And he also didn't see any telltales. But if he left a single thing that Alnes spotted, the guy would vanish in an instant.

"If Alnes finds out, he'll be in the wind. Otherwise, they'll call NYPD. NYPD will send a flyer team. And we'll explain why we're breaking in. Then Alnes will find out and he'll disappear. So, hope nobody looks up."

He started mouthing the *Mission: Impossible* theme as he worked the latch.

"Duh, duh, duhduh, duh, duh, duhduh, duh, duh..."

"That is going to get so annoying," Sasha said.

"Everybody always says that," Mike replied.

He got the window unlatched and very carefully opened it.

He turned himself horizontal and drifted into the room. Sasha gracefully followed.

"Don't touch anything," Mike said. "Especially the window frame."

"I'm just starting to wonder why I'm here," Sasha said.

"Company?" Mike said, hovering over the chair. He turned so his feet were vertical and gently started swabbing the chair with a Q-tip. "I needed a sidekick?"

"I am *not* a *sidekick*," Sasha said.

"At least *you* can go out at night," Mike said. "My last sidekick, his mom tracked his phone constantly. And you're the lookout. Duh. That's what sidekicks do!"

"Shouldn't we be whispering?" Sasha asked.

"There is literally no one in these offices," Mike said. "I waited 'til the janitors left. We're done. Let's go."

They slid out the window, then Mike closed it and ensured that everything was in order.

"I need an apprentice flying cat burglar?" Mike said, heading upward like a vampire leaving behind his victim. "I'm trying to show off to my future wife, to prove to her that I am a virile and successful potential mate? That my genes are worthy? I get bored talking to myself?"

"I get bored *listening* to you," Sasha said.

"Imagine what it's like to *be* me, then..."

"And that is how you break into an office," Mike said as they walked out of the alleyway in midtown where they'd landed. "At least if you can fly. Or climb really well."

"I'm pretty sure this is illegal," Sasha said. A figure, female by her

WELCOME TO THE JUNGLE

bone structure, passed by the end of the alleyway and did a double take in their direction. Any intelligent New Yorker would actively ignore a couple people in an alleyway, regardless of the situation. Of course, tourists were always in abundance, and they were a curious lot.

"It is," Mike said. "It's called breaking and entering. B and E. It's like a misdemeanor juvie. Even if we get caught, it will just increase your street cred. Also, they'd have to explain how we did it."

The woman headed toward them and Mike barely had time to silently warn Sasha.

"Hey, uh, hi," the woman said, walking up to Sasha. She was in her forties and a little drunk. What she was doing on East Seventy-second at three A.M. was the question. "Are you Sasha Nikula?"

"Um, yes, I am," Sasha said, her eyes wide.

"Do you want to get a picture with her?" Mike said. "Let me take it."

"Sure!" the woman said.

When they were done the woman thanked her.

"My daughter wants to be a model," she said. "You seem very grounded."

"I try to be," Sasha said, nervously.

"But she soars to great heights," Mike said.

"Why are you dressed like a, uh...?" the fan said, suddenly noticing Sasha's distinctly non-chic attire.

"She's considering taking a role as a teenage secret agent," Mike said. "You know, one of those 'spies like us' things?"

"Yeah," Sasha said, brightly. "So, I'm just getting the feel for it, you know?"

"You haven't said *anything* about getting into acting," the fan said. "I follow *all* your social media."

"Yeah, well, keep this one quiet, okay?" Sasha said. "I'm not sure I'm right for the role."

"Oh, you'd be fantastic!"

"What are you doing out at three in the morning, if I may ask, ma'am?" Mike said.

"I dunno... I think I'm a little lost..."

"Let's get you back to brighter climes, shall we?"

"You are going to lead me into a life of sin and perdition," Sasha said.

They'd found the lady an Uber and gotten her headed back to her hotel on East Twenty-seventh and Second Avenue. Dyslexia can be deadly.

"I certainly hope so," Mike said. "But *is* it sin and perdition if we're legally married? And we have done proper superhero good deeds this night. That counts..."

"You have to appear in court," Derrick said at breakfast the following morning.

"I'm pretty sure I didn't get caught," Mike said.

"The judge has ruled that your identity is public domain," Derrick said, "since your suit affects the stock price of Fieldstone. And the defense has called for a competency hearing. So, you have to appear."

"Yaay!" Mike said. "That means I'm going to need a suit!"

"You're also going to need a psychological evaluation," Derrick said. His eyes were narrowed, with a hint of concern.

"Because I want to get a suit?" Mike asked.

"Thanks for going shopping with me," Mike said. "I figured you'd know the good resale shops."

Mike and Sasha were poring over various suits at one off East Sixty-eighth Street. Mike greatly preferred New York at night when fewer people were around and that blinding light in the sky wasn't there. But stores had a tendency to be closed just then. At least he had good company.

"How'd you figure that?" Sasha asked.

"The minute that Laura got her money she started buying clothes and shoes like they were going out of style," Mike said, pulling one of the suits off the rack and holding it up. "What do you think?"

"Too banker," Sasha said.

"Your clothes scream resale," Mike said. "Refitted nicely. But resale."

Even dressed down in those resale clothes, someone would occasionally recognize Sasha. Thankfully, they would just point and whisper. So far, none were brave enough to approach like the woman the night prior.

"I don't like to spend money," Sasha said with an uncomfortable shrug. "My parents spend enough."

"What's going to happen when you're on your own?" Mike asked.

"I'm going to put them on a stipend," Sasha said, sounding a little distant. This particular matter had clearly been bothering her for a while. "It will be a decent one. My dad's a businessman; he isn't going to go broke. But they're not going to be spending like they have been."

"You're not broke, are you?" Mike asked as he held up a navy blue sport coat with gold buttons. "This one?"

"Too ship captain and . . . not you," Sasha said. "And no. I made sure of that. Plus, all the escrow. When I turn eighteen it will be interesting. I'm going to invest it and probably just quit modeling."

"Tired of being a dress dummy?" Mike asked.

"Hey!" The shout came from a guy in his thirties, wearing a T-shirt and jeans. He was pasty and could stand to eat some fruit. Also, starstruck.

"Are you, uh, Sasha Nikula?" he asked.

"Yes, I am," Sasha said, smiling brightly.

"Can, uh, can I get a picture?" the guy said, pulling out his phone.

"Why don't you get one together?" Mike asked. "I'll take it."

"Sure!" the guy said, handing over his phone and standing next to Sasha.

"No hands, okay?" Sasha said.

"No! No . . . not . . . no!" he said.

She posed smiling brightly as the guy looked dumbstruck.

"I'm your biggest fan," the man said after the picture was taken. "This is going to be . . . wow . . . Uh . . ."

"What do you think of this one?" Mike asked, pulling out a slightly oversized black suit with white pinstripes and turning to the fan.

"Uh, I don't know . . . much about . . . suits . . ." he said.

"It's, uh . . ." Sasha said, considering.

"Black preacher, right?" Mike said. "Screams Jesse Jackson?"

"That, yes," Sasha said.

"Perfect," Mike said. "That's one. The rest I agree don't work. Where else is good?"

"Maubry's?" Sasha said.

"Uber?" Mike replied.

"We can probably walk it," Sasha said.

"Hey, it was great meeting you, man," Mike said, shaking the man's hand. "May God walk with you in all the dark places you may go . . ."

⊕ ⊕ ⊕

"You handled that well," Sasha said as they managed to break free from the fan. "And *that* is what I'm getting tired of."

"Understandable," Mike said. "When you're a public figure, you always have to have someone to say no. Someone to be the bad guy. That way you can be nice and someone else can tell them to take a hike."

"That," Sasha said. "They just all want to be your friend! And it's not that most of them are bad people, it's just..."

"How many friends can you have?" Mike said. "And each of them don't realize that those few seconds you spend on them, extrapolated to the entire fan base, is your entire life. No one raindrop thinks it's responsible for the flood. Do you know why? Do you want to know?"

"One of your long explanations?" Sasha asked.

"I can do it in one sentence, but it won't make sense," Mike said. "Or I can do it in five thousand words, and it might."

"What's the one sentence?" Sasha asked.

"We are evolved to never leave high school," Mike said. "It's why high school never ends."

"You're serious," Sasha said, laughing. "Just live our entire lives in high school? That would suck."

"You're going with an ascot?" Sasha said. "Those...aren't exactly in style."

"It's a cravat, not an ascot," Mike said, testing out cravats in a mirror. "I intend to set a trend."

"Really?" Sasha said.

"They're releasing my name and basic fake background tomorrow," Mike said. "The marshals aren't all that happy. The background was never designed to stand up to scrutiny. But by the time we have the hearing I'll be known as the modern Oliver Twist. The hearing is live-streamed and it's going to be covered by some of the bigger law streamers. I intend to be the height of fashion in my own personal idiom.

"And I've already been seen in the company of Sasha Nikula," Mike added. "Which is status by association."

"Please tell me you weren't just hanging out with me to be noticed," Sasha said. "I hate it when people do that."

"I wasn't," Mike said. "Do you recall what else we've been doing?

I'm still waiting on the DNA results. Plus, we shall be wed. This is a thing. But by hanging out with you and being noticed it's already warmed up the information mill. Think about Mike Truesdale for just a second, Sasha. Am I or am I not the *strangest* person you've ever met?"

"You're certainly different," Sasha said.

"Dropping the essential Mike Truesdale onto the public without warning is likely to cause brain meltdowns," Mike said. "They needed some warning and I thank you for allowing that warning. It's liable to save some lives from stroke and thus we've done our job as heroes saving lives. Notice how except for our one foray into crime I've always been well dressed when I'm out with you?"

"Yes. You dress better than I do," she admitted.

"Maybe I can get some of my generation's males to put on something other than jeans and a clean T-shirt," Mike said, contemplating a light violet cravat. "I think this one with the Jesse Jackson suit."

He held them both up to her.

"What do you think? With the suit fitted, obviously."

"That . . . might work," Sasha admitted. "The violet is good but a bold choice. You're going to need to get it fitted pretty quick."

"Ooooh, Kevinnnn . . . ?"

"Whatever are *you* two doing here?" Kevin asked. His workspace was a strange juxtaposition between an otherwise immaculate and somewhat spartan modernistic room, but with a table of pure chaos before him. Scattered drawings, pieces of fabric, multiple pairs of scissors, and various writing implements were laid out haphazardly, with measuring tape draped around his shoulders. He was overseeing the redesign of one of the Corps costumes. He liked to change the regular Corps members' costumes about every two years. "I saw where you'd been seen in public lately. Do I need to know something?"

"We're just friends hanging out," Sasha said. "Mike needed some help shopping."

"I have a competency hearing coming up," Mike said. "What do you think of this suit with this cravat?"

Mike tied the cravat then put the suit up in front of him.

"I need your expert opinion," Mike said.

"The cravat is a bold statement," Kevin said, examining the ensemble. "Very daring."

"I'm a daredevil," Mike said.

"It's tremendous!" Kevin said. "But be warned: Once you make a bold fashion statement like that, you're going to be under a microscope for the rest of your life. *Everyone* will be judging your look."

"There is a group in far lands called the Monks of Cool," Mike said. "In distant lamaseries found only by treacherous secret paths, they study for years to determine the true nature of cool. When it is time for their mastery test, they are taken to a room full of clothing of every style throughout the centuries and asked, of all of these, which is the coolest. The only proper answer is, of course: Whatever *I* am wearing."[1]

"You *understand!*" Kevin said, putting his hands on either side of Mike's face. "Not only my little Michelangelo's *David*, but my little apprentice of cool!"

"I need to know who I can see—not you—to get the suit fitted," Mike said. "And well fitted."

"I know just the person," Kevin said.

"Wait," Mike said, holding up his hand. "Is he black or Persian? 'Cause I'm racist. Black and Persian tailors are the *only* people I trust their fashion sense. In general, white people don't gots none. You being an obvious exception. And I really need just the right *shoes*..."

"I understand from Kevin you only trust black tailors?"

Mr. Plimpton was exactly what Mike had been looking for in New York: a sixty-year-old black tailor who had probably started as an apprentice tailor when he was a child.

The small, discreet tailor's shop was tucked away in an older but charming townhome on West 144th Street in Harlem. Counter to Kevin's workspace, the shop was both packed full of Plimpton's work and meticulously maintained.

"Black or Persian, sir," Mike said. "I was raised in the ghetto and have come to have great regard for the fashion sense of well-dressed black men and the tailors who supply them. I was doing business

---

1 This is stolen blatantly and unashamedly from the late and much-lamented Sir Terry Pratchett. The author strongly recommends that his gentle readers start reading the Grand Master and be prepared to laugh and cry. Do so unashamedly. It is recommended they start with *Wyrd Sisters* or *Guards! Guards!* From there you have much enjoyment ahead.

consulting back home before I moved here. One of the first gentlemen I consulted with was a tailor such as yourself, sir."

"Business consulting?" Mr. Plimpton said. He wasn't measuring Mike for the refitting himself. He was overseeing a teen male, also black.

"I have already taken numerous college courses, sir," Mike said, "including in the field of business and finance. It was a way to make money that did not involve standing on a corner dealing drugs."

"Wise of you," Mr. Plimpton said. "Where are you from?"

"Discreetly, sir?" Mike asked.

"Everything in this shop is discreet."

"Baltimore, sir," Mike said. "East Baltimore. Raised in foster care. I am ABE, though I rarely attend these days as it's hard to explain why a white kid is in the congregation. Everyone I knew growing up was black. I have a hard time distinguishing white faces. White people all look alike to me."

"Really?" the teen said. He was pinning the hem and leaned back to check if Mike was lying.

"Really," Mike said. "You develop the ability to distinguish faces between four and seven. I saw approximately *no* white people on a day-to-day basis between four and seven. So, they all look alike to me. I also don't *get* white people. They think weird. I do get black people including, especially, those who are raised in bad circumstances. 'Cause that was my life growing up. Bad circumstances in a ghetto."

"Are you sure?" Derrick said, looking at Mike's outfit back at the apartment.

"I'm sure," Mike said, removing the pocket scarf. Add accessories until you're done, then take one away.

"This *is* a competency hearing," Derrick pointed out. "And that looks a tad ... um ..."

"Outré?" Mike asked. "It will work. Trust me."

"I'm not sure I should," Derrick said. "But it's a bit late to get a tie."

CHAPTER 9

"Familiar Taste of Poison" —Halestorm

"Your Honor, this is nothing but a delaying tactic on the part of the defense," Ahuvit said. "The plaintiff's father will have control of the funds in question. The heir's father is a career soldier, a Georgetown graduate, and a member of the bars of Virginia, North Carolina, and Montana. The heir will have no control of the funds until he turns eighteen. If there are questions about his competency then, it will be a matter for another court."

"Objection, Your Honor," Rich Lowe replied in his usual, nasally tone. "The plaintiff has not been determined to be the heir, therefore the plaintiff's counsel's reference to him is premature and prejudicial."

In the earlier, largely inconsequential proceedings, the courtroom had been chock full of reporters. They had dwindled as the case dragged on and now just a single, bored intern sat in the front row to take note of the highlights. However, the horde of Trust attorneys hadn't diminished in the slightest, even though only Lowe ever actually spoke. Conn sat with a smug expression and arms crossed, as if he knew he'd already won.

"Your Honor," Ahuvit said, "referring to the plaintiff other than as the legitimate heir creates a counter prejudice. I will remind the court and the defense that there are not only the statements of the plaintiff's father, a member of the bar, but a positive DNA test. We really should just be proceeding to probate."

"I think the term 'heir' is prejudicial," Judge Mickelson said. He had the face of a bulldog, which was only exacerbated by his perpetual scowl, and his robes did little to hide his extra weight. "Sustained. Whether the defense sees this as a delaying tactic is moot. There is a question of competency. Young man?"

"Your Honor," Mike said, looking at him.

"You are potentially the heir to a very large fortune," the judge said. He leaned forward and spoke slowly as if talking to a much younger child. "That money affects many other people. It is currently primarily in stock in one company. Simply the public notice that there is a potential heir has caused that stock price to fall. People have their life savings tied up in similar stock. There are pension funds tied to it. This decision affects *many* people. Not solely yourself. Do you understand that?"

"Yes, Your Honor," Mike said. "May I comment on that at some length, Your Honor?"

"You may," the judge said.

Mike paused a moment in thought. It took significant effort to block out his intense desire to simply kill Conn and then leap out the window to escape. A glance at Derrick, who sat with rigid posture and perfect poker face, immediately grounded Mike.

Death is too good for him. Beat him in his world. Humiliate him.

"I recognize that, Your Honor," Mike said. "The question for this hearing, however, is: Am I competent to manage the funds? If I am found incompetent for any reason, the Trust will argue that they should continue to manage the funds. I would like to speak to that matter as well."

The longer Mike spoke, the wider the judge's eyes got.

"I will refer to my counsel's argument that that question is moot. My father will be in charge of the funds and thus *my* competence, either my psychological competence or my intellectual competence, is moot.

"However, we will entertain the defense's argument for a moment to consider it carefully," Mike said. "The question of competence also arises in the defense. Are *they* competent?"

"That's not an argument we are addressing here," the judge said. He was starting to glance around at the various lawyers in mild panic. The child was not only speaking but speaking intelligently.

"But it is part and parcel of the argument, Your Honor," Mike argued. "And I think a review of that competence may define the question of *my* competence in Your Honor's mind.

"The Trust chose to convert *all* of my family's assets, save a few personal housing units here in New York, into Fieldstone stock. First of all, it is a common axiom to never put your eggs into one basket. It is certainly a common axiom in finance. You should *always* have a distributed portfolio. And then there is the question of placing them all in Fieldstone's basket."

The collection of Trust employees was breaking down into a torrent of whispering that grew into muttering, with expressions ranging from irritated to worried.

"The first issue in the question of *their* competence, is that they were *specifically formed* from the original Follett Trust for the purpose of holding the Follett fortune in the event that the potential heir should appear. When it was announced there was a potential heir, the sudden question of disposition of a large amount of Fieldstone's stock caused a large-scale sell that caused the stock to drop."

"Quiet!" Mickelson said with a bang of his gavel. The chattering ceased.

"Had the Trust *spread* the money, had a distributed portfolio instead of putting all my family's eggs in one basket, that would have *never happened*. Part of it in stock here, part of it in bonds there, part of it in ETFs, part of it in commercial properties, possibly a high-risk portion, say ten percent, invested in tech and commodities.

"If the fund had been *competent* fund managers, Fieldstone would never have taken a hit! It is not *my* competence which should be on trial, Your Honor!"

"Objection!" Lowe said. "That is the point of this hearing, Your Honor."

"Your Honor?" Mike said. "I would ask that you allow this line. There is a specific reason that directs to the point of this hearing."

"Overruled," the judge said. "Go on. But please don't waste the court's time."

"I assure you, Your Honor, *this* is not a waste," Mike continued. "Then there's the issue of taxes. At least *half* of this will go to taxes. That would happen no matter *who* inherited. The Trust was *specifically* set up to search for an heir. An heir was presumed from its inception.

Any heir would *have* to pay inheritance taxes. Where *is* the money to come from? Oh, that's right, *Fieldstone stock*! Because there is *no other source* of funds due to the Trust putting *all of it in one basket.*

"So, it is guaranteed that at some point there will be a sell. If we spread the sell over time, it will have less effect. If we're forced to hurry into a sell and dump half a billion in Fieldstone, it will be particularly painful to those investors you are worried about, Your Honor."

Lowe had stayed out of his entourage's conversation, but now he leaned back to pass one a quiet message.

"All of which could have been alleviated if the soi-disant trustees had *bothered* themselves to do all the hard work of managing a *distributed portfolio.* Heaven forbid they actually have to work!

"And then there is the issue of it being all in *Fieldstone* stock," Mike said with an aggrieved sigh. "From the point that they converted *all of my family's assets*, hard won over *centuries*, into nothing but Fieldstone stock, the stock price has only gone *down.* And that has nothing to do with my sudden appearance. *That* is *all* on *Fieldstone."*

Most of the Trust's lackeys were still fidgeting nervously, but one was sitting smugly with his arms crossed, as if Mike was saying things he'd already told them himself more than a few times.

"I find Fieldstone's continual creation of novel ETFs charming in a naïf, loving sort of way. I tend to think of it as the Humbert Humbert of investing. But their international investment strategy is something from a Three Stooges movie!

"Fieldstone is heavily invested in China," Mike said. "There are many issues with investing in China, not the least of which is losing money to contract breach and having no real remedy in Chinese court. Which has happened to Fieldstone *several* times."

Conn waved Lowe over. The lead defense counsel leaned it to hear him. Conn jabbed a finger into the air and practically spat while talking. Lowe shrank away and nodded in obeisance. He turned to the judge and looked like a deer in the headlights trying to find words but failing.

"But the real issue of investment in China, currently, is demographic. The Chinese population is graying rapidly, and their total population is declining. Due to the one-child-policy that was in effect for so long and the cultural changes in childbirth it caused, the population of China is approaching a crash point.

"An economy depends on people. You literally cannot have an economy without humans. An environment without people is called *ecology* not *economy*. Economies and thus business wealth do not grow in a condition of declining population. Just ask the Japanese. The economy eventually stagnates and even regresses."

The rest of the lackeys scoffed and shook their heads, but the one man shrugged and waved a hand as if to say "Exactly!"

"But Fieldstone *continues* to invest in China. They recently made a pronouncement about another multibillion-dollar investment that is, based on their recent history, probably going to go south in a big way.

"Do you know where Fieldstone does *not* invest in any significant fashion? India. Which is financially insane! If anyone should be in a competency hearing, it's the leadership of Fieldstone!

"India has common law courts, which means that, unlike China, you can *occasionally* get a fair hearing. I will point Your Honor's attention to the case of *Allegheny v. Uttara* as an example. The Allegheny Financial Corporation sued Uttara Chemicals for fiduciary breach, won in Indian court, and was financially compensated."

Derrick had actually straightened with some pride and cracked the slightest approving smile—though it disappeared the second Mike noticed it.

"Show a *single time* when the same has happened with China. How many American companies have been ripped off by the Chinese and been laughed out of Chinese court? Hundreds? Thousands? Fieldstone has been ripped off *multiple* times, but they just keep going back to the well like Charlie Brown with Lucy and the football.

"And I must point out that every time they toss money into the firepit called China, that is *my family's money*! That is *my* legacy they are burning like the Allies burned Dresden! Not to mention all of those other investors for whom you are reasonably concerned, Your Honor.

"Further, India has a similar population to China but a *fraction* of the GDP—literally only three percent of China's. India has nowhere to go but up whereas China is reaching a combination maximum equity condition coupled with population limit. On the subject of demographics, India's population continues to grow, slowly but steadily. People equal an economy. Its GDP continues to grow, slightly but not explosively ahead of its population growth."

Judge Mickelson was staring at Lowe as if willing for some rescue.

Lowe, looking somewhere between lost and distressed, remained silent.

"Right now, Indian IPOs—initial public offerings—are in the same condition as US IPOs in the 1980s. Not every company is a success story. But right now, you can more or less put all the names of Indian IPOs on a dartboard, close your eyes, throw three darts, and you're going to make money. A well-run fund that is familiar with Indian business could be making returns similar to what Peter Lynch made with Magellan in the 1980s. The Indian Home Depot awaits, Your Honor!

"So, why isn't Fieldstone investing in India? And the defense would question *my* competence? When *they* put all of *my* family's money in a company whose stock is on the decline and is so purblind it cannot see the biggest financial windfall since the *internet*? What, is India too far to *fly*?

"So, at this very moment, Your Honor, my family's fortune is being frittered away by people so *in*competent, I am surprised they can tie their rather vulgar shoes."

Mike then sat and looked at the judge, who was looking a tad confused.

"Does that, uh, complete . . . ?"

"I said, Your Honor, that the defense's objection was to be put to rest," Mike said. "That diatribe against the management of *my* family's money should prove this hearing as well as their objections are moot. The question is not *my* competence, Your Honor, but Mr. Conn's."

Conn's casual dismissal of the proceedings had evolved to quiet, angry stewing. But now he locked onto Mike with a death glare, as if trying to slice Mike to pieces with eye lasers. Mike, on the other hand, felt oddly relaxed, almost zen.

"I am competent to manage the funds both psychologically and *intellectually*, Your Honor. Am I PTSD? Yes, eighty-eight points, which is *extremely* high. Do I wake up at night screaming? Yes. I have a lot of bad things in my past to scream about. So did Oliver Twist. Am I ADHD? Very. Am I ODD and various other letters? Yes. Do I also have an untestable IQ? Yes, I do. Have I studied business and finance? I audit college courses for fun. I have taken and *passed* courses from *Wharton* at graduate level, Your Honor. I specialize in international finance and economics.

"So, what the defense is doing, Your Honor, is wasting your time,"

Mike concluded. "That is *all* they are doing. While it's fine to waste *my* time, Your Honor, you should be rather offended that they are wasting *yours. That* concludes my statement."

"Okay, we're here with Edward Folsom, who's an investment counselor with Folsom and Folsom Investments. Yes, this is a law stream but we're trying to sort out something that Mike Truesdale, the potential heir that just burst onto the scene, said during his presentation at a competency hearing. First of all, hi, Ed. Welcome to the podcast."

"Thanks, Hank."

"I think that Mike Truesdale's competence in general was probably proven in court with his statement. He wasn't reading from notes, either."

"No, I watched that, too. Not so much from the law perspective but a lot of analysts wanted to know who this kid is. And wow! I was howling at his presentation. I've been warning people about Fieldstone's international fund management for a long time, so this was right where I work."

"Right, which is one of the reasons I asked you to be on. You've said similar things about Fieldstone in the past."

"But I never managed to slip in a Vladimir Nabokov reference. I was howling at that one! I literally was laughing so hard I couldn't even follow the next part."

"Can you walk us through that? What the heck is a 'Humbert Humbert of investing' mean?"

"Let's back up to the thing about ETFs. Can we play the whole clip?"

"Sure:"

"I find Fieldstone's continual creation of novel ETFs charming in a naïf, loving sort of way. I tend to think of it as the Humbert Humbert of investing."

"Okay, you're laughing again."

"Yeah! Okay . . . Uh . . . First, what's an ETF? It stands for Exchange Traded Fund. An exchange traded fund is, well, a fund that you can trade on an exchange. That fund might be a fund of, say, agricultural stocks. Instead of investing in one stock, you're investing in a group of them. And unlike a mutual fund, that does something similar, you can buy and sell your ownership of the fund on a trading floor, just like a stock. Does that make any sense?"

"Sort of got it."

"Okay, so what's a novel ETF? A novel ETF is when someone comes up with some new field to create an exchange traded fund. So, I used the example of agricultural company stocks. That's fairly obvious. But then you get into things like an ETF that invests in a range of blockchain coins. Or an ETF that's based on a range of ETFs."

"Is that a thing?"

"That's a thing, yeah. And Fieldstone is famous for setting up novel ETFs that are sort of out there. They have to have some think tank that sits around going 'What's the craziest thing we can think of to set up as an ETF?' I mean, like, they'll say, 'How many times do financial podcasts mention ETFs? Can we set up an ETF for that?'

"So, Fieldstone will set up the Global Fund for How Many Times Financial Podcasts Mention ETFs with some of their money. Then people who seem like they will invest in just anything will buy shares in that fund, buying them from Fieldstone, and start trading them. Fieldstone sells the shares at a profit, then manages the fund for a fee.

"Mostly people end up losing money on it. And most of them are people who don't know what they are doing. Sometimes it's big-money managers but it's more likely to be individual investors who just are investing in some hot new thing and lose their money. So . . . yeah, the entire reference is to the Nabokov novel Lolita."

"Right, and the main character and narrator is named Humbert Humbert and he, well, Lolita is his stepdaughter and her mother dies and they enter into a . . . shall we say inappropriate relationship."

"It's basically an entire novel about him screwing a fourteen-year-old girl."

"Right."

"So, yeah, so setting up novel ETFs and screwing naïf investors with them is sort of being the Humbert Humbert of finance. It's the best one-liner I've ever heard about novel ETFs. See why I was laughing so hard?"

"Yeah, I sort of get it."

"Wow, was it an insider financial joke! I mean, it's one of those things . . . If you've got to explain a joke to somebody it's not funny. But to anybody who's working in finance and who knows who Humbert Humbert is, it was hilarious. I called up a couple of other advisors who were watching and they mostly were wondering who the hell is Humbert Humbert . . . ?"

⊕ ⊕ ⊕

"I generally don't prefer my clients talking much in court," Ahuvit said as they drove back in the limo. "But I'm going to say that was a very nice presentation. 'The Humbert Humbert of finance.' Wow! That's obscure in two *different* fields!"

"It just popped out," Mike said, laughing. "It wasn't really part of my mentally prepared statement."

"I'm not getting the joke," Wilder said. "I heard some laughs from the courtroom, and you grunted, sir, but..."

"It's too hard to explain," Ahuvit said, still laughing. "I think if his honor had been able to parse it out, he'd have probably had words to say. But even *he* didn't get it. You could see him trying to figure out what you'd said when there was a titter in court."

"No one studies the classics anymore," Mike said with a sigh. "He's still going to require I go through all this stuff. Motion to enter my results from the very complete psychological evaluation in October."

"Wasn't that the one that found you nuttier than a fruitcake?" Derrick asked.

"I *am* nuttier than a fruitcake," Mike said. "But it also found me competent. And we'll have their psychologist say I'm incompetent and ours will say I'm competent and maybe we will get Dr. Michelle to chime in, and in the end the judge is going to find me competent. Or if he doesn't, then we'll have to go to appeal. They're just delaying the inevitable."

"They may be able to delay it for some time at this rate," Ahuvit said.

"Then I'll just enjoy the Big Apple and try to stay out of trouble," Mike said.

CHAPTER 10

"The Phoenix" —Fall Out Boy

"Ta-da!" Mike said, handing over a sheet of paper.

"What am I looking at?" Sasha asked. Other than fairly indecipherable writing at the top, the paper just seemed to be covered in marks.

They sat alone at a small table in a hole-in-the-wall coffee shop named Burnt Grounds. The place was known for its horrible coffee and worse service, which was exactly why Gondola funded it. It was the perfect spot for these sorts of transactions.

"That is a DNA profile," Mike said. "The actual technical readout. I'm going to skip what all the marks mean but it's the new international standard. A computer would normally be used to make a comparison, but you can do it by eye with another equal-size sheet that uses the same exact layout."

Mike slid another sheet across.

"Hold those up together and toward the light," Mike said.

Sasha did as bid, then looked at him and frowned.

"See how all the marks line up?" Mike said. "Look at the second one I handed you and the individual name."

"Jost Alnes," Sasha said after a moment then looked at the other page. "Unknown subject. So . . . that's definitely him?"

"That's him," Mike said. "We got him."

"So, what do we do next?" Sasha asked.

"Funny you should ask that question," Mike said looking behind her. A man in a cheap black suit pushed the door open and stepped inside, followed by another. "Hello, Special Agent, have a seat."

"Oh, we're meeting with the FBI?" Sasha said, turning to see them. "Lovely. You forgot to tell me that!"

"Special Agent Hinkle," said the first through the door. He nodded toward his partner. "Agent Starr."

"Mike Truesdale and Sasha Nikula," Mike said. "You know our other identities."

"You're the ones who grabbed Cannibale," Hinkle said. They somewhat awkwardly remained standing beside the table.

"I knew I recognized you from somewhere," Sasha said. "Sorry it took me a second."

"No problem," Hinkle said. "You said you had something for us that was big?"

"CI, right?" Mike said. "'Cause there might be some irregularities in how it was obtained."

"How irregular?" Starr asked.

"Little light B and E," Mike said. "Is that going to be a problem?"

Starr half chuckled, while Hinkle shrugged.

"If it has anything to do with who you talked about, not a single issue," Hinkle said. "What do you know about him?"

"That he's right here in New York," Mike said.

"Seriously?" Starr said, frowning. "Here?"

"Sasha, mind giving the special agent the unknown subject page?" Mike said. "Now, compare that to the profile you hopefully got from CODIS without anyone noticing."

Hinkle put the papers together and held them up to the light.

"Okay," he said, handing the papers to Starr. "You're not fooling around here? Tell me you're not."

"We're not," Mike said. "We got the DNA and I had it tested on an offline machine that matches the international standard test. That is his DNA collected, fresh, right here in New York City."

"Where?" Hinkle asked.

"Sasha?"

"An office on Seventy-ninth and Second."

"Address?" Hinkle asked.

"Grabbing him is not going to be easy, Special Agent," Mike said. "I promise you if you put this on the general database, he'll vanish. He's got contacts. Look what happened with Bear. He was on his way out of town, wasn't he?"

"Speaking of Bear," Hinkle said with a raised eyebrow, "that's an interesting connection."

"You want to collar this guy or not?" Mike asked.

"Yes," Hinkle admitted. "So, what's your plan?"

"Sasha will pull a fly day with Iron Eagle," Mike said. "We'll read him in. They pull him out of his office and hand him to you on the street. She knows where the office is. I can definitively locate that he's there. You have to ask Iron Eagle and to keep it quiet.

"You got a tip from a confidential source and rather than wait you spoke to a flyer about grabbing him. You can possibly, quietly, mention that with Bear getting a tip you were after him, you didn't want the same thing to happen with this guy. But we're just an anonymous tip. Confidential Source. And we remain anonymous. Yes?"

"Yes," Hinkle said, thoughtfully. "How did you find out about this?"

"I was the person who was followed into Two-ninety-one Broadway," Mike said. "I'd spotted *two* tails. The male got popped. I then turned around and followed the second tail. She met with a guy in Harlem, not far from my tailor's office coincidentally, and I followed him back to Seventy-ninth. He's still working in that office as of today. I checked. But he's known to up and disappear at a moment's notice."

"Right," Hinkle said.

"You get with Iron Eagle and tell him about this," Mike said. "And Sasha will pull a day fly and work to get the target. They then turn him over to you. And it *is* our subject. I'll be able to spot if it's not."

"How?" Starr asked.

"Superpowers," Mike said, perfectly deadpan. "I found him, didn't I?"

"When?" Hinkle asked.

"Sooner the better," Mike said. "After we have him, then shut the office down and get a team and a warrant. There's going to be illegal stuff."

"I've met Iron Eagle," Hinkle said, "but I don't exactly have his number."

"I do," Sasha said. "When do you want to do this?"

⊕ ⊕ ⊕

"Now you know why I was flying around, Patrick," Mike said.

Iron Eagle, Ivory Wing, and Stone Tactical were fully suited up and standing on the roof of the building, waiting for Hinkle to get into position. It was midmorning on a crystal clear, slightly chilly day. Pedestrian and car traffic was nonetheless heavy on the street far below, though Mike could only see him with his eyes. His Sight didn't extend quite that far. *Yet.*

"Still being cool about the Sight?" Mike asked.

"Yes," Patrick said. "I'm one of the faction that thinks we don't train our powers enough. But the Secretary is of the other mind. Just don't let it on too much."

"Will do," Mike said.

"This guy is serious?" Patrick said.

"Very," Mike replied. "But remember he's a normal. He's tough but breakable. And we need him alive."

"I've arrested normals before," Iron Eagle said. "I will not break him."

"*In position,*" Hinkle radioed.

"He's in his office," Mike said. "You're up."

"Ivory Wing!" Patrick boomed in his best superhero voice, putting both hands on his hips and sticking out his chest. "Let us go apprehend this wicked individual!"

Sasha chuckled and rolled her eyes. "Every time," she said softly.

"So, you do that as a *joke,*" Mike said.

"Yes, I do, Stone Tactical!" Patrick boomed, lifting into the air. "And I do it so well, no one ever seems to get it! Up, up and awaaay...or, rather, up and down and away...Whatever! Follow me, Ivory Wing!"

"Holy Frog Guts, Iron Eagle!" Sasha said in a falsetto as she lifted into the air. "Let's go snag an international criminal!"

"So, some of these people are actually pretty cool," Mike said, musingly. "That's a surprise."

In a joint operation today, the FBI and Super Corps arrested notorious criminal and terrorist Jost Alnes, a former officer of the Norwegian Navy...

New York Post: INTERNATIONAL CRIMINAL NABBED ON UPPER EAST SIDE
Gotham Herald: THE SURPRISING DOWNSIDE TO RECYCLING

⊕ ⊕ ⊕

"Well, that worked out well," Conn said with a growl. He'd had to cancel his morning tee time for an emergency meeting with Dion. "So much for Mr. Kindred being of any use. What else do we have?"

"We can keep trying the competency angle," Bafundo said, "but we're just using up time. The kid's Stone Tactical. He's still caught up in that transphobe thing. What if we . . . ?"

"Even the *Herald* won't breach super confidentiality," Conn said. The dumbass was grasping at straws, and there weren't even that many straws left to grasp. "If anyone who doesn't have access to the supers list does it, the FBI comes down on them. If someone who does does it, they lose access. So, it would have to be some obscure site and it would get pulled from everywhere. Even Twitter is okay with keeping super confidentiality. Next."

"We push him, so he has a public meltdown as Truesdale," Bafundo said. "Get a reporter to ambush him with some question that's going to get him to go off. Something the *Herald* can tag as racist or whatever. It won't necessarily stop the suit, but it can cause him heartburn. We need to push him from all angles. But we need an angle and right now we don't got one."

"I'll set it up," Conn said.

Mike was walking down Broadway, headed for Central Park, when three people, a young woman and two males, approached him. None of them were armed, but one of the males had a camera.

That was more dangerous than a gun.

"You're Michael Truesdale," the woman said, harshly, holding out a microphone. "Do you denounce white supremacy?"

"*Asul ang langit karon,*" Mike said.

The sky is very blue today.

"What?" the woman asked. "Do you or do you not denounce white supremacy?"

"*Pharavā māṭē sārō divasa chē,*" Mike said. "*Tamē āṭalā gus'sāmāṁ kēma chō?*"

It is a nice day for a walk. Why are you so angry?

"This is serious!" the woman said. "White supremacy is the most dangerous threat to the world today!"

"*Bagaimana pula dengan pemanasan global?*" Mike asked. "*Laut akan naik! Kucing dan anjing akan hidup bersama!*"

What about global warming? The seas will rise! Cats and dogs will live together!

"Do you even speak English?" the woman asked. "Are you Mike Truesdale?"

"No," Mike said. And kept walking.

"Michael Truesdale, who stands to inherit more than two million shares of Fieldstone stock, has made some interesting points about Fieldstone's recent investment strategies. Would you care to comment on investments in India versus China, and are we assured that this recent Hang Sun Financial deal will not result in lost returns?"

The quarterly Fieldstone investors meeting was lit. The stock was down again, the quarter had been no great shakes, institutional investors were not happy, and the CEO was not appreciating the questions.

"While Mr. Truesdale's comments were appreciated, I'm not sure I'm going to take investment advice from a thirteen-year-old. As to Mr. Truesdale's comments in regard to taxes, that is recognized and accepted. In the event that Mr. Truesdale inherits, I'm sure that we can work out an equitable manner to move the stock."

"Have you spoken to him, personally? In the event he inherits, he's going to be one of the larger personal investors in Fieldstone. His actions could seriously affect stock price, and he currently does not seem too enamored of Fieldstone."

"We have not spoken personally. I do hope to have some persons meeting with him in the near future..."

"Fieldstone wants us to meet with one of their executive vice presidents for Investor Affairs," Derrick said, his eyebrow raised. He'd just ended a phone call and waved Mike over to the kitchen table. "I guess they've decided you're going to inherit."

"Do you know what that means in terms of a company like Fieldstone?" Mike asked.

"EVP is fairly high up," Derrick said.

"In a regular division, like Tenth, is lieutenant colonel kind of important?" Mike said.

"Yes," Derrick said. "They're battalion commanders."

"How about in the Pentagon?" Mike asked.

"Not so much," Derick said. "Is that germane?"

"Vice presidents in places like Fieldstone are lucky if they have an office," Mike said. "Not a *corner* office, just an office. If a person isn't a managing director, they're basically carrying the piss bucket. It's an insult to someone who's about to hold their balls in his tiny little super hands. And I'm pretty sure they think I'd think it would be a great honor to meet with a *vice president*! Especially an *executive* vice president!"

He thought about it for a bit, then shrugged.

"We either tacitly indicate that I sort of get that it's an insult or we go with it," Mike said. "Start with tacitly pointing out that it's insulting to fob off someone with two million shares of stock to an EVP. Not as a first meeting. You want to set a good impression so someone much more senior spends a bit of their time schmoozing the potential heir, *then* you fob them off on the EVP. An EVP of investor relations might as well be fobbing me off on a used car salesman.

"We can indicate that we know that and show I'm a child of the world. Force them to get a managing director or the CEO out of his chair to go to a nice dinner with a mouthy kid.

"But that is only useful if I'm going to be trying to redirect Fieldstone using the relatively small shares I'd have after the taxes. Sort of pointless. Why waste time?

"Besides, I'm planning on dumping Fieldstone. Hard. Not much is going to turn me away from that. But it looks bad if you just do that without a reason. However, one of the reasons that financial and inherited wealth people *will* get is that it was *insulting* to get fobbed off to an EVP for a first meeting given, you know, two million plus shares of stock.

"I'm fine *after* I've dumped it with pointing out that as a reason. Quietly, in the background, people who understand know it *was* an insult and a studied one. In the meantime, I'm not planning on making *any* more comments about it. We don't have it in hand, yet. Best to let them think I've decided to just roll with it. What do you think?"

"I think I saw a squirrel one time that was more on track than your brain," his father said. "I say keep it simple. Take the meeting. Don't mention you're planning on dumping the stock, obviously. Try to mostly listen."

"I'm good at that," Mike said.

CHAPTER 11

"Snake in the Grass" —Midnight Star

"Mr. Truesdale, Mr. Sterrenhunt, John Garret! Pleasure to meet you! Call me Smiley! Everybody does!"

John Garrett, Fieldstone Executive Vice President for Investor Relations, was about six foot two with amber eyes, steel-gray hair, and a firm handshake. The suit he was wearing wasn't off the rack. Mike, having priced out custom suits, was thinking around twelve grand. The custom dental work for the, yes, extremely broad smile had probably cost quite a bit more.

Crocodiles smile, too.

"This is Scott," he added, introducing his aide. "Hope you like this place! The Odeon is a Tribeca landmark!"

Scott Haney was just under six feet tall and had the young, bright-eyed look of someone just out of college. At a guess, he'd gotten his position through family connections and was wholly out of his depth.

"We almost got lost," Mike said, smiling. "Which is weird since we're right down the street. But whenever someone says 'Tribeca,' I hear 'Trifecta' and start looking for a jai-alai place!"

"Oh . . ." Garrett said, puzzled.

"Let's eat!"

The Odeon had obviously started as a diner. From the exterior it had the look, including a big CAFETERIA in neon as part of the signage.

The interior was anything but diner-esque, with warm lighting, white linen, wood paneling, and fine china. The room was crowded with diners, men in suits and women in dresses, to the point it was a bit suffocating. They'd obviously gone for the "pack in as many tables as possible" look.

They'd been led through the throng, having to navigate some tight passages, to the bench seats at the side. There were a few other groups of businessmen having lunch meetings as well as a few dates, two families, and a quartet of women straight out of *Sex and the City*.

"Mind if we sit on the inside?" Mike asked.

Mike no longer cared if his back was to the room. His Sight allowed him to watch his back. But his father was long-term special operations. He'd appreciate being able to watch anyone approaching.

"Of course," Smiley Garrett said, waving.

Mike slid over so his father didn't have to, and Smiley took the seat opposite him.

"Can I put in a drink order?" the hostess asked.

"Macallan," Garrett said. "The Twenty-five."

He seemed overly eager to act like a big dog, with a wide, flashy smile and relaxed, cavalier attitude. But small tells of nervousness—minute foot-tapping, a super subtle gnashing of his teeth—were obvious to Mike.

"I'll have the same," Haney said.

"And for you, sir?" the hostess said to Derrick.

"Water will be fine," he said.

"I'll take a glass of milk, please," Mike said.

"Water?" Garrett said. He said it almost like a challenge, as in "Come on, drink like we important people do."

"I'm Native American," Derrick said. "Alcoholism is a plague among Indians. My father is a recovering alcoholic and I dealt with *way* too many drunks in the Army."

Garrett reluctantly waved a hand in acquiescence.

"And I'm thirteen," Mike said. "Besides, it doesn't affect me. Neither does caffeine. I still like the taste of sweet tea, but you can't get that in New York. Not the real kind."

"They have iced tea," Haney said, smiling and gesturing. "And sweeteners!"

"I'm sure they do," Mike said, trying not to wince.

People who were unfamiliar with the *ambrosia* that was properly sweetened iced tea, much less the chemistry as Mike was, really didn't get it. The worst thing that someone could say was "You can put sweetener in it!" That was not sweet tea. That was dreck, defined as whale feces dredged off the bottom of the ocean.

"Bless your heart," Mike added.

"You have a very interesting background," Garrett said, looking at Derrick. "We, of course, have access to credit records and so on and you . . . don't have *any* for nearly twenty years. You just did not seem to exist."

"I didn't," Derrick said. "I was put into a glass case and frozen that entire time."

"And yet, somehow in that time in the glass case you managed to amass . . . what is it, fourteen Bronze Stars, Silver Stars and . . . what exactly *is* a Distinguished Service Cross?"

"The medal directly above the Silver Star in the hierarchy," Derrick said. "And other than that . . . that's the only description. I will say that one of them can be considered a double award.

"It takes a board time to determine the award of a DSC. So, if it seems at that level, in the meantime you get the Silver Star. You keep the Silver whether you get the DSC or not. However, if the DSC is later upgraded to the Medal of Honor, you retire the DSC."

"Is that likely?" Garrett asked. "That you'd get the Medal of Honor?"

"I hope not," Derrick said with a slight shake of his head. "I don't think I deserved the DSC. Or any of the rest of them, for that matter. I was just doing my job. And as to being invisible for all that time . . . I preferred it. I really don't like visibility. I certainly would not like the visibility of 'The Medal.' Which I have stated quite firmly. Besides that, the mission was classified and remains classified. That was one of the reasons I was not considered for 'The Medal.' And, again, I don't want it, nor the others. I was just doing my job."

"Is he always like this?" Garrett asked.

"Yes," Mike said. "And so are all the people he used to work with."

"And you can't talk about any of it?" Garrett said.

"Nope," Derrick said. "I don't really remember any of it. Glass case, remember?"

"But he does have some awesome golf stories," Mike said.

"You golf?" Garrett said. "I've got a few myself!"

"Not like his," Mike said.

"I have drinks," the waiter said. "And would you gentlemen care to order...?"

"So, golf stories?" Garrett said. "Ever been to Pebble Beach? One of my favorites!"

"I have, yes," Derrick said. "As a very junior enlisted man."

"No, no, no," Mike said. "Just start at the first one. Second deployment. Come on."

"The first one?" Garrett asked.

Derrick took a sip of water.

"When you are first in the Unit, you're constantly being judged," Derrick said. "Are you good enough to stay?"

"The Unit?" Haney asked.

"Delta Force," Mike whispered.

"Oh," Haney said, his eyebrows raising.

"That's what we call it," Derrick said. "The Unit. As if there is no other unit in the world. Because to us, there isn't. But once you have some in-country time under your belt, once you're considered made, you can express some individuality."

"I know the feeling," Garrett said with a smile and sip of scotch.

"So, we're packing our gear on pallets to deploy," Derrick said. "And just about the last thing, I walk out carrying a set of golf clubs and toss it on top of the pallet. The other guys just look at me and I shrug.

"When I joined the Army, I never intended to return to Montana," Derrick said. "I was going to stay in the Army the rest of my life. My father and I did *not* get along when I was a teen. I never wanted to see Kalispell again in my life."

"What made you go back?" Garrett said.

"I'd calmed down being stuck in a glass box?" Derrick said. "But when I was still a junior enlisted, I was chosen for the Battalion Color Guard. The guy in charge was the sergeant major of the battalion. At one point he suggested that someday I'd make a decent sergeant, which was a high compliment from a man who rarely had a good thing to say. I told him that I intended a career in the Army, and I hoped to someday make a good sergeant major. And I asked him, since we were having a moment, what was one thing that I should do to advance in my career—not to sergeant but beyond. He told me: Learn to golf."

"Same thing in business," Garrett said. He finished his drink and waggled the glass in the air at the waiter. Coincidentally, his nervous twitches were diminishing.

"So, I did," Derrick said. "Generals have to golf with politicians to get money for us to jump out of airplanes and shoot guns. Since they need somewhere to golf, every base in the US military has a golf course. The Air Force has the best ones, hands down. The Air Force pretty much has the best everything.

"Since it would be a waste of the taxpayers' money for it to be *solely* for generals, they encourage others to golf. There's very cheap club rental, greens fees are very low, there's a golf pro on staff who gives free lessons to beginners, and so on.

"So, I started golfing and found I enjoyed it," he said. "I'd go down on Saturdays and sometimes Sundays and wait around for a threesome. Then I'd generally join them. Often, they were officers. I'd be very polite and emphasize that I heard nothing. Ensure that I called them 'sir' every time.

"But I would hear what they talked about, and it gave me an inside view of higher ranks that was very useful later in my career. And I'd sometimes get useful advice. It probably doesn't mean much to you, but it is very unusual for a full colonel to take an interest in a private first class and give him some cogent mentoring."

"I can imagine," Garrett said, in a tone that said he actually had no clue.

"Golf, rather than being something that advanced my later career, very much assisted my early one. And one time that my pay was absolutely screwed to the point *nobody* could figure it out, having a golf buddy who was a major in finance came in handy.

"In addition," Derrick continued, "you can travel anywhere in the world in what is called 'Space Available' on military aircraft while on leave. For free."

"Really?" Haney said with genuine curiosity. "Anywhere?"

"Well, except for classified bases," Derrick said. "Unless you have the security clearance to go there. Kwajalein has *excellent* scuba diving. No golf course. Since I was not going home on leave, when I took leave,

I'd take a long one. You get a month off a year, and I'd generally take the whole month at once.

"You have to travel in your dress uniform," Derrick said. "But you can take pretty much as much luggage as you can carry. You're flying on transport planes designed to carry tanks. There is space for personal luggage. So, on my first real leave I walked to the airfield at Fort Drum, waited for what is called a Space A, loaded up my luggage and golf clubs, and took it wherever it was going.

"I was *trying* to get to Hawaii," Derrick said, "but I ended up in Guam instead."

"Guam?" Garrett said, laughing. "Isn't that . . . ?"

"Well, it's in the Pacific and it's tropical," Derrick said. "And the Air Force base has a *fantastic* golf course. Also, one heck of a dining facility and great temporary accommodations. Of course, most Air Force bases have all of that."

The waiter dropped off another scotch for Garrett. Haney looked at the glass with mild concern.

"Since one cannot spend all one's time golfing, I also took a scuba course while I was there and got scuba qualified. Then I left in plenty of time to wend my way back to Fort Drum. Traveling Space-A is not direct.

"That's also how I ended up golfing at Pebble Beach. With a colonel who was an acquaintance of an acquaintance.

"So, we fast-forward to I'm in-country as a made member of the Unit," Derrick said. "And at one point there is nothing to do. Usually, you are *too* busy. Sometimes, you are waiting to be too busy. But sometimes . . . there is nothing to do and nothing is going to happen that involves you for some time. At least a day.

"So, I walk out of my hooch wearing my full combat rig and golf cleats," Derrick said, miming holding a golf bag and making a *clitch, clitch, clitch* noise. "I walk up to the gates of the combat action base and look at the contractors guarding it. They look at me like I'm insane. I'm obviously going out into a dry and dusty place filled with hostile locals . . . golfing."

"You're serious?" Garrett said in between sips. "Like . . . Iraq, Afghanistan . . . ?"

"A dry and dusty place with locals who are hostile to an American presence," Derrick said. "It was *not* a training base in Nevada.

"So, they open the gates and I walk out. *Clitch, clitch, clitch.* Drop a ball on the road, look off into the distance and yell 'Foooorrre!'"

"Two hours later I'm belly down in a wadi," Derrick said. "That's a dry streambed. My lie is just over there," he pointed off to the side. "But it's covered by a sniper and I'm *not* taking the five-stroke penalty!"

Garrett burst out into laughter.

"YOU'RE KIDDING ME!"

"I'm not taking it, I tell you!" Derrick insisted. "Screw that guy. So, I'm stuck. I can't figure out how to play the lie without getting shot."

Garrett and Haney both laughed at that.

"You hate five-stroke penalties, huh?" Garrett said. "I'd have taken a mulligan."

"Never trust anyone who takes a mulligan," Mike said.

Garrett shot Mike an annoyed side eye and quickly returned his attention to Derrick.

"So, I'm stuck and I'm not sure what the rules are here," Derrick said. "So, I had a sat phone and it had internet connection, so I looked up the number for the R and A."

He mimicked speaking on a phone while lying sideways.

"Hello? Is this the R and A? Hi, Cecilia, this is Staff Sergeant Hunter. I'm in a bit of a pickle involving a rule of golf. Is there anyone there I can ask a question? Oh, thank you ..."

He paused for a moment and nodded.

"Sir Ian! Hello, this is Staff Sergeant Hunter. I can't tell you my exact location, but it is rather dusty and dry and has hostile locals who don't seem to care for golf. At the moment I'm in a bit of a pickle.

"You see, my lie is covered by a sniper, and I don't want to take the five-stroke penalty ... Oh, so there's a rule for that. Okay ... So ... yes, this *would* be what *is* referred to as a beaten fire zone. So, I *have* to play the lie? Right, I either have to remove the hostile enemy force or take the five-stroke penalty or risk the chance of being shot in my backswing ... Well, yes, a good backstroke *is* important ... Yes, that did cover it, thank you, sir, much obliged ... No, going to have to take out the sniper then ... Right ... Good luck to you *as well*, sir ..."

"So, you can't just do a drop?" Garrett said. "You *have* to play the lie?"

"Many of the rules of golf were developed during World War One,"

Derrick said. "The Germans and British used to have informal local truces and they'd go out and play each other in no-man's-land."

"Seriously," Haney said. He'd been nursing his scotch but finally sipped that last bit. Garrett finished his second as well and waved for the waiter again.

"There's a lot of waiting around in combat," Derrick said. "So, you're playing in the trenches and your ball ends up somewhere covered by German fire. What do you do? Arranging a truce so you can play your lie is nearly impossible with Taliban.

"You've got to take out the enemy position. Simple as that. Which is, after all, what you're being paid to do.

"So, I pop up and get a bead on the guy and use the sat phone for its proper purpose.

"Base, this is Hunter," Derrick said, his tone much more professional. "Hostiles located, request Reaper support. No Reaper available? We've got an F-18, though? Roger, sending location... JDAM locked..."

Derrick hummed and looked up and over as if over the side of a wadi, then ducked back down, checked his watch, hummed a bit more, then went:

"KABOOOM!"

He looked up again and made a motion of dusting himself off.

"Fuck *you* covering *my* lie!" he said, flipping a bird.

As Garrett and Haney laughed, he made a motion of a golf swing. "FOOORE!"

"You're serious?" Haney said, howling.

"It was put down in the official after-action report as a solo reconnaissance of enemy territory," Derrick said. "Which I suppose was true."

"That is *insane*," Garrett said. "Okay, so much for my Pebble Beach stories. That tops them all!"

"All his stories are like that," Mike said. "They're all 'Hi, Cecilia, it's Sergeant First Class Hunter... Yes, I did get a promotion, thanks! Is Sir Ian available? I'm in a bit of a pickle...'"

"I ended up contributing to three new rules," Derrick said.

"Seriously," Haney said, looking incredulous. "That's kind of a big thing."

"They mostly were in reference to IEDs," Derrick said. "There were plenty of well-written rules regarding mines and so forth but fewer where there was a potential IED. So, yes, three. Also, got a couple of them modified. I think the old rules were a bit ... restrictive on some things."

"Like what?" Garrett said.

Derrick put his hand up to his ear again like he was talking on the phone and hooked his left arm as if he were holding onto something.

"So, I'm hanging in a tree on the sat phone ...

"Hi, Cecelia? This is Master Sergeant Hunter. Did Joey try that math workshop I suggested? He did? Good, glad to hear it. And it is helping? Good to hear ... that? Oh, that's a hippo ..."

"A hippo?" Smiley said as Mike started snorting.

"Yes ... That's a hippo you're hearing ... a rather ... *angry* one ... Is Sir Ian availa—Oh, okay ...! Sir Ian! Pleasure to speak to you again as well, sir ... Sir Ian, I think we have to discuss seriously the rules regarding hippopotami. I think that the one-hundred-and-fifty-foot buffer outside of which you *have* to play the lie is a tad ... small. I'm thinking the rules committee *meant* one hundred and fifty *yards* because oh, my God! *These things are fast!*"

"You were hanging in a *tree*?" Garrett said, wiping his eyes.

"I barely made it!" Derrick said. "Those things are huge but they can move like lightning! And they *hate* golf!"

"Sounds like my ex-wife," Smiley said. "I'm *dying*!"

"In the middle of my *backswing*?!"

"So, we really should talk some business," Smiley said with his characteristic crocodile smile. The waiter was replacing his third glass of scotch and collecting a few appetizer plates from the table.

"You didn't appreciate my analysis of Fieldstone's investment strategies," Mike said.

"Everyone has an opinion," Garrett admitted with a dismissive shrug.

"And there are much larger holdings in Fieldstone than mine who have different opinions," Mike said. "The New York State Teachers Retirement System comes to mind. I understand, and it was perhaps a tad unhelpful. But I'm mostly annoyed at the Trust for putting it all in Fieldstone. Not because you're a bad company but because it puts us in this situation no matter what."

Haney shot a nervous glance at Garrett. He'd barely touched his second glass of scotch.

"Let's talk some numbers," Mike said. "And we'll use some round figures. So, rounding, I've got two million shares of stock in Fieldstone. Bit more. Federal death tax is fifty percent. When that eats into it the rounding may possibly leave me with one million shares. Whether I transfer those to the Feds or whatever, half of it goes away. Then there's New York State taxes, which I could argue about being a resident of Montana but probably won't bother. That's more taxes.

"I'm assuredly going to have to sell at least one of the properties..."

"Any idea which one?" Haney asked, curiously.

"They're all impossible to replace if I do," Mike said. "Try to buy a Fifth Avenue penthouse on Museum Mile. I'll wait. I'm not even sure that Eisenberg's will go on the market. If it gets sold by his estate, it's more likely to be a private transfer.

"I have no real *personal* interest in *any* of them," Mike said. "But since realizing Annabelle was my biological mother, I've been studying the Folletts. They were quietly powerful when the child of some guy named Red Shield was dealing shekels out of a hut..."

"Sorry...?" Haney said.

"Red Shield," Mike said. "As in the Rothschild family. Klaus Schwab ring a bell? It means 'Red Shield.'"

"Oh."

"We were amassing money and power all the way back to *Charlemagne*," Mike said. "Yes, ups and downs, the Terror was a bit of an issue. But we've been a power since there *was* power."

Mention of the Folletts' history had finally gotten Smiley's attention and sobered him up. The smile was gone, and the man was now watching him with cold, calculating eyes.

He's wondering how much I really know.

"You don't simply sell all that off and toss it into an account," Mike said. "Those properties mean very little to me but that may not be the case of my children or grandchildren. I'd like to hold onto them for that reason alone."

Switching back to business talk had the desired effect—Garrett relaxed a little and the smile returned.

"But the issue is the stock," Mike continued. "I have to get rid of approximately half to pay taxes. More, but it will leave me with about one million shares. I was serious about one thing, which is that you should always have a distributed portfolio. Not tied up entirely in any one thing or firm. That's simply good financial sense. That Conn et al. put all of it into one basket is terrible management. I don't care what basket that may be.

"Generally, it's advised that you only have at most twenty percent in one basket. So, at the end of the day, I'll probably only hold *at most* two hundred thousand shares. Ten percent of current. At most."

"So, how are you planning on disposing of them?" Smiley said, not smiling.

"That will be up to my pater familias," Mike said. "I'm a minor."

"Who will be consulting financial advisors," Derrick said. "As well as my son who has, obviously, some knowledge of this field. As do I. I have a distributed portfolio—small, but I do have one. I was investing while I was in the Army."

"These are the realities as they are, Mr. Garrett," Mike said. "The big chunk will be the taxes. But a distributed portfolio is a must. Sorry."

"I can see where you're at," Smiley said. He repeatedly glanced at Derrick while mostly addressing Mike and was now really forcing the smile. "But I'd like to politely request you avoid dumping the stock all in one go and perhaps reconsider dumping so much on the whole. Once you're a majority stockholder, we'd be more than interested in hearing your investment and diversification ideas. Would you consider hanging on to the stock until we can discuss better options?"

Mike imitated Smiley's smile. "Obviously nothing's happened yet, so of course I'll keep my options open."

Smiley sighed and relaxed as if he'd won something. "I appreciate it. And if even if you return to the plan you outlined, we can probably help somewhat. The investment will appreciate. On the taxes, have you considered a loan? We'd be more than happy to front one."

"With current interest rates?" Mike said. "I'd have to have my frontal lobes taken out by a number two pencil shoved up my nose to lose that many IQ points. While I'm sure you have a number two pencil, I don't suggest you try it."

"Wouldn't think of it," Smiley said, holding up his hands.

"You, of course, know what I am," Mike said.

"We have the List," Garrett said, nodding.

"These are realities, Mr. Garrett," Mike repeated. "Sorry that it had to work out this way..."

"I listened," Mike said as they were walking home. It really was around the corner in New York terms.

"You did," Derrick said.

"You have good stories," Mike said.

"Penny for your thoughts?" Derrick said.

"They're worth more than that," Mike said. "And not on a city street. Too many cameras, too many eyes..."

CHAPTER 12

Original "Theme from *Mission: Impossible*"
—Lalo Schifrin

"Hey, Dad?" Mike said, walking through the living room. "Gotta do some Gondola skullduggery."

Normally, for skullduggery he'd be wearing mostly black. In this case he was wearing a suit with the collar undone. He even had a tie in his pocket. It was late evening, and the apartment lights were taking over as sunlight faded.

"Okay," Derrick said, not looking up from his book. "If you get caught, don't talk 'til the lawyers get there."

"Will do," Mike said. "Take care yourself."

"Roger," Derrick said.

Having a dad who was read in, and former Delta, was awesome.

Mike walked to the corner of Broome and West Broadway and got in the car that pulled up. To any observer, it would look like he was catching an Uber.

He put in his earbud as they passed West Fifty-second and tested the Bluetooth connection.

"How we doing?" Mike asked.

"You're up on commo," Celsius said. Celsius 22 was his usual partner when they were doing online work for Gondola and was running the op with backup from Titanium Asteroid. "I can't believe you get to do merc work."

"Trained as a thief at a young age," Mike said. "I've got all the necessary skills. Plus, easiest for me to get into the building. And I can afford my own attorneys if I get caught."

"Don't get caught," Diarrhea said. He was Gondola's head of ops and intel and the guy who ran all the organization's mercenaries.

"Don't let me," Mike replied, putting on a surgical mask. Mike hadn't fully considered it before, but there was a chance Derrick and Diarrhea knew each other, as the latter was definitely former US Special Operations and, more specifically, rumored to be a former Delta.

The driver dropped him at 9 West 57th Street and left.

Mike walked casually down the street for a bit, briefcase over his shoulder. He might look a bit baby-faced but just another upper tier office worker on his way home. He scanned all around, both visually and with Sight. No one nearby struck him as suspicious, and he'd gotten really good at spotting tails and lookouts.

"You're clear on all cameras," Celsius said.

With that, Mike took off into the air. Fast. It was dark. Even if someone got their phone out in time, they'd never catch it.

When he landed on the rooftop of Nine West, he took a headcam out of his briefcase and put it on, then contemplated the target. Central Park Tower was well lit. He needed some height.

He examined it under Sight. He'd already checked it out from Central Park more than once. Since he could stand at Umpire Rock and examine the entire building inch by inch with his back turned, it hadn't been particularly hard.

There were only a few people in the building. Two were lower-level employees working late, though one was sleeping at his desk. Neither would be anywhere near where Mike was going. The last was a janitor, but he looked to be done with his rounds and was cleaning his things in the basement.

Conn was definitely gone.

"Flyer patrols?" Mike said. He couldn't See any, but the sky was a big place and flyers were small.

"Over in Queens," Celsius said. "No helos in the area. You're clear."

He took off and headed for altitude, well above the top of the building. Shortly he was on the roof of Central Park Tower.

He walked to the security door and just looked at it.

"Alarm bypassed," Celsius said.

Mike keyed in the code to open the door and started humming the *Mission: Impossible* theme again.

"Duh, duh, duhduhduh, dah, duhdah . . ."

"That is going to get *so* annoying," Celsius said. "I can put on the actual music if you'd prefer."

"I'm good," Mike said while heading to the service elevators. "*Where's* my elevator, Celsius? Do I have to do *everything* around here?"

"Just about there," Celsius said. "Hold your cats."

"Horses," Cleopatra said. Cleopatra was one of the newer recruits to Gondola. Mike didn't know much about them except that they'd been poached from the Society.

"Herd your cats, hold your horses, Celsius," Mike said as he entered the elevator. "Duh, duh, duh, dadadadaaaaa, dadadadaaaaa, dadadt!"

"That's not the current one," Diarrhea said.

"Sixties," Mike replied. "I'm into the classics."

Without touching the buttons, the elevator descended four floors as he put on rubber gloves. The doors opened on a service area. He pushed open the swinging doors, then went down a fine paneled hallway to 9605.

"Alarm bypassed," Celsius said.

First, Mike checked carefully for telltales. Conn didn't seem like the type, but you did. Then he keyed in the code for the high security door, opened it and walked into Wesley Conn's personal residence.

"Bump, bump, bup, bup, bup, bup," Mike said, blowing out his lips in the *M:I* theme.

"That is officially worse," Cleopatra said.

The first thing that a visitor saw on entering the spacious condo was a nearly two-story-tall Warhol-style painting of Conn.

"Of *course*," Mike muttered.

"Oh!" Celsius said. "I've seen some horrible things in this job but . . ."

"Yeah," Mike said, going through the apartment to the home office. Check for telltales again. Open door. "And he didn't even rape *your* mother."

Mike knew military veterans would sometimes have an "I love me" wall with patches, awards, and plaques from their various units. But Conn was not former military, and this was much further along the spectrum of narcissism. Wesley Conn was trying way too hard to look like someone wealthy and important.

The man had way too many paintings and pictures of himself by different artists and a range of styles. There were also countless pictures of Conn with different famous people—actors, actresses, billionaires, politicians, et cetera.

Funny, but your stepdaughter/my mother had pictures and videos of some of these same people, but in a drastically different context.

The house safe was on the back wall behind still another painting of Conn.

"*That* is getting *old*," Mike said, checking very carefully for telltales. The headcam had a light and he keyed it on to get a good look as well as using Sight. Nothing.

"Sure way to spot Society," Cleopatra said. "Look at Fauci."

"When oh when are we going to have some *real* competition?" Mike asked.

"There's always China," Cleopatra noted.

"Point," Mike said, carefully taking out materials from the briefcase and laying them out. He opened up the pad and turned it on along with pulling out various cables and laying them out. "Alarm?"

"Taken care of," Celsius said.

"Where's Conn?" Mike said, carefully swinging the painting out, checking for telltales or secondary alarms they didn't have hacked.

"Still at the party," Celsius said.

Mike stuck the suction cup of the electronic stethoscope on the safe, stuck the black box on as well, and pulled out his earbud.

"You're going to have to just watch the master work," he said talking into it. "I need quiet. Buzz my phone if something's going on."

He cracked his neck, put on headphones, closed his eyes and proceeded to crack the safe.

"The combination is 05-11-19-94-11-19-08-22-20-11," AutokId said about thirty seconds later. Gondola's predominant AI had a tendency to show up unannounced to operations and help out. There was still considerable concern over the existence of an AI that had named itself and executed operations on its own, but Faerie Queen treated it as an equal, so everyone else followed suit.

The electronic tone enhancer was Wi-Fi enabled and tied into Gondola's system. The AI had figured out the combination first. Naturally.

"God damnit!" Mike said, dialing in the combination. "I was almost *there*. Is that actually my mother's birthday, how old she was when he first raped her, how old she was when she died, and the date of her death?"

"Yes," AutokId said. "By the time you'd gotten to the second nineteen it was obvious."

"Jesus," Mike said, opening the safe. "This guy is *obsessed*."

Mike took off the headphones, put his earbud back in, took a photo of the interior of the safe with his phone and started checking for telltales.

Money, a cloth bag probably of gems. Some general papers like deeds. False passports. This guy was always one foot out the door. Not what was important.

On the top shelf of the safe were two small ledgers and a hard drive. Bingo.

Mike removed the high-security hard drive and set it on the desk, then attached it to the pad. It had a USB connection, so he didn't need any of the cables.

"You got that, Celsius?" Mike asked.

"Hackin' and crackin'," Celsius said. "But it is one of ours."

"Nice when you design the security," Mike said, carefully pulling out the ledgers. He turned slowly through the pages of the account book. The camera was picking everything up so no need to take photos.

"Certainly makes things easier," Cleopatra said.

"Did we check to see if the old accounts are still operating?" Mike said. "This looks as if he's only changed one account based on Annabelle's photos."

"We did and they are," Cleopatra said. "And based on the money trail, he's not just embezzling from you. He's been embezzling from the Society."

"This guy is too much," Mike said, getting done with the account ledger. He flipped through the next book and shook his head. "They've changed about five members in his division. That's it. Not much turnover."

"Tell the Society he lost this and there will be," Celsius said. "Hard drive mirrored."

"Oh, but I want to kill him *myself*," Mike whined. He went back and turned the pages slowly, keeping his head still. "Status?"

"Nominal," Celsius said.

When he was done with the hard drive, he put everything back, then considered his photo of it. His memory had been right.

"See anything out of place?" he asked.

"Looks exactly the same," AutokId said.

He closed the safe and turned it to the same number it had been on. That was probably as close as Conn got to a telltale.

Then he repeated the entire operation and walked to the elevator.

"We need more capable enemies," Mike said as he walked into the waiting elevator.

"China," Cleopatra repeated.

"There's that . . ."

"How'd it go?" Derrick asked. He was still reading the same book.

"Cakewalk," Mike said. "Our enemies are *morons . . .*"

"God is building an army," Mike said when his phone rang the day after the operation in Conn's apartment.

"God has an Army," Titanium answered.

Mike was riding the subway again, despite the filth, because it gave a fantastic overview of the geology of New York. Not nearly as interesting as Montana but it was something to see. He was also occasionally interfering with the various unpleasantness. "Youths" who decided to harass passengers, especially female passengers, were having mysterious pains in their bones. Generally, just their vestigial coccyx bone but the really nasty ones were in for bone spurs in their knees.

It was a way to pass the time. Mike was in the process of restricting one such "youth's" activities when Titanium called.

"Update," Titanium said. "One thing is, whether you want it or not, you've been promoted. You're going to have to go through Level Four clearance protocols."

"Joy," Mike said while moving to a more isolated spot at the end of the subway car. "My life is literally an open book so that should be easy."

"Conn's black accounts are still there, and we've got a monitor on them in case he moves anything," Titanium added. "Further, the take from Alnes was interesting. The FBI, of course, has lost most of the *most* interesting things but they did look at them, first.

"Alnes has been the Society's black ops and wet-work specialist for quite some time. The take was very good. The FBI who were looking at it, who were cleared and also work for the Society, were still a bit put out to find out how many agents or former agents had 'committed suicide' under duress."

"Welcome to the jungle," Mike said.

"Some of them are probably going to try to run," Titanium said. "We may offer them protection to get what they know."

"You lie down with dogs, you wake up with fleas," Mike said. "The survival or death of corrupt FBI is one of those conflicted things. Alive, they're a source of information. Dead, they're getting what they deserve."

Mike had left the "youth" alone since receiving the call, but the guy was rubbing his back and returning his unwanted attention to a midthirties woman in a waitress uniform. Mike tweaked his coccyx again and the youth retreated once more.

"He also had notes of meetings with various individuals of the Society," Titanium continued. "More confirmation there than original intel. On a sort of personal note, he was the person who managed the issue of the two FBI agents that your mother contacted. Also, who arranged for the actual pickup."

"Which Mom was bright enough to avoid," Mike said. "Not that in the end it mattered to her much."

"She had you," Titanium said. "I think that mattered to her."

"Sorry," Mike said. "Having a down day. So *many* of these assholes. And if you took them all out most politicians throughout the world wouldn't know what to do. It would be a huge problem. The *Herald* still can't quite figure out what the narrative is with Eisenberg gone. Take them all out and all their brainwashed NPCs would be lost."

The subway jerked to a stop. The waitress got out and a group of people flooded in around him, so Mike got out as well and headed to the quietest spot he could find to continue the conversation.

"We found one thing on the servers that was very interesting," Titanium said. "The Society, of course, mostly uses paper for its records."

"Right," Mike said.

The Society had never really switched to digital technology. About the time there were members who were computer-versed, they'd realized it was too easy to hack.

The best way to defeat Gondola was a three-by-five-inch card and duct tape.

"We've known that they had archives," Titanium said.

"Every member has their records somewhere secure," Mike said. "Generally, a legal firm's offices. Thus, the reason so many firms are Society. Besides their control of most of the world's financial companies."

"Yes," Titanium said. "But we found two items in the servers which the FBI sort of no longer has."

"We extracted it before they could look at it?" Mike said. Another horde of subway passengers streamed down the escalators, so Mike shifted. Both visually and in Sight, no one seemed to be watching him. There were a few of New York's standard mentally divergent individuals lurking about, but none struck him as watchers pretending to be crazy.

"Yes," Titanium said. "The first is we found their secure archives. They're in an old limestone mine in Missouri. Underground mine."

"Alnes red-teamed the facility," Titanium said. "He was able to penetrate it but not get much out. The records are moved from paper to microfiche. Do you know what . . . ?"

"Micro-photos of the paper records," Mike said. "A predecessor to scanning."

"Yes," Titanium said. "Some of them are kept as paper but they are all microfiched. Now that we know we're looking for companies that use microfiche materials in Europe and Asia, it may take us to the other archives."

"Hard to get into a mine," Mike said. "Unless you're an Earther and can fly underground."

"The Vishnu are on it," Titanium said. "But if we get another administration that is interested in going after the Society, we now have a complete members' list as well as all the records a grand jury would need."

"To really clean up would require multiple," Mike said. "Practically one in every court district. And without the FBI you'd have a hard time doing all the arrests."

"There's a plan being worked on," Titanium said. "But it will require the right administration."

A particularly twitchy homeless man staggered past Mike, glaring the whole time. Mike avoided eye contact and was ready to act, but the man continued on without incident.

"Right," Mike said.

"And it will require other things," Titanium said. "We'd have to have Super Corps on our side, not theirs."

"We've discussed that," Mike said when the man was well clear. "Flipping the Secretary is a guarantee based on what *actually* happened to James King. Then you'd have most of the Corps except the hardcore Society supporters like Electrobolt. Civil war, but if you flip them in the right way, it would be at least five to one if not ten to one."

"And then there's you," Titanium added.

"And then there's me," Mike agreed. "At this point I can take on at least a quarter of the Corps. Give me enough time and it will be the entire Corps. Granted, I hope it doesn't come to that like it did for King. Different circumstances, of course, but... Anyway, I can only be in one place at a time."

"Understood," Titanium said.

"I won't ask what the full plan is regarding the archives," Mike said. "Above my pay grade. I will say that these powers are overpowered for anything involving normal policing or even skullduggery. I am especially now not looking forward to the Storm. But if some kaiju don't turn up soon, I'm going to get bored just practicing for them. I can see why so few Vishnu make master..."

Mike was checking out some of the tunnels under New York when his phone buzzed with a text from his father.

DS: FBI wants to meet.
MT: When?
DS: Tomorrow.
MT: Meet at attorney's office. See if Ahuvit available. Name of agents?
DS: Hinkle. Starr.
MT: Roger.

CHAPTER 13

"Spanish Harlem" —Herb Alpert & the Tijuana Brass

"Special Agent, welcome," Counselor Brauer said, nodding to Hinkle and then Starr. "Agent Starr. Please, have a seat. Coffee? Water?"

The conference room had a classic oval wooden table but more modern, very comfortable office chairs. An aide stood by for Hinkle's response to Ahuvit's offer.

"We're fine," Hinkle said, sitting down. "This isn't a hostile interview. You really don't need an attorney, though your father obviously has to be present. It regards some information we've developed from an investigation that relates to your client."

As usual, Hinkle was the primary speaker while Starr's job entailed sitting quietly, reading everyone's reactions, and taking constant notes.

"There are reasons," Mike said. "And it's not the right wing 'You cain't trust ther F-B-Arh!' Other reasons."

"Alright," Hinkle said.

"Why don't you go over why you *are* here, Agent?" Ahuvit said. Rather than his usual relaxed posture, Ahuvit was straight-backed and stern.

"We were recently involved in the arrest of a Jost Alnes," Hinkle said. "Do you recognize the name?"

"It was in the news," Mike said. "At least in the *Post*. International terrorist or something."

"Yes," Hinkle said. "When we raided his offices, we were able to get some information about his activities. Some of his staff have given statements. Most of them were aware that they were working for a security firm that might be a bit shady but not that they were working for an internationally wanted criminal. Others . . . we're unsure what they know.

"But we did recover a file that indicated that Mr. Alnes had been hired by persons unknown to investigate Mr. Truesdale and attempt to find as much dirt as possible. You were being tailed, but you knew that, since you led one of them into Two-ninety-one Broadway.

"He was also to investigate this firm, suborn persons working for it, and generally play dirty tricks. There is even discussion of potential assassination methods. They were aware that you are a super.

"What we are currently investigating is *who* hired him. We're following several leads, but this is one. So, the question is, who would hire him to investigate you and possibly try to suborn persons at this firm?"

Mike looked at Ahuvit and got a nod.

"I'm currently involved in a billion-dollar inheritance suit," Mike said.

Hinkle and Starr briefly glanced at each other and Starr scribbled something. "So, you suspect the Trust?" Hinkle said.

Mike looked at Ahuvit, who shrugged.

"Can Agent Starr put down the notepad for a moment?" Mike asked. "'Cause if he doesn't, you're going to end up dead of a self-inflicted gunshot wound. Or autoerotic asphyxiation. Sudden death is popular these days. Let's hear it for the vax."

Hinkle looked at Starr and nodded. Starr set the notepad on the desk.

"Were you working here in New York eighteen years ago?" Mike asked.

"No," Starr said. "I was at a fairly remote field office back then."

"Then you didn't know Special Agent Henderson and Agent Sternback," Mike said. "Have you ever checked to see if there were any contacts with the FBI by Annabelle Follett?"

Starr froze and actually looked mildly shocked.

"Why?" Hinkle asked, his eyes narrowing for half a second. "You're asking a lot of questions."

"And you ask questions, you don't answer them," Mike said. "Even to a CI? Or was it an anonymous tip? They're both read in," he added, nodding to his father and Ahuvit.

"We went with anonymous tip," Hinkle said. "A confidential source under certain conditions has to be revealed."

"And there's a reason for that that's not what they say," Mike said.

Starr shifted uncomfortably and raised a finger. "Okay, my question. Were you behind the personnel getting trapped in the offices?"

"Are we entirely out of school?" Mike asked.

"Yes," Hinkle said.

"Then, yes," Mike said. "Which is revealing something to you that could get me severed. You go back to NK at least, Special Agent, right?"

"Yes," Hinkle said. "I had a piece of that investigation."

"We're not supposed to train our powers," Mike said. "Everybody's afraid you'll go NK. NK! NK! NK! Which, given that someday the Storm *will* come, is crazy. But if Corps—or rather the people who were running Jost—find out I've got Sight and the *range* I've got, they'll gin up some investigation to sever my powers. It will be bogus, turn out to be much ado about nothing. But once they are gone, they are gone permanently. I'd rather keep my powers, thanks."

Hinkle and Starr shared another concerned look.

"So, you *know* who was running him?" Starr said.

"Everyone was looking for Alnes in Europe or Africa or South America at least," Mike said. "And he was right here the whole time under our very noses. Let me guess. The guy had a legend from hell, right? These days it is hard to create a legend that's totally secure. Ask the marshals how hard and they've got every tool available. How *do* you create a legend that good?"

"*Do you know who was running him?*" Hinkle asked.

"In general?" Mike said. "Of course I do. I'm surprised *you* don't. Starr I'd assume was clueless. But you've been at this too long to be *entirely* clueless."

Hinkle blinked but otherwise held a perfect poker face.

"Annabelle Follett came to the FBI when she was seventeen or eighteen," Mike said. "Around that age anyway. She alleged that she had information about a large-scale conspiracy that was suborning the federal, state, and local governments and extensively engaged in pedophilia.

"She alleged that she had been sexually trafficked by, among others, Wesley Conn and the chief of security Eric Bear. That she had solid information, a hard drive full of videos and documents. She had one video she showed which was of recent origin in which Conn and she had sex and Conn admitted that he had raped her at an earlier age.

"The agents that she dealt with were Henderson and Sternback. They reported this information honestly to their superiors and arranged a deal for protection through the DOJ. Instead of them going to pick her up they were told other agents would handle it. She never made the pickup and disappeared.

"Henderson and Sternback pushed for the investigation. They said they believed she was honest and not hysterical. That this was the real deal. She'd named names. *Big* names. They wanted to know which agents had gone to pick her up.

"They were both pushed off the investigation and eventually pushed out of the FBI. Six months after leaving, both agents were dead of self-inflicted gunshot wounds. A few years later, Annabelle Follett was dead in Philly, almost assuredly at the hands of Eric Bear."

Under the table where no one but Mike could See, Starr's foot twitched.

"Have you ever checked to see if there was a contact with the FBI by Annabelle Follett?"

"Yes," Hinkle said. "There isn't any listed."

Derrick crossed his arms and sighed. He was uncharacteristically tensed up. In fact, he looked like he might pop a blood vessel or spontaneously fly into a rage. It was still outwardly subtle, but clear as day to Mike. He'd never seen his father like this.

"But she did," Mike said. "Which means it got scrubbed. Who can scrub something like that? I'd tell you to ask Henderson or Sternback but they're both dead."

"You think this pedophile ring was running Alnes?" Starr asked.

"Oh, it's far more than a pedophile ring, I assure you," Mike said. "Alnes was more than their dirty-tricks guy. He was running some of their assassination teams.

"Pretty soon there will be a team from Washington here to take over the investigation. You'll be given a hearty handshake and a pat on the back. There will probably be a ceremony and medals. You'll be ordered to turn over all evidence and all notes.

"And if you push to continue with it, you'll have a choice: Join the Evil League of Evil or die. And you probably won't be asked to join the Evil League of Evil. So . . . you'll die. Very dramatic but it's real life. Ask Henderson and Sternback. You really didn't have any hint about this, Special Agent?"

"Remember when you asked why I never got promoted?" Hinkle asked Starr. "This is why."

"This is a real thing?" Starr asked. He clenched and unclenched his fist.

"Yeah," Hinkle said, sighing. "Those guys, huh? I *hate* those guys."

"You just want to be a gumshoe," Mike said, nodding. "You're good at investigations and it pays better than the NYPD. Way better. And there's a need for that. As corrupt as the FBI is, it still does some good. So, don't get yourself killed or pushed out. Keep your head down and do your job as well as you can in the environment. Ever seen *Citizen X*?"

"The movie about the serial killer in Russia?" Starr said.

"Love it," Mike said. "Probably Donald Sutherland's best role ever as the cynical police colonel who knows how to get things done even in the corrupt Soviet Union. And by the end of the movie, he's discovered he has a passion for finding the actual bad guy.

"One thing that I drew from that movie was that even in the most corrupt and horrible system you *have* to have the guys who just get the job done. I'd like to see a Netflix movie or something about a homicide detective in Nazi Germany. He's not a Nazi, doesn't particularly like them, but he just wants to get the job done. There's been another bombing raid and he's trying to convince his superiors that one of the victims is actually a victim of a serial killer who turns out to be a high Nazi official."

"That sounds like a winner to me," Starr said.

"So, what *do* we put in our notes?" Hinkle asked. "Since, yeah, I know what you're talking about now and I don't want to end up eating my own pistol while another is pointed at my head."

"Pick up the notebook again," Mike said.

Starr did so but looked a little hesitant.

Mike cleared his throat and looked at them seriously.

"If you want me to point a finger, I'll point it at Wesley Conn," he said. "Conn probably hired Alnes. We've been looking at the Fund as closely as we can without internals, and it appears that there's a good bit of money gone missing. He's desperate to try to keep that from becoming public. It's embezzlement and he's at the center of it."

As Starr scribbled furiously, Derrick finally relaxed a smidge.

"Further, based on analysis of my mother's Facebook memorial page, I believe that he was sexually assaulting her from a young age. And I think there were others. It was an Epstein thing. She was being trafficked. Not just here in the New York area but to other destinations. And I think that Conn, again, was involved as well as the late Eric Bear."

"Do you have any specifics on the embezzlement?" Hinkle asked.

"There doesn't seem to be any reinvestment of the dividends from Fieldstone stock," Ahuvit said. "Not that we can find. And the annual return is well in excess of what is necessary to support the properties retained here in New York. So...where *has* the money gone?"

"Okay," Hinkle said. "That's certainly a motive. We'll look into it. Thank you for your time."

He nodded at Starr to put away the notebook.

"Do you have hard data on any of this?" Hinkle asked.

"I've got the hard drive," Mike said.

"The one your mother allegedly had?" Hinkle said.

"Yes," Mike said. "And it will do you no good except to get you killed. Taking out that group is a very long-term project, Special Agent. You'll be retired before it can have any chance of success. Which is one reason for you, Agent Starr, to keep your head down and just do the job. Someday, maybe, there will be a chance to bring them down. All of them, all the way. That is not today."

"What do you know about the death of Eric Bear?" Hinkle said.

"Are we out of school?" Mike asked.

"Depends."

"Bratva," Mike said. "The hooker, Nataliya Komarova, was carrying the child of Feliks Morozov. He was less than pleased that she was killed for just some fucking tissue samples."

"How do you know that?" Hinkle asked.

"Who do you think pointed Morozov at him?" Mike said. "Bear raped and murdered my *mother*, Special Agent. There are three rules of the street: Big boys don't cry. Never snitch. *Always* get revenge. But

I assure you, Special Agent, if something nasty happens to Conn, I will be in front of *impeccable* witnesses. I'm one of the good guys, Special Agent. But I'm not *that* kind of good guy."

"How'd the interview go?" Supervisory Special Agent Brock asked, standing at Hinkle's cluttered cubicle. "Did he lawyer up?"

"No," Hinkle said. "He pointed the finger at Conn. Thinks the Trust was behind it. His lawyer pointed out that it appears money is missing. Gives Conn a pretty good motive to hire a dirty-tricks guy. Also thinks Conn may have sexually assaulted his mother at a young age. Possible trafficking across state lines. How's the computer forensics going? We into their servers, yet?"

"It's on hold," Brock said, making a clicking sound with his tongue. "The investigation is moving to D.C. That comes from the seventh floor. There's a team taking over right now. You're to turn over all notes, reports, evidence, everything."

"Okay," Hinkle said.

"Just that?" Brock said. "*Okay*? You bust Jost Alnes and just *hand over* the investigation?"

"I saw the beginnings of what we were looking at," Hinkle said. "This has counterintelligence all over it. Figured it would get pulled to D.C. No point in bitching. So, I'll start the handover."

"Okay," Brock said. "See Agent Erickson . . ."

"Son of a bitch!" Starr said, leaning on Hinkle's cubicle.

The "team from Washington" had gone, taking all the notes, reports, and evidence with them.

"Sometimes the only satisfaction you get in this job is a job well done," Hinkle said. "If you want to keep going, the one thing to know is stay away from *any* investigation that has this smell. If the 'team from D.C.' shows up, just hand over your notes and try not to think about it. I was already wondering about Alnes."

"I was thinking something," Starr said.

"That might be a bad idea in this case," Hinkle said.

"It's about Bear," Starr said. "The coroner was able to identify that many of his injuries came from something like a baseball bat. But he also had some that were consistent with something like a bowling ball being slammed into him. Hard. Probably when he was being held with his hands over his head. Now, who could throw a bowling ball that hard into a human body?"

"That *is* a puzzler," Hinkle said. "And I just realized that I really don't *care* who could do that to someone who raped and murdered at least seven women—one of them almost assuredly Annabelle Follett, biological mother of a pretty powerful Earther who obviously knows Morozov. I know *nothing*."

"What *are* you thinking?" Starr asked.

"I'm thinking...Chinese food..."

CHAPTER 14

"They're Coming to Take Me Away" —Napoleon XIV

"You're scheduled to meet with the psychologist for the defense," Derrick said as Mike got home from another expedition. "Dr. Swanson has agreed to testify on your behalf."

"Joy," Mike said. "When am I meeting with the hostile shrink?"

"Two days," his dad said. "You gonna be able to handle this?"

"Oh," Mike said. "It'll be as fun as lemon juice in a paper cut. For them."

"Welcome to Spies R Us, how can I help you?"

The man behind the counter was tall and spare with a nearly blank expression and black eyes.

"I'm looking for a device," Mike said. "I'm going to be meeting with someone and I want to be able to record certainly audio and preferably audio and video. Whatcha got . . . ?"

"Dr. Andrews will see you now," said the languid male receptionist at the psychologist's office.

"Be ready to call 911," Mike said. He was dressed in the height of his particular fashion, including an ascot with a faux ruby stickpin holding it in place.

He was accompanied by a paralegal from the firm, since it made no sense for his dad to hang around while he was evaluated.

The middle-aged brunette woman just looked at him quizzically.

Dr. Talia Andrews was every awareness class squeezed into one. Very squeezed. From the bad blonde wig with the pink bow to the unnecessarily over-the-top makeup to the *hideous* pink, frilly little-girl dress that clashed with the bow to the Mary Janes, she filled the therapist's chair like Jabba the Trans.

Change of plan. Time to bring in Dr. Mike. 'Cause this chick's got issues.

"I understand you are transphobic," Talia said in a singsong falsetto. "But I want you to understand, *this* is a *safe* space."

"A safe space for transphobia?" Mike asked.

"In here *everyone* is safe," Talia said, though her disdainful expression and aggressive posture disagreed.

"Even *transphobes*?" Mike said. "Under the circumstances that seems a tad odd. Your assumptions are showing, Doctor. Don't they tell you in shrink class to check your assumptions at the door?"

"Are you claiming you are *not* transphobic?" Talia asked, angrily. She clearly hadn't liked "shrink class."

"I was found in an alleyway with my umbilical cord attached," Mike said.

"Oh, that must have been so *terrible* for you," Talia said, unconvincingly. She even rolled her eyes.

"Is interrupting your patients constantly some new therapy technique of which I've never heard?" Mike asked. "Is that a thing? Aren't you supposed to be doing an evaluation which, presumably, would mean you'd need to hear what *I* have to say? Or am I supposed to sit here and let you lecture me on trans awareness? Is this a trans awareness class? Did I miss something?"

"I'm here to evaluate *you*," Talia said, tightly. "Not to be *berated*."

"Do you want to know why I might *not* be transphobic?" Mike asked. "'Cause there's a point here if you'll let me speak. Are you going to?"

"Yes, *of course*."

"I was found in an alleyway with my umbilical cord attached," Mike said. "The lady that found me wanted to adopt me but the state wouldn't let her. Wasn't 'cause she was black; all my foster parents were black. Probably wasn't 'cause she was six-four in her fishnet stocking feet and talked in a deep baritone. Was because she was a drug addict and a street ho. But that's the lady I called Mama right up 'til MS-13 kilt her."

Talia's expression finally softened.

"So, you're saying that a kid who called a six-four trans 'Mama' his whole life is a *transphobe*," Mike said. "Wanna check *that* assumption, maybe, Doc?"

"Well..."

"Look," Mike said. "I am *not* the guy who raped you when you were nine, okay?"

"*What* did you say?" Talia said, angrily.

"He was an adult," Mike said, leaning forward and looking at her closely. "Not a relative. Coach? Neighbor? *Neighbors*. Ouch, more than one?"

"How *dare* you!" Talia snapped, trying to heave to her feet.

The paralegal stiffened and her mouth dropped open. She seemed to be wondering whether she should intervene.

"It's what you're *supposed* to tell your *therapist*, Talia!" Mike said. "How can *any* therapist not have *seen* that? You're weighed down by the shame to this day! You need to grasp that it's taking you to dark places! You don't have to live with the *pain*, Talia!"

"How did you...?" Talia said, starting to sniffle.

"I have *eyes*, Talia," Mike said, softly, shaking his head. "I can *see* the pain. It's written in every line. But the thing is, you're trying to normalize it and as a therapist you *know* that's a bad thing."

"It's not *normalizing*..."

"How else do you say it?" Mike said. "What happened to you, what happened to me, is *not normal*, Talia! And it never *should be*! Children are *not* naturally sexual creatures! You know the pain and the shame and the feelings of complete lack of ownership of your own body.

"I know you try and believe that it's okay. That you say that. That this is okay. That it's just part of life. But you *know* that it's a lie, Talia! You know that it's more children being hurt, as *you* were hurt, Talia! You have to stop the cycle! You have to stop the pain!"

Talia recoiled, and a tear streaked down her cheek.

"What you went through *no* child should have to suffer," Mike said. "And you *know* it's not okay. You want it to be okay. You want to feel as if it's normal. But it's not and you know it. And you never will feel normal. But you have to stop perpetuating the cycle. You have to stop the pain from coming to others. And you have to start dealing with your *own* pain. You need to tell your therapist the truth, Talia."

"I...can't..." Talia said, sniffling. She pulled out a tissue and dabbed the corners of her eyes.

"You can, Talia," Mike said. "You're strong. You can do it. You must. You have to if you're ever going to start to relieve the pain."

"I really...I can't..." Talia said, breaking down to full on blubbering.

"We hold onto the pain, don't we, Talia?" Mike said, knowingly. "It's our friend. Sometimes our only companion is our pain. But it's a false friend, Talia! It's a deceiver! It holds onto you, clinging, like the vicious girlfriend who won't let you go. Like those men who hurt you! And it hurts so much when you lance that boil. When you finally force yourself to say their names. Their loathsome names! It *hurts* like hell to relive it all over again, but that's the only way you'll heal..."

"Thank you," Talia said, giving him a hug in the door. "Thank you so much!"

"You'll be okay, Talia," Mike said, trying to get his arms around her. "You need to talk to your therapist. Promise me!"

"I will," Talia said, her makeup running.

"You've got the strength, Talia," Mike said. "You're strong! You can do it! And you need to report them to the police. It hurts but it's healing. Promise, girl!"

"I'll try," Talia said, nodding. She grabbed him again and hugged him hard. "Thank you!"

The paralegal, however, was doing her best to stifle laughter.

"You'll be okay, Talia," Mike said, trying to detach himself. "This is the beginning of healing. But I've got to go now, okay? You'll be okay..."

"That...seemed like it went well," the paralegal said as they got on the elevator.

"I've got M·A·C smeared all over my suit," Mike said, sighing. "I'm not sure the dry cleaner can save it. That lady has *issues*..."

"Got an email from our psych," Bafundo said. "She's not willing to take any amount of money to testify against the brat. She said she's going to testify on his behalf for free."

"Are you fucking *kidding* me...?"

⊕ ⊕ ⊕

"So, the evaluation went well," Derrick said over Korean takeout at their kitchen table. "She's willing to testify that you are of sound mind."

"Oh, my *God*!" Mike said. "That session was a *nightmare*!"

"Didn't seem that way?" Derrick said, surprised.

"Talia has so many issues she should be *Time* magazine," Mike said. "I feel for her therapist but whoever it is is lousy at their job. I don't think anyone has ever forced her to confront her issues before. It's all been hand-holding and handing out tissues. She's like a giant psychological pus ball nobody is willing to lance! I get why. Lord, does it smell. But she really needs a better therapist."

"So you..."

"I just analyzed her and started her on the path," Mike said. "I could barely scratch the surface in an hour session. So much pain. But, yeah, I totally flipped her. I was going to just get the therapist to assault me or something. But I really couldn't with poor Talia. She needed the help. Call me an old softy.

"It's times like this that you wish you had more competent enemies. Where are the really *brilliant* supervillains? Sending me to a therapist who's *trans*? They were probably depending on the *Herald* for accurate information and thought that would throw me. 'Ooo! He's a *transphobe*! Let's send him to a *trans* shrink who's as nutty as a fruitcake!' That's the problem with lying all the time: sooner or later, you lie about important things to yourself..."

"Your Honor, my client attended the evaluation of the psychologist chosen by the defense and she found my client to be of sound mental health," Wilder said. "Why should my client attend still *another* session with *another* psychologist?"

At defense counsel's request, the conversation was taking place in Mickelson's chambers. It was in their best interest to keep the results of the evaluations quiet.

"We really don't feel that was a thorough evaluation, Your Honor," Counselor Lowe replied. "We really feel that it's appropriate to get another opinion."

"Is the defense going to be allowed to troll through every psychologist in New York until they get the answer they want, Your Honor?" Wilder asked. "This is just a waste of everyone's time. *Two* qualified psychologists have presented evidence of my client's competence, Your Honor. How many more is it going to be? This is just another delaying tactic, Your Honor!"

"I understand your argument, Counselor," the judge said. "But I think that the defense argument has some merit as well. I'll consider this and rule on it shortly. Good day."

"Okay!" Mike said, bursting out of the therapist's office. "Yeah! *We're done, here!*"

"He assaulted me!" Dr. Ernst said, coming out behind him.

"I assaulted *you*?" Mike said, gesturing at his face. "I'm the one with a cut lip! Take a picture of this and call 911! This guy is nuts!"

"You little son of a bitch!" Ernst said, hitting him on the head.

"And now we have witnesses!" Mike said loudly. "This is your kid's therapist! This is who you're sending your kids to! You really think they're going to get better with this nutcase?"

"I'm going to kick your ass, you little . . . !"

"Your Honor, as of this point the defense has been allowed to send our client to *three* psychologists. The first of those is eager to testify that our client is of sound mind, the second has had his license suspended and was arrested on charges of assault on a minor, and the third has been arrested for attempted *sexual* assault of a minor, to wit our client. How long are you going to subject our client to this barrage of insanity, Your Honor . . . ?"

"This is closing in on end game," Mike said as he and Derrick were eating some really good Italian.

The one thing he was going to miss about New York was the delivery. You could get approximately everything delivered. He'd hardly been cooking.

As his Sight range increased it was also fascinating under Sight. New York went down nearly as far as it went up and the underground portions were complex. There were subway tunnels, steam tunnels and tunnels he was pretty sure that nobody even knew existed anymore. He'd found a complete subway line that looked as if it had gone out of business in the thirties. Some of the tunnels he suspected were old mines or something. *National Treasure* wasn't an entirely crazy movie. He was pretty sure the Chamber of Secrets was down there somewhere.

"It is, yes," Derrick said.

"We swept?" Mike asked.

"Clear," Derrick said.

One reason for his father more or less inhabiting the condo full-time was to prevent it from being bugged. They'd convinced the owner they could manage the housekeeping themselves, which, since they were both neat freaks, was true. The manager had come by one time unannounced and determined that it was looking better than with the regular help.

"I'm still unsure about getting rid of the houses," Mike said. "I'd prefer to keep them if possible. They're a legacy."

"Agreed," Derrick said.

They'd had the discussion before.

"The problem is the help," Mike said. "As in, they're presumably Society help. Good help is hard to find but...I'm probably going to have to switch them out. The question is...who handles something like that? I'd think it would be something like a super personal assistant, but I don't know. I'm going to go out of my depth quickly there."

"I know a guy," Derrick said.

"You know a guy?" Mike replied.

His father often "knew a guy." His career in the Army had had him encounter a host of unusual and very high-end characters. Though Mike might have been able to lean on Gondola for an electronic security specialist, his father "knew a guy" who Gondola was enthusiastic about. They'd pegged him as a new asset.

But knowing a guy who knew something about high-end "help" was a surprise.

"I know a guy," Derrick repeated. "English. May only be available to consult but he's an English butler. They're called house managers these days. 'Butler' is considered an insulting term."

"Okay," Mike said.

"I'll send him an email, see if he can at least consult on it," Derrick said. "But, yeah, I know a guy..."

CHAPTER 15

"To Glory" —Two Steps From Hell

"Do I get to know what we know about Dad's guy?" Mike asked, sitting at his laptop in his bedroom.

"Mark Alger," Titanium said, throwing up a photo of a man in British camouflage uniform. Alger was stocky with broad shoulders, blue eyes, and black hair. His nose was slightly crooked from punches.

"Markings for Regiment," Mike said.

"Yes," Titanium said. "Medically retired SAS color sergeant. Lost both lower legs to a mine on a joint mission with Combat Activities Group, Charlie Troop, Third Platoon."

"My Dad's unit," Mike said.

"Your father's platoon," Titanium said. "When your father was platoon sergeant. Nearest secure LZ was fifteen miles away. The SAS and Delta squaddies put on tourniquets and packed him out. Two others, including your father, were wounded by the blast. Nonetheless, your father was one of those who packed him out on his back."

"That would tend to indicate a possibility of trust," Mike said. "He's a butler now?"

"He's very much the traditionalist, I suppose you could say," Titanium said. "It's something that wounded soldiers used to do quite frequently. At least in Britain. Took the courses to go 'in service' in the traditional term and started off as a footman."

The photos had continued along with written data: date of birth, age, blood type, psychological evaluations. Alger was homosexual.

"The jokes write themselves there," Mike said.

"He apparently made them himself," Titanium replied. "He completed a fair term in his first position but declined to extend his contract. He moved to the employ of Lord and Lady Beckham-Smythe and has remained in their employ ever since."

"So . . . downsides?"

"His first employer was Sir Charles Edgerton, Twenty-eighth Baron Crumley. Recognize the name?"

"Big-time British Society," Mike said. "Either top of the heap or close. Raging homosexual pedophile. Almost assuredly a Dark Hand. Somebody we'd bump off if it he wasn't British."

"The same," Titanium said. "While there are not precise internals, we believe he left due to distaste for the baron's lifestyle. He'd be unlikely to reveal it—it would be both a violation of an NDA and a violation of the code of the in-service. But it's probably why he didn't renew his contract.

"He also had a report during an earlier tour in Afghanistan. He took exception to one of the tribal chiefs they were working with."

"Lemme guess," Mike said. "Boy play?"

Boy play was a translation of the euphemism that Afghans used for sexual assault on young males. It wasn't considered by Afghan tribals to be homosexuality, which was a sin in the Koran. It was just *boy play*. It frequently involved the rape of young males between the ages of nine and twelve.

"The same," Titanium said.

"So, he doesn't like pedophiles," Mike said. "That doesn't mean he's safe. Current employer Society?"

"Most members of the British and Continental aristocracy could be described as such," Titanium said. "None of the inherited titles are notably *anti*-Society. Or at least not openly. But the Beckham-Smythe couple is about as far away as you can get. And very definitely not pedophilic."

"I wonder if that was intentional?" Mike said.

"It appears to be," Titanium said.

"So . . . read?"

"Definitely possible," Titanium said. "But his association with the Society is troubling. Reality, though, is that any British help is going to have some Society association. You'll need to feel him out before he's read in on anything serious and cannot be read in on Gondola until we determine his position."

"Roger," Mike said. "Hope he works out."

"Good help is hard to find," Titanium said. "Trust me."

"I may have an in there besides Dad's 'guy,'" Mike said.

"Oh?" Titanium replied. "I'd like to know. Good help really is hard to find."

"Wouldn't work for you," Mike said. "I assume, anyway. I'm a Vishnu. I may be an American super but that counts as Vishnu. Religious fanatics tend to be very loyal. It's just a matter of finding some that are competent 'in service.'"

"That, yes, would not work for me," Titanium said with a sigh. "Oh, well. I'll keep looking."

"Mr. Alger," Mike said over the video link. "It's a pleasure to make your acquaintance."

He still looked more like a thug than a butler.

"Mr. Truesdale," Alger said, nodding. "I understand you are in need of a gentleman?"

"Bit more complex than that, sir," Mike said. "I'm on the verge of inheriting three properties here in New York: a rather large apartment across from Central Park; a large townhome, thirteen thousand square feet, in Riverside; and an estate on Long Island. The house there is a sixty-two-bedroom French-style chateau.

"The current employees with those properties were chosen by people it is reasonable to describe as enemies," Mike said. "I'm going to have to decide which properties to keep, which will depend on various issues. But I also have to decide which *employees* to keep. And if I let them go, where to find good ones to replace them. I have a surprising number of abilities for a thirteen-year-old, but at that point I'm totally out of my depth."

"I see, sir," Alger said, nodding. "What you need is the 'valet.'"

"I . . . ?" Mike said. "I need a tailor? I like my tailor."

"The 'valet' is a rather old-fashioned term, sir, for a supervisor of the employees of various homes," Alger said. You could cut diamond with his vowels.

"When a young heir was coming of age, he would tend to find a personal servant, usually from one of the families who were in-service.

Someone he'd grown up around, may have horsed around with as a child in dresses or, once they became more common, short pants.

"As the clothing of past times were sometimes hard to assemble, that person would among other actions help the young gentleman dress. A valet. The valet would then tend to follow the young gentleman around through his life. If the young gentleman went off to war, the valet would be his servant on the lines, making sure the young master ate even if it was by stealing food from other valets. Assuming both of them survived, not guaranteed, he would then return with the young master.

"As time went by, he'd be trained to run the household and eventually *households* eventually becoming not just *a* valet but *The* Valet. Do you get my meaning, sir?"

"I do," Mike said, smiling slightly.

"So, the present-day term for what you are looking for is a general manager of personal properties and personnel," Alger said. "But that has so many P's, does it not? Being rather old-fashioned, I prefer the old-fashioned term. The valet."

"Would you be available to consult?" Mike asked. "Or, potentially, take the position of the valet?"

"I would be available to consult, young sir," Alger said. "To take the position would require me leaving my current position and I would have to be assured that that is an action of worth. A contract would be required, and it would have to ensure a decent severance if things did not work between us. There is many a slip twixt the cup and the lip, sir."

"What is your current position if I may ask, sir?" Mike said. Even dealing with Alger he'd started to affect the proper diction.

"I am the assistant house manager for the country estate of Lord and Lady Beckham-Smythe, sir," Alger said. "It is assumed that I will eventually take over the position of house manager. Being the valet to three such homes would be a promotion, that is assured. You question keeping them, however?"

"I'm going to have to look at the finances," Mike said. "They're expensive to keep and the taxes on this are going to be ludicrous."

"You do not understand the term 'ludicrous,' young sir, until you deal with *British* tax authorities," Alger said. "But I do understand the difficulties of inheritance taxes."

"I, however, intend to *increase* the financial holdings, if possible," Mike said, "as well as acquire some other properties. One in Montana is more or less a necessity. I'm also considering one somewhere in the Caribbean. So, I think the position would be commensurate with your expertise. What are your desires in terms of compensation...?"

"Since we have determined the subject is of sound mind, the real issue before the court is a lack of evidentiary DNA," Judge Mickelson said. "It would be easier to rule if there was evidentiary DNA available..."

They were in the actual courtroom this time, as they were whenever Lowe thought he held an advantage.

"There is evidentiary DNA, Your Honor," Wilder said.

"There *is*?" Lowe said. "Where?"

"The FBI has not been able to find the sample they took from Washington state in their evidence," Wilder said. "Sadly, it appears to be lost. However, that was not the *full* sample. A portion of it was held by the lab in Washington."

"It sounds like the FBI should..."

"And *that* portion is currently in the care of the US Marshals," Wilder continued. "You may recall, Your Honor, that our client is under a light protection order of the marshals. Also, his identity has, yes, been changed. As such, his DNA cannot appear on any database. Since it is possible to reconstruct from familial DNA, it's important that his mother's DNA not be available. Thus, the reason it was removed from CODIS. Though you will recall, Your Honor, that there was a match.

"However, the marshals picked up the remainder of the sample in Washington, and since the primary area that Mr. Truesdale is being managed is here, they have a sample here. And we've checked. It is available any time. However, Your Honor, because of the security nature of the sample, they will only turn it over to you, personally, to be tested."

"That's... rather irregular," Judge Mickelson said, perhaps a touch nervously.

"It's the federal government, Your Honor," Wilder said with a sigh. "What are you gonna do? They have offered to walk it to the lab here in the building, Your Honor. Your Honor could observe the test yourself in person. Just name a time. But it has to be done on an offline system. Which is available. So, they can deliver it to you, and you can sign for it and have a bailiff do the test or they can bring it to the lab here in the courthouse and you can observe. Up to you, Your Honor. Either way, it has to be in *their* possession or *yours*, Your Honor."

"Okay, uh..." Mickelson said clearing his throat. "Let me, uh...I'll rule on that shortly. Next case..."

"What the hell do you want me to *do*?" Mickelson hissed. "He's the freaking *heir*! There's no way to cover that up! And the marshals have the DNA? Can you...you know...?"

The judge was starting to fear Mr. Anson, his Society contact, would no longer be buying him steak dinners at fancy restaurants if this case continued on its current path.

"Not with them," Mr. Anson said, calmly. "The marshals are... difficult."

He took a bite of rare, aged steak and contemplated the matter.

"We've reached the point that it's no longer possible to delay," Anson said. "I will pass that on. Do the DNA test. This was a lost cause from the beginning. Most of the cleanup has already been effected. We'll just have to cut the Trust loose."

"Your Honor, Marshal Goddard," the US marshal said, nodding to His Honor.

The group had gathered at the DNA testing lab in the basement of the courthouse. It was usually used for paternity tests, but it could hum the tune of maternity. The lab was clean, orderly, calm, and quiet. It lacked the frenzied activity and chaotic mess Mike had seen in other DNA labs.

It wasn't just the judge present. Conn, Bafundo, Lowe, and Packard were all there from the Trust as well as Ahuvit, Wilder, Derrick, Mike, the chief of the testing facility, and the poor DNA clerk. The room was crowded.

Mike still had to fight both the physical tension and the homicidal desires he got from being this close to Conn, but it was getting easier. It helped that Conn looked perpetually pissed off of late. Derrick had subtly placed himself between Mike and Conn. Mike knew he didn't need protection from the evil man, but it still meant a great deal that Derrick had done that.

"This sample was given into the hand of Marshal Ellsworth in Washington state, Your Honor," Goddard said, noting the hand receipt. "It was sworn and attested to be a subsample of the toxicology sample from Kennebunk of Annabelle Follett by Dr. Hlavacek. There is a copy of the original evidentiary documents attached. I can either hand the sample to the DNA tester or you can sign for it, Your Honor."

"I'll allow you to hand it to the tester," Judge Mickelson said. "Absent objections from either party."

"Without objection, Your Honor," Ahuvit said.

"Without objection, Your Honor," Packard managed to strangle out.

The sweating DNA clerk took the sample and looked at Mike.

"I need a cheek swab," the clerk said.

Mike hated people sticking things in his mouth, but he just squatted down and held it open.

The clerk managed to not have his hands shake as he prepared the samples. Then he put them in the machine.

"About five minutes," he said.

"Mr. Conn," Mike said, smiling. "We are currently in a rather cramped loft in SoHo that, nonetheless, is costing us about five grand a month. I'm aware there is still probate but I do hope that once His Honor has ruled in my favor, we can use one of the houses here in the New York area. As a gesture of goodwill."

"I believe that would be up for discussion should there be such a ruling," Conn said, tightly. "You're going to need someone who can manage these sorts of funds. I'm aware that you have some training, but you will probably need an experienced fund manager. I would offer my services."

The greatest human example of evil personified was "offering his services." On reflection, it was actually kind of comical.

How dumb do you think I am? Even if I didn't know what you did to my mother?

"Thank you for your delicate inquiry, sir," Mike said, acting a combination of friendly and thoughtful. "That had been a consideration. You've been with the Folletts, man and boy, for quite some time. But, alas, we have chosen a firm to do the management."

"I see," Conn said while casually putting his hands behind his back.

"Now that the attorneys are about done, time to bring in the accountants," Mike said with a sigh. "Your Honor, one shouldn't schmooze a judge when involved in a case before him. That being said, I read your opinion in *Lazar versus Krumwalt,* and I found it in places quite lyrical. Decidedly different from most judicial opinions. Pity the Supreme Court overruled. I thought your reasoning quite cogent."

"Well, thank you, young man," Judge Mickelson said. "I thought my reasoning quite cogent as well. The current court is somewhat activist in my opinion."

Lazar created rights out of whole cloth but, sure, call them *activist.*

"As a person from so many different cultural influences I find some aspects of the current world logically uncomfortable," Mike said. "Are you aware, Your Honor, that I am published in the field of intersectionality?"

"I was unaware, no," the judge said. "That doesn't seem . . ."

"To be quite as I'm perceived?" Mike said, smiling. "I'm a puzzle wrapped in an enigma to even those closest to me, Your Honor. Don't be surprised if you find me confusing. But I was particularly drawn as someone who has studied that field to your argument that those who represent the smallest of minorities are those who require the greatest support. That their lack of power due to their numbers requires the courts and the government in general to protect them."

"Do you disagree?" Judge Mickelson asked.

"It is the *very* basis of critical oppression theory, Your Honor," Mike said. "Which, in turn, is the very basis of civil rights law in the United States. You surely agree with that?"

"Obviously," Judge Mickelson said.

The longer Mike engaged intellectually with the judge, the tighter Conn's hands clenched into fists behind his back where he thought no one could see. But Mike could See. By now, Conn's fists could've turned coal into diamonds. The more pissed off Conn became, the calmer Mike felt.

"That is the basis of intersectional theory as well," Mike said. "Take myself, for example. Though I appear white and am about to inherit what can only be described as obscene white-privilege wealth, I am legally Native American as well as being, as most present know, a super. That puts me into an intersectional point that is *extremely* small. That's in the range, pardon me, of a Jewish paraplegic lesbian. Smaller, in fact. If one takes the traditional approach to oppression theory and add in an intersectionality for 'born in poverty,' then that puts me into an even smaller group.

"But at present, essentially *anyone* can claim the same."

"Excuse me?" Judge Mickelson said.

"*You* can check a box that you are Native American, Your Honor," Mike said. "Whether you take the term 'falsification' for it, persons can and do claim Native American ancestry all the time who have not a drop of Red Indian blood in their veins. And before anyone says, 'You can't say Red Indian,' Counselor Sterrenhunt, what do Red Indians call themselves as a group?"

"We call ourselves Indians by and large," Derrick said. "'Native American' is for activists and white people. One of the reasons it's okay to call yourself a Native American is, if you were born in the Western Hemisphere, you are a Native American."

"You call yourselves Indians?" Judge Mickelson said, looking confused.

"We generally just reference our Nation or tribe, Your Honor," Derrick said. "Am I a Native American? Yes. I was born in Montana. But if you're asking my *race*, I'm a *Lakota*. Which is a very different ethnicity than a Cherokee or a Cree or an Algonquin. But if we generally refer to aboriginal Americans, we use the term 'Indians' or more commonly 'Injuns.' That somewhat distinguishes us from persons from India. The federal *government* refers to us as Indians. Bureau of Indian Affairs. The Indian Child Welfare Act."

"My point being that in the current times *anyone* can call themselves *anything*," Mike said. "Mr. Packard can state that he's a currently male-presenting homosexual female who is of African genetics and identifies as a tree. That puts him squarely in the same intersectionality as mine."

"Well, I suppose," the judge said.

"Which means that the very *basis* of the Civil Rights Act evaporates," Mike said. "If anyone can claim an intersectionality minority, then there is no such thing as a minority that needs protection from the majority. There *is* no majority and there *is* no minority. It's just a random mass of individuals.

"So, how does one say that, for example, Mr. Lazar of the previously mentioned ruling deserves protection from Mr. Krumwalt on the basis of Mr. Lazar's minority status in comparison to Mr. Krumwalt's? Mr. Krumwalt could have simply stated he was a blind homosexual dwarf rabbit. In the current case law environment, he therefore would have been more of a minority than Mr. Lazar and therefore Mr. Lazar's argument that he deserved protection was moot."

"That's a novel legal approach," Packard said. He frowned at first, but reluctantly shrugged agreement after a moment's thought.

"I'm surprised that Mr. Krumwalt's attorneys didn't think of it," Mike said. "But think of it in terms of sexual harassment allegations. A manager is accused of sexual harassment. They state that they cannot have sexually harassed that person because their sexuality is in conflict. A male manager who is accused of soliciting sex from a female employee states that they are homosexual and therefore uninterested in women. That it is entirely impossible even though there are multiple witnesses.

"Do you take the position, Your Honor, that they are not in fact homosexual?" Mike asked. "I'm not asking for a reading, obviously. But if you do so then you are accused of not being sufficiently understanding of homosexuality. You bigot."

Micklelson now looked a little lost and glanced at Packard as if asking for help. Packard was no help.

"This is a *critical* issue in modern intersectionality theory," Mike said. "It is just one aspect that is touched upon in the Three Goat Problem. When you have a Fred, things start to go off the rails."

"That is a point," Judge Mickelson said.

"What is the point of Title Nine if anyone can be a woman?" Mike asked. "What is the point of the Civil Rights Act, for which the reverend doctor gave his very *life,* if anyone can be black? What is the point of civil rights at all, if *anyone* can be a minority of one and thus protected against the other three hundred odd million? Why have specialized civil rights at all if they apply to everyone?

"It's almost as if we'd have to treat everyone as individuals with no reference whatsoever to intersectionality! It's madness!"

"We've got the results . . . ?" the DNA clerk said.

"Ah," Judge Mickelson said. "And the results are . . . ?"

"Positive," the DNA clerk said, pulling a sheet out of the printer and signing it. "The received DNA is the biological mother of Mr. Truesdale."

Conn tensed up just a little more before slowly releasing a breath and completely relaxing.

"*Et voilà,*" Mike said. "So, about that apartment . . . ?"

⊕ ⊕ ⊕

"'It's almost as if we'd have to treat everybody as *individuals!*'" Ahuvit mimicked, giggling. They were in a small meeting room preparing to receive Mickelson's judgment. "The horror! The horror!"

"I never saw you as a giggler," Mike said.

"'It's madness!'" Derrick added, then laughed. It was more of a snort, but it counted.

"Holy shit," Mike said. "I got a laugh out of Chief Stone Face!"

"All rise!"

Judge Mickelson swept into the courtroom and took his seat behind the bench.

Mike sat down and assumed a composed mien.

"Having received evidentiary DNA of the deceased Annabelle Follett, which was, in my presence, tested and confirmed to be the DNA of the biological mother of the plaintiff, Michael James Truesdale, I hereby rule that Michael James Truesdale is the biological son of Annabelle Follett and the grandson of Dela Follett."

He banged the gavel.

"Case is closed. Next case..."

Mr. Truesdale appreciates the well-wishes sent to him by many people in this hour...

He asked me to add that while he is nonjudgmental, he is a Believer in the One God and was raised African Baptist Evangelical. While this may seem to be a wonderful thing, and it is, he reminds believers that it is easier for a laden camel to thread the eye of the needle than a rich man to enter Heaven.

He asks that those who believe pray for him. And he specifically asks that you pray to whomsoever you pray to, to send the angels to guard and guide him as he takes up this task.

New York Post: FOLLETT HEIR CONFIRMED!

Gotham Herald: IS BASEBALL THE NEW FACE OF WHITE SUPREMACY?

CHAPTER 16

"Today, the Junior Super Corps will be demonstrating an important development in the Super Corps' ability to keep us all safe and respond quickly to natural disasters and other emergencies," Bonfire said in front of the podium on the small stage in the center of Central Park's Great Lawn.

Shortly after they'd started patrolling together, Mike had dreamed up a way by which Laura/Fresh Breeze would be able to fly using an air tank. The concept easily translated to many of the other supers with elemental powers, and the concept had now spread throughout the Super Corps.

Metalstorm was displaying his new metal body harness. Fresh Breeze showed off the realization of Mike's original concept. It was an air tank on a custom-made parachute-like harness that would better support flying than a regular scuba vest. Stone Tactical had a similar but slightly simpler rig that carried a large, flat stone on his back. Of course, he hadn't needed that kind of setup to fly since his very early days with powers, but it really wouldn't serve to let the general public know that.

"Using these custom-developed harnesses, supers will be able to use their natural powers to lift themselves into the air for far-improved mobility and drastically reduced response times."

Out of the whole team, only Hombre de Poder remained flightless, as Invulnerable Ground powers didn't directly offer up a means of flight. He *could* jump pretty high and pretty far, but only a few degrees beyond Olympic gold medalists. It was nothing anywhere like the comic book Hulk. On the other hand, he could always be carried, as he had been on the El Cannibale raid.

However, it hadn't taken too much to fashion a metal rig for Jorge as well, with the belief that once Josh had mastered his own flying, he could learn to also manipulate Jorge's rig.

Naturally, it was unnecessary if Mike was around, as he could already lift and transport Jorge with great proficiency if he wanted. But once again, the public couldn't know that.

All three of the flying rigs had been adapted by Kevin to better match their outfits. Josh's, Jorge's, and Mike's outifts hadn't need much modification to fit their existing costumes. For Laura, however, the addition of the harness required a more extensive fix. This was mostly because the tight straps around her thighs greatly accentuated her already prominent cameltoe.

"Their training will be monitored by our very own Iron Eagle, but primarily led by their peer, Ivory Wing."

Patrick and Sasha stepped forward with smiles and waves. Laura looked just about ready to explode while fighting to keep her eye from twitching as Sasha took center stage yet again.

"So the junior supers, and supers on the whole," a reporter shouted, "are expanding their powers? Isn't that a dangerous precedent, a slippery slope? What's to stop them from going too far and heading down the path that—"

"To be clear," Bonfire interrupted, "this is *not* an expansion of powers, just a new way of using the powers they already had. As I said, the increased mobility will be a godsend in times of need, when we need as many competent supers with a wide range of powers on location in the shortest time possible."

"Is it really a good idea to increase the capabilities of a kid who's currently embroiled in litigation for assaulting an innocent member of the trans community?"

"How fast can they go?"

"Can you confirm reports that other supers, and maybe even some of these junior supers, have already been observed flying unsupervised around Manhattan?"

"Can they survive a fall from high altitudes?"

"Does this mean the flyers will no longer be the top of the proverbial supers food chain?"

"Are you going to have some sort of burning harness to fly around?"

"Nebraska Killers in training! Nebraska Killers in training!"

Bonfire nodded to Iron Eagle and jerked a thumb back toward the baseball field behind them. Then, he launched into a bland, Secretary-approved statement about not commenting on ongoing cases, nonspecific generalizations about potential capabilities, and assurance that the flyers would still be the masters of super air travel.

A couple police officers moved in to escort out one particularly disruptive individual who was trying—and failing—to start a chant.

Patrick led the group to a cordoned-off baseball field, where they'd be conducting public flight training. Josh was still entirely new to flying with his rig, so Patrick personally took him under his wing—literally. Sasha was primarily in charge of training Laura and Mike. Laura had some experience already, but she'd been told to go slow and downplay her abilities.

Mike, of course, was nearly as comfortable in the air as Sasha—if not quite so fast—but he had to play at both needing the stone to fly and being completely new to the experience. In actuality, he was acting as a subtle safety net for both Josh and Laura. If one of them lost concentration and took a tumble or just came down too fast, he'd grab hold and slow them just before impact. It was tricky to do so in a way that wouldn't be obvious on video, but the key was to grab their skeletons in a way that made it look as if they'd briefly caught themselves before hitting.

He only needed to do it a couple times for each of them, and no one seemed to question how they'd landed. Iron Eagle and Sasha had some tips and advice for flying in general, but there was a tremendous gap between how they flew and how the others were learning to fly.

A flyer simply felt themselves into the air and went. Most of their training centered around heroic poses and postures for flying, hovering and landing. It was another thing entirely to take hold of one's respective element and move it in a way that also moved you with it. On that score, it was theoretically easier for Josh since he simply had to grab his metal harness and move it around without crushing, squeezing, or bending the metal.

Laura, on the other hand, needed to grab hold of that *particular* tank of air and *not* all the air around it or—heaven forbid—any of the air inside her. That could be devastating. To her credit, Laura had taken to flying with the tank very well. Mike suspected it was largely out of spite to prove herself as capable and wonderful as Sasha.

Jorge spent his time jumping as far as he could and as high as he could—which was a spectacle in and of itself. Mike respected that he was showing zero signs of disappointment in being the only one who still didn't have a means to fly. Mike had some ideas on that front, but they were a bit more complicated.

Since the training, such as it was, was none too intellectually stimulating, Mike scanned around in Sight as he usually did. The watchers were still there, and it was remarkably simple to discern them from tourists and fans trying to get pictures of the junior supers in flight training.

It wasn't too long before Patrick decided Josh and Laura needed a break, even though Jorge was the only one showing any signs of exertion.

Patrick left to join up with Bonfire, and the junior supers all relaxed under a large tree. Laura went straight into her phone, Josh picked Sasha's brain on the differences in how they each flew, and Jorge flopped down next to Mike.

"So, Señor Stone," Jorge said, "last time you mentioned you had a big family now, but we didn't get to talk about it too much. You said your father was Mr. Sioux Nation? That's pretty badass, huh?"

"You don't know the half of it. Impressive as that is—and it is—it could be argued that's one of the least impressive things he's done. He spent a whole career in the Army, has stacks of medals, and most of his service record is redacted."

"Whoa, you mean he spent all that time doing, uh, spooky, secret squirrel sh—stuff?"

"No comment," Mike said with a wink, "though I don't have many details myself beyond knowing he was a Delta."

"A Delta?" Josh said. "Wow, that's, just . . . wow."

Sasha nodded agreement as well. That had gotten the attention of everyone except Laura, who was still buried in her phone.

"Damn, your dad is a super badass," Jorge said. "Bet his parents are proud, huh?"

Mike shrugged. "His mother, my grandmother, maybe. But my grandfather Jacob doesn't act like it. I'm sure he is proud, he's just really funny about it, like he can't admit his son's achieved anything."

"Yeah, dads are funny that way about sons," Josh said, and Jorge nodded.

"At least he knows his child exists as something other than a cash cow," Sasha said wistfully. She looked at Mike. "Although that might be your fate in the near future, with the inheritance and all."

Mike shook his head. "No, if anything the family's gonna think my money is cursed and refuse anything I might offer. And, truth be told, it might actually be cursed. Remains to be seen."

He'd mostly meant it as a joke, but it did get him wondering. No one seemed to know how to respond to that, so silence lingered for an awkward moment.

"So, Stone, your dad got a girl?" Jorge asked.

"Oh yeah, her name's Jane and she's awesome. Little blonde spitfire. Pretty sure she used to be a cheerleader back in the day. Now she's a CPS investigator."

"CPS investigator?" Sasha said. "Really?"

"Yeah, that's why I met her right after telling Derrick he was my biological father. He walked me straight to her office. But it was partially just pretense to see her. They're really cute together. When I met her, they thought they were keeping their relationship a secret, but it was pretty obvious to me and the entire town already knew."

"What the hell?" Laura shouted.

The entire group jumped in mild surprise and looked at her.

"What is it?" Sasha asked, leaning toward Laura.

"I'm seeing us on social feeds, right now, but somewhere else in the park," Laura said. "People are tagging me as if they just met me, but in the North Meadow Baseball Fields instead of here. And WAIT!! They say I'm charging forty bucks for an autograph!"

"Show us," Sasha said.

The group crowded in around Laura's phone to watch someone's feed. The account had the username "JSCfan69," and it was a simple pic of a cute girl with glasses and bobbed, black hair in the middle of a group of supers who looked *sorta* like the five of them. To an even mildly trained eye, they were clearly just cosplayers, but they at least had the right body types and general features. Times Square was riddled with people dressed like supers who'd offer a photo and then demand money. But that was a well-known scam, and it was obvious none of those people were the actual supers. But this seemed intended to make people think it really was the Junior Super Corps on patrol to milk money out of real fans.

"But aren't our fans tracking us here?" Josh asked. "Isn't it public that we're here training?"

"Apparently, the internet is now confused as to which baseball fields we're at," Laura said. "People are already flocking there instead of here as a result."

"Should I fly over there and stop it?" Sasha said.

"Yeah, we can all go," Josh said. "Come on."

"Wait," Mike said.

"What's wrong?" Josh asked.

Mike looked around, semi-dramatically for effect. "Last time we were here, I got the impression we weren't finding any drugs or rapists or anything because someone set up a network of lookouts. I mean, look around. There's at least a few people watching us who don't exactly look like fans. Homeless people, kids, et cetera, with really nice phones just eyeballing us?"

Jorge stood and started scanning around.

"Jorge, bring it back in, let's not make it too obvious we know," Mike said. "Just trust me on this."

"I can be there faster than someone can call," Sasha said.

"Yeah," Mike said, "but they'll all still scatter when we show, and then the big, mean Junior Super Corps is pushing around innocent people just trying to enjoy Central Park."

Josh frowned and sighed in frustration. "Then what do we do?"

"Here's the plan . . ." Mike began.

A few minutes later, the patrol casually headed off the Great Lawn and beelined for the Winterdale Arch, near West Eighty-first Street and Central Park West. They passed through it and continued west into the trees until Mike was certain they only had one watcher chasing them. The poor kid was out of breath by the time he got to the Arch, where he tried to make a call. Unfortunately, both the camera and faceplate cracked right before he could unlock it.

"We're clear," Mike said.

"You sure?" Josh asked.

"Haven't you learned not to question this guy?" Jorge said.

They hurried north until they reached the shore of the Jacqueline Kennedy Onassis Reservoir. There, Mike spotted a homeless man in torn jeans and heavy, scraggly facial hair jogging after them and frantically tapping at his phone. That phone, sadly, cracked as well before he could call.

"Still clear, let's go," Mike said.

Sasha grabbed hold of Jorge, and the five of them lifted to fly low and fast along the reservoir's western shoreline. Mike added his own "help" the one time Josh faltered, and they were soon over the north shore just southwest of the tennis center. They stayed airborne and threaded the trees—where both Josh and Laura needed a little more "guidance." As they approached the North Meadow Baseball Fields, two small kids spotted them and turned to warn someone. Both kids found they couldn't move their jaws to shout or their arms to wave until the patrol had moved past them.

The quintet landed gracefully at the edge of the crowd. Heads turned, and confused mumbles turned to a wave of cheers as people realized the real junior supers were the ones who'd just flown in. The fake supers braced for a confrontation, already sputtering about rights and racism and cowering as if they were about to be assaulted.

But the Junior Super Corps, under Mike's suggestion, instead approached to kill them with kindness.

"Oh. My. God!" Laura squealed as she walked up to her counterpart with a wide smile and hands out as if offering a hug to a friend. "You look incredible. I'm so honored a fan went to such trouble to make this."

"Love the mask, *mi amigo*," Jorge said, laying the accent on *thick*. He offered a fist bump, which his counterpart matched on instinct, looking completely dumbfounded.

Mike simply strutted up to the kid in the Stone Tactical costume, gave him a once-over, then made a thumbs-up. "Looking good."

The real supers held tight and demanded photos from everyone around with their "cosplayer fans." The fake junior supers glanced at each other in panic but stood and posed with forced smiles. They'd all rightly concluded that running was a horrible idea.

Then Mike figured out the real game. It was about more than just making a few bucks off phots by pretending to be the junior supers.

Some New Yorkers said that pickpocketing was a thing of the past in New York, and they were mostly right. There'd been a crackdown by the police in the eighties and nineties and professional pickpockets had largely disappeared. It was also true that few people carried a lot of cash anymore, and credit cards could be canceled with a few taps on an app if a purse or wallet was stolen.

However, purse snatchers had never really died out and there was a growing trend of pocket or purse *slashing*. Simply cutting a purse strap or a pocket open and collecting the contents was faster than pickpocketing and easier to learn. As an added bonus, if you got the phone along with the wallet—best of all were the people with credit cards in a clip attached to their phone—then you had a lot more time to use a credit card before the owner could cancel it.

And this crowd was *thick* with the little pocket and purse slashers. The fake supers had largely been a front to gather a big crowd for the little buggers to go to work. In Sight, Mike could see them sweeping through the crowd of fans and tourists like an infestation. They were both admirably stealthy and incredibly brazen as they were still working the crowd even with the real Junior Super Corps on location.

He *could* stop them all at once, but it'd be tricky to do it without being too obvious. Here and there, he slowed their progression by holding a hand back until they'd missed their opportunity, but it was just treating the symptom rather than the disease.

Instead, he kept track of the worker bees and followed them back to the hive. Or hives, rather. There were three adults—one woman and two men dressed like women who were probably more disguised than trans—pushing covered baby strollers that Mike could clearly See did not have babies but did have a growing collection of phones, wallets, and other stolen items.

"Hey, Ivory Wing," Mike said in his cheesiest superhero voice, "I know how much you like babies, should we go say hi to some?"

He jabbed a thumb toward one of the baby strollers, whose owner was now casually moving away from the crowd. Sasha narrowed her eyes in confusion and searched for a second before catching on. She rose into the sky and shot toward the departing "mother." Mike similarly lifted his stone and let it carry him to one of the others.

"Oh, how old is your baby?" he said sweetly, gushing and motioning at the cover. "Can I see her?"

The "mother's" eyes darted every which way like a trapped rat. In the cheesiest of fake, high-pitched voices, he said, "Sorry, uh, she's taking a nap and I gotta get her, uh, home."

While he engaged with this one, Mike knocked over the third stroller with Earth Move. Its contents scattered across the grass. Jorge leaped over the crowd and across the lawn to "help" her.

"Ma'am, is your baby okay? Can I help with—*Dios mio*," he said as he landed beside the tipped cart. "Looks like you've been pretty busy, huh?"

The owner of that cart bolted, but Laura landed directly in his path. He took a swing at her, but she blocked it with ease. Half a second later, Jorge wrapped a gentle arm around the man's waist and just held him in place. There was a lot of flailing and cursing, but there wasn't much anyone could do when they were restrained by an invulnerable ground.

"Wait a second," Mike said with his very best shocked face. He lifted the cover off the stroller, then raised another thin blanket to reveal their score.

"Help! This boy's attacking my baby!" the "mother" screamed.

"Do you really want even more attention over here?" Mike asked with a grin.

The "mother" turned to run, but Mike caught her ankle with Earth Move just enough to trip him up.

"What the hell?" the man said, dropping his fake woman's voice entirely.

Sasha had similarly exposed the stash in the stroller she'd gone to. That woman tried to run, but she yelped and dropped, clutching her ear. At a guess, Metalstorm had yanked on her earring.

The kids were scattering, but Mike let them go and none of the other junior supers made a move to stop them either. If they collected them up, they *might* get a better life somewhere. But Mike knew they'd just go into the foster care system and odds were they'd actually wind up worse off. Hell, some of them might have wound up here after fleeing foster care.

Getting the three principals would have to do for today.

Iron Eagle swooped in to take control of the situation, and a collection of police flooded in shortly after.

New York Post: JUNIOR SUPERS BUST CENTRAL PARK ROBBERY RING

Gotham Herald: SHADES OF THE NEBRASKA KILLER IN TODAY'S SUPER YOUTHS!

⊕ ⊕ ⊕

"Mr. Alger," Mike said, waving to a seat in the condo's main living room. "Please have a seat. How was your flight? Accommodations satisfactory?"

"Very nice, sir," Alger said. "You are aware of my military service, I am sure. I really don't need to be cosseted, sir."

Alger had sharp eyes that took everything in but were primarily gauging Mike at the moment. He sat ramrod straight and his outfit was meticulously maintained in a way Mike hadn't been able to fully appreciate over the video call.

"Good people are hard to find," Mike said. "That is the case in every endeavor. I have been fortunate in that I've been able to access excellent people throughout this... I would say 'ordeal' but I have a different concept of the meaning of that word. Perhaps... minor annoyance? But the good people have managed to reduce it from the point of minor ordeal to minor annoyance."

Counter to Derrick's perpetual stone face, Alger was practiced and specific with his expressions and body language to be perfectly proper and amenable to whomever he was with.

"And if you take care of good people, they take care of you," Mike said. "A long way of saying if a business-class ticket and a suite get me a qualified British house manager who is also a friend of my father, it's worth every penny."

"That *is* a position, sir," Alger said. "I would go so far as to say a refreshing one."

"Problem with your last employer?" Mike asked.

"Not at all, sir," Alger said. "If this does not work out within a reasonable timeframe, I was invited to return to service and received an excellent recommendation. But he understood the circumstance and approved of an early termination of my contract."

"Current terms are acceptable?" Mike asked.

"Quite, sir," Alger said. "The compensation is quite acceptable, and I look forward to the work."

"And there we get to the bone of the matter," Mike said. "And while I'll allow you to obviously not betray any confidences, you left the employ of Sir Charles at the completion of your first contractual period. Why?"

"I did not feel... comfortable in service to Sir Charles, sir," Alger said, carefully.

"When you were in *the* service versus in service," Mike said, "you took issue with a tribal chief who had a taste for young boys."

Alger's face barely revealed a flicker of surprise, but it was there.

"I didn't get that from my father," Mike said. "Not even sure if he's aware. Without betraying any confidences of a former employer, would that tend to have had some bearing on your leaving his employ?"

"That would seem to be asking to reveal a confidence, sir," Alger said. "Not that I am either confirming or denying the implication. The question I would ask, sir, admitting that I do take issue with assault on young people, as one should, is if that will be an issue in this household?"

"Ah," Mike said, shaking his head. "No. You've got the stick a bit backward there. Rather the opposite issue. I've been a sexual assault victim, at least orally. The one person who, when I was nine, decided to go for the full treatment ended up with eighty-six stitches."

There was a calculated flash of sympathy in Alger's expression. Even using Sight, Alger had almost no tells in his body language.

"The problem is that I need to ensure that all of my confidences remain confidential," Mike said. "Obviously, I have access to information that is surprising for someone of my age and not yet inherited. Your classified military service record, for example. Had to do qualification for the Regiment twice. Did quite well both times, just a bit of a slipup on the first round."

"You do have good information," Alger said.

"Which means that I know that the baron was an active and aggressive pedophile," Mike said. "I don't have to ask you, and you don't need to violate a confidence. I also know that he is part of a conspiracy called the Society. Every Society member is a pedophile. It's required for admission. And its purpose is the long-term overthrow of all this silly democracy stuff and a reimposition of a self-selecting elite. Ring a bell? The Society bit?"

"Yes, sir," Alger said with a cautious nod. "I shall admit to some knowledge of that of which you speak."

"Various groups are in opposition to the Society, whether they know about it or not," Mike said. "The MAGA types here in the US are composed of those who are led around by the nose by it or those who are truly and intelligently in opposition, though they tend to call it the Deep State.

"Then there are those who know about it, in detail, and are opposed.

"The Chinese know and are opposed. The Society is truly white supremacist. The Berlin branch, which more or less leads it, is still stuck on Aryan purity, for God's sake! They are also neocolonialist. They don't actively colonize but they still consider third-world countries as nothing but extraction zones. They consider all other races and nations outside Europe and Britain as the other and unimportant. That includes both the US and China. And the British branch was responsible for the Opium Wars *and* stabled their horses in the Palace. That last is something the Chinese will never forgive in a thousand years.

"Last but not least, the Chinese fully intend the same thing: take over the world and rule it with an iron fist. There can be only one world master. I am sure that if nothing else while serving drinks you've heard conversations. Am I getting ahead of where you're at, Mr. Alger?"

"No, sir," Alger said.

"I'm not sure if you would consider this a violation of confidence," Mike said. "But are you aware of any other groups other than China who are aware of the Society and who are in opposition?"

Alger thought about that for a moment and nodded.

"Several nation-states," Alger said. "Besides the Chinese, the Indians are notable. Especially the Vishnu. The Society does not care for Vishnu and the other way around."

"We haven't covered this," Mike said. "And I'm not sure if you are aware..."

"That you are Stone Tactical?" Alger said. "I am aware, sir."

"The Society hates all supers," Mike said. "How dare we have power when we are not the proper sort? Other than nation-states, any other groups? An NGO perhaps?"

"Nongovernmental organization?" Alger said. "Most of those are *created* by the Society for their purposes, sir."

And, ironically, heavily funded and controlled by Society-run government entities. I'll assume you know that as well.

"Okay," Mike said. "Point. Another *conspiracy*?"

"Ah," Alger said. "You may be talking about Omega."

"That," Mike said. "Yes. And what do you know about Omega, if I may ask?"

"Hackers," Alger said. "Not betraying a confidence to a great degree but the term I heard was 'snooping little buggers.' They're involved in rescuing children from child trafficking and generally fighting child porn and that sort of thing. They also hire mercenaries. I've heard of them through contacts with squaddies. Most just take usual sorts of contract work but a few have worked with them, so I've heard. Say they're top notch at operations."

"You hinted that there might be a problem if I was into young people," Mike said. "I'll point out that being thirteen, it's sort of okay if I bang thirteen-year-olds. Though that would be girls, not boys. But any thirteen-year-old girl who is sexually active has already been through a lot. So, no issues there because I've got an issue with that sort of thing."

It was his turn to pause and think.

"I'll go so far as to say I've been an Omega asset," Mike said. "They do use very young assets. Baker Street Irregulars, if you will. So, I'm aligned *against* the Society."

"And you or Omega are afraid I might be a Society plant," Alger said, nodding. "That would be an issue, sir. Also, might explain your information source."

"Which it does," Mike said. "And, yes, that question has been raised. It's still an open issue and will remain one, absent some way to close it. The point was made that virtually any British in service was probably working for the Society simply because of their omnipresence in the British upper class.

"However, be advised that Wesley Conn, the chief trustee, is Society. Also, that he began raping my mother, Annabelle Follett, his stepdaughter and beneficiary of the Trust, when she was eleven. And last, be advised that I am going to take away his power, take away his money, take everything from him including his self-respect, ego, and hubris, rake him over hot coals for years and *years* before I *allow* him the sweet, merciful release of death."

"Sir," Alger said. "I understand that there are some questions as to my loyalty. I will simply state that if I am in service to you, I am in service to you and no other."

Mike nodded in response.

"I will add, sir, that you seem to be the sort of employer for whom I would very *much* like to work . . ."

CHAPTER 17

"Roots" —In This Moment

"So, now we have to prove I'm even entitled to the inheritance," Mike said, shaking his head.

They'd borrowed the car and driver from the law firm for the tour of New York properties. It wasn't the swank limo they'd traveled in for the legal proceedings, but it was a comfortable luxury town car. They were getting closer to the apartment on Fifth Avenue, based on reaching Central Park. The leaves were fully out. When they'd first arrived in town, the trees were bare. There were a few clouds in the sky, and Mike had the window down to catch the scents of early spring and the occasional waft of the Hudson.

"Law is a slow business," Derrick said. "At least Judge Mickelson agreed that you were entitled to tour the properties and temporarily use one of them. Like the proof of maternity, it's essentially a done deal. But law is a slow business."

"Yes, but that leaves an abundance to pull more dirty tricks," Mike said absently.

"You knew that was the game before we started playing."

"Yes, I did."

Derrick and Mr. Alger were along for the tour of the family homes. For the first inspection Derrick had chosen to wear one of his standard "disappear in New York" business suits. Mike was wearing a plum Glenn plaid sport jacket and gray dress slacks with a light salmon ascot. A cravat was too formal for a house visit.

"Can't wait for the accountants to get their hands on the books," Mike said. "Though I'm sure they're in the process of trying to hide everything."

"Be a bit hard," Derrick said. "I suspect 'everything' is a bit much."

They pulled up at the front of the apartment building and their door was opened by a uniformed doorman.

Mike stepped out and looked up at the building, shaking his head again.

"It's a nice design, at least," he said.

The front lobby of the apartment was more like a high-end hotel than an apartment building. There were two people standing behind the front desk. What did they do all day? Surely people had their own keys.

A representative from the Trust was waiting for them in the lobby. He was average height, a little overweight, and had a wolfish grin plastered on his face. Something gave Mike the impression he was someone who liked to abuse his authority whenever possible.

"Mr. Truesdale," he said, holding out his hand. "John Rossman. I'm an associate with the Trust."

Mike considered just looking at the hand, but the guy probably didn't deserve that, so he shook it.

"Apartment?" Mike asked.

"Right this way," Rossman said, leading the way to the elevators.

"There is a separate elevator for the penthouses," Rossman said, gesturing to the end elevator. "The apartment shares the top floor with only one other, which formerly belonged to the late Butch Eisenberg."

"Understood," Mike said.

Rossman swiped a card across the access panel and the doors opened.

"Each of the penthouse apartments has its own private rooftop pool," Rossman continued. "There are, in addition, two other rooftop pools which are accessible to other tenants. However, they are separated from the private pools. The building has a full gym and a restaurant. Tenants never need to leave."

He swiped the card again and pressed the only button, which was marked 14.

Not too surprisingly, the elevator was all fumed oak and gilt. Despite only servicing two apartments, it was big enough to fit an Indonesian family of twenty.

"I don't intend to be a high-living shut-in," Mike said. "I'm not even sure how much I'll be in the City."

"You don't intend to make New York your primary residence?" Rossman said.

"With the crazy taxes in this state?" Mike said. "Hell, no. But I'll probably keep at least one of the properties. Just depends."

"Alright," Rossman said.

The elevator opened into a short hallway with several doors.

Mike pointed to them as they stepped out and Rossman turned to the left.

"Those are primarily for the service personnel," Rossman said. "This is the main entrance to the apartment."

The electronic locked door led to a short foyer. Beyond was the main room of the apartment, which stretched up three stories. The floor was marble tile, the walls were decorated in oil paintings and murals, while the ceiling was a fresco of clouds and what appeared to be cherubs.

Waiting for them was a gentleman in his sixties with thinning gray hair and blue eyes. He was dressed in a white linen day suit very similar to Alger's attire.

"And this is Mr. Pelton," Rossman said.

"Mr. Pelton," Mike said, nodding.

"Sir," Pelton said, clicking his heels.

"Mr. Pelton is the house manager," Rossman said. "Though I see you have one of those."

"Mr. Alger is the valet," Mike said.

"Oh?" Rossman said, looking confused.

"Shall we tour?" Mike asked.

The "apartment" was seven thousand square feet, double the size of most large single-family homes. It contained—besides the mentioned small indoor/outdoor pool with adjoining hot tub—six bedrooms, including a master in the corner that was the size of the loft they currently occupied. An office with seating area with a magnificent view of the park. A library. A sauna. A steam room. A small and rather antiquated gym. A dance salle. A grand dining room adjacent to the main room. And large kitchen with an enormous pantry.

All of the walls were covered in paintings that, while not to Mike's taste, were well chosen. Many of them were of the Folletts over the time they'd owned the apartment. The building had been constructed in the 1920s and the Folletts had been the primary investors in the building. The Eisenberg family had bought into it after it was constructed.

The main thing that Mike noticed about it was that it could best be described as "frou-frou." It just gave off the aura of an apartment of a woman. It definitely was not manly. It also had a lighter feel than he'd expected.

When they'd completed the tour, Mike suggested they round out at the study.

"Mr. Rossman," Mike said, holding up his hand as they reached the study. "Could you give us a moment?"

"Of course," Rossman said, looking a bit nonplussed.

Alger shut the door in his face.

"Right," Mike said, walking over to the seating area. "Mr. Pelton, take a seat if you will, please?"

"Sir," Pelton said, sitting uneasily in one of the florid satin chairs. Pelton acted properly in the same calculated way Alger did, but he looked far more worn out than Alger did.

Mike braced himself for the conversation. It was going to be painful for both of them, but it needed to happen.

"Mr. Pelton," Mike said. "You are, pardon me, rather late in life."

"I am, sir, yes," Pelton said.

"How long have you been employed by the Trust?" Mike asked.

"I was originally hired by the Family, sir," Pelton said. "I was hired shortly before your great-grandfather passed away as an assistant houseman at the estate."

Alger remained standing and took a respectful position to the left and slightly behind Mike.

"Continue," Mike said.

"Well, sir," Pelton said, "your grandmother had a liking for me. Not in any inappropriate way, sir. She just thought I was a good assistant. So, when she took over living in the apartment, she asked me to be the manager. I have been here most of the time since."

"So, you're sort of a career Follett man," Mike said.

"I am, sir, yes," Pelton said. "I've never worked for anyone else. Save, I suppose, the Trust. But like your mother I held out hope there would be another Follett."

"And so, he appears with a flash of fire and a smell of brimstone," Mike said, grinning. "I'd gathered this was my grandmother's apartment. It has that feel. Were you working here when she passed?"

"I was, yes, sir," Pelton said. "I was the one who found her."

"Story?" Mike said.

"There is not much of one to it, sir," Pelton said. "I do not reside here. I have my own small place. I had had the night off. We do take some time, sir. I came in the next morning, prepared her breakfast as normal, carried it into the room . . . and there she was."

"I'm sorry for your loss," Mike said. "I'm sure that was hard. I can tell that despite your personal sexual choices you had some feeling for her."

"You noticed, sir," Pelton said.

"Alger," Mike said. "Wasn't it the Queen Mum or someone that said that if it wasn't for queens, we'd have no one to serve queens?"

"It was something like that, yes, sir," Alger said. "And it was indeed the Queen Mum, sir."

"I don't have an issue with that sort of thing," Mike said. "But you did like her in a bit of a way, yes?"

"Yes, sir," Pelton said. "I was in an odd kind of love for her. It was hard to find her like that."

"Yes," Mike said. "I've dealt with a lot of dead bodies in my time. And some I even cared for. Did my grandmother return the feeling, at least to seeing to you in her will?"

"She did, sir," Pelton said. "She was quite generous in that matter. I could have retired already but . . . I don't know that I held out hope, but it is what I do."

"And I suppose you're somewhat worried about a new broom sweeping clean," Mike said, sighing. "That is an issue. Depending on too many factors to discuss, I may have to sell some of the residences. As such I may have to let some people go. But you have been with the family for a long time and if you need to leave service, I shall ensure that it is with a generous severance package."

"You are too kind, sir," Pelton said.

"You knew my mother?" Mike said.

"Oh, yes, sir," Pelton replied. He tensed up a little.

"What was she like?" Mike asked.

"She was a bright spark, sir," Pelton said, smiling. "She was just so much fun as a child. I did not see her on a regular basis. She mostly stayed at the estate. I ... Dela was ... Dela ..."

"She'd forget from time to time she even had a child?" Mike said. "Not maliciously, she was just ... Dela."

"Yes, sir," Pelton said, shaking his head. "Dela was wonderful as well. Vivacious. Charming. Sophisticated. But also a bit ..."

"Scatterbrained?" Mike said.

"You said it, sir, not I," Pelton said. "But ... I heard that Annabelle left you in an alleyway, sir. Please don't judge her by that, sir. Please. She was such a kind and wonderful and smart and *such* a wonderful child."

"And then she changed," Mike said.

"She did, sir, yes," Pelton said, looking mournful. "She just ... changed, sir. Dela didn't know what to do about her. Drugs. Alcohol. Boys. Disappearing for *days* at a time. Finally, she just disappeared. When she died, Dela did *not* forget she had had a child. Not one day. After that it was all about finding the heir. But ... she mostly hired psychics and that sort of thing. Ouija boards were all over the house."

Mike forcibly calmed himself as imagery of his mother flooded in. He knew, probably far better than Pelton, what had been happening, but hearing Pelton's perspective still stung like a dagger to the heart.

"Then she was gone."

"And you were left all alone in this museum to her to mourn them both," Mike said.

"That is ... an apt description, sir," Pelton said.

"Pelton, I grew up on the street," Mike said, his diction changing to slight ghetto. "Only thing I ever wanted in life was what I only ever see on the tee-vee. Clean house, clean yards, clean cars, clean people. A wife who loved me, some kids, maybe a dog."

He thought about it for a moment and shrugged.

"Time I was twelve, I was a state's witness," Mike said. "For once, they had the good sense to move me out of Baltimore, which is where I'm *actually* from, to a town called Marysville.

"Saw something there I'd never seen before: girls who was sweet. On the street time they're twelve, girls are either hard or broken. They've been through too much. Been too much done to them."

Pelton's face turned pained and sympathetic.

"There was this girl there in the school, name of Mary," Mike said, his face full of memory. "She was one of the ones was sweet. Sweetest girl you'd e'er see, Pelton. I was all street, like, 'Hey, babe, you be fine! Wass your name?' And she's like, 'I'm Mary! And this is *my* town 'cause it's *Marysville*! And this is *my* land 'cause it's *Maryland*!'

"Man, I just thought that was the *cutest* thing I'd ever seed," Mike said, shaking his head. "She was a honey little blonde, got her boobs tad early. Little on the chunky side but that was okay. Man, my heart, and hate to say other parts, was just *full*.

"But maybe I was a touch too scary," Mike said. "There were lots of rumors 'bout me. Some of them close to true. Most less than truth, truth told. I had scars and word got around. That fella scary. He dangerous. Which true, Pelton. I am a dangerous person.

"But she liked this boy, Hector Marchado," Mike said, smiling tightly. "Hector was thirteen and he was *Latin* and he was *handsome* and smooth and he was MS-13.

"Hector convinced her to come over to his uncle's house, play some video games or something. And he and his uncle and a bunch of other guys raped her and then they pimped Mary out, Pelton. Right under her parents' *noses*. Her *and* her younger sister.

"So, then she weren't sweet no more," Mike said, his face hard. "She was broken. And I could see the signs, Pelton. I *knew* what had happened. Didn't know *who* right away. Didn't have to ax. Arms crossed over her chest. Head down. That light of innocence died in her eyes. She was broken."

Pelton sighed and tilted his head sorrowfully.

"So, I axed some questions, Pelton," Mike said. "New in town, didn't know rightly who to ax. So, I had to ax a good few people. Some of them probably didn't deserve what they got. Others did. But I got me some answers, Pelton.

"Thought about going all Boogie Knight on their asses," Mike said, his eyes cold. "Didn't have the contacts. Couldn't figure how to do it and walk away clean. And where the fuck was I gonna get the guns, right, Pelton? Wasn't like I had a problem with cleaning up that fucking house. Just . . . gonna need at least *two* pistols and a shotgun or AR . . . six of them usually, one of me . . . Could use some body armor . . .

"Call it common sense, call it cowardice, call it being twelve and in a town I didn't rightly know where the local gun dealer was at, I did the thing that made the most sense: called a marshal I'd worked with before. I'd found some of the girls was trafficked cross state lines. Made it marshal territory.

"Marshals and Maryland State Police raided the house," Mike said. "Got all the girls out. I talked Mary into giving state's. Marshals moved her and her family into WitSec and whisked them off into the night. Last I ever seed of Mary of Marysville.

"Older guys got a few years," Mike said. "Deportada after that—leastwise, gotta hope. Then probably right back across the border to do more raping poor innocent girls, pimping them out.

"That fucker Marchado got *six fucking months* juvie and they even suspended *that* for probation.

"Every time MS-13 dude commits a rape, gets a tattoo of a rose. Did you know that, Pelton?"

"I was unaware, sir," Pelton said with wide eyes.

"Motherfucker already had *four*," Mike said, shaking his head. "And they don't lie about that shit. You put on a tat you ain't rightfully earned, they'll take it off with a *knife*. Mary was the *fourth* girl he'd raped wasn't but thirteen.

"The point to that sad, angry-makin' story, Pelton, is that your new boss has gots the knowing," Mike said, looking at the elderly house manager. "He gots the street eye. So, you want to maybe say anything at this juncture 'bout my momma other than she jist '*changed*'?"

Pelton shifted uncomfortably in his seat.

"I'm really not sure what I could say, sir," Pelton said.

"A'ight," Mike said, standing up and slapping his legs. "Good talk, Pelton. Hope to see you 'gin sometime soon. We'll see what we see and if there is a partin' of ways, I'll make sure such a long-time associate is adequate compensated for your years of service."

"Thank you, sir," Pelton said.

"Think the townhome next," Mike said, walking to the door.

They were walking to the entrance foyer when Pelton cleared his throat.

"Sir," Pelton said. "Mr. Truesdale. A brief moment of your time before you go?"

"A'ight," Mike said, still in Boogie Knight mode.

Pelton gestured for him to come into the main room.

"I believe, sir, that, yes, your mother was being sexually assaulted," Pelton said, quietly.

"Did you know that at the time?" Mike asked.

"I did not *know* that it was happening, sir," Pelton said, a touch desperately. "I just . . . There were rumors, sir."

"A'ight," Mike said.

"Ms. Kennedy at the estate was quite definite about it," Pelton said. "She tried to tell Dela, and Dela just . . ."

"Couldn't hear it," Mike said. "Because it didn't fit into her worldview that anything like that could be happening."

"Yes, sir," Pelton said.

"A'ight," Mike said. "Ain't gonna ask who. Water over the dam. Probably already dead of old age."

He stuck out his hand to the house manager and Pelton lightly shook it.

"Welcome to the firm, Pelton," Mike said. "I understand you have some experience at this. I'm looking forward to working with you, if you'll put up with me."

"Oh, yes, sir," Pelton said, tearing up slightly.

"And, yes, you just saved your job," Mike said. "If you'd kept lying to me, Alger would ensure that your feet did *not* touch the ground on the way out."

CHAPTER 18

"Vater Unser" —E Nomine

"That's not a *town house*," Mike said as the town car pulled up alongside a towering building. "That's a *castle.*"

The town house on Riverside Drive was enormous. Built in 1910, it had been regularly and extensively renovated on the interior. But the exterior, thank God, was original architecture. And it was absolutely gorgeous. His ancestors might have been Satan-worshipping, demon-possessed, child-murdering and -raping, slave-trading *scum*, but they had *exquisite* taste.

Twelve thousand square feet with an additional two-thousand-square-foot wine cellar, pre-stocked as part of the inheritance, it was six stories tall and took up a spacious corner lot.

What it did *not* have was parking. Apparently, the carriages were kept elsewhere. Probably at the stables with the horses. They passed through a large metal gate and immediately came to a stop at the entrance.

The door was opened as they walked up the front stairs and they were greeted by five people standing in a line. Their uniforms indicated their respective jobs.

"Mr. Truesdale, I am Wesley Otoy, house manager," the man said, bowing slightly.

Wesley was about six feet tall, heavy set, with dark black skin and chocolate brown eyes, dressed in an off-white morning suit. From his accent he was from somewhere in the Caribbean.

"If I may have the pleasure of introducing the staff?" Otoy continued.

"Of course," Mike replied. They'd managed to shake Rossman since from here on out they'd be around Fund people.

"Ms. Van Hamen, the housekeeper," Otoy said.

Ms. Van Hamen was a black woman in her fifties in a standard housekeeper uniform. She was a plump five foot nine at a guess and had light green eyes.

"Good morning, sir," Ms. Van Hamen said. Islands accent again.

"Ms. Van Hamen," Mike said, nodding.

"Mr. Friedman, the chef."

Friedman had a couple inches on Ms. Van Hamen and was very heavyset and fair skinned with a series of double chins squeezed into a chef's whites. Blond hair and blue eyes, set deep. At a guess he was in his sixties.

"*Guten tag*, sir," Friedman said in a heavy accent.

"*Sind sie Deutscher?*" Mike asked.

"I am, sir," Friedman said.

"*Zer gut*," Mike said.

"Mr. Ortillo, the gardener and handyman," Friedman said.

"*Buenos dias*, sir."

Ortillo was fortysomething, five foot six and stocky with a quick grin that revealed a gold tooth. He was wearing a dress shirt buttoned to the neck with long sleeves buttoned down.

Mike was curious what tattoos he was trying to conceal. He could just barely make them out in Sight. He could tell they were old.

"*Buen dia*," Mike said.

"And the maids, Consuela and Devera," Otoy finished.

Consuela was in her twenties, five foot four or so. Devera was older, forties or so, and shorter, closer to five feet even. Both were in gray maid outfits with functional aprons.

"Thank you," Mike said, nodding at them. "I'm sure we'll get to know each other well in the future. A tour, Mr. Otoy...?"

The tour took a great deal of time and required a lot of walking. They even stopped in the parlor for refreshments halfway through.

There was no pool but other than that it was more sumptuous than the apartment. The floors were parquet wood and most of the rooms were wood paneled. Mike knew just enough about wood to see that it was all hardwood and fine-grained, meaning that it was from old, very mature trees. There were several original, functional fireplaces.

The top floor was an open patio with a glassed-in gazebo that had some spectacular views of the Hudson River. In the distance, you could just see the George Washington Bridge.

The whole thing was beautiful at that level. But then you got to the furnishings and art.

The furnishings were primarily, in Mike's opinion, hideous art nouveau style. There was a lot of curved tube steel and angles to everything. It looked as if it hadn't been redecorated since the 1970s.

The paintings and art in general were all postmodernist and even then, it wasn't good postmodernist. The art was all "most expensive in the gallery" crap. If the artist has to pontificate for hours explaining it, it wasn't art in Mike's opinion.

The entire place had a heavy feel. Mike recognized it. It wasn't just that it was haunted, it was demon *infested*.

It also had some ugly secrets. There were three people who had been walled up in the basement and apparently left to die. The bodies were old, just skeletons, and even then the bones were mostly decayed. Plus a hundred years at a guess. Just post the house being built. He was wondering how to both remove the literal skeletons that were buried in the walls as well as explain them. And explain how he knew they were there without referring to Sight.

It wasn't just Mike, he could tell that both Alger and Derrick were getting creepy vibes at numerous locations.

This was going to take some major spiritual cleaning. And clearing out all the crap furnishings and art would be a good start.

"All very nice, Mr. Otoy," Mike said. "You've clearly done an excellent job managing the house and it is appreciated."

They'd repaired to the study again.

"Thank you, sir," Otoy said.

"Please, have a seat," Mike said, gesturing to a chair.

"How long have you been with the firm?" Mike asked as they both sat. Once again, Alger assumed a position at Mike's side.

"I was hired as house manager eleven years ago, sir," Otoy said.

"Direct to house manager?" Mike asked.

"Yes, sir," Otoy said.

"Previous experience?" Mike asked.

"I was assistant house manager to a Mr. Powell, sir," Otoy said. "He has a place, still, in Long Island as well as Palm Beach."

"Very good," Mike said. "The house manager before you here?"

"A Mr. Portnoy, sir," Otoy said. "He had passed away and I was asked to step into his shoes."

"Must have been rather a trial at first," Mike said. *Wonder what Portnoy knew?* "The apartment did not seem to have been extensively used by the Trust. Did they use this home often?"

"Not *often*, sir," Otoy said. "During the winter when there was a Trust meeting some of the trustees who lived out of town would stay here, and there would generally be a formal dinner here. And, occasionally, there would be dinner parties during the winter season. During the summer they used the estate."

"Eleven years," Mike said. "You were hired after my mother had passed. But my grandmother was still alive. Did you know her well?"

"Not well, sir," Otoy said. "She rarely visited the house. This was, as I understand it, your great-grandfather's primary residence before his death. She stuck mostly to the apartment or occasionally the estate. Before, of course, her untimely passing."

"Alright," Mike said. "Well, your work here is appreciated. There are too many factors at present to determine if I'm going to sell any of the homes and if so which. Tell the staff I wish I could say more but it is impossible at this time. If anyone has to be let go—if, for example, I choose to sell the house—there will be a decent compensation package. I don't believe in just tossing people out in the snow with a sack."

"Thank you, sir," Otoy said, evenly.

"Well, that's all," Mike said, standing up. "I hear it's a long drive to the estate. Very much appreciate everyone's work. Looks great..."

When they were back in the car, Mike crossed himself and said an Our Father under his breath.

"Jesus, Jesus, Jesus, be with us now," Mike finished. "Either of you even vaguely Sensitive?" Mike asked. "Believers?"

"I am not a churchgoer, sir," Alger said.

"Demons?" his father asked. "Ghosts?"

"Lots," Mike said. "You always get one with the other. And you can put that down to nerves, though generally I've got nerves of steel. But there are literal bodies in the walls."

"Literal?" his father asked.

"Not new," Mike said. "From around the original build at a guess. Sealed up 'Cask of Amontillado' style. They were either put there to unconsecrate the ground or were just problems that were dealt with. Also, secret passages, servants' passages, that I'm not sure Baron Samedi even knows about."

"Baron Samedi?" Alger said.

"If that guy hasn't got the full costume sitting in his closet, I'm a monkey's uncle," Mike said. "Alger, I haven't covered this but I'm a Believer. And I'm not just a Believer in God, I'm a believer in angels and demons. Real things that exist right here in this world and have an effect.

"There are all sorts of angels, but everyone gets one assigned at or near birth," Mike said. "They hang around maternity wards. Babies can see them and maybe when they're there in the incubators looking around, they pick one out. Dunno.

"Ever hear that thing 'Whenever a soul is saved, an angel gets its wings'?"

"I think that's in a movie, sir," Alger said.

"Also a real thing," Mike said. "Angels have wings. The job of the assigned angel, the guardian angel as it's called, is to shepherd their charge though life. Not sure if they directly get additional wings when their charge has made it to heaven but the holier their charge is, the more they bring good to others, the more powered up they become.

"Demons also come in many forms. They generally don't attach to someone, but they're there all the time. The more evil, more death, more grief there is, the more they're attracted, more they're powered up. Sin draws them.

"The Society practices literal human sacrifice. Mostly children. That's not about giving the children's souls to Satan. Children are innocent. They go to God's arms. That's about ensuring the damnation of the members.

"The Folletts were Society in the US before there was one," Mike said, looking out the window at the passing buildings. "They brought it with them from France as aristos escaping the Terror. And while there's not generally a demon that's attached to a person at birth, there are families that have familial demons. Ancient. Powerful. There's every indication that the Folletts had one. What is called a cursed family. But the curse generally falls on anyone who comes up against them.

"And all indications are it was attached to the male line. That's generally the case. By my mother leaving me in the ghetto, she broke the chain. I don't think she really knew about this, or believed it. But she managed to hide me from that demon just as she hid me from the Trust.

"So, if that demon is still around looking for its lineage, it's probably going to be at the estate, where my great-grandfather, the soulless bastard, died.

"It's hard to know what demons and angels know, what they think, what they understand," Mike said. "Using Sight I get a glimpse of how the angels and demons, and God, might view the world. But they're seeing souls not bones. Souls trapped in a fleshy prison. Sent here to be tested against the world. To be tested for proof. Are you going to go to the side of God or the side of Satan? Tempted by demons. Protected by angels. We are all sinners, but we are saved. It's quantum."

He sat and thought in silence as they drove.

"Contact the estate," Mike finally said. "Tell them that when I arrive, I'm going to need a moment."

"A moment, sir?" Alger said.

"I'd like everyone to gather outside the main house," Mike said. "I need to step inside for just a moment by myself. Perhaps with my father but none of the help nor anyone but myself and my father. It will only be a moment."

"Yes, sir," Alger said, pulling out his phone.

"Are we scheduled to eat at the estate?" Mike asked.

"No," Derrick said. "We're scheduled to stop somewhere. Possibly another studied insult."

"Eduard," Mike said to the probably now freaking-out driver. "Is there a Chik-fil-A more or less on the route? Not too far out of the way?"

"Yes, sir," Eduard said.

"Let's go there," Mike said.

"Chik-fil-A?" Derrick said.

"If I'm going to face down an ancient and powerful demon," Mike said, "I'd rather do it with Jesus Chicken in my stomach..."

⊕ ⊕ ⊕

The Dosoris Estate comprised two hundred acres, the entirety of Dosoris Island. There were six homes on the property, most of them on what people would consider separate estates. They included a 1920s-era dowager cottage that was bigger than the town house, as well as two caretaker cottages and a gatehouse. But the centerpiece was the manse, a classic French chateau-style building with sixty-two bedrooms and pretty much everything else one could need, want or desire.

As they pulled up on the pea-graveled drive, the entire household staff filed out on the steps, waiting. It was at least a couple dozen and, again, they were dressed to show their positions. Fortunately, it was a nice day.

A footman wearing a day coat and white gloves opened his door and Mike stepped out.

The house manager was waiting in front of the throng.

"Mr. Truesdale, I am Evan Wyll, house manager. Welcome."

Wyll was the spitting image of Otoy. Black, six foot two or so with dark black eyes and graying hair cut extremely short. He was dressed in an off-white linen suit and white shirt with a cream bowtie. Islands accent, again.

"Mr. Wyll," Mike said, shaking his gloved hand. "You were informed there will be a brief ceremony, yes? Then introductions, if you'll pardon."

"Not at all, sir," Mr. Wyll said, gesturing to the open doors.

"Father," Mike said, walking up to the doors. He paused, closed his eyes, and breathed deeply to settle himself. Then he and Derrick passed through the entrance and shut the doors behind them.

"What are we doing?" Derrick asked.

"Something that is going to give me away as a Gondola asset," Mike said. He walked into the main foyer and looked around. Then, in a very loud voice but not shouting he said, "The Faerie Queen is *coming*!

"That's it," Mike said, turning around and going back to the doors. It was getting hard to breathe.

He opened them and walked down to the bottom of the stairs.

"Now, Mr. Wyll," Mike said. "Introductions..."

The manse was too big to do a full tour. It would take months to just poke into every nook and cranny and it was clear Wyll was less than thrilled with the idea. He particularly preferred that Mike stay away from the basement.

But under Sight, Mike could see that everything hadn't been cleared out. There were computer servers in the basement as well as what he had to assume was the sacrifice room. That still had an elaborately carved stone altar as well as bas reliefs. Since for once it was all stone, he had an unfortunately clear view of what was depicted. There was also a body buried under the altar. He wondered if people knew it was there.

But they did tour the extensive wine cellar, music room, ballroom, enormous formal dining room, the upstairs suite where his grandfather had lived and died, the massive library and study.

Then it was time to visit the family memorial.

Mike had been getting the sense that the pronouncement had not been entirely successful. He was getting angrier and angrier, a sure sign in his estimation of demonic presences. He was resentful of his father all of a sudden and hungered to increase the wealth and power he was about to inherit.

While he did intend to do so, he had a specific reason. This was just greed, and greed for power.

When they reached the mausoleum, the feeling had become particularly strong.

"This is where your ancestors are interred," Wyll intoned. "Your mother's ashes are in this niche."

The sensation was overpowering. It was like choking on vomit. Mike had a harder and harder time breathing.

Since taking up the public persona of Michael Truesdale, Mike had set up a Twitter account. Michael Truesdale was a fan of Central Park and looked forward to doing philanthropy with his inherited wealth. He was also a fan of traditional architecture and frequently took pictures of notable buildings. He'd taken one of the town house and had posted about it after they left. He didn't want people to gather around when he visited. He, obviously, liked to dress up and explained that as being from a black cultural background. "Wealthy black men dress better than most wealthy white men. It's a black-culture thing."

He'd gotten a huge number of followers instantly just from being in the news. He hadn't mentioned angels or demons since the brief public announcement after his family background had been proven in court.

As he stood there in the mausoleum, though, he pulled out his phone and brought up Twitter.

Right now is when I particularly need the angels. I thank anyone who is reading this and ask them to pass the request to other people of faith. In Jesus' name I ask. Send angels. Send them all.

As he stood there, he started to feel like a live wire. It was similar to when Electrobolt had tried to electrocute him to death, but not unpleasant. Buoying. The feeling of oppression fell away, and he stood a little straighter.

"This is not directed at you, Mr. Wyll," Mike said. *Much.* "*IN NOMINE DOMINI JESU CHRISTI. DEI CONSECRATUS SU, NON SATANAM! NIHIL TIBI EST POTESTAS! Hic frangitur potestas tua!*"

Mike took a breath, sighed then tapped his phone.

Thank you. The Adversary will not win. This land shall not fall.

"Sir?" Mr. Wyll asked.

"I'm a believer in things like ghosts and demons, Mr. Wyll," Mike said. "And if there's ever been a place with a demon hanging around, it was right here. Sad to say. Shall we continue?"

CHAPTER 19

⊕

"Thank you, Mr. Wyll," Mike said. They'd returned to the foyer of the manse. "That was quite the tour. This is all a bit overwhelming. I suppose we should be going."

He'd already covered the "I might have to let some places go" and "There will be compensation if there are layoffs." He hadn't bothered to have a sit-down with Wyll. No point. The man's antipathy for Mike after his banishing was evident.

"Before you leave, sir," Mr. Wyll said, "there is one small matter about the house."

"Sir?" Mike said.

"There is a room in the basement," Mr. Wyll said. "We mostly keep it shut. Your great-grandfather apparently had some . . . peccadillos."

"Oh?"

"It's a bit of an odd room. But when you inherit, this will all be yours and we will leave it as is. He . . . well, you're a bit young but men of the world, your great-grandfather included, liked to spank willing ladies. And he had a bit of a . . . dungeon created."

"Oh," Mike said, grinning. "When I get older that may be some fun. Think nothing of it. And mum's the word, of course."

"Whew," Mike said, sitting in the town car as they cleared the gatehouse. "Feet wet. Jesus, Jesus, Jesus. Do either of you . . . are either of you even vaguely . . . ?"

"I'm not, sir," Alger said. "It's just a creepy old house to me. Served in more than one."

"Funnily enough," Derrick said.

They both looked at him.

"First, I'm an Indian," Derrick said. "I was raised Catholic, but the Sioux know there are dark and light spirits. We're not quite as dichotomous on the subject as Christians, but we know."

As they drove out, they passed a line of similar estates. Mike wondered if they were all as soaked in evil as the one they'd just left.

"Then there's my military background," Derrick said. "There's a split even in the Unit. To the ones who come entirely from Ranger background, it's a bunch of silly superstitious nonsense. Then there's Special Forces. There are more or less two branches in SF. One of them is the straightforward commando branch that is into the recon aspects. They're like the Rangers: 'Why are we talking about ghost stories?' Then there are the ones who are more oriented to the cultural side and training indigenous forces.

"That last group tends to have some who are heavily into the supernatural," Derrick said. "They study the beliefs of indigenous people. They tend to believe more. They also tend to be the ones who are the intellectually brightest.

"It's a subset of the Unit," Derrick said. "And it's a subset that's considered a bit weird by the rest."

"Like going golfing in country?" Mike said.

"Yes," Derrick said. "But ... I was part of that subset. Not on the extreme end but in it. And, surprisingly enough, the ones who tend to end up in the higher ranks in the Unit almost always tend to be from it as well. The ones who think the world is just a bunch of random events can go over to a regular unit when they get ranked out."

"Interesting," Mike said. "The estate and, I think, particularly the mausoleum, are on a power point. A power point is where an angel fell to earth. It holds a residue of the power of the Fallen. There were at least four Falls. The main one, the first, was the one that's in the Bible.

"The more powerful the power point, the more powerful the angel. The only big ones that fell, fell in the first wave. Unless I'm much mistaken, there was a very powerful angel that fell to that spot. And I would not be at all surprised if it was not the one that was attached to the Folletts for so many centuries.

"Bottom line: We're not just going to have to have persons of faith come in and seal and consecrate that ground, we're going to have to practically hire a crop duster and spray the whole estate with holy water."

"Is that a literal desire, sir?" Alger said, puzzled. "We endeavor to provide...?"

"Being honest, I don't know," Mike said. "We're at the edge of my expertise, again. Unlike most people of my level of IQ I am not a Seer. Sensitive, yes, but not a Seer. We'll live at the apartment until I fully inherit and take possession. Then we'll get them cleaned up and consecrated. That should seal out that nasty. Just the Faerie Queen pronouncement should have done that. But apparently it only worked in the house, not the mausoleum."

"That I found...interesting," Derrick said.

"The Faerie Queen is the head of what you know as Omega, Mr. Alger," Mike said, trying to think how to summarize.

"God likes prayer, but at a certain point it's immaterial. It's more about the person's soul than God. God is infinite. No amount of prayer increases God's possession. God possesses all.

"Neither angels nor demons can be destroyed, only attracted or repelled. Though in the case of demons, if their name is known they can be trapped in hell and removed from this earth they fell to.

"Angels are empowered and attracted by prayer to God, while to demons it's like nails on a chalkboard. The stronger the faith and the greater the innocence, the stronger the power.

"*That* is why the Society sacrifices children. Why Lucifer hates them and always has. They are the strongest in faith and the greatest in innocence.

"What you know as Omega has rescued over four hundred thousand children from evil..."

"That many?" Alger said.

"That many," Mike replied. "So, those children pray for the Faerie Queen. And that gives the Faerie Queen serious God mojo. Since the Faerie Queen is also a Believer and of true faith, if not innocence, that means that God has given her the power to command angels. Even very major ones.

"So, by stating that the Faerie Queen was coming, which was what I did when I entered the manse, it gave warning to the demons that a host of angels was about to descend. That should have cleared off most of the riffraff. Possible that not having full ownership limited the effect. Or language.

"Demons don't learn very well," Mike said. "Nor do angels. Humans are like mayflies and human languages constantly change. English is particularly new. So, I suppose some of them might not have understood it. That wording is used in India to clear out demons from old estates that they turn into orphanages. But those languages are old, and the demons have been around for them changing over time.

"I probably should have used Algonquin or something? French? But that was the reason for the Latin in the mausoleum. The ancestral demon was lurking there, waiting for me.

"I doubt he's going to just quit," Mike said, thoughtfully. "The Folletts belonged to him for centuries. They've been corrupted generation upon generation. So... that's an issue. Even if I keep him off of me for the rest of my life, he's going to be hunting my male descendants. He won't just quit. The only answer is to find someone who can find his true name and bind him. That's a toughy.

"For now I'll stay at the apartment," Mike said. "That's the lightest of them. And I'll handle all the woo-woo side. Don't sweat that. I know who to call."

"You can probably speak to the local archbishop," Derrick said.

"I will," Mike said. "But he'll want to send an exorcist and those are hard to find. I know a guy," he added, grinning at his father.

"What I said when Mike brought up the problem of having multiple estates," Derrick said to Alger.

"On the rest," Mike said, "virtually all of the furniture and art in the house has got to go."

"Sir?" Alger said.

"It's God awful," Mike said. "That's possibly a real term. Postmodernist is progressive is Marxist is Satanic. There's a reason it's all so ugly. Satan hates humans. And a couple of those paintings, the ones that really stir the soul, are straight-up evil. The artist was a real artist. You can feel the soul of the artist in them. And that artist was, if not possessed, then very close. Those I might just burn. Seriously. I'll take the hit on the value to get rid of them permanently. Couple of the sculptures as well. Gimme a second to think..."

Mike looked out the window at the spring foliage for a few moments, then grunted.

"So easy," he said, distantly.

"So easy?" Derrick said.

"I was wondering what to do about the human remains," Mike said. "You're required to report them even if they are old. And I'd prefer to keep this out of the *Post.*"

"There are ways to do that, sir," Alger said. "One of them is to promise a large ad buy."

"Aware," Mike said, smiling. "But it's easier than that. I could remove them and burn them quietly. Once we have our people, they won't talk. But it's still easier. I personally can heat bone to the point it sublimates. Just remove them and heat the bones up to gas. Remove any ash and scatter that on consecrated ground. I'll make a point of being worshipful about it. I don't know who they are, and I doubt it would be possible to find out. But I shall treat them with respect and with luck we can get their souls released.

"The manse is less God awful, but I'll go through and designate art to get rid of," Mike said. "Got to pay the taxes somehow. If we dump it all on the market, it might dilute the value. Get someone to deal with that.

"There's more in the manse than bodies. There's an entire part of the basement that's sealed off. From the bottles in it, I'd guess it's an old wine cellar. He said the wine cellar had been added after Prohibition."

"Yes, sir," Alger said. "I noted that."

"I think they sealed up the old one to keep it away from the revenuers," Mike said, "and somehow forgot about it. There's also servant passages, some of which are sealed, not sure who knows about them.

"I'm wondering if I have to do a complete change of staff with the exception of Pelton. Certainly, the managers have to go. Wyll, Palmer and Otoy all scream Twenty-one Divisions . . ."

"Sir?" Alger said.

"Dominican Vudú," Mike said. "It's spread throughout the Caribbean. They are all from Saint Croix and I know it's on Saint Croix. Otoy screams full-on Black Division witch doctor. I think Palmer and Wyll are his apprentices. Whatever the case, they all go."

He thought about it a bit more and sighed.

"Just plan on a complete replacement," Mike said. "Down to the gardening and estate staff. Do compensate them and give them a good reference but they all go. It would be impossible to sort out who's who.

Look for Vaishnava primarily as replacements but if that's impossible to find in things like gardeners . . . Use your judgment. I know a good lawn-maintenance company if it comes to that. Though I'd feel odd about using them."

"Sir?" Alger said. "Sorry to keep asking questions but . . ."

"You need to get to understand this crazy guy you now work for," Mike said, grinning. "Hombre de Poder, Jorge Canejo. His father runs a lawn-maintenance company."

"Ah," Alger said.

"But use your judgment," Mike repeated. "Again, getting out of my field of expertise. Ah! A billion dollars is a billion *headaches*. But speaking of areas of expertise, we're meeting with the accountants tomorrow, yes?"

"Yes," Derrick said.

"That should be interesting," Mike said. "We've got dinner on Saturday with them and the law firm, right?"

"At The Grill," Derrick said.

"I need to make a call. Later . . ."

MT: Hey, Sash, got a minute for a quick call?
SN: Gimme an hour? I'm in the middle of a shoot. I'll call.
MT: Kay.

"Hey, Sash, how's tricks?"

"I don't do those," Sasha said, smiling over the video call. "No matter how much money is offered. What's up with you? Did you see the houses?"

"Yes," Mike said. "And my distant ancestors had remarkable taste in architecture. My more recent ones have horrible taste in furnishings and decor."

"And it's all about taste, right?" Sasha said.

"So, couple of times I considered asking you for a favor," Mike said.

"Did the favor involve a felony?"

"No," Mike said, chuckling. "I'm meeting with the new accountants this week. Saturday we're going out with the lawyers for a celebratory dinner at The Grill . . ."

"And you want me to play arm candy?" Sasha said, tossing her hair to the side.

"Just as friends," Mike said. "But ... yes?"

"Whatever happened to 'we shall have many children'?" Sasha asked.

"We shall," Mike said. "In the fullness of time. But this is just friends. I know you don't owe me anything and I know this is ... Guys probably ask you all the time ..."

"I'd be delighted," Sasha said. "I owe you for telling me about the supersonic thing."

When flyers went supersonic in cloth clothing, it tended to blow apart.

It had happened to California Girl when she was fourteen. Since then, it had become a joking rite of passage for junior flyers. They weren't warned and it was extremely embarrassing for most of them.

Mike had warned her about it and suggested that she pack along some clothing, anything, in her commo pack, which had a small personal effects compartment. Which she had. So, she was able to fly back to the support ship in a leotard instead of nekkid.

"That feels like a thousand years ago," Mike said.

"And you never did properly explain what you were going on about ... stellar nucleo ... something."

"Don't sweat it," Mike said. "So that's a yes?"

"I think I could have my arm twisted into promenading at The Grill with a young billionaire," Sasha said. "Oh, the horror, of just one of the best restaurants in New York! It never comes easy when you're digging for gold, am I right?"

"Right," Mike said. "So that's a yes?"

"Yes," Sasha said. "That's a yes."

"Great," Mike said. "Uh, reservation's a bit late. Eight. I'll pick you up around seven-thirty?"

"Sounds great," Sasha said. "I may even be on time."

"Mr. Ben Avidan," Mike said, shaking his hand. "Good to see you."

He and his father had moved into the apartment after it had been *thoroughly* swept by his "guy." So, they had room to meet with the New York general manager of Asuda Financial Management and his entourage.

Asuda, based in Tel Aviv, was a small but powerful financial management firm with offices in cities scattered across the globe including, to Mike's surprise, Dubai.

"Mr. Truesdale, Mr. Sterrenhunt," Avidan said while motioning to one of his associates, "This is Benjamin Goldblatt. If things work out, he'll be your primary account representative."

"Mr. Goldblatt," Mike said, shaking his hand. "I'm sure things are going to work out famously."

Goldblatt was five foot four and wiry with curly hair and dark eyes.

Under Sight, Mike was gonna go with another Israeli paratrooper.

"So, please, sit," Mike said.

They were holding the meeting at the dining room table as the only place with enough seats and flat surfaces. But it was set up much like a boardroom, anyway. Alger had graciously provided drinks and hovered nearby to refill or collect glasses as needed.

"Okay," Mike said. "One, the room has been swept. Not as good as a deal room but it will have to do for now."

"Understood," Avidan said.

"Electronics, I've got a team monitoring for snoopers," Mike said. "That's computers, tablets, phones, the works. If someone is listening in, we'll get alerted. Currently, no one is listening except my people, who are solid."

"Aware," Avidan said.

"We already had a meeting with an EVP from Fieldstone trying to convince me to keep their stock," Mike said. "I pointed out that I was going to have to dump most of it just to pay taxes. Maybe."

"Maybe?" one of the men asked.

"Sorry," Avidan said. "Moriah Schecter. Chief accountant."

"Morry," Schecter said.

"Sir," Mike said, nodding. "Maybe. I'm going to dump it and I'm going to pay taxes. But how is the question. We should get full access slightly before the upcoming Fieldstone quarterly announcement. Unless it looks to have been a fantastic quarter—and right now it looks to be, if not dismal then not great, certainly below their prediction—I intend to dump the entire stock shortly before the announcement and short the hell out of it."

"Oh," Moriah said, blowing out. "You don't like them, I take it."

"Everyone is not read in on everything," Mike said. "But no. However, you brought up taxes. I'm going to have to pay more than half of this in taxes. Federal death tax plus New York state. I can argue I'm from Montana or something but I'm not sure it's going to be worth the hassle in the end. Either way, lots of taxes.

"But I don't have to pay them 'til next year. As long as I don't go under, I'll have the cash. Doing a big drop-and-short on a marginal quarter will recoup much of the tax burden. Depends on market reaction but if the quarter is dismal versus meh, then it could go as high as doubling. Benjamin, suggestions or thoughts? Am I off?"

"No," Benjamin said. "But if you bring out some just short and we set some options, it will set up a situation of leveraged arbitrage. Be hard to get to double on just one short. If you dump, and you have to to drop the stock price, then you're not going to get the full value of the stock back. Especially since if the feel is it's going to be a bad quarterly, there will already be people shorting.

"So, as soon as we get the stock, we trickle some out to build up a cash position. Then when the quarterly is coming up, quietly set up some options ahead and go in hard that morning. That should get you the best return."

"That," Mike said, smiling. "What he said. But, yes, Mr. Schecter, I fully intend to pound them. When the SEC investigates, as they will, one of the things I'm going to point out is that for a first meeting they sent an EVP to schmooze a billionaire. An EVP is for day-to-day contact. First meet should have been at least a GM or C-suite. Not an EVP. I don't really care, but I know an insult in business when someone throws one at me."

Alger stepped in at that moment to refill Mike's glass of water, as if to demonstrate that Mike was important enough to have a valet.

"After that, distributed portfolio," Mike said. "But . . . there's stuff. Details. One of them is that I've been working on an algorithm in commodities. I've reversed modeled it. It works . . . pretty well. It could be better. But it gives an over under previous year's yield that's accurate, when factoring in other variables, about four times out of five. So, take a good predictive letter or an aggregate, throw this on top, and it improves the prediction.

"Again," he said, looking at Benjamin. "It's been reversed modeled. Works fairly well. I'd be willing to talk to some of your quants under a really strict NDA about it. I know how it works on my side but fully feeding it in . . . I know my current limits and I'm at my current limit."

"Okay," Benjamin said, nodding thoughtfully. "I've seen that you've had some classes..."

"I'm not a commodities guy," Mike said. "I'm more international finance and economics. But I can hum the tune. This needs somebody who's a pure commodities guy.

"Everything that is used as a standard method in every market started as a trick," Mike said. "Rule of five eighths. Reverse short sell. Rule of small numbers. Every quant trick. This is just another one. Specifics? Too many people at the table, sorry. But I've modeled it, and it works four yields out of five. I even know why it will never be better than that.

"Distributed portfolio," Mike said. "I want to lean heavily to Indian investments."

"I saw where you spoke about that at your competency hearing," Benjamin said, nodding. "I'm not sure about throwing darts at a blackboard, but..."

"Nor am I," Mike said. "It was hyperbole but not huge. India is growing; China is stagnating. There's still growth to be found in China but it's small. And there's another side."

Mike thought about how to phrase it.

"Everyone here should know what I am," Mike said. "For those who don't: Hi! I'm Stone Tactical. Earther. Pleased to meet you."

Avidan and Benjamin didn't show any signs of surprise, but Moriah and the others recoiled in mild shock.

"When you hear the Words, you don't have any question that the Storm is Coming. It may take a while, but it is coming. And if I'm going to have investments, I'd like them to be somewhere that should survive. 'Cause if India doesn't survive the Storm, nobody will."

"That is a point that others have made," Mr. Avidan said.

"So, stocks and bonds that are long-term buy hold, I'd like to focus on India," Mike said. "Properties. To be clear: real estate. I'm less interested in commercial in general than most and I have little interest in residential rental. I'm interested in farmland: crop, ranch, tree farming. One thing on that is that I'm interested in getting some land near Kalispell, Montana. That area is not optimum for crop lands, though they are there. My grandfather runs several fields. But I'm interested in a large purchase of land somewhere in the area. Large.

"There is no federal law against using your powers for prospecting,"

Mike said. "Again, everything here is NDA. I have been training my powers and it's possible I could use them similar to the Vishnu to find ore bodies."

"That would be a *fantastic* way to make money," Avidan said.

"But it takes forever to open a mine in the US," Mike said. "And I'd like more return than one percent. If I own the land, then it's all mine. Pardon the pun. And given that Montana is literally 'the Treasure State,' I'm pretty sure if I buy a big enough parcel, there's going to be something on it. Whether I can find it, another question.

"I also want a large parcel, and large is a general term but at least ten thousand acres, as a place to put a very-out-of-the-way ranch. Again, think Storm."

"Understood," Avidan said, making notes.

"I'm thinking the area up around the Fisher River," Mike said, looking at Derrick.

"That's a thought," Derrick said. "Right now, most of it is owned by a company in Chicago. They bought it to log it. There was some talk of doing developments but last I heard that fell through. They're probably going to sell it back to the state at some point. You could probably pick up some parcels that way."

"Do you know the name of the company?" one of the two women in the group asked.

"Perla Krauz," Avidan said as he gestured toward her in introduction. "Real estate management. Pearl."

"Ms. Krauz," Derrick said, nodding. "East River Colonial Management."

"Them," Perla said, distastefully.

"Oh, agree," Derrick said.

"Same here," Mike said. "They don't care about the long-term health of the forestry in the area since they know the state will buy it back when they're through raping it. And it's not even necessary. You can make just as much money doing it right. They just don't care.

"If it's known that I'm picking up a big parcel people may consider the mining aspect," Mike said. "We may want to do a buy through a shell if possible. And I'd consider essentially anything that Morry feels I can support. Sorry, Benjamin, but financial people make more money, accountants keep you from losing it and attorneys keep people from taking it."

"Right," Benjamin said, smiling.

"So, Morry would have to determine if a buy would be out of my league," Mike said. "But if it's not, buy. As long as it's contiguous."

"There's probably some money to be made even if it's been logged," Morry said. "And if there are no minerals."

"There are minerals," Derrick said. "It's a known silver area. There are two mines there, now. Both are just about played out. They're not owned by East River. They're both owned by Helicon. And they're just in the area. It's a big area. There are plenty of parcels to choose from."

"What I'm thinking is that they've probably looked for other ore bodies," Mike said. "But it's possible there are ones that they haven't found. It's hard when they're underground. So, possibly, I slip over into the area and check it out. If I find another ore body that's accessible from the existing mine..."

"That would limit most of the problems," Avidan said, looking around. "We don't have an exact mine expert."

"You're still going to have to do *some* permitting," Derrick said. "And I can speak on that because I've *done* the permitting. The main thing is the issue of surface and ground-water contamination. If it's in a *completely* new area, well away from the current body but still accessible, there will have to be a hydrology study. If it's in the same hydrology and if you intend no major expansion... couple of pieces of paper. The definitions of major and new area are exact, by the way. Not details worth going into."

"Right," Mike said.

"If you work in law in Montana, you more or less have to study mining law," Derrick said. "Half of Montana's bar exam is mining law including the environmental law. Fortunately, Helicon is *not* one of our clients. Or I wouldn't be able to discuss anything about it."

"What are they like?" Pearl asked.

"Evil big mining corporation, one each," Derrick said. "Funny thing, in areas like South America or Africa: as soon as some local village starts complaining about the cyanide in their river water, a bunch of them suddenly die of lead poisoning and the rest leave."

"Weird that," Mike said. "It would be nice to screw people like that."

"You're already going to screw Fieldstone," Benjamin said. "How many enemies do you want to make?"

"All of them?" Mike asked.

"Fieldstone is one of their big investors," Derrick said.

"And that says it all, in my opinion," Mike said. "So, once we have full control, Benjamin, you understand the gist of the plan with the quarterly, yes?"

"Yes," Benjamin said.

"Up to you to execute," Mike said. "After that we see what we invest in. I'm big on keeping money moving and building. But distributed portfolio, farmland, stocks, bonds, whatever you want to work in as long as it makes money. Lean to India for all the reasons. Oh, but farmland in the United States, to be clear. And keep an eye out for land in the area around the Fisher River valley.

"Morry?" Mike said. "How are you at forensic accounting?"

"My favorite field," Morry said, rubbing his hands. "I've heard there are some questions about where the money has gone?"

"Quite a few," Mike said. "I'm hoping you and a team can track it down. And as soon as you're done showing that there's money missing, I very much look forward to suing the crap out of Conn, et al. I won't get into why I have reasons to thoroughly hate Wesley Conn, but I do. I plan to make the rest of his life as miserable as possible. And I'm just going to delegate it . . ."

CHAPTER 20

"If I Were a Rich Man" —*Fiddler on the Roof*

"Oh, wow," Mike said under his breath. "There goes my brain."

Sasha had chosen to wear a little black dress, the tactical nuclear weapon of the female wardrobe. And she wore it extremely well.

"Miss Nikula," Mike said, formally.

He was standing by the door of the stretch limousine while Carl held the door.

"If I might introduce Carl," Mike said. "My father assigned him to keep people from pestering me."

Sasha looked up, then looked up again.

"How's the air up there?" she asked.

"Thin," Carl answered.

Carl Thronton was six feet, eight inches of solidly muscled former Army Ranger.

"I need a Carl," Sasha said. "Are they available 'male' order?"

"Good one," Mike said.

"I might be free from time to time, miss," Carl said. "I admit to being a fan of both yous, if I may be so bold. I wasn't aware until recently that there were two yous. Nothing salacious, just a fan."

"Thank you," Sasha said.

"And I have never had a position like this one in which I felt so *entirely* superfluous," Carl said.

"You're not superfluous, Carl!" Mike said. "If something goes down, you'll make an excellent projectile."

"My life would be complete, sir," Carl said.

"Shall we?" Mike asked.

Sasha made a graceful model entry to the limo, then scooched across the seat.

"I've mentioned before that you scoop my brain out with a spoon, Sasha," Mike said, resolutely not looking at her. "This was just a tad unfair."

"You're the one wearing the ascot," Sasha said. "And I'm not super into being seen. I've said that. But if you're going to do the strut across the floor of The Grill, you've got to dress to impress. And I *do* intend to do the strut. It never comes easy when you're diggin' for gold, right?"

"Right," Mike said, smiling.

Don't look down the dress! Don't look down the dress! Damnit! I looked. I'm stone again . . .

Simultaneously working out Conn and the Trust's next legal and nonlegal moves, ruminating on the wide range of investment options once he won his inheritance, determining what to do both spiritually and financially with the various properties, as well as revisiting the old stellar nucleosynthesis chicken-and-egg problem were not occupying his brain nearly enough to distract him from the green-eyed goddess next to him.

He focused even more attention on sweeping his Sight out far and wide around them. With luck, there'd be an entire clan of Society-paid ninjas hot on their tail for an assassination bid, or maybe MS-13 might've sent an army for another long overdue attempt at revenge.

No such luck, at least as far out as he could see, which was pretty damn far by now. But then he realized he'd been sitting there, looking zoned out for some time. Sasha was awkwardly and uncomfortably examining the limo's interior.

"So, it's hard to even get reservations on a Saturday," Sasha said to break the silence.

"Right," Mike said, taking a breath and putting his hands in his lap. "Especially for a party our size."

"How many?" Sasha asked.

Putting his hands in his lap suddenly felt awkward, so he relaxed them to his sides.

"About a dozen or so, I think?" Mike said. "It's people from the law firm and the financial firm with plus-ones. My dad's girlfriend flew in for it. So, you get to meet Jane."

"She's the CPS investigator," Sasha said.

"Yes," Mike replied. "And both firms had connections, so they were able to arrange it. And we don't have to worry about who gets the check. It's one of them."

"Which financial firm did you go with?" Sasha asked. "Not that there aren't hundreds in New York."

"Asuda Financial Management," Mike said. Hands to the side was a little too relaxed, so he crossed his arms.

"Never heard of it," Sasha replied. "But, as noted..."

"Yeah, they're Israeli," Mike said. Nope, crossed arms was too defensive or aggressive or... something, so his hands went back to his lap. At least he'd kicked his habit of tugging at his ear during his time in Montana.

"Oh."

"It's not like *that*," Mike said, looking at her.

Warning! Warning! She's turning you to stone again! The eyes! You looked in the eyes!

Damnit! You can complete another sentence! Just power through! Where the hell are those damn ninjas?

Nothing but normal traffic all around. There wasn't even anything remotely resembling a tail. No threats of any interest whatsoever except the remarkable bone structure of the stunning young medusa in her Little. Black. Dress. Little as in short, at both top and bottom.

"They...I..." Mike said, clearing his throat.

Brain re-railer, don't fail me now! Power through! Power through! MAXIMUM EFFORT!

"You okay?" Sasha asked.

"No?" Mike said. "Really. Brain freeze. It's... there's *things*, Sasha."

No, you cannot confess to being an international criminal.

"Things?" Sasha asked.

"You remember Cannibale," Mike said.

"How can I forget catching a notorious international criminal?" Sasha asked. "Oh, wait, that's because we keep *doing* that."

"Yes, we junior supercorpsians have actually been doing superhero stuff of late," Mike said.

"Junior supercorpsians?" Sasha said.

"Yes," Mike said. "What I said. But when we were planning the Cannibale raid I had surprisingly detailed information, you might recall."

"You said you had 'sources,'" Sasha replied. "I do recall that, yes. I didn't even ask where you got Alnes's DNA because 'sources.'"

"The same," Mike said. "Yes. Well, my sources suggested the firm."

"Ah," Sasha said. "I need your sources."

"That would be a bit tough," Mike said. "They're shadowy. They're like that groundhog. They only peek out from time to time. So, how's modeling been?"

"Lots of bright strobe lights," Sasha said. "And people who want me to take off too many clothes."

Wait, what's going on over there?

"Eduard," Mike said, suddenly. "Pull over up here and just stop somewhere. Anywhere."

"Sir...?"

With nothing of interest on the streets, he'd increased his Sight scan to include the buildings they passed by. There was a man who had followed a woman off an elevator in an apartment complex two blocks away. He wasn't sure if...

The woman had made it to the door of her apartment and the man rushed at her, his hand extended. The hand was curled around something. It mattered if it was a knife or a gun and Mike couldn't quite make it out—which probably meant it was metal.

The man grabbed her and pushed her against the door. By the way he was holding his hand, it was a knife.

Mike thought about it for a moment and pulled back on the bones of the hand, pulling the knife away. Simultaneously, he extruded some concrete from an open patch down the wall and wrapped some around the rapist's neck and more around his wrist. Then he—gently—pulled him away from the woman.

"Come on," he said, shaking his head. "Open the damned door..."

"Mike?" Sasha said.

Finally, the woman had the door open, got inside, closed it and locked it.

"Okay, go," Mike said.

There wasn't anything to do about the guy. He just released the concrete and let him go.

"What was that?" Sasha asked, eyebrow raised and looking a little spooked.

"You know I've been training my powers," Mike said. "Guy was trying to rape a girl in an apartment that way." He gestured to the west. "Stopped it."

"With powers," Sasha said. "From here?"

"Yes," Mike said. "Do you have any idea how much bad shit goes down in this town *all the time*? *Everywhere*? You know that thing where Superman can hear all the distress calls from all over the world all the time? Got any idea how *ugly* that would get when you can only help *one person at a time*? I have to pick and choose what I'll interfere in and what I won't. And I can do it from a *distance*. I can get the cat out of the tree from five blocks away, and let me tell you, I'll never waste time helping out a cat when there are so many *people* who need help!"

Now it was Sasha crossing her arms, and looking away uncomfortably. Her gaze went to the window, as if she was looking outside wondering what might be happening out there that she didn't know about.

"It's the reason I ride around on the subway," Mike said. "There's always somebody hassling someone. But I could just sit anywhere pretty much and sit there stopping crimes all day long. And there's no real point. Even if I could direct the cops to it, the perpetrator would be out before I'd finish the damned paperwork. And most of them are recidivist. Guarantee that wasn't that guy's first rape or attempted rape in this case. He might have gotten scared off by suddenly having a stone collar but probably not. He'll just find another victim. It's frustrating as hell."

"Wish I had it," Sasha said.

"You're fifteen?" Mike said.

"Yes," Sasha replied.

"You might be able to get it," Mike said. "It's probably going to be hard. And with flyers, what you see is movement. And everything has movement. The problem for flyers is the air moves. So, you have to look through it for stuff that has limited movement. Everything has harmonics. Brownian motion. So, flyers can see pretty much everything. And that, again, is the problem. But you can probably do it."

"How?" Sasha asked.

"I usually lie and say that I just got it when I Acquired," Mike said.

"But what you do is sit somewhere with a blindfold on and try to see through it. Rummage in your brain. Just do that until it clicks or it doesn't."

"Oh," Sasha said. "That's it?"

"That's it," Mike said.

"How do you know these things?" Sasha asked. "Sources?"

"And we're here," Mike said as they pulled up at The Grill.

The Grill in the Seagram Building was a New York landmark. It was not the original chophouse, but it harkened back to a bygone era of fine dining and fine presentation. It was the sort of place to Be Seen.

"Hello," Ahuvit said as they reached the bar. He and his associates had taken over a sizable area. "Miss Nikula, what a pleasant surprise! I'm Ahuvit Brauer, one of Mike's attorneys and the host for this evening. You look radiant!"

"Thank you," Sasha said, posing. She'd gone from depressed and contemplative during their discussion to bright and smiling as if flipping a switch. "Do I look good enough to be on the arm of a billionaire?"

"You do indeed," Ahuvit said. "I take it you two met through . . . volunteer work?"

"We did," Sasha said.

"If I might introduce my wife . . ."

"Jaaane," Mike said, giving a big hug to a short, athletic, blonde woman. "Welcome to the party!"

"I feel under dressed," Jane Carson said. She was wearing a simple cocktail dress.

"Never," Mike said. "Unless you're not wearing anything at all. And if I may introduce Sasha Nikula?"

"Hello," Jane said. "I was already informed you don't like to shake hands."

"I've broken too many?" Sasha said, grimacing.

"I don't want it broken, so," Jane said, drawing back defensively. "So . . . *you two* are the talk of Kalispell."

"Not much to talk about in Kalispell," Mike said. "No big surprise. And we're just friends."

"So I hear," Jane said, looking over at Derrick.

"We're young teens," Mike pointed out. "That's a time when

relationships form and break up with the rapidity of a chain nuclear reaction."

"That is true," Jane said. "You should think about coming out sometime this summer, Sasha. The mountains are beautiful."

"I could get away from the city," Sasha said. "I'm a country girl. I miss it. But there are mountains in Missouri, too."

"Not like Montana," Mike said. "I'm not sure the Alps meet the standards of mountains in Montana. It's literally called . . . wait for it . . . *Montana*."

"Pretty big mountains?" Sasha said.

"It's pretty much what it is, yeah," Mike said.

"I'd rather come out in winter and snowboard," Sasha said.

"You snowboard?" Jane said.

"I do," Sasha said. "I barely got any time this winter. I started pretty young. But it's a little different these days, what with being able to fly. You don't have to worry about falling down, that's for sure."

"Or breaking anything if you do," Mike said.

"You're dressed quite nicely," Jane said, looking Sasha up and down.

"Well, it's The Grill," Sasha said, shrugging. "It's a place to be seen. It's not really a teen place to be seen but . . . I'm not that into the narcissistic aspects of modeling. My stepmother forced me into modeling and pageants young. Then I started to make money and I was like 'Okay. I can do this.' But I'm actually getting pretty tired of it."

"Why?" Jane asked.

"You're a CPS investigator?" Sasha said. "Any idea how many predators there are in modeling? I managed to avoid getting raped before I Acquired but it was a near-run thing. Twice. And I was . . . Stuff happened. It's filled with complete assholes. Then there's the fans," she added with a sigh.

"Assholes?" Jane asked, relaxing her shoulders and tilting her head sympathetically. Mike feared she was going into professional mode.

"They're mostly nice but there's so many of them," Sasha said. "You can't move without someone wanting your autograph or your picture."

"I will attest to that," Mike said. "We've been out shopping a few times and it's constant."

"Papparazzi and all the rest," Sasha said. "I sort of like to be noticed. It's a girl thing. It is. But it gets really old really quick to not be able to finish a meal without somebody wanting to be your friend. And then there's the ugly side."

"The predators?" Mike asked.

"You didn't hear?" Sasha said. "I got deepfaked."

"Porn?" Jane asked. She was fully engaged now and looked ready to start making phone calls. "Isn't that child pornography?"

"According to my attorney, it's not," Sasha said, angrily. "There were no actual children physically harmed. The fact that it's . . . me as far as anyone can tell is . . . I refuse to let it get to me. There've been girls who just totally melted down about it. I won't. I won't give them the satisfaction."

"Good for you," Jane said. The answer was apparently sufficient, as Jane calmed back down.

"A person can only control your emotions if you let them," Sasha said. "But it really is a form of rape. They're just rapist wannabes. That's what I said on my post about it. That they're tiny little men who can't get it on with a real girl, so they make up these fantasies."

"That sort of thing doesn't usually get very widespread if . . . you might have wanted to just not mention it," Mike said.

"Oh, it was already going all over," Sasha said. "There's this asshole, Keith Silverdon. He used to be a photographer here in New York and he's always talking about how all models are a bunch of whores. Really misogynistic bastard. There's a reason that he's not a photographer anymore, and they allow photographers to get away with lots of crap. And even he was too much. But he has about a bazillion psycho misogynist followers, and he spread it out to his list, and it went viral.

"I'd heard about it and was ignoring it. I agree about that. But it was already viral. So, I just said, 'People can do this. It's legal. But they're just tiny little men with no girlfriend and big fantasies. They're rapist wannabes. They're nobodies. They're trying to rape me emotionally and I won't let them. No person can harm you emotionally if you don't let them. So, they can go to hell but I'm just going to ignore it.' And I did."

"That's . . . Okay, yeah, I'm in love," Mike said. "That was fantastically mature and truly strong of you."

"Thanks," Sasha said. "But I'm still angry about it. I won't cry about it. But I'm angry about it."

Mike saw the significant look from Derrick.

"It doesn't rise to the level..." Mike said. "It's the same as the law. No actual minors were harmed. It's like hentai that way."

"It's *not* like *hentai*," Sasha said, angrily. "Good God, Mike! That's a cartoon not...!"

Jane looked just as shocked at what Mike said, but Derrick briefly cracked a tiny smile when no one else was looking.

"Wait, Sasha," Mike said. "Please. I was having half a conversation with my dad. My sources, okay? They go after child pornographers and stuff. What I was saying to my dad was this is bad, okay? Yes, it is. But there's only so many man-hours and if it's a choice of tracking down someone who is physically abusing kids or someone who does deepfakes, which do you do?"

"Oh," Sasha said. "I guess..."

"On the other hand, Counselor," Mike said, cocking an eyebrow, "if you ain't cheatin', you ain't tryin.'"

"If you get caught, you ain't SF," Derrick finished.

"Okay, coded conversation again," Jane said, sighing. "They do this."

"I might know a little bit about something that sounds like a cat coughing up a hairball," Mike said. "Haaaack... Hack, hack!"

"You're a hacker?" Sasha said, quietly, looking around.

"I'm a teen super-genius who used to spend all my time on computers," Mike said. "Guess. I can't get rid of every copy out there. But I might be able to track down the person who did it originally and they might have some issues with their computers and that other guy... Silverdon. And I can't believe I'm saying this in front of people who are not *privileged*!

"But I'll see what I can do," Mike said. "It's still going to be out there. But the word might get around that if you download it, bad things happen to your computers."

"You might be a little cooler than I thought," Sasha said.

"It's the ascot, isn't it?"

CHAPTER 21

"Wouldn't It Be Nice" —Beach Boys

"Remember when I said I had a secret I wanted to share with you?" Mike asked. "About not losing all your clothes at supersonic?"

The party was in full swing. The table was a little delayed, but nobody cared because they were enjoying the atmosphere of the bar.

Sasha leaned back on the railing over the main dining area, spread her arms to either side, and posed.

"*Yes*," she said, looking at him coyly.

"Here's a similar secret," Mike said, as quietly as he could in the noise of the bar. "Never lean against a railing like that when you're wearing a miniskirt. Especially if there's nothing underneath."

Sasha looked at him quizzically for a moment, looked over the side of the railing, and blanched.

"Oh, shit," she said.

"Come on," Mike said, smiling. He led her a little way from the railing through the crowd.

"Thanks," Sasha said. "I'm still getting used to the whole sort of grown-up thing."

"I don't think anybody saw anything," Mike said, chuckling. "But a couple of the guys were leaning over so far, their ties were in their steak. They were like owls, trying to turn their heads around to look over their back. Some of them were with wives. It was gonna get ugly."

Sasha laughed and shook her head.

"You have the oddest way of putting things," she said.

"Watch the bartender," Mike said. "The one tossing bottles around."

"Very cool?" Sasha said.

Mike waited until he was spinning one behind his back, caught it, and waited for him to turn around in a panic, then swung it around to the front again. The bartender spun around in a circle looking for the bottle in what was clearly bafflement, then reached for it as it hovered in front of him. Mike moved it away, then back. Bartender reached for it again and it moved again.

Then Mike, figuring that the drink in front of the bartender was for the bottle, did a perfect pour into the drink, and landed the bottle on the counter next to it.

The bartender cautiously reached for it, picked it up, and put it away.

As he reached for the next bottle, it moved just out of reach. Then again. And again.

Mike could hear the patrons around the bar laughing as the bartender tried again and again to grab the bottle.

Mike set it down again and just let him get back to his job.

"That was cruel," Sasha said.

The bartender reached for a glass and Mike handed it to him. Then raised several bottles and lined them up for him to choose. Oops, none of those, huh?

"Okay! What the hell is going on?" the bartender yelled.

"Hey, Sasha Nikula, right?"

The speaker was a beefy fiftysomething guy, six foot four or so in a very fine suit, holding a glass of dark whiskey.

"We met at the Spring Fashion Show," he added.

Mike set down all the bottles as if clearing the decks. He knew a situation that was going to require deconfliction.

He was planning on deconflicting this one the easiest way possible: violence.

"Right," Sasha said, nodding. "Good to see you again."

She clearly had no idea who he was.

"You're lookin' really good tonight," he said, rubbing her upper arm.

Sasha bit her lip and slid aside, trying to avoid the hand.

"Yeah, well, out with a friend," she said, looking over at Mike.

Derrick laughed at something Jane may or may not have said and, in the process, shifted backward to stealthily move closer.

"So, how've you been?" the man said, shifting to push Mike out of the space and not stopping with the hand.

"Yo, unintroduced dude," Mike said, loudly. "You must be a nobody."

"Excuse me," the man said, turning to look at him angrily. "Do you know who I am?"

"Not a fuckin' clue," Mike said. "Don't care. Somebody who's a *nobody*. 'Cause if you were *somebody*, you'd know the young lady you're feelin' up can rip your arm off and beat you to *deaf* wif it."

"Mike," Sasha said.

"What?" the man said, his brow furrowing.

"Run along," Mike said, tiredly, waving his hand idly in the opposite direction. "Take your fiftysomething 'Hey, if you ever need a hand' shit to some twentysomething model wants a meal ticket."

"Listen, kid..." the man said, starting to get angry.

"A'ight," Mike said. "Don't say I dint warn you."

The man's face went white, and he dropped the scotch glass.

Mike caught it with his powers and took it in hand as asshole sank to his knees, then hands and knees.

People were looking, whispering and laughing. Derrick scanned the crowd with a grim expression. Mike had zero read on what Derrick thought of the stunt.

"What did you do?" Sasha asked.

A waiter hurried over to help the patron.

"He gonna be okay soon he can get over the pain," Mike said, hovering the glass in the air for the waiter. "Give him some of that. Might help."

"Mike?" Ahuvit said, coming over.

Derrick returned to his conversation as if nothing had happened.

"Asshole was being asshole to Sasha," Mike said as the man was helped to his feet. "Didn't want to run long. Look, he runnin' long now."

"*What* did you *do*?" Sasha asked.

"Ahuvit, know what a coccyx bone be?" Mike asked. "Bone be stone."

"Oh, ow!" Ahuvit said. "Ow. Yes, I broke mine once. Ow."

"What is the... that?" Sasha asked.

"Let me take your... come to think of it, wrist," Mike said. "May I hold your wrist?"

"Okay," Sasha said.

Mike put considerably more pressure into Sasha's tailbone than he had the man's. The real problem these days with tweaking a coccyx was that he had to use tremendous finesse. With Sasha not so much.

Her face went white, and her knees started to buckle. Mike held onto her wrists to keep her upright.

"It's okay," Mike said. "Pain will pass. You'll regen."

"Ow!" Sasha said, leaning in to speak quietly. "How in the *hell* did you do that? I'm an invulnerable! That's the first time I've felt pain since I *Acquired*!"

"It passed?" Mike said.

"Yes," Sasha said, breathing out. "Oh. Still woozy. That hurt!"

"Sorry," Mike said. "Hug? Don't squeeze me in half?"

"Yeah," Sasha said, accepting a hug. She was careful squeezing back.

"Okay," Mike said, patting her as they released. "*That* is the coccyx bone. Also called the tailbone. Remnants of when we had tails. That is what I did to the guy. Just with a lot less power."

"But I'm an invulnerable," Sasha said.

"There's no such thing," Mike replied. "You're not *invulnerable*. You're just *very resistant*. Drop a JDAM—that's a Joint Direct Atack Munition, or big, guided bomb—on you and you'll survive. Drop a nuke on you and you're plasma."

Sasha shuddered and reluctantly tilted her head to concede the point.

"The way it works is an internal telekinetic field," he continued. "How the hell that works and your metabolism at the same time is the weird part. But your telekinetic field is your power level. I don't want to do this here because it could cause issues. But if you tried to punch me, I could stop you. Put up a fist pointed at me."

"Right in the kisser," Sasha said, holding up a fist for a jab.

Mike mildly pushed back on her bones and could feel Sasha starting to strain into the pressure.

"We've got to be careful letting down," Mike said, slowly backing off on the pressure. "Remember that time I held you up like a fly in amber?"

"Yes," Sasha said. "And I didn't like it."

"That shows I can overcome your telekinetic field," Mike said. "And the bone is a very small spot to focus powers. Easy enough to overcome it in a small area. And that was before I went out to Montana. That was six months ago. I barely had trained my powers."

"How do you train them?" Sasha asked.

"Same way you do," Mike said. "Use them. Most supers don't. The reason that flyers are the most powerful is they fly. And they start flying around regularly when they are young enough to keep building their powers. If we just used our powers all the time, we'd get more powerful. I do. Use them, that is."

"Doing what?" Ahuvit said.

"Nothing noticeable," Mike said. "Corps is very down on supers building their powers since NK."

"So, how do . . . ?" Sasha asked.

"The way I do it is various," Mike said. "Depends on where I'm at and what I'm doing. For you, it's easy, but the main thing is to keep it from being obvious. When you're just sitting around, cross your ankles then try to pull them past each other. Grip your hands together. Push your fist into your palm. There's no point in lifting weights. You'd have to use a tank. Just use your muscles like isometric but do it as hard as you can all the time. The more you use powers, the more you get. Simple as that. Reason Cali's so powerful was she used to fly all the time, every day, flying around LA. That's the secret. Use your powers."

"Okay," Sasha said. "And you've got Sight."

"That's . . . easier and harder," Mike said.

"This is fascinating, but I think our table is ready, finally," Ahuvit said.

"Meat!" Mike said.

"Sasha," Mike whispered in her ear while tugging at her arm. "Come on."

As they were being led to their table, Mike saw someone they just *had* to introduce themselves to.

"What?" Sasha said, her model strut interrupted.

She *was* getting looks. Many of them from women were particularly catty.

"We need to introduce ourselves to Senator Drennen, don't you think?" Mike said.

"Oh, shit," Sasha said.

Tara Drennen was the ranking Democrat on the Super Affairs

Committee and had been one of Electrobolt's biggest supporters. She had not appreciated Bolt being arrested for sexual battery on Stone Tactical. Especially the *day after* Bolt had been an invited guest speaker at a fundraiser for her campaign. Nor did she like the suit that was brought by, eventually, *all* the members of Junior Super Corps for being forced to deal with an aggressively grooming pedophile every freaking patrol.

"Come on," Mike said. "Head high. Confident..."

They approached a table of four women. One, the obvious queen bee, was a short but roundish woman with bobbed brown hair and a wrinkly, sourpuss face even though there were signs of Botox treatment. Two of the other women were of similar age and unpleasant demeanor, while the fourth was an attractive thirtysomething redhead.

"Senator Drennen," Mike said, holding out his hand. "Mike Truesdale. Please don't get up."

"Mr. *Truesdale*," Senator Drennen said, thinly, taking his hand lightly. "Such a pleasure to meet you, finally."

It was amazing she could speak at all with her teeth so tightly clenched.

"And you as well, Senator," Mike said, nodding and smiling at the other people at the table. "Girl's night out?"

"My aide, Doreen," Senator Drennen said, gesturing to one of the women. "Congresswoman Sanchez and Assemblywoman O'Bannon."

"Ladies," Mike said. "I'm sure you know Miss Nikula. You've at least seen her gracing the cover of magazines."

"Of course," Senator Drennen said, smiling as brightly as she could manage. "And we've met. Hello, again, Sasha."

"Senator," Sasha said, smiling brightly and posing again. "So nice to see you again."

"Just thought we should say hello," Mike said, in his most friendly tone. "Good luck on the upcoming election, Senator! Ladies," he added, nodding.

"Are you *nuts*?" Sasha asked through smiling teeth as they walked to their table.

"Jury's out," Mike said.

"Oh, I am so full," Mike said, getting in the limo. "I can't believe I ate the whole thing!"

"I brought a doggie bag," Sasha said, holding up the plastic bag.

She suddenly swung around as they pulled out and, keeping her knees tightly pressed together, laid her legs across Mike's lap. His brain glitched out again.

"The conversation at dinner was great," she said. "Your attorneys and money guys are so much more interesting than mine. All mine can talk about is law, money, or golf."

"Uh," Mike said, holding his hands in the air like he had guns pointed at him. "Um..."

"Don't get up near the bottom of the skirt," Sasha said. "Otherwise, yeah."

"Oh," Mike said. "Okay."

He cautiously put his left hand well below the skirt, but *definitely* on thigh, and started stroking her shin and calf with his right. She was very shaved.

"What's up with this?" Mike asked.

"You're a little cooler than I'd thought, Michael Truesdale," Sasha said.

"It's the ascot," Mike said. "Or was it the hacking?"

"I'm thinking it was the hacking and that I've never experienced pain since I Acquired," Sasha said. "It's weird to like it. You know, most people want to avoid it. But... I hadn't realized I'd missed it. It's so hard to feel..."

"Anything," Mike said.

"I can feel a breeze on my skin," Sasha said. "But you always feel as if you're wrapped in plastic. Or in a box or something."

Don't. Give. The. Lecture.

"Can I show off a little?" Mike said.

"Sure?" she said.

"Eduard, can you take us around to the house?" Mike said.

"Yes, sir," Eduard said.

"Just one thing, Mike," Carl added, turning around. "We got direct orders to make sure the divider stayed *down*."

"Okay," Mike said then turned back to Sasha. "Ever discussed the neurochemistry of love? Ever heard of oxytocin?"

"No...?" she said. "Is that Oxy the drug?"

"Might as well be," Mike said. "When your body experiences pain, a flood of neurochemicals start dumping. Two of them are dopamine and oxytocin. Oxytocin is also triggered by touch and a few other things. Essentially, any abuse will tend to trigger it. It's part of the body's response to damage. But it's also triggered when a person is sexually aroused. One reason is that there's damage that occurs in sex. But dopamine and oxytocin are both part of the cocktail that gets released when a person is aroused. Got all that?"

"Yes," Sasha said, shifting in her seat.

Mike raised his hands.

"No, it's okay," she said, frowning a little. "Just..."

"When you start to discuss things at an intellectual level, resources move away from the survival and sex centers of the brain and to the higher levels," Mike said. "Thus, the reason that my hand was less interesting on your leg, now. I took the conversation to where your non-romance parts of the brain were engaged and your oxytocin levels, which reduce higher-level brain function, reduced. So, all of a sudden, I was less interesting as a potential mate. That's why I stopped stroking. That's interesting if I'm a potential mate but not if I'm a nerd."

"So, you just adjusted my... neurochemical levels intentionally?"

"Mine too," Mike said, grinning. "I was right on the edge of showing you just *how* interesting I could be as a mate. As in having-babies mate."

"Okay," Sasha said. "How?"

"By showing you I could *flood* your body with dopamine and oxytocin," Mike said. "There are ways to *make* a woman fall in love with you. Like hypnosis. If you know what you're doing, and I do. But it's manipulative. It's not being a friend. And please, don't ask me to prove it. It's sort of a one-way trip and you'd end up either addicted or hating me and possibly both and I prefer that you not hate me. Even though, yeah, we might just have to run off to Arkansas to get a quicky marriage. What with you being pregnant with our first of many children."

"Okay," Sasha said, chuckling. "That's remarkably mature for a..."

"A guy?" Mike said. "Or a thirteen-year-old? We wield way too much power. With great power *should* come great responsibility. Some would tend to disagree. And I wield more because I *do* know how to turn a girl around my finger. Nerd and all. But I don't want that. It's anathema to me. But the demons are whispering, right? 'Go ahead. Be the romantic. You can make out with Sasha. She's beautiful and she's smart and you like each other.'"

He closed his eyes, not wanting to continue. It was a major crossroad, and he'd hoped they could've delayed this talk a little longer. But it needed to happen.

"But at our age, what's the difference between 'Hey, we can just make out' and some guy who nails a girl just to say he did? 'Yeah, I nailed Sasha Nikula once!' isn't that much different than 'I made out with Sasha Nikula once.'"

"Oh, I'd say there's a difference," Sasha said.

"In degree but not in kind," Mike said. "We're going to be dealing with each other for a long time. Who knows how long we're going to live? So, in fifty years, which would be better: 'Yeah, we've been friends since we were teens' or 'Yeah, he's my ex'?"

"When you put it that way," Sasha said, laughing, "as usual you have a point."

"I'm going to kick myself for it," Mike said. "I'm going to bang my head on a wall. But it's not right to just kiss and go. Not for us. It's not like ships that pass in the night. Like it or not, we're two of only three hundred and change in the US. So, kicking myself mentally as I say this . . . Friends?"

"Friends," Sasha said. "I'm not sure if I'm disappointed or relieved."

By her expression, it was more of the former. He couldn't agree more.

"If we had that down," he said, "we'd be adults or something."

CHAPTER 22

"Ahem," Carl said. "Sir? We're approaching the house."

Mike braced himself for Sasha's reaction. She casually looked out, but then her eyes went wide, and she glued herself to the window.

"Oh, my God!" Sasha said. "That's not a house, that's a castle!"

"My words exactly," Mike said, laughing. "Fantastic view of the Hudson from the roof patio."

"Of course there's a roof patio," Sasha said as they crawled past along Riverside Drive. "That's not where you're staying?"

"The decor is hideous," Mike said. "All postmodernist crap. I had to choose one and since the apartment is slightly better decorated, I went with that. There's about to be a flood of postmodernist furniture and art on the market."

"If that's the *town house*, what's the *estate* look like?" Sasha asked.

"Sixty-two-bedroom French chateau," Mike said. "Plus, several other houses. Two hundred acres, private island in Glen Cove."

"Good Lord," Sasha said, then started ticking off her manicured fingers. "Lessee . . . superrich. Good-looking. Has some *really* nice pads . . ."

Mike sang the first few lines of The Beach Boys "Wouldn't it Be Nice."

"Yeah," Sasha said. "Okay, we need to non-seriously discuss the baby thing. I'm not planning on a big family, okay?"

"Well . . ." Mike said with a sigh. "Can we compromise on ten?"

"Ten?" Sasha said. "Ten? What part of 'I'm not planning on a big family' was unclear?"

"It's down from forty!" Mike said.

"Are you serious?" Sasha said, laughing as they finally passed the enormous townhome.

"We've got all this space to fill!" Mike said. "Seriously. I'm thinking about turning some of them into orphanages. The problem is that orphanages in the US are a nightmare. Social services and all the activists are totally against religious orphanages and the other kind generally ends up having too many Electrobolts. Though that's been a problem with religious ones as well. And the paperwork is a nightmare. And I can support ten orphans in, say, Brazil for the cost of one in the United States."

"You could sell them," Sasha pointed out.

"I've got enough money, I don't need to sell orphans."

"That was *not* what I meant," Sasha said, chuckling. "Three houses is probably a bit much."

Per Mike's direction, Carl slowly drove them north on Riverside Drive, with the waterfront on their left and swankier homes and apartment buildings to their right.

"Agreed," Mike said. "Sort of. I really don't need or want three. But my family built these up over centuries. The manse on the estate was built in the late 1800s, replacing a previous house that burned. That one was built in 1910. The apartment was built in the twenties. You can't just buy something like that these days. I'm thinking about the legacy of the family. It may be an evil legacy but it's a legacy."

"*Is* it an evil legacy?" Sasha asked.

"Oh, all that and a bucket of sauerkraut," Mike said. "Slavery. Really crappy treatment of workers. Pollution. Eviler than that. The Folletts were virtually demonic."

Not just virtually.

"But that was them," Mike said. "I *am* a Follett, but the legacy is broken. I can choose not to be demonic and pass that down. The thing to do is to try to instill decent respect for others into your kids and teach them to pass that down. Not . . . lefty 'Love not hate!' while beating someone and shouting them down. Decent morals. Do unto others as you would have them do unto you is simple enough."

"To forty kids?"

"So, you're getting okay with forty?" Mike said.

"I do want to have kids, someday," Sasha said. "But I'm thinking more . . . two."

"Okay, so we compromise," Mike said. "Forty plus two is forty-two. Divided by two is twenty-one. I'll settle for twenty-one. Since it's you."

"Oh, my God," Sasha said, laughing. "*You* don't have to carry them."

"That is a point," Mike admitted. "Reality. I do want a trad wife or a mod trad."

"Trad wife?" Sasha said. "Seriously?"

"Why would I want a career wife?" Mike said. "I'm not going to force her to be trad. I'm *looking* for a trad. Someone who *wants* that. That's their goal. Not someone who goes 'Oh, I can marry a billionaire and then shop all the time!' Someone who *wants* a large family."

"Aren't you worried about overpopulation?" Sasha asked. She waved her hand at the world outside, from the crowded buildings of Manhattan on one side and the thick lights of New Jersey across the Hudson.

"Seriously?" Mike said. "You realize that the world's population is about to experience a major *drop*, right?"

"I was about to ask, 'are you sure' but then I realized that you've always known what you were talking about," Sasha said. "My teacher was just talking about it the other day, how we're overrunning resources."

Mike sighed and shook his head.

Fucking Society.

"Over the next thirty years China is going to see a population decrease of two hundred million people," Mike said. "By the end of the century they are going to have at most five hundred million. Which is a lot. China is about the size of the US. But it's less than half their peak. They stopped having population increase a few years ago and it's declining.

"India is still growing, slowly. They have net population increase still. Africa is growing fast but even there the rate has leveled off. South America as well.

"As people get into even African middle class, the rate of population growth decreases until it flatlines and starts to go down. Any group that gets into reasonable wealth, the population stops growing and starts shrinking.

"You want two kids," Mike said. "You realize that doesn't even replace you, right?"

"I think it does . . . ?" Sasha said.

"You have to factor in the father," Mike said. "So, two kids, one replacement for each parent. But in the aggregate, to have zero population growth each woman has to, on average, produce two point one children."

"How do you produce point one children?" Sasha said, grinning.

"You're smarter than that or I wouldn't be out with you," Mike said. "We reached a peak in the 1960s, worldwide, of *five* per female. A guy wrote a book, *The Population Bomb*, which is what all the *Soylent Green* and *Stand on Zanzibar* books and movies were about. The world was going to be completely overrun. We'd die of pollution and starvation and running out of resources."

"You're saying we're not going to?" Sasha said.

"We're more likely to run out of people than resources," Mike said. "As people become richer, they want more stuff. Look at food. Imagine a multigenerational family in, say, Indonesia. Father of the first generation is a day laborer. First generation, they survive on soy. But the next generation the dad has a small business and things are better and they eat chicken. Then the next is richer and they eat pork, if they're not Islamic. Or mutton. The next eats beef."

A motorcycle rocketed past with a roar, weaving through the lanes, and Sasha twisted to see it on instinct. Mike had seen it approach in Sight, so he knew it was just a jerk speeding rather than an obvious tail. He was tempted to mess with the driver but didn't.

"That's all increased resource use," he continued. "Richer generations eat foods that require more resources to produce. And it's generally that case across *all* fields. Better housing. Better transportation. More electrical consumption. Who has more money consumes more resources. See also the big house we just passed and this limo. Got that?"

"Yes," Sasha said, sitting up.

"But as those generations get more resources, there is generally a slight baby boom," Mike said. "But *after* that generation, they stop reproducing at above replenishment rate. So, the day laborer dad has ten kids by his, at most, maid wife. She probably has to stay home and take care of the kids. But the next son, who has something that is better than day laborer, he and his wife have five. The next generation that's still better, they have two. Eventually you have the daughter that is a career woman who never has kids.

"And then there's the issue of generation time," Mike said. "And that's the complex bit."

"This isn't complex?" Sasha said.

"You getting bored?" Mike asked.

"No."

Carl had finally reached the point where Riverside merged onto the West Side Highway and traffic was backing up behind them, so he initiated the complicated process of routing back around to go south rather than north.

"Be fruitful and multiply," Mike said. "There are two components. 'Be fruitful' is how many children a woman has. She has to have more than two point one children to replace her and her mate. Otherwise, it's stagnant growth. But how *fast* is the growth? That's the 'multiply' part and that's generation time.

"Generation time is the time between when a woman is born and when she has her first child," Mike said. "The shorter the generation time, the faster the growth. By the same token, the longer the generation time, the slower the growth. With me?"

"Sort of," Sasha said, frowning.

"Say you wait 'til you're thirty-six to have two children," Mike said. "Not uncommon in current America. We'll make it four 'cause otherwise there's zero growth. Your two daughters have four children at thirty-six. Their two daughters have four. Et cetera. That's twenty-eight total children in one hundred and eight years. Got it?"

"Okay," Sasha said.

"Let's say that you have four when you're *eighteen*," Mike said. "That's half the age, right?"

"Right."

"You'd think that would be twice the kids but it's not," Mike said. "It's two hundred and fifty-two children."

"Are you joking?" Sasha asked.

"No," Mike said. "In one hundred and eight years there are nearly *ten* times as many children. I won't get into the population growth equation, but the power portion is one over generation time. The power portion is always the most powerful part of the equation, and one over means the smaller the number the faster the growth.

"Bangladesh in the 1970s had to have set some sort of record," Mike said with a sigh. "The average birthrate per female was nine point two and the generation time was thirteen point five. That's growing like yeast. It also means that the average Bangladeshi woman was having her first child at my age, thirteen and a half."

"That's disgusting," Sasha said, angrily.

"It was cultural," Mike said, shrugging. "It was a primarily small farm agricultural society and Islamic. They were virtually all married at very young ages, which was common throughout history until recently. Mary, the mother of Jesus, was twelve when she had Our Lord and Savior. That was common."

"I . . . guess," Sasha said. "Really? She was twelve?"

"Yes," Mike said. "That was considered a thing of value in a woman. It was a high-status thing in that society. She might not have been, for real, and it was tacked on to make her more of a mother and a woman than she actually was. Like that Jesus had thirteen brothers and sisters 'cause that is suspiciously like the Disciples and it would be another thing to make much of Mary in that society. She was very fertile. But early marriage was common and standard and all that up until very recently, historically, in Western societies."

Sasha shuddered and crossed her arms.

"Now, that's the way to make a lot of babies, but not necessarily healthy babies. The optimal time for that looks to be roughly late teens through the twenties. But developing and pre-industrialized peoples aren't exactly tracking the statistics. So we used to have babies too early, now we're edging toward too late.

"Points being these: Population is now actually headed for a crash. It is especially crashing in Western societies. While there is a resource bulge when wealth increases, it is less threatening to the human race, long term, than that we are headed for extinction due to a lack of breeding. And my personal solution is to find a wife who wants to bear many children, be fruitful, and start relatively young, multiply, generation time. Young being eighteen or so, not thirteen. And a wife that will instill the same values in her daughters. 'Cause unless people start doing that, there ain't no reason to *bother* about a future. The human race does not have one.

"That woman who wants a huge passel of children is not *you*, Sasha," Mike said, shrugging. "It's not how you were raised. It's not what you think is the thing to be. It is *essentially* not you. Which is why making out with you would have just been putting a notch on the limo, getting married would be the wrong thing for me *and* for you. Get involved with someone with the same goals rather than trying to change them."

"So, you want some girl to just cook and take care of the house," Sasha said, shaking her head. "I thought better of you."

He sighed and his gaze wandered to infinity. "You know, a year back, I didn't think a family was even possible in my future. I knew the odds were strongly stacked against my surviving to adulthood. Even if I did survive that long, a relationship with . . . anyone was entirely unthinkable. No family, my few friends always disappeared or sometimes died, and you'd run screaming if you saw what counted as 'relationships' in that world."

He returned to himself and glanced at her, still a little melancholy.

"And that's where you don't get it and won't," Mike said. "I was out in Montana for a couple of months. All of a sudden, I was part of a family, and a huge one at that. Each of my aunts save one had five or six kids. And they all homeschooled, gardened, and were all homemakers. Many of them were not affluent. They had to scrimp. And they were all into it, personally.

"This thing about population growth I just explained to you? I didn't have to explain it to the kids there. I got into a discussion of generation time with one of my female cousins. She was explaining it to *me*. She was *ten*, Sasha. And she was using the sort of equations I *avoided* using with you because they would be confusing. You don't have the math.

"You can say they're 'indoctrinated' but *you* were being taught *false* information by your tutor to indoctrinate *you* into 'do not breed.' *They* are being taught *real* information and shown why it's important to bear children. Some will have large families, some won't. That's up to them. But they make the decision with the *knowledge* to do so rather than indoctrination into 'The World Is Coming To an End Due To Overpopulation!' Which is a past crisis if it ever was one.

"Resource questions are a different question. But most of the resources that people scream about us running out of, we've always found more."

They finally emerged back onto the West Side Highway going southbound, so now the Hudson and New Jersey beyond were on the right, with the parks along the waterfront on the left.

"I don't want to *force* some woman into having a large family," Mike said. "Or manipulate her. I want it to be her choice before I even meet her. And please don't ever tell some interviewer that that's what I'm looking for. Please. Because there are women that will look at the houses and go 'I'll do that!'

"And even if they are sincere, if it's not who they are it won't work. But there *are* women who have decided that the modern woman thing is not for them. To be honest, I think they're smarter than the ones who fell for it. I think the whole 'modern woman,' 'I am woman, hear me roar' is a trap. And that's what I'm looking for. Because I've got all this *stuff* and might as well use it for kids. And because the population is crashing. And I love kids and want to raise a bunch of them."

He paused while considering whether or not to bring the Storm into the conversation, considering it was almost guaranteed to render the entire philosophical discussion meaningless. He ruled against it.

"That's who *I* am," Mike finished. "It is not who *you* are. Let me be me and you be you."

"Yeah," Sasha said. "It's not me. I still think they're indoctrinated."

"They think *you* are," Mike said. "Laura *certainly* is. But we can agree to disagree. I think most things that are 'known' among the right people are just lies and indoctrination. Don't get me started on why wind and solar are just a way for rich people to get richer and screw over poor people."

"They're good for the environment," Sasha said, then looked at his face. "They're not?"

"I just did a long thing on the population fizzle," Mike said. "You do not want me to explain how much *waste* is produced by solar power versus nuclear. Or how safe nuclear is. Or that when power goes up, rich people make more money and poor people get their lights turned off. I could go on at length. Don't tempt me, seductress. I will 'splain!"

"I think you're the seducer," Sasha said with a sigh.

"I went easy on you," Mike said, smiling.

"You're so smug," Sasha said.

"You're so beautiful," Mike said. "And smart. But your tutors are indoctrinated into certain thought processes, and they pass them on to you.

"*Every* culture is based upon indoctrination. The question is, is the basis of the indoctrination real information or is it simply lies built upon lies? 'We're stripping the world like locusts!' is one of those lies that really annoys me. Because the answer is *always* poor and middle class are supposed to do without, but rich people can go right along flying around in private jets and living on estates and looking down their noses.

"Having grown up very poor, *that* one annoys the *fuck* out of me," Mike said. "I'm supposed to eat bugs while you dine on Wagyu beef? Fuck that, asshole.

"Ditto wind and solar are the answer and most other so-called answers the Left has for every problem *they've* created. It always comes down to somebody else who has to suffer while the rich get richer. They pump in poison then say, 'Reelect us and we'll give the antidote!' And the antidote is *always* more poison."

"I can see why you're going to Osseo," Sasha said.

"My old name got *hard* canceled by *all* the elite academic institutions," Mike said. "Despite being a child genius and from poor circumstances. For being an eleven-year-old who *did not want to die.* That was it. I chose to *not* die by surviving the only way I could: killing the people trying to kill me. And I got canceled. Hard. Does that make sense?"

"No," Sasha admitted.

"Whenever some professor tells you something, think about that," Mike said. "Just that. That professor, personally, may disagree. But they have to preach the party line, or they know they'll get cancelled.

"The professor I collaborated with at Stanford on the Hawking radiation paper went to bat for me over the thing with the Fifth Street Kings. Tenured professor. Well-respected astrophysicist. And he nearly got fired for it. There were protests at his classes. Most of the people protesting weren't even Stanford students but the Dean of Diversity was right there in the midst.

"I told him to save himself. Throw me under the bus. Make the apology, just say he had no idea I was such a horrible person. Because he was a good astrophysicist and a good teacher, and the world needed that.

"So, he did. Reluctantly. He threw me under the bus. Because it was that or his career. And I forgive him for that. I told him to do it.

"They preach the party line whether there is a rational basis to it or not. Because the lunatics have taken over the asylum."

They passed by his town house once again, but a little further removed this time. Mike didn't bother to point it out.

"When you take a postmodernist philosophy course, wonder where the stopping line is. What is the stop code? If you're supposed to overthrow the institutions, doesn't that mean that new ones will arise? Do you then overthrow *those*? If you don't, what about the next generation? Where is the stopping point? What is the stop code? What is good enough?

"And since postmodernist philosophers will say there is no such thing as morality, ask yourself what is wrong with rape?"

"Excuse me?" Sasha said.

"There are plenty of postmodernist philosophy professors who can explain there is no such thing as morality therefore there is no problem about killing," Mike said. "There is nothing wrong with sex with children. That's a favorite. Then they say they don't mean you should but prove there is something wrong with it. What's wrong with it? That's the mentality, the philosophy, that Bolt came out of. So, okay, then what is wrong with rape?"

"It's . . . wrong," Sasha said, angrily.

"Agreed," Mike said. "But prove it logically to someone that says it's okay to have sex with a child. They will twist logic into pretzels.

"When you hear them saying lighter things—the reason that riots are good, the reason that criminals are the real victims—remember that Bolt was saying that everyone is innately homosexual, and I had to get over my homophobia while flailing me with his *dick*. That he justified his actions because I wasn't sufficiently progressive. I didn't want to have sex with a random trans. And that made *me* transphobic because I wouldn't have sex with *him*. That I wouldn't let him just rape me. That I wouldn't just let him rape me makes *me* a transphobe in his eyes and the eyes of trans activists. Think about it. *Really* think about it."

Sasha crossed her arms again and looked away uncomfortably.

"Is that wrong?" Mike said. "Yes. Absolutely. But people will twist themselves into pretzels to prove Bolt is the victim. Because that's their indoctrination. When you go to some elite college, you are there to be indoctrinated into the party line. Period. Dot. Didn't used to be that way but it's the way it is now. You shall conform or else."

She reluctantly nodded agreement.

"Osseo, believe it or not, is *not* into indoctrination," Mike said. "There are so many things you just cannot say in leftist circles. You *cannot* question the party line. Ever. You can question, seek, explore, at Osseo. It's classic liberal, not Bob Jones conservative. It's what college *should* be and no longer is. It's what Stanford *used* to be like. Maybe someday it will be again. Maybe. Hopefully.

"They'd take me now," Mike said, grinning. "Stanford administration is tacitly aware that Michael Truesdale is my old name, the child genius that got canceled, not to mention a billionaire. They don't care as long as it doesn't get out. Billionaire is the magic word. They'd *love* to have me now. Hell, they wouldn't care if people found out my old identity. Billionaire is the magic word."

Outside, the river view ended and was replaced by a never-ending string of massive piers.

"I don't play that game. Forget that I've already been canceled, and I'm still pissed about it. I was dodging them back then because I didn't want to deal with the pod people. I'm sure as hell not going to go *now*.

"And at Osseo I'm much more likely to find some young lady who is getting a math or science degree who wants to be the math and science teacher in a homeschooling pod," Mike added. "And have a big passel of children. You're not going to find that at Stanford.

"And who *wants* that. Wants to be a wife and mom. Wants to have a large family. Her body, her choice. Who sees her career as creating a home and big family. Not she's interested because billionaire. I wish that word wasn't attached, honestly. And I definitely don't want anyone to know that's my goal. Not because of the *Herald*, et cetera, though the Left will flip out. But because I don't want some woman that that's not her goal to go 'Oh, I'll have twenty kids if I can marry a billionaire.'"

"Right," Sasha said, making a moue. "I guess..."

"We'd be a horrible couple long term anyway," Mike said. "You would get *seriously* tired of explanations and, honestly, I get tired of them as well."

When Mike got back to the apartment after dropping Sasha off, he got out of his zoot suit, got into comfortable sweats, propped himself on the bed, and opened up his laptop.

He couldn't use Gondola's resources for this, but he had his own network. Not as extensive, not as thoroughly hidden. But it should work.

First, he searched for "Sasha Nikula fake time porn."

He tried to ignore what he was watching but he was a heterosexual male. Yes, it did look like Sasha.

Then he traced who had spread it, found the "misogynist," and did some research.

Yeah, the guy was a total creepazoid. Sometimes the term *misogynist* was tossed around like *transphobe* as just a generic insult. Then there were the people who were truly wannabe or actual rapists.

Then he started tracking who had actually done the deepfake. He finally found the guy in part through dark web research and asking some questions of contacts. No one he recognized as Gondola, but possibly they were Gondola. You had multiple names when you worked in the dark web.

With the targets identified, he closed his computer, comforted himself, and went to sleep.

CHAPTER 23

"Hero" —Skillet

"Alger," Mike said as he was eating a delicious plate of eggs Benedict.

He wasn't used to someone just standing there while he ate. That was going to take some getting used to. Not to mention it was Pelton who'd prepared the breakfast.

He'd gotten up before Derrick banged on the door, done an hour of yoga and Powers study, gone out for a run in Central Park in the predawn darkness, and come back to a cooked breakfast.

It was weird.

The nice thing about running in Central Park that time of day was that there weren't many other runners, so he could open up to full gallop. Normally, he kept his speed down. But as a super he could go as fast as a sprint for miles.

There *were* other joggers out that time of day. A few. Including his dad. And he kept lapping them around the lake. It was fun. Good way to give away that he was a super, but what the hell.

"I'm going to need a room set aside for a full computer rig. I'll order the equipment, but we'll need a contractor to set it up. See Mr. Fulmer about that."

"Yes, sir," Alger said.

"I have the funds still from the reward," Mike said. "I'm sure my father will clear it. Also, I'm going to buy that Razer I wanted. The laptop my dad bought me is nice, but I need something faster if I'm going to do astrophysics modeling. But I still need the full rig. You've probably got a full plate. You can feel free to delegate working with Mr. Fulmer to Pelton if you feel comfortable with that."

"Sir," Alger said.

"Last item for now," Mike said. "I'm going to talk to Dad about having dinner with the archbishop or a monsignor. We need to discuss the spiritual purification of the properties—including this one. I've got my own sources for most of the spiritual heavy lifting but I'm going to need to get some specialty stuff done. So, we're going to need to set that up. Small party. Think that's all for now."

"I shall endeavor to provide, sir," Alger said.

"Since the next meeting with the estate attorneys is tomorrow," Mike said, "I'm going to be on my computer today. I'll set up in the study. That will do until we have something better set up."

"Where do you want the full rig, sir? The study?"

Mike thought about that.

"The back parlor," Mike said. "That's got essentially no view. And I don't need a view for what I'm going to be doing. The study is too nice to clutter it up with plasma screens and servers. We may need to work on the cooling there. I'll speak to Mr. Fulmer about it."

"Sir."

Mike set up his laptop on the desk in the study at first, but it wasn't really comfortable, so he moved to a couch and laid the laptop on his lap with a pillow to keep it from heating up his legs. Then he got to work.

First order of business was to check in to Gondola and get some work done.

There was a whole list of individual taskers and he started with the oldest: metatagging some collected intel. Not fun work. Boring and tedious but necessary. And somebody had to do it. Also, it was in Hangul, so it took someone who read Hangul. Which he did.

Much of it was handled, these days, by the AIs. But even they couldn't keep up with the mass of intel that Gondola collected every day, so humans helped out. There was talk of bringing up another AI beyond the three they were already running. But that was up to the Faerie Queen, and it would require a mass of new servers. Getting the servers wasn't the problem. Finding someplace safe enough to put them was the problem.

He set a timer and worked on it for four hours. At his level, four hours was all he was required to volunteer a month to maintain his status. He usually tried to do more because there were never enough man-hours available for all that Gondola did. If he got moved to Level Four it would mean more hours. But now that he had some stability in his life and a secure place to work, he could probably put in the time.

When he was a couple of hours in and puzzling over a term that he suspected was cultural, there was a discreet tap at the door.

"Come!" Mike yelled.

"Did the young sir have a preference for lunch?" Pelton asked.

"That's so weird," Mike said, looking up at him and smiling. "Uh . . . no. The young sir leaves it up to you. Surprise me."

"Sir," Pelton said, nodding and closing the door.

Mike poked into one of the chat rooms that were frequented by Koreans. It was eleven P.M. in Seoul but since most of Gondola did their time after work, it was busy.

MT: I need some cultural translation help with a Hangul phrase I don't recognize.

WHUTAN ELECTRIC: I'll help with that.

It took less than a minute to sort it out and he was back to tedious, tedious metatagging.

Lunch was Dover sole in wine sauce with a side of asparagus and garlic mashed potatoes.

"This is very good," Mike said. "Did you order this or cook it?"

"I cook, sir," Pelton said.

"This is excellent."

And, perhaps forewarned, he'd made enough that Mike was a bit full when he went back to work.

He'd done enough collating of data. Time to do some hacking.

He pulled completely out of the Gondola system and went to his own server.

Most of his "system" was zombie servers that he was "borrowing" from various owners. He knew it was a bad idea to have a pattern, but he'd found that library servers in small towns tended to have *really* bad cyber defense. He didn't just take them over, while allowing continued full use by the librarians and clients, he also cleaned them up—as they were generally loaded with viruses—and secured them. It was a public service, really.

But at that point he owned them.

Most of them existed as potentially disposable servers that were there to create a buffer between him and whatever he was doing. He didn't keep important "stuff" on them. They were too likely to get moved out or something. Important "stuff" he kept on servers that were semipermanent and much more heavily guarded.

But the library servers acted as a very nice buffer.

So, Silverdon first. 'Cause that guy was an *asshole*.

Once he found Silverdon's private phone number it wasn't hard to get in. He set up a website that had "dirt on Ekaterina Golub," another teen supermodel, and texted the link to Silverdon's phone. Most of it was known stuff. But there were some pics of her that weren't widely known. A couple of them were nudes.

They weren't real. They were more deepfakes he'd found on the dark web and suspected that Silverdon already had.

Silverdon hit the link and a tiny little line of code went into his phone along with one of the nudes.

Then Mike waited. Most of hacking was waiting.

When Silverdon used his phone to connect to a different website the code popped up and said "Hello!" to one of the library servers. Since it was already in the phone and not a known virus—it was custom made—the phone allowed the server to send more malicious code into the phone.

At which point, Mike owned Silverdon's phone. And if you owned someone's phone, you pretty much had their entire lives at your fingertips.

Oh, he used a password generator to generate random passwords. Wasn't that sweet. Doing real good cyber defense there. *You might have enemies, Mr. Silverdon*. The password generator also listed all the generated passwords and what they went to.

So, now Mike had all his passwords and the location of all the servers he used.

Tum-tee-tum . . .

Give Silverdon credit. He was either afraid to have child porn or didn't support it. More likely afraid to have it. Based on everything else in his life, the guy was at least a wannabe rapist. And he concentrated on younger models to hassle. Child porn was his natural métier. But Mike wasn't finding any on any of his systems.

"Okay, what to do to this guy?" Mike muttered.

He had three girlfriends who each didn't know he was dating the other two.

Start there.

"Hey, Sasha," Mike said.

It was nearly dinnertime, and his dad was on the way home, so time to update Sasha on the latest news.

"Oh, my God, Mike!" Sasha said, laughing. "You know how we were talking about that asshole Silverdon last night?"

"Yes?" Mike said.

"It turns out he was dating two different girls," Sasha said, grinning. "And neither of them knew about the other!"

"Three," Mike said.

"What?"

"Three different girls," Mike said. "You already heard?"

"One of them ambushed him at Bloomingdale's while he was out with the other!" Sasha said. "There was a big catfight right in public!"

"Wait 'til the third gets involved," Mike said. "Were the two at Bloomingdale's Sarah Cohen and Tshwala? I knew he was going shopping with Sarah. Or which two?"

"Sarah Cohen and Lindsay Jameson," Sasha said. "Who's Tshwala?"

"His third girlfriend," Mike said. "I would have expected it was Tshwala that would do an ambush. But in her case, he'd better be worried about getting shot. She's pretty violent."

"How did you . . . ?" Sasha said, puzzled.

"Who do you think *told* them?" Mike said. "I was calling you to update you. He's also about to get sued by his business partner for embezzlement, which might mean jail time, and the IRS is going to be investigating him. You're welcome."

"Are you serious?" Sasha said.

"I'm good at what I do," Mike said. "But that gets us to the guy who made the deepfake."

"That mother . . ." Sasha growled. "Tell me who it was, and I'll rip out his heart, I swear I will."

"Really shouldn't be that way about Daniel," Mike said. "Daniel Duffee is just a guy who loves to do video. He works in the industry, and he just loves it. And he didn't do it maliciously. He just does not *get* that it's hurtful."

"That's hard to believe," Sasha said, angrily. "I can't believe you're taking his side!"

"I have to *analyze* these things, Sasha," Mike said. "This is a lot of power, and you have to use it responsibly. Silverdon deserves everything he's going to get. Duffee is another case. He doesn't even get into porn. He did it because someone asked. And he's neuro-abnormal enough that he truly doesn't *get it*. 'Spectrum' is one way people put it.

"Bottom line is, I'm going to have to figure out what to do about Duffee. He's not a bad *guy*, he did a bad *thing*. I've got to show him *why* it's a bad thing in a way he can comprehend and convince him not to do it again. That's my take."

"I guess," Sasha said, shaking her head. "I still want to kill him."

"Understandable."

"Did you watch it?" Sasha asked.

"Had to," Mike said. "To get the information I needed. I've ... seen a lot of that sort of stuff. Not because I watch porn all the time. Because I work with people who track child pornographers. I can distance myself from it. Want to know what got me about it?"

"Do I?" Sasha asked.

"The guy in the video, it's a het-sex porn, would have been dead if it had been you," Mike said, grinning. "Couple of things that went on I was like 'Welp, if that had *actually* been Sasha, he'd be dead now. 'Cause that particular move would have killed him.'"

"Funny," Sasha said, drily.

"There's other stuff that's going on I can't get into," Mike said. "Once it's out there, it's never all going away. It's going to be out there forever like those kids who are in memes who are in their twenties now. I'm sorry you're going to have to deal with it your whole life. And I'll see what I can do about reducing it and getting Duffee to not do any more. But there's always some technically competent neuro abnorm or asshole, or often both, who can do something to ruin people's lives. The world is not an easy place."

"Well, I appreciate that you tried," Sasha said. "And whatever it is you did to Silverdon."

"Oh, there'll be more," Mike said. "It won't stop the video getting around. But ... there's going to be more. Just not stuff I can talk about.

"Talk later?" Mike concluded. "It's about dinnertime."

"Sure," Sasha said, sighing. "I guess I'll just handle it."

"Every time I go out as Stone Tactical, someone is going to ask me about being a transphobe," Mike said. "Every time you do something public, someone is going to either ask about or be thinking about that porn video. Life sucks."

After dinner, he followed up with something he was curious about.

Silverdon's server had had a log of everyone who had downloaded the Sasha video with their IP addresses.

He loaded those into a wardialer—a program that automatically connects to a series of phone numbers—and waited while it pinged the systems, looking for a weak port.

When it found one, he carefully picked his way into the system.

Sasha Nikula was fifteen, but the fake looked more like twelve or thirteen. She was nearly hairless in the nether regions, for one thing. The video was for all practical purposes child pornography.

People who viewed it were likely to have some actual child porn with real physical victims on their computers.

He hit jackpot on the third one and flagged it for Gondola. Then another. About every fourth was someone with masses of child porn.

The Sasha Nikula video might as well have been a honeypot trap for people into child porn.

That was worth bringing to Gondola's attention.

"And that completes my analysis, ma'am," Mike said.

Lady Autumn was the on-call senior officer of the day. Mike had been continuously exploring the Sasha video downloads as the report had run its way up the chain.

"So far I've found sixty-two individuals with valid child pornography on their computers," Mike said. "I think this may be worthy of a follow-up."

"Agreed," Lady Autumn said. "I recognize the personal aspect to this, but do you think you can run a team?"

"Yes, ma'am," Mike said. "I've had team lead experience in the past and now that I have a stable and secure location to work, it's doable."

"Agreed," Lady Autumn said. "Disco, assign a team."

"Will do," Disco said. The assistant supervisor was Indian from his accent.

"Secondary item, ma'am?" Mike said, diffidently.

"Go."

"The originator of the video is the type of neuro abnorm that just doesn't realize that this is hurtful," Mike said. "He also is incredible with this type of video. Some of his other stuff is excellent. I know we do fake videos. He's a potential recruit if someone can figure out how to explain why it's a bad thing."

"We'll look into that," Lady Autumn said. "I know the type. Anything else?"

"No, ma'am," Mike said.

"Sorry your friend got pulled into this," Lady Autumn said. "It's a place where it's about time we had some laws. Deepfake takes it to a whole new level. But that's something to persuade politicians about. Okay, if we're done, I'm off to see the Wizard . . ."

"I'll assign a team," Disco said. "Any preferences?"

"I'd like Celsius, sir," Mike said. "Just someone I know. If you're asking for my full preferences, Celsius 22, Blushing Duster, Guilty Eyes, and Pink Badger. I'd also like permission to use the Network and apps to penetrate Duffee's server to get another download log."

"Approved," Disco said. "I'll send notes to them to see if they want to be on the team. Remember to watch for interaction between participants. Look for networks."

"Roger that, sir," Mike said.

"I'm out."

The probate was "proceeding" and if he was going to call in some spiritual mojo, he needed put that up on the schedule.

So, the next morning during a break in the Gondola action he made a call.

"Henry's Barbershop."

"Big Tom, that you?" Mike said, standing on one of the apartment's balconies and taking in the view. "It be Boogie Knight."

"Man! Good to hear from you! Long time. You didn't even call 'bout the funeral! If you callin' 'bout Miss Cherise, Preacher Man done her good. It was a good funeral. Everybody said so."

"Nah," Mike said, trying not to tear up. *Big boys don't cry.* "I watched it stream, Big Tom. It was. It was a good send-off. Preacher Man said good words. That's who I gots to talk at. Preacher Man. He round?"

"He right here, Boogie. Yo, Henry, Boogie Knight want to talk you up."

"Hello, Michael," the preacher man said in his deep basso profundo. *"How have you been young man? Are you safe?"*

Preacher Henry Thomas was the minister of the East Baltimore Church of Zion of the Cross. A former convict—murder—he had found God and become reformed while serving a twenty-five-year sentence. As an eventually trusted member of the prison population, he was trained to be a barber.

Prisoners had to have their hair cut, and to cut hair you had to have a barber's license. So trusted prisoners were trained as barbers. They had to be trusted. Most of barbering involved sharp objects. Prisoners would use any weapon they could find or make to cut on each other.

When he'd finished serving his sentence he'd returned to the hood, which was usually a bad idea, and asked the owner of the barbershop if he would accept a reformed convict as a fellow barber. The man had, and later Preacher Henry had bought the shop as well as investing in other businesses in the area.

By the time Mike met him, he was a solid and respected citizen of East Baltimore who worked to keep kids out of gangs and tried to make peace. It rarely worked but his reputation as an "old lion" went before him. And any young buck who thought that just because he was a preacher man he'd lost the edge, tended to learn differently.

Mike had preferred to go to Preacher Henry's barbershop to get his hair cut when he could arrange it. There is a significant difference between cutting white hair and black. As prison barbers, Preacher Henry and Big Tom knew how to cut white hair. They were the only barbers in the ghetto areas of Baltimore who did.

"I am well, Preacher," Mike said. "I am very well. My name was changed by the marshals so I'm going to be out of sight from what I was there. And that's for the best."

"It is. I know you always wanted to make it out. I am glad you did so."

"So, Tom's still there," Mike said. "How are Willy and Speedbump?"

You didn't just jump right in with Preacher Henry. Asking about the fortunes of others was The Way.

Big Tom, Willy, and Speedbump were all ex-cons. Big Tom had been done up for confidence trickery and also was a trustee-trained barber. Mike wasn't sure he was reformed. As a kid he'd lost many a nickel and dime to the barber until he learned the only way to win at three-card monte was to be the one dealing the cards.

Willy and Speedbump were definitely not reformed. Between them they probably had a hundred previous convictions ranging from armed robbery to a petty theft. They were just too old for thugging.

The foursome had been in a barbershop quartet in prison. They didn't mostly do the really old stuff, tending more to the Four Tops and doo-wop. Willy was a not bad rapper. So, they just hung out like they had in prison, Big Tom working as a barber and Willy and Speedbump just hanging around the barbershop, reading the paper and arguing sports. Willy and Speedbump paid their way cleaning up and such like.

So, if you went to Preacher Henry's barbershop you were guaranteed of a good cut for a fair price and you often got a serenade thrown in.

"Speedbump is well, he is here and gives his regards," Preacher Henry said. *"Willy, sadly, has been taken by the Big C. He's at chemo today. Speedbump is going to pick him up soon."*

"I will pray for his recovery, Preacher," Mike said. "And, uh, I gots to thank you for doing a real good service for Mama. It was fine. And thank the choir for singing for her. I know she wasn't of the faith, but she had a good heart and she treated me well."

A ruby-throated hummingbird chose that moment to zip up to a box of flowers Alger had arranged on the balcony. It hovered as if frozen in place and seemed to be watching Mike more than inspecting the flowers.

"We were more than happy to welcome her to God's arms, Michael. How are you handling it?"

"I've put that aside for another day, Preacher. I gots too much on my plate to open that box. If I may talk about that somewhat?"

The hummingbird zipped off again, so fast Mike wondered if he'd imagined it.

"Of course."

"Preacher Man, this bit I gots to be careful about," Mike said. "Ax that you don't be talkin' 'bout it to no one."

"I am a man of the cloth. It is under the seal, Michael."

"Finally gots me some of that white privilege everybody talkin' bout," Mike said. "Turns out I'm an heir to a vast fortune. Try not to let that on to Speedbump; he'd be lookin' for what he can get out of it."

"That is an issue of that sort of thing."

"I intend a bequest to the church," Mike said, "once the money comes through. But it will be a trust. If you just drop money on a congregation, it tends to cause issues. So, it will be a trust set up to provide money over time. That way it just keeps going."

"That is well thought of you, Michael. My thanks. And, yes, you are correct on that issue. I have seen it many times."

"There are houses that are part of the inheritance," Mike said. "We spoke once on the subject of belief. On the subject of demons and angels and haunts and such. Do you recall?"

"I do. You were knowledgeable beyond your years in that matter."

"The problem is, my mother's family, which is the inheritance, was pure evil, Preacher. Not my mother. She was a victim. And she *didn't* leave me in the alley. She left me with Miss Cherise, yes. But that was to hide me from bad people and, I think, from the demons that had held my family in thrall for generations.

"But the demons of this family are not just seeking me. They infest *all* of the houses. I need some prayer warriors. Not just I need prayers my own self, which I could always use. But I need some to come in and cleanse these dwellings. They were sites of pure evil for a very long time."

"I see. Where are you, if I may ask?"

"New York," Mike said. "You've probably heard of it in the news: Michael Truesdale and the Follett fortune."

"Good Lord. I had heard of that. That is quite the ... Yes. I understand why you wish this to be quiet. Hmm ... I do know some good people in that area. I could put you in touch with them."

"I would be much obliged, Preacher," Mike said. "I walk in the light of Jesus, but it's some evil places."

"I'll make a call. Can I use this number?"

"This is my current cell," Mike said. "Much of this matter I have to delegate, but this one I'm going to have to handle myself. And there will be adequate compensation."

"You've always been a generous soul, Michael."

"May God walk with you, Preacher," Mike said.

"You as well. Goodbye."

CHAPTER 24

"Feel Invincible" —Skillet

"That'll do," Mike said, looking around the back parlor of the apartment.

The back parlor had been built in a time before skyscrapers or, notably, the Mount Sinai Center for Advanced Medicine building.

It had probably once had a pretty good view. These days it was of the windows of the Mount Sinai building.

So, covering the back window with curtains was no big deal. Though what he'd really have preferred was a SCIF. But double paned, insulated, and blocked against electronics was the best he could do.

The rig was everything he'd dreamed about and more. Multiple large screens, every kind of input up to and including gaming pads and more computing power than most major nation intelligence services.

"You should be able to get some work done on it," Mr. Fulmer said. "Not as secure as it could be, but we work with what we have."

His father's "guy" was a former Army chief warrant officer in electronic and cyber warfare. His retirement job was as a cyber defense, electronic intelligence, and computer contractor.

"Once we're done with probate, I'm going to need one at every house I keep," Mike said. "Which houses are still up in the air. But I'll need more."

"Oh, I will happily provide," Mr. Fulmer said. "And you'll need upgrades."

"Oh my, yes."

⊕ ⊕ ⊕

"Sir," Pelton said. "There is a delivery?"

"Hmm...?" Mike said. He was deep in thought tracing the electronic communications of one of the targets.

The Sasha Nikula video had been a *godsend*. While not every person who downloaded it had had child porn on their systems, there had been a fair number. And they'd found communications between groups of them that were very active in the *production* of child porn. They'd so far found *three* rings that were involved in manufacturing and distribution. One of them, it was their own stepchildren or children. Some of it was brutal, involving beating and torturing the kids.

The team required expansion. Mike was still running his team but two more had been brought in under the general direction of Titanium.

They needed to build the full case, though, before authorities took over officially. The groups were in multiple countries, which meant Gondola would have to build the international cooperation. He'd just gotten off the phone with one of the senior people in Interpol. Fortunately, it was someone he'd already worked with and they got along. But one of the main producers was in Morocco and part of the Moroccan government. That was going to be sticky. There had been a "frank discussion," including one of the senior members of the Moroccan General Directorate for National Security, about whether to just use Mercenaries R Us and take the guy out.

The one he *really* wanted to take out was the foster care social worker in England. But the British *national* authorities were pretty good about taking down people like that. It was local cops who hid these types of things for fear of being called racist.

They needed all the different countries to move on them more or less at once, which was the tough part. If you hit one part of a ring and the rest learned of it, they'd start destroying evidence. Getting all the countries to work together was the problem. The lower-level people were generally fine. Just leave it to them and it would be a done deal. But when it got international, or multistate in the US, the bosses *had* to get involved. It was the upper-level people who generally caused the most issues.

Everyone wanted credit for it. *International* credit. Everyone understood Gondola wasn't going to be publicly credited, so *they* wanted to be the main player. The Moroccans wanted it to have been *their* investigation that *they* brought it to the attention of the French National Police and British National Crime Agency and the FBI. So did the Azerbaijani, Chadian, *and* Indonesian police. Nobody wanted to even *mention* Interpol except in passing.

"A delivery, sir?" Pelton repeated.

"Is it my ball bearings?" Mikes asked, rubbing his forehead. The freaking politics in this thing was the real nightmare. No, the child porn was the real nightmare. The politics just had to be done to get rid of that.

"I believe it may be, yes, sir," Pelton said, curiosity written on his face.

"Great. Lemme at 'em," Mike said. "I need something to distract me or I'm going to fly to Morocco and *strangle* a minister of justice..."

New York Post: CHILD PORN INTERNATIONAL!

An international joint investigation into the manufacture, distribution, and possession of child pornography has led to the arrest of six hundred people in fifteen different countries. The investigation, which was initiated by the French National Police...

The investigation was initiated due to investigation of a deep-fake video of an unnamed teenage supermodel...

Persons arrested in the New York City area include...

Mike looked at the article in the *New York Post*, hit SHARE, and sent it to Sasha.

It turned out your video did some good in the world for what it's worth...

Gotham Herald: ALARMING RISE OF RACISTS AND TRANSPHOBES IN THE HACKER COMMUNITY

Mike hovered in a lotus position in midair in the study, his wrists resting lightly on his knees, hands cupped inward. Between the hands there were two objects hovering. One was a chunk of simple pyrite, iron sulfide ore. The other was the chalcocite ore he'd picked up in Montana wrapped around a three-eights-inch steel ball bearing.

It bothered him no end that iron was a big part of the earth's crust, but metallic iron wasn't an Earth power. Only metallos could manipulate metallic iron, which made up the majority of steel. Though he got the issues of the electron fields, it made no sense to him. Iron, *metallic* iron *should* be one of his chakras. And he intended to find it.

In Sight, within the ball of chalcocite was a spherical gap. There was, apparently, nothing there in Sight.

He rummaged in his mind, trying to put aside all other thoughts. Breathe deep. Zen...

They'd all look fabulous in red and white...

Breathe...

Tiffany already has a bonnet...

Feel the iron...

I wonder what Pelton's fixing for dinner. He's a better cook than I am, damnit...

Zen...

In the same way he'd learned to put every muscle in his body to sleep, he slowly shut down all the tracks, becoming the pyrite. Why was the iron in the pyrite visible in Sight and he could Sense it but not the iron in the steel?

Become the pyrite... Feel the iron... Feel its electron spin... Search your mind...

Suddenly it clicked and the iron in the steel ball bearing was there. Visible in Sight and he could Sense it.

So was *all* the steel in every direction. Cars going by down in the street. The steel in the buildings. The Mount Sinai building. He could flip from Earth to iron easily enough. It wasn't part of Earth, but it was a chakra. And now he could Sense steel.

That should be useful.

He pulled the chalcocite away from the ball bearing and plucked it out of midair.

"What else that is earth can I find?" Mike asked, quietly. "Aluminum makes up a good bit of Earth matter. So does *oxygen*..."

"You said you had something regarding commodities you wanted to test out?" Benjamin Goldblatt said.

Mike and several associates from Asuda Financial Management were going over plans on how to invest the money from the estate after it was through probate. It was a team meeting in their largest conference room that included all the specialists that would be working on the distributed portfolio. Laptops, coffee mugs, and pitchers of water were scattered across the table, with two large flat-screens mounted at one end to display charts, data, and news regarding whatever stocks or market they were focused on at any given moment.

He was going to owe half of it in federal death taxes and more to the State of New York. He'd decided it was going to be essentially impossible to fight that one. He was just hoping Maryland didn't jump in.

But the more money they made in the remainder of the year off of the full estate, the easier it would be going forward. So, investments in the first year were, after some discussion with his father, going to be leaning to growth. Which meant risk but that was the best strategy. It was just a matter of managing the risk.

"What's the one thing that *every* investor who knows diddly about commodities, or weather, or climate, thinks is *super* important, and every expert knows is a bunch of hokum?" Mike asked.

"Oh, there's *so* many of those," Lee Miles said. "Take your pick."

Lee was an older gentleman with glasses and slightly graying hair. He was their commodities guy.

"Think sunspots," Mike said.

"Oh, those," Lee said, grinning. "Yeah. Don't know how many people have insisted that the answer to making it big in commodities is sunspots."

"Every *expert* knows that sunspots are hokum," Mike said. "Had that in several commodities classes. Absolutely have no effect. You know what: When all the experts are in agreement, check the horse's teeth."

"You think they do?" Benjamin said.

"I know they do," Mike replied. "With due respect to commodities experts and houses, they don't understand solar physics..."

It took about an hour for Mike to work through the entire sequence.

"So...what it gives, if you take all the known factors into account, is a tighter fit for high, low versus the last year in yields," Mike said.

Lee looked at the figures that he'd brought out on the plasma and furrowed his brow.

"You want me to cover the middle bit again?" Mike asked. "The reason you can at best get four out of five correct responses is that cosmic rays come in from all over the place. And the solar wind holds back most of them at the heliopause. So, you'd have to have a mass of satellites *outside* the heliopause in every direction to get some aggregate of the solar wind. *Voyager* is barely there. We're not going to have that in a thousand years."

"Yeah, I'm not getting the physics," Lee said, looking at the numbers. "But the results are good on the reverse model. You don't mind if I crunch these myself, do you?"

"No," Mike said. "But if, if, if. If we get the money before the Fieldstone quarterly and if it's anticipated that it will be worse than projection, then we can dump on them hard. And the early spring Ontario yield results are announced not much later."

"So that would have us with significant funds in hand to play the market," Benjamin said.

"Exactly," Mike said. "And, yes, sunspots do have an effect. The reason they've been dismissed was everyone was looking at it backward, essentially. It wasn't a direct effect."

"Let me crunch these," Lee repeated, furrowing his brow again. "You do have a general grasp on this stuff. I mean, the training. It shows."

"I'd make a great pickup as an intern in a commodities house, right?" Mike said, smiling. "I can handle that. We're not going to bet the farm on it. But if we make out with the Fieldstone short, I'm willing to bet the entire return on it. How do you feel about that, Benjamin?"

"The return, yes," Benjamin said. "But not the principal."

"Absolutely not," Mike said. "Too risky. Okay, next area . . . Bonds, is it . . . ? This Vietnamese bond sale you suggested? I checked with one of my Vietnamese friends who's in business over there. He's really leery of it. Ong Thi Thom has had a bad run of luck lately . . ."

Mike was at a quiet dinner with his father when he Saw the rape in Central Park.

It was already ongoing by the time he noticed it. It was near maximum range and that was something like a telescope you had to move around rather than continuously in Sight. One of the women's bathrooms. The girl looked to be a teen by her growth plates.

When the guy was done, he took a picture of her with his phone and pulled up his pants. Then he took off with her phone, headed in the direction of Fifth Avenue.

The rapist dumped the girl's phone in a storm drain and kept trotting. Across Fifth, up to 103rd and eastward into the projects, taking up a walking pace. By then he was obviously looking at the photo or video he'd taken of the victim. He was enjoying himself.

The actions had been rehearsed, practiced. This wasn't a chance event. The victim might have been by chance, but the guy was a repeat rapist.

Mike traced him until he got into one of the stairways—not under any cameras and out of sight of people—and hit him with Death Wind. Then he simply buried the body under the building. Deep. Even if the entire area was reconstructed, it would never be found. The body was deep in Manhattan schist.

That was his last rape.

"I have come to the conclusion, Father, that there is one way in which I am *not* Bruce Wayne," Mike said.

"What's that?" Derrick asked.

"I am *far* less lenient. Batman was a sissy . . ."

"Sister Beulah," Mike said, bowing to the middle-aged black lady and gesturing to the settee in the parlor of the apartment. "Welcome. Is there anything you ladies would care for? Tea, coffee. Ask."

Sister Beulah was at the head of a party of five, all black women dressed for church in dresses, gloves, and hats. They stood respectfully in a small, tight cluster. A few cast nervous glances at their surroundings.

"I'll take a cup of tea," Sister Beulah said.

Orders were made all around and Pelton silently left.

"So, some introductions are in order," Sister Beulah said. "I am, as you noted, Sister Beulah. This is Sister Joynisha."

"Hello." Sister Joynisha was also middle-aged. Very dark skin. Possibly an immigrant.

"Sister Lalique." Thirtysomething. Very light-skinned.

"Sister Jabrielle." Twenties. Dark-skinned. Fine features. Some Arabic mixture at a guess.

"Sister Meridian." Early twenties. Very nervous. It wasn't social anxiety at being in a fine apartment on Fifth Avenue. She was trying not to look around.

Seer.

"You've done quite well by yourself, young man," Sister Beulah said.

"It is easier for a laden camel to thread the eye of the needle than for a rich man to enter heaven," Mike quoted. "I will admit that this is definitive white privilege. And that my family came about its fortune through great evil. It doesn't mean I have to perpetuate that."

"That is a good approach," Sister Beulah said as Pelton entered the parlor bearing a tray laden with goodies and drinks.

Once it was laid out, with the sisters seated on a couch and chairs around a large coffee table, Mike said, "That will be all, Pelton."

"Sir," Pelton said, nodding.

"Nice to have servants," Sister Jabrielle said, archly. She was on the couch between Joynisha and Lalique. Beaulah and Meridian sat in chairs to either side. All sat up very properly.

"It is," Mike said. "I grew up fighting to survive in the ghetto. This is a bit of a change. But I don't think Pelton should be in this conversation. He's a bit freaked out by my insistence on the existence of the invisible.

"I assume all of you know that I'm Stone Tactical, the junior super?" he asked.

Sister Meridian, still studiously avoiding looking at anyone or anything, gave a slight nod.

"I was unsure whether you were comfortable sharing that," Sister Beulah said.

"Just did," Mike said, grinning. "But you should be aware that I have super sight. X-ray vision, if you will."

"That's unusual in American supers," Sister Joynisha said.

"Yes," Mike said, shrugging. "It is. But what I do *not* have is the Sight of the invisible. I'm somewhat Sensitive but that is about it.

"The Folletts, as I mentioned, did not get their power through being sweetness and light," Mike said, sighing. "From what I can glean, and based on recent experience, they had a generational demon attached to them. A powerful one that drew still others to it. This apartment is not, I think, totally infested. The town house is bad. The manse and the mausoleum on the estate are literally God awful. Unless I'm mistaken, all the house managers are hoodun. In the manse there is a full-up Satanic temple with a child's body buried under it."

"Oh, my God," Sister Joynisha said, holding her hand to her chest.

Meridian closed her eyes and shuddered. Lalique tentatively offered a hand to Meridian. Eyes still closed, Meridian took Lalique's hand and settled.

"There are three bodies buried in the town house," Mike said. "Four including the one on the estate. That's beside the mausoleum. Buried in the walls. All I can See, all that's left really, is the bones. But they're there."

Several of them visibly shuddered.

"As to the demons," Mike said, shrugging, "I also have association with a person who is very much favored by God. They can summon the angels, and angels descend in their name. I used their name—which is, I assure you, a name of power—to somewhat clear out the manse. But the entire thing needs to be thoroughly gone over and cleansed. It will take a fair number of prayer warriors. The manse is pretty big."

"Spiritual janitors?" Sister Jabrielle asked.

"I have considered turning it into an orphanage," Mike said, "but I probably won't. I was an orphan. This is all very *Oliver Twist*. I care about American orphans, but I can support ten in Brazil for one in the United States. And children are children, Sister Jabrielle."

"That is true," Sister Beulah said.

"So, I may sell it, I may keep it," Mike said, shrugging. "It's an annuity to my children eventually. But whatever the case..."

He told them the story of the oppressive attack at the mausoleum. Joynisha and Lalique appeared shocked and pained through most of the telling, but the others remained calm and largely expressionless.

"That's a major demon," Mike said. "And the site of either the mausoleum or the manse is a power point. It used to be an Indian spiritual center, which pretty much says it all. Clearing it out and consecrating it to God is an important action, Sister Jabrielle. I hope that you agree."

"I agree," Sister Jabrielle said, looking around. "But I do hope that you contribute some of this toward the work of the Lord."

"I'm going to set up a trust for the ABE in general," Mike said. "I was ABE. It's just a tad weird, a white kid showing up so I'm moving over to Catholic, which the rest of my family is. I hope you are comfortable working with the Roman Catholic Church. I'm hoping to involve them as well."

"I can work with them," Sister Beulah said. "Though it depends on the priest."

"We'll have to see who the monsignor assigns," Mike said. "Getting an actual exorcist these days is tough. But I'm confident that prayer warriors can handle it.

"General plan of action: Once everything is signed over, I'll move the bodies out and deal with them through the Church. I'll also get all the worst of the evil artwork out. Some I may miss. I'll have to have you determine that.

"Then, once the major issues are removed, bring in as many priests, nuns, and prayer warriors as can be found and clean out everything— including this place. Seal all the portals and I'll try to find a way to clear the entire grounds of the estate. Is that something that you would countenance?"

Sister Beulah took a moment to gauge the reactions. There was some hesitancy throughout the group, but one by one they seemed to steel their resolve and nodded their heads.

"I believe we can accommodate you," Sister Beulah said.

CHAPTER 25

"Archangel" —Two Steps From Hell

TA: Tomorrow at the end of your run. 6:20 AM. Meet the asset, bridge by south gate house.

Mike slowed as he got to the South Gate House in Central Park, and turned toward the bridge. There was an African American male on its north side.

Mike walked slowly, breathing as if he were walking off the run. The male, who had been looking at his phone, turned toward him and did a brush pass of something as Mike walked by. It would have been nearly invisible to anyone even if they had been looking.

Mike waited until he got home to check out the package. It was a tiny bone wrapped in plastic with a small note, apparently a scrap from a three-inch-by-five-inch card, written in a woman's hand.

"Proximal phalanges Fortunato."

"Holy . . ." Mike said, cradling the relic. "—bone of a *saint*," he finished.

Fortunato had been one of the Faerie Queen's most favored mercenaries when she'd first taken over. A former South African naval commando, he was one of their best when they needed the best. There had been an early operation where he'd performed above and beyond tracking down some real bad guys in the bush of West Africa. The slavers that they'd been associated with hired witch doctors to curse him for it.

Sorcerers were possessed. To be possessed required first losing your personal angel. Demons hated and feared angels and it was impossible to be possessed without both accepting the possession and performing acts that permanently and irrevocably damned the soul. Murdering children was high on the list of "your soul isn't recovering from this" actions.

At that point the powerful demons of the possessed could command lesser demons to bedevil people in various ways. The demons could cause depression to the point of suicide. Various bad things just happened. They were cursed.

The problem for the possessed was that their demons were in some way tied into their nervous system. And powerful as the demons might be, angels were *more* powerful.

The Faerie Queen had heard about it and sent a host of angels against the sorcerers, including Michael the Archangel.

Even *Lucifer* would take off when he saw Michael coming. Michael had become *more* powerful since the Fall. He was the biggest of all thermonuclear weapons of the angel pantheon. And his one true love was hunting Fallen and beating up on them. He was kind of a bully about it, to be honest.

When Michael leading a host of angels descended on the place, the demons took off like scalded cats. Which meant ripping out of the possessed like ripping out their spinal columns.

From the point of view of the sorcerers' apprentices, their masters went into a room, locked the door, and started the ceremony. When they hadn't come out after a few hours, the apprentices broke down the door. They found four of the six dead and the other two in a coma. All of them had blood coming out of their noses and ears. They'd all stroked out. Hard. Simultaneously. In a locked room.

Since it was *obvious* that Fortunato did this, he had to have some *serious* mojo. That was powerful magic they thought they could use.

Sorcerers all over Africa started hunting bald black men until they found him in Zanzibar. He didn't go down easy. He'd been ambushed but still took seven of their mercenaries with no more than a handgun.

The sorcerers who had caught him fully intended to use his bones in their black magic. Here was really powerful juju.

When the Faerie Queen found out, she was furious. With

permission of God and the pope, she bound Michael the Archangel to Fortunato's bones, essentially making the career mercenary a saint. Michael wasn't required to be wherever his bones were full time. Michael's primary job was guarding the Tomb of St. Peter. But *any* black magic in the area of Fortunato's bones, meaning any powerful Fallen, would summon him immediately. And woe betide anyone who thought to use his bones for blood rituals.

When the sorcerers had cleaned his bones, they took his skull into another room, locked *that* door, and started *their* ritual.

There went six more. Same symptoms. Blood coming out of their nose and ears. All six dead this time.

That time the Faerie Queen's mercenaries turned up to collect all the bones. They were kept in a *very* safe place.

Now, Mike was holding one of them. It was the bone of a saint. A talisman that would literally summon Michael the Archangel.

"Hee-hee-hee," Mike said, grinning. "I can't *wait* to place this where it will do the most good."

Mike floated in a lotus in the apartment, holding up a can of oxygen with his mind. The container was aluminum and he'd already found that chakra. But the interior still appeared simply empty.

Breathe ... Zen ... Search your mind ...

The gas inside the container suddenly popped into view. Also, all the oxygen in the room and beyond in Sight, making everything misty. He turned off Oxygen Sight and everything cleared. Back on: Misty.

"That's oxygen down ..." Mike said. "Now on to water ..."

"All parties having come to agreement, this probate is complete," Judge Mickelson said in the packed courtroom, banging his gavel. "Next case ..."

"Michael J. Truesdale," Mike muttered, signing still another sheet of paper on a conference table. "Michael J. Truesdale ... How many of these *are* there?"

There was a near constant flow of assistants traveling through to deliver new documents and collect the ones he'd signed.

"Only four more," Derrick said, taking the sheet and signing. "This is the rest of your life, Mike. Get used to it."

"Think this is bad, wait 'til you do a really big business deal," Ahuvit said, passing the sheet on. "I've done ones where there are over a *hundred* pieces of paper to sign."

"That's just insane," Mike said. "Michael J. Truesdale ..."

"Mr. Conn," Mike said, looking into the eyes of the man who had raped his mother of her virginity at the age of eleven. "Thank you *so* much for your excellent work maintaining the estate of my late mother and grandmother."

"You didn't sound like you thought much of my work in court," Conn said, dyspeptically. Outwardly, he appeared relaxed and even carrid a slight smile. But there was pure hatred in his eyes. If Conn could kill Mike with a look, he would.

It warmed Mike's heart to know how much he'd enraged this man.

"It's called being *polite*, Mr. Conn," Mike replied, clapping his hands together. "Honestly, I think you're a scumbag and I have a virtual army of forensic accountants lined up to find out how *much* of a scumbag. *So*, it's time to hand over the passwords for the primary servers and then your labors here are *complete*. I wish you due regards and *good luck* in your future endeavors. I even have a pocket watch to help you on your way ..."

"Oh, they're *so* clever," Mike said, laughing.

"What?" Abraham said.

Abraham Eban was the chief forensic accountant assigned by Asuda to go over the books.

"So ... when people are making up numbers, they tend to choose three and seven, right?" Mike said.

"Yes," Abraham said.

"So, I did this Java app a while back that goes through pretty much any spreadsheet and counts the individual numbers," Mike said. "Number one. Number two. Number three. Then it averages them. If it's an honest spreadsheet, they're going to average out to point one more or less. You always get some divergence from perfect. With me?"

"That sounds useful," Abraham said.

"You can have it," Mike said. "So ... yeah. Threes and sevens are at point two. Five is over point one. All the rest are *way* low. These accounts are *totally* screwed. I mean, I thought *everyone* knew not to use three and seven when making up numbers."

"Everyone who diddles the books thinks they're the first ones to ever do it," Abraham said. "The real question is, where did the money go?"

"First find out how much was stolen," Mike said. "Then we'll track it down. We have time. All the time in the world. And I've got so many *other* things to do first."

"Can I borrow that app?" Abraham asked.

"Oh, definitely," Mike said. "I gotta head to the town house. It's spring-cleaning time..."

"Sell, sell, sell..."

Mike was going through the Riverside Drive town house, selecting the artwork to be sold. The answer was "pretty much all of it" but then there were some...

"Burn," Mike said, pointing to a postmodernist painting in the style of Pollock. Just splatters of paint on canvas.

"Burn, sir?" Pelton asked. "You're sure? That's a Kaamaakhan. It's quite valuable."

"So is the throne of Satan," Mike said. "Send it to the estate to be burned."

"Pelton," Mike said. "Again, sit. You're not in trouble."

"Sir," Pelton said, taking a seat on the edge of the chair.

"You said there was a Ms. Kennedy that complained about what was happening with my mother," Mike said. "I didn't ask more at the time. I was afraid the Trust would retaliate against you."

"I...was afraid of that as well, sir," Pelton said.

"I don't expect courage out of the staff, Pelton," Mike said. "Just loyalty and, to me, honesty. Courage is my charge. Who was Ms. Kennedy?"

"She was the housekeeper of the manse at the time, sir," Pelton said. "With Miss Annabelle, governesses and nannies would come and go. Mrs. Kennedy was there her whole life. And, yes, Dela was...not the best mother. She really seemed surprised sometimes to remember she had a daughter. Ms. Kennedy was a constant.

"When...things appeared to happen with Miss Annabelle, Mrs.

Kennedy tried to tell Dela and she just couldn't handle it. Ms. Kennedy was fired without recommendation."

"Ms. Kennedy have a first name you remember?" Mike asked. "Any idea where she went?"

"I do not know that, sir," Pelton said. "But her first name was Marge. Just that. Marge."

"Marge Kennedy," Mike said. "Okay. It's water over the dam but she stood up for my mother when nobody else would. She probably hasn't fared well. I'll see if she's still alive and how she's doing."

"Ms. Marge Kennedy?"

The duplex off South Orange Blossom Trail in Orlando was not in the best neighborhood. It was probably the worst. Terence Porter hadn't been in this rotten of a neighborhood in a good while, if ever.

"If I owe you money, you're trying to get blood from a stone," Marge said, starting to shut the door.

"The opposite, Ms. Kennedy," Porter said. "The opposite."

"Nobody owes me money," Marge said, looking him over.

"My name is Terence Porter, I'm an attorney," Porter said, handing over his card. "I represent Michael Truesdale, who recently inherited the Follet fortune. Did you follow that in the news?"

"I did, yes," Marge said, curiously. "What does that have to do with me?"

"Mr. Truesdale wasn't clear on that," Porter said, "but we are to make arrangements for better conditions for you. He only said that you had been on his mother's side in something and that you were fired for it. As such, while he cannot undo these last years, he would like to ensure that you have a comfortable retirement."

"A Follett male with a soul?" Marge said. "Will wonders never cease..."

"You've got her eyes," Marge said.

"Others have said the same," Mike said over the video link. "You tried to go to bat for my mother and lost. That took courage and caring. That is rarely rewarded but it should be."

"I'm not sure what you know, exactly..." Marge said. In her background, Mike could see spots of black mold on the ceiling, and wallpaper coming apart at the seams on the wall. There were hints of clutter behind and around her.

"Conn raped my mother," Mike said, "then later passed her around like an appetizer tray. I think that was probably after you were fired."

"She'd call me sometimes," Marge said. "I was the closest thing she had to a mom. There wasn't anything I could do."

"Given that you had direct knowledge, I'm frankly surprised you're alive," Mike said. "I was expecting that you'd committed suicide or got caught in a random street shooting or something."

"I don't think I was important enough for them to bother," Marge said, bitterly. "Even if I tried to tell people, I'd figured out long ago there was no one to tell."

"No, there really wasn't," Mike said. "That may be changing but even then, you wouldn't know who to tell."

"I'm not sure what that means," Kennedy said, confused.

"Doesn't matter," Mike said. "If you will, the general idea is this: You should have been able to retire in a semi-middle-class fashion instead of on food stamps. You were there for my mother. You shouldn't be where you are. As I understand it, you have no heirs?"

"Anna was the closest thing I ever had to a child," Marge said. She lowered her gaze sorrowfully.

"I'm sorry," Mike said. "The lady Anna left me with was a six-four black transgender street hooker. I, too, was the only child Mama would ever have. And at least I made it out alive. MS-13 killed her as a way to get at me."

"I'm sorry for you as well," Marge said.

"So, I'll buy a house for you," Mike said. "Somewhere decent. And set up a trust to ensure you have a comfortable life. When you pass, the house will revert. Among other things, that way you don't have to handle all the issues related to a house. But the stipend will be enough so you can travel. As much as you want. Have a decent retirement. Retired quite comfortably instead of poor."

"Thank you," Marge said, trying not to cry. "You're a credit to your mother."

"More than you know," Mike said. "Or, rather, my mother was probably more than you realize. She almost made it out alive as well."

"At least you took the Trust away from Conn," Marge said. "That's something. He was all about the Trust."

"Oh, I'm going to take far more than *that* from Wesley Conn, Ms. Kennedy," Mike said. "We're just getting into the juicier details of the embezzlement that went on. The lawsuits against *all* the Trustees are going to be *legendary*.

"I have said this before, and I'll say it again: I grew up on the street. So, at a certain level I'd very much like to go full Boogie Knight on Wesley Conn. But honestly, I'm hoping Mr. Conn lives a *very* long time. Because I am going to make every single day of the rest of his life miserable. And I won't even *bother* with doing so myself. I'm just going to *delegate* it."

"Mr. Edward Alvard?"

The Follett trustee was just leaving his favorite lunch bistro and wasn't in the mood to deal with some person pestering him to invest. He nonetheless took the proffered papers.

"Why?" Alvard asked.

"You've been served, Mr. Alvard," the process server said. "Good day."

"Wait, what?" Alvard said, opening up the document. "What the hell?"

"It's not just you, Wesley," Bafundo said sitting in Conn's office. This was a discussion to have in person. "It's every trustee and all of the C-suite that were in place since Dela's death."

"That little bastard," Conn said, looking at the suit.

"They found the missing money in record time," Bafundo said. "And they have a point about some of the sales of property."

"There were reasons for that," Conn said, grimacing. "We'll settle."

"I don't think he's planning on that," Bafundo said. "That bastard Brauer says he's planning on taking this all the way to court. And some of the items in the suit are reasonable grounds for charges of embezzlement. And you're about to get calls from all the people who were involved. And I'm not talking about the trustees."

"Mr. Conn," his EA said over the speaker. "Senator Drennen is on line one."

"God *damnit!*" Conn said. "There wasn't supposed to *be* an heir!"

"This is a nightmare," Conn said, then drove the ball straight into the woods. It was a miserable day for golf, with a slight drizzle and too much wind. It also wasn't his favorite course, but he'd booked it on short notice as he needed to clear his head. "FUCK! The Group has to figure out something to do about this. I'm at my wit's end. Losing the Trust was bad enough, but now the little bastard's coming after *me*!"

"The real problem is the trustees, Wesley," Hamlin Devlin said. "Their primaries are not taking the suit well."

"Since he's trying to recover all the money that's missing by taking it out of the hide of anyone who touched it, I think not," Conn said. "Because it trickled over to the primaries. But I got saddled with all those useless scions and diverted all that money to support the Group. So... what is the Group going to do?"

"We're considering that," Fieldstone Holdings' CEO said. "It may be time to call in the big guns. But the problem is, killing him probably won't stop anything. His family could just continue the suit. However, it may be necessary to take that route."

"Good," Conn said. "*Please* kill the little bastard. Even if it doesn't stop the suit, we can get at least a little satisfaction."

"When are you meeting?" Devlin said. "I assume the judge has ordered a settlement meeting."

"Next week," Conn said. "I'll be meeting with them as chief trustee, but a bunch of the other trustees are going to be there."

"That should be interesting," Devlin said. "We need to get this shut down. Do whatever it takes. We will be doing so as well."

"God is building an army," Titanium said.

"God has an army," Mike responded from his command room. "What's with the emergency code?"

"Wow, you *really* know how to make friends," Titanium said. "And, yes, I've heard the chemical facility story."

"Which friends did I make this time?" Mike asked.

"*So* many," Titanium said. "You've now got a hundred million euros on your head, my boy."

"Whaaaaat?" Mike said, grinning. "Get *out*! That's more than what's on Elon Musk! That's in *Faerie Queen* range! Over *my* little lawsuit? Gosh. I am both humbled and... humbled. I would like to thank the Academy... My fifth-grade teacher, Mrs. Summers, who said I'd never amount to anything... *Somebody* is running scared."

In certain circles, how much you were worth dead was a way to determine status. A hundred million euros was a *lot* of status if that was your thing.

And it kinda *was* Mike's thing.

"I'm glad you find this amusing," Titanium said. "But the real problem is that the Society is bringing in their heavy hitter: Stormsurge."

"Oh," Mike said, sobering up a bit. "That's . . . less than good. Unless I can get the drop on her. She's been notoriously hard to find."

"We're keeping an eye out," Titanium said. "They want you taken out before you get to the financials of the trustees. If the judge will let you get them."

"It's going to take time," Mike said. "But the judge isn't Society. They also could take her out."

"And we're watching for that," Titanium said. "We've informed the marshals of the threat as well."

"You can't get anything done without rocking the boat a little," Mike said. "Stormsurge, huh? Well . . . that's a thing. My dad is going to be sooo happy about this . . ."

"Thank you for the meeting, Your Honor," Marshal Garrick said over the video link.

"When the chief marshal of the Court says there's a security issue to discuss, it's stupid to not listen," Judge Teresa Perkins replied. "I try not to be stupid. What's up?"

"It regards the suit *Truesdale v. Follett*," the marshal said. "We have many sources of intelligence, obviously."

"I would hope you would," Judge Perkins said. "I'd expected it to be something about cartels not a suit from an heir."

"We don't have specific information regarding a threat to *you*, Your Honor," Garrick said. "But according to chatter, there are numerous hits landing on Michael Truesdale. It appears someone or someones do not want something to come out from the suit. That in no way should affect your rulings, Your Honor, but you have to be advised of this matter.

"Further, and again, I do not want to affect your rulings in any way, Your Honor, but it is possible that if you rule in certain ways that some of those contracts may be directed at you. Since it appears, as stated, that some persons do not want certain information revealed in this suit. Since that would probably be in discovery by the plaintiff ... We truly do not want to affect your rulings, Your Honor ...."

"That is recognized," Judge Perkins said. "How much *does* it cost to kill a teenage billionaire?"

"Our intel is that there is over a hundred million dollars on his head, Your Honor," Garrick replied.

"A hundred million dollars?" Judge Perkins said, leaning back in her chair. "Oh, my God. That poor kid. That's insane!"

"It indicates the degree to which persons do not wish certain information revealed, Your Honor," Garrick said. "However, our brief is *your* safety, Your Honor, not whatever may or may not be turned up in this suit. As such, and as a purely precautionary matter, we request to assign you a regular security detail. A driver. A marshal bodyguard as well as marshals and NYPD to watch your home. They will be as nonintrusive as possible, but we do consider this to be a legitimate threat situation."

"Not going to turn it down," Judge Perkins said, thoughtfully. "And you think that if I were to, say, rule that a certain person's financial records could be subpoenaed that contracts might be let on me?"

"I do not want to in any way affect your rulings, Your Honor," Garrick said. "But ... yes."

"Hmmm ..." Judge Perkins said. "I suppose it's a bit of a test. As a knee-jerk reaction, I'd like to see what discovery turns up. But that would not be fair to the defense, either. So ... I'll have to consider this at length. And, yes to the bodyguards. That will make my mind clearer on the subject. Thank you for your time and your professionalism, Marshal."

"Your Honor," he said with a nod.

CHAPTER 26

"Sympathy for the Devil" —The Rolling Stones

"Well, that's great to hear," Derrick said. "First thing we need to do is start changing your routine to *no* routine."

They were sitting at the main dining room table of the apartment, which was substantially larger than the kitchen table they'd had in their previous accommodations.

"Not sure that's the right path," Mike said. "If I could explain, sir?"

"Go," Derrick said.

Alger, as always, hovered nearby. Mike had briefly considered asking Alger to leave for this conversation as he had Pelton, but there was really no point since odds were the man already knew full well the details of both the price on Mike's head and the super-assassin who'd taken the contract.

"With my schedule, the obvious time to take me out is while I'm out running," Mike continued. "Just walking along the path, minding your own business, on your phone, I come running past and bam! I'm dead."

"Yes," Derrick said. "Which is *why* you should change your patterns to no pattern."

"Checked Stormsurge's file," Mike said. "She's never done a kill beyond about thirty meters. That's in the fairly standard range. No indications she has Sight. No indications she has increased her range or had *any* training. Which means I *easily* outrange her."

Mike wasn't even telling his father the full range of his Sight, but he'd gotten to the point where he was always scanning around in a roughly hundred-meter sphere, and his maximum range was far, far beyond that. In fact, it had become somewhat common for him to locate and neutralize a robbery, an assault, or even, in one case, a murder somewhere within his range as he traveled through the city.

"And supers are *very* noticeable in Sight. They stand out in a crowd.

"So, I go running along the trail. I see her well away from me, take her out. She's the one who drops."

"That easy," Derrick said.

"Honestly, yes," Mike replied. "Especially if Gondola can spot her before she gets into range. Once we're on her, we won't lose her. Not in New York. Too many cameras."

For dramatic effect, he waved at the expansive windows facing the infamous skyscrapers of Manhattan.

"If we can locate her somewhere, I'll just go there and get vaguely close and take her out. Might even be able to hide the body. Depends. But I've got range on her. She's got a pistol that can't shoot through walls. I've got a Barrett that can shoot through five hundred meters of rock. And the difference is, she *doesn't know* she's outclassed."

"I'm not comfortable with the plan," Derrick said. "It would be better if she had to find you. That way, if your friends *can* find her, you can then attack without warning as you said. But putting yourself out as bait is not a good move. It really isn't. It's not just that you're my son and I'd prefer you alive. Professionally, it's tactically unsound. If you're being hunted, never give your enemy a clean shot if you can possibly avoid it."

Mike turned to Alger.

"Your thoughts?"

Alger politely dipped his chin. "Are not you Americans always saying that the best defense is a good offense? Is that not a term from your American football? On the converse, if you wait around hoping to get shot, you probably will be. So I'm inclined to agree with your father, and not just because I prefer to remain in your employ."

Mike looked back to Derrick and nodded.

"You have a point. So ... ? I need her to be sure I'm in the New York area. And all three of my homes are known."

"Then we move you somewhere else," Derrick said. "This is New

York and you're a billionaire. There are a *million* places for you to be not here. Best bet is to move you around."

"Very well, sir," Mike said. To Alger, he said, "Make the arrangements."

The valet nodded curtly.

"That brings up another issue," Derrick said. "You need a chief of security."

"I agree," Mike said, making a face. "You know all the stuff I'm into. It's going to have to be someone that Gondola clears because a chief of security that doesn't know what his boss is into is not worth the money."

"Since I have a number for them, I can handle that," Derrick said. "And I know a guy . . ."

vv: You forget about your friends so quickly?
mt: Not sure that being close is wise right now. Reasons.
vv: Need to come by the restaurant.
mt: Roger.

"Mikhail!" Feliks Morozov said. "You never call, you never write!"

The Russian mob, Bratva—the Brotherhood—was never popular. Like the Fifth Street Kings, they were respected from fear rather than liking.

Everyone knew they were terrible people. Michael knew they were terrible people. The Faerie Queen knew they were terrible people. But they were also useful and for terrible people they had one small code that meant that Gondola could abide them: No kids, no slaves.

It was a small thing but telling, and it wasn't because of their association with Gondola. From what Michael had heard, back in the nineties one of their low-level guys ran into a situation that sickened him so much that he drew up that personal rule: No kids, no slaves. No trafficking child prostitutes, no forcible prostitution, no forcible trafficking, period.

Which was better than, for example, MS-13, which was all those.

As that guy rose through the ranks, generally by killing everyone who disagreed, he enforced that rule across the Bratva groups he controlled. Anyone who disagreed either kept it to themselves or got the choppy chop.

Eventually, he ended up running the main Russian mob. He had since semi-retired—from what Michael had gleaned. His heir in the position was even more determined to maintain the rule. They both hated child traffickers and slavers with an unbounded passion.

Since Bratva operations stretched across much of the globe, they were useful allies to Gondola. Gondola's weapons caches were often supplied by Bratva. They also provided forgery services. Occasionally, it had been Bratva teams that showed up at an orphanage that was having problems, and Gondola orphanages in Russia were under their direct protection. Those were the interactions that Michael *knew* about from being involved in ops. There were probably more.

Gondola worked in the shadows because pretty much every government on *Earth* had, at one time or another, tried to ferret them out and eliminate them as a "terrorist organization." A "terrorist organization" that had informed pretty much every government on Earth of an upcoming terrorist attack and even stopped several personally. The Society had originally just seen Gondola as a thorn in their side. As time had gone by they'd begun to view them as legitimate competition. So, every government and administration they controlled was anti-Gondola despite the good that Gondola did. Gondola had informed the FBI *and* the CIA about 9/11 to the point of locating the terrorists *in the United States* before they found out, years later, that both groups had leadership working *with* Atta and UBL.

And pretty much every government on earth had also, at one time or another, come to them for help. The Society had come to them for help and if it was for the good of the world, they helped. It was like that in the shadows.

You found allies where you could.

In the case of Feliks Morozov, head of Bratva on the East Coast, Mike had been authorized to reveal that he was part of Gondola, which was beyond unusual. But he was bringing Morozov intel that the prostitute he had gotten pregnant years before, Nataliya Komarova, had been killed by the late chief of security of the Follett Trust, Eric Bear, to provide tissue samples to be substituted for Annabelle Follett's. Morozov had had a vasectomy and had never expected to have a child. And with the killing of Nataliya, while she was pregnant, he never would.

He was less than pleased about both the killing and why. Which was why he'd arranged for Bear to end up chained to a ceiling in Flushing. After which he and Mike had taken their time beating the former SEAL to death.

Beating an enemy to death is a very bonding experience. He was clearly less than happy that Mike hadn't checked in since he returned to New York.

They were meeting in his office, which was over an upscale Russian restaurant in Brighton Beach, Brooklyn. It wasn't quite the offices of the lawyers and financial advisors he'd been working with, but it did have its charm in an old, Mafia boss sort of way. It was filled with older, classic wooden furniture and it was well kept without any clutter.

"Feliks," Mike said. He'd worn one his nicer suits, cravat and all, to better blend in with the clientele. "Now that it's known I'm distantly associated with Bear, if we were seen together, it might raise questions you don't want."

"Or *you* don't want?" Morozov said. "Big-shot *billionaire*! Fucking oligarchs are all the same."

"Pfff," Mike said. "*Vor, ukravshiy dve kopeyki, poveshen. Vor, ukravshiy poltinnik, khvalitsya!*" *A thief who stole two kopecks is hanged. A thief who stole fifty kopecks is bragging.* "Who is going to accuse a billionaire and super of beating to death the former SEAL who killed his mother? But *many* would accuse a Russian man of many businesses."

"True," Morozov said.

"I'm still a friend," Mike said. "You were a friend when I was in need. You remain a friend. I don't forget a comrade."

"There are things to discuss," Morozov said. "Vodka?"

"Please," Mike said. "If we're not drinking, I know I'm in trouble."

"You *are* in trouble, my friend," Morozov said, pouring drinks for three. "Big trouble. But not with me."

"The contracts?" Mike said, smiling. "You going to put neo-ket in the vodka? Be careful. Getting it on your hands will kill you."

"You heard?" Feliks said, handing him a glass. "You've got more money on your head than my boss. He's pissed about that. 'How do I get that many rich people to try to kill *me*?'"

"Open a lawsuit that has the potential to kick up a lot of dirt," Mike said.

"How bad is it?" Valerian asked.

Valerian Vadik was five foot nine, 170 pounds, with blue eyes and black hair. He was the Bratva executive in charge of New York operations and as such the heir apparent to the East Coast.

"The bounty?" Mike said. "So far up to a hundred million euros. *Prosit!*" he added, downing the vodka. "Aaah...wish this had *any* effect at all."

"A hundred million?" Valerian said. "My God. My friend, I would *gladly* kill you for *far* less!"

"As I would kill you for a kopek, Valerian," Mike said, toasting him with his empty glass. "We're such good friends."

He picked up the bottle of Belvedere and poured another drink. For a super it was like drinking slightly tasty water. The Russians hated that a thirteen-year-old could drink them under the table.

"The contracts are not all," Feliks said. "Stormsurge is heading to town."

"Do you know when and where?" Mike asked.

"No," Feliks said. "Not yet. But we got the word that she is coming to New York. And you may not be the only target."

"You?" Mike asked.

"They may have an idea who killed Bear," Feliks said with a shrug. "It is not Bear that is the issue. It's Conn. They protect him still. Moscow won't clear killing him."

"Leave Conn to me," Mike said. "As to Stormsurge, leave her to me as well. Conn...*please* don't kill him."

"He needs to die, Mikhail," Feliks said, his face hard. "For what he did he *will* die."

"Yes, but not *yet*, Feliks," Mike said, clasping his hands in prayer. "Be *patient*. Death is less to be feared by someone like Conn than being *nothing*. And I intend to make him *nothing* before he dies.

"I have taken the Trust from him. The lawsuits will take far more. He will find he has no friends when all of this is exposed. *And* I know where his offshore accounts are, Feliks. So, when he tries to flee... suddenly his secret money will...poof! Disappear! And the Trust? Half the politicians in New York and Albany who are in the pocket of the Society had family as trustees. I am going to be investigating all of *them* as well to see where my family money went.

"And since I should be able to dig into *their* finances, that means when my money went to their corrupt senator and congressman and governor brothers- and sisters-in-law and parents . . . I get to dig into *their* finances . . ."

"*Boze moi*," Valerian said, laughing. "You *can't* be serious! Going after all of them? One hundred million isn't *enough*!"

"I cannot *wait* to *personally* serve Senator Drennen," Mike said, grinning. "Of course, I'll let the process server handle it. But I want to be there to *watch*."

"And I thought *I* played a dangerous game," Morozov said, shaking his head. "You really love making enemies, don't you?"

"The more powerful the better," Mike said. "So far, they have sent one of the top criminals in the world—after yourself, of course—after me. Tried to destroy me in the court of public opinion. Tried to defame me. And we haven't even *started* the defamation suits. And now they're sending a super-assassin. Who, with luck, will simply disappear.

"Disappearing Stormsurge is more frightening than some big battle in the streets. Evil will never love me. Let it fear me."

"I am suddenly glad we are friends," Valerian said.

"What do you think of your houses?" Feliks said, pouring himself another drink.

"Gah!" Mike said. "Speaking of *evil* . . ."

"Father," Mike said, shaking his hand. "Come on in."

After dinner with the archbishop and a monsignor, Mike had been assigned a personal father confessor. The Church liked to do that sort of thing with billionaires when it could.

Father Samuel Constanza was Argentinian and, as requested, had extensive experience working with Catholic Relief Services. When asked, he'd admitted that he'd joined the priesthood about the time the last pope was elected, but he knew people who knew him.

Father Constanza had been informed of the various bodies scattered around the house and the manse. Mike hadn't checked the rest of the houses on the estate, yet. Alger and some hired security were busy moving out the occupants.

But it was time to manage the bodies in the house. To finally put them to rest. And the father agreed that such actions didn't need to come to the attention of authorities.

Mike led the way down to the wine cellar and walked to what looked to be just another section of wall. Then he opened up the wall using Stone Shape to reveal a small cell. There were crumbled bones and bits of cloth in the compartment. It also released a whiff of foul air.

"Can you tell anything about . . . them?" Father Constanza said, squatting down.

"Female, lower teens," Mike said. "Poor nutrition. I don't think she was part of the Follett family. Probably a servant. I'm going with scullery maid. And from the fact that her pelvic girdle is slightly separated, I'm going with she got pregnant, and this was the easiest way to deal with it. Just say she ran off and disappeared."

"May God have mercy on her soul," Constanza said, softly and shaking his head.

"The question becomes, how do we handle her appropriately?" Mike asked. "I can just burn the bones. I have that power. Or they can be placed in consecrated ground. If that can be arranged."

"Burn them," Father Constanza said after a moment. "After due ceremony and consecration. I wish we knew her name."

"She's not the only one."

"*In nomine Patris et Filii et Spiritus Sancti,*" Father Constanza said, crossing himself at the Satanic temple in the basement of the Manse. "Oh, good Lord. This needs an exorcist not a counselor."

"Have faith, Father," Mike said, looking around. "The question is, can I take out all the stones and get rid of them? The altar is easy enough."

He started by simply morphing the altar like clay until all the engraved, horrific, carvings were gone. He lifted the ball of rock out up to expose the small crypt underneath and the bones of the victim.

"I'm guessing that was the sacrifice that desanctified the place," Mike said, clinically. "Another female victim. Young teen. Caucasian. Again, not in good health. No spreading to the pelvic girdle so had not been pregnant at any time."

"Virgin sacrifice," Father Constanza said.

"There are old records around," Mike said. "Most of them burned with the fire in 1868. But there are a few around. I think this chamber dates from the original house. So . . . finding record of her will be tough."

"Well, let's get her to her final resting place," Father Constanza said. "What about . . . ?" he said, looking around at the carvings.

"They're all stone," Mike said, wiping the horrific images away with

Stone Shape. "I'll get rid of the actual stones later. For now, let's get this poor girl some peace."

They'd gathered all the bones at the house and the manse. There were even a few at the secondary houses he could now See with his longer ranged Sight. None of them looked to be less than fifty years buried. There was no point in bringing in authorities. All of the criminals who'd murdered them were long dead and with any luck burning in hell. That definitely included his great grandfather.

It was just a matter of what to do with the bones.

They took them down by the water at the estate. There, Father Constanza said a prayer for them, then Mike held them out over the water and applied Earth Heat. In a few moments, there was barely ash left, which scattered as dust in the wind.

"Ashes to ashes, dust to dust," Father Constanza said.

"We are all made from stardust," Mike said. "Let them be lifted to the arms of Jesus. Let them return to the stars."

"Amen."

"Are you *sure* about burning these?" Alger said, looking at the pile of modern art. "There's, combined, nearly a half a million dollars' worth of artwork here, sir."

Mike thought about the "artwork" in the Satanic temple in the basement. Not all art was good art.

"I'm not sure what you use as a measure of evil," Mike said, looking at the art. "But there's at least a billion sins in that pile."

He applied Earth Heat to the pile and watched it burn.

"This is *literally* good riddance to bad rubbish," Mike said. "I probably should have done it with *all* the postmodernist crap because it was *all* rubbish. Just not evil rubbish."

Mike didn't feel the oppressive weight at the family mausoleum this time. He wasn't sure if that was because the major demonic presence had taken off or because of what he was carrying. Or that it took off because of what he was carrying.

He had put the bone of Fortunato in his personal safe at the apartment until it was time. Now it was time to take it to its final resting place.

He stood in front of the small niche that held his mother's ashes.

"Mother," Mike said. "Annabelle. I'm sorry for everything that happened to you. I'm sorry I couldn't be there to help but, hell, I wasn't even born, yet. And I'm especially sorry for all the things I said about you when I was a kid. Mama was right—you never know why people are the way they are on the street. But . . . I'll pray for you every day."

As he was speaking to her, he started to feel the presence again. A weight of depression dropped on him, a feeling like he had no worth and no purpose and he started to get enraged at . . . well . . . everything. The death of Mama. His mother's death. All the hurts he'd suffered in his life. It was everyone's fault. Everyone needed to pay. He just needed to be powerful enough to make them all pay.

Being enraged at what had happened to his mother was fairly normal. When it came to grief, he tended to get stuck on rage. But he also knew that this wasn't his normal anger. He was having a hard time breathing again. Starting to full-on see red.

Yeah, well, time to summon some *righteous* anger.

He reached into his pocket, withdrew the bone, held it up over his head and released his full aura.

It was bright and very large. His power had increased enormously. It was probably going to be noticeable to other homes in the area and was certainly visible to boats on the Long Island Sound.

"*Digitus Sancti Fortunati. Hoc os Michaeli tenetur. In nomine Domini nostri Jesu Christi Michael hic adesto, patroni et patroni mei Fortunati! In nómine Patris et Fílii et Spiritus Sancti, relinquáte locum istum servum Satanae!*" *Finger of St. Fortunatus. This is the mouth of Michael. In the name of our Lord Jesus Christ, Michael, be present here, my patron and patron Fortunatus! In the name of the Father and of the Son and of the Holy Spirit, leave this place, servant of Satan!*

He felt the weight fall away. The anger faded and he felt that feeling like a live wire again. He turned off his aura, wondering just how noticeable it had been.

"Thank you, Lord," Mike said, opening up the niche that his mother's ashes were in. He recited the Our Father as he opened up the urn his mother's ashes were in and carefully laid the precious bone on top of them.

"Lord, I ask that you allow this relic of Fortunato, fallen champion of the Faerie Queen, protect this place from all unclean spirits from this time to the End of Times. Bind this place to Your Name. I ask this in the name of your Son, Jesus Christ the Risen Savior. That the angels reside here in peace and harmony from now until the End of Times. And I beg, Lord, that you allow my mother entrance into heaven. She suffered greatly in this life and may not have known the love of your Son. But . . . she protected her child, and *he* knows your Son's name. In Jesus' Name I pray. Amen."

He closed the niche and looked up.

"Thank you as well, Michael," Mike said. "And parenthetically, I cannot imagine a better thing than to be a curse upon all evil even *after* your death. Amen."

New York Post: UFOS IN GLEN COVE?

CHAPTER 27

"Citadel" —The Crüxshadows

"These issues you raise are simply paperwork," Larry Packard said.

The conference room was large, with an obnoxiously long table in the center, and every single seat was occupied. Beyond that, the room roughly matched every other large conference room they'd been in for all the other various legal proceedings going back several weeks.

The fine firm of Bruck, Kadish, Packard and Ulmer was back for the suit entitled *Michael Truesdale v. the Follett Trust et al.* Packard was the lead counsel and representing Conn while the same firm represented about a third of the named defendants. The rest were represented by a motley collection of the dregs of the legal industry.

The Trust had twenty-five trustees. Three were "management trustees" who ran the day-to-day business, whatever it was. Those were Conn, chief trustee; Douglas Spoon, the comptroller; and Robert Engle, chief of operations.

In addition, there were twenty-two Joe Blow trustees. Those members of the Trust were supposed to be keeping an eye on the management trustees to ensure they didn't divert or peculate funds and put them in a Cayman Island account, just as a random example. For that, they were paid five thousand dollars a month and required to appear at quarterly meetings of the Trust to go over the books. If they suspected anything they were authorized to call an audit while large actions on the part of the Trust, such as selling off most of the Follett assets, required their vote.

Each of those persons was supposed to be fine, upstanding citizens of the State of New York who were carefully selected for their trustworthiness.

The reality was that each of them was selected for their relationship to some politician. As an example, Edward Alvard was the brother-in-law of Senator Tara Drennen, currently ranking member of the Super Affairs Committee as well as a senior member of the US Senate Finance Committee. It was that relationship rather than the fairly unimportant Super Affairs that got her brother-in-law a job as a trustee.

And Mike knew, via Gondola, that part of the deal was, in most cases, they had to kick back some of the money to their primaries. The Big Guy gets ten percent sort of deal.

Politicians made money on big book deals, sure. Book deals financed by publishing companies controlled by the Society. And that was nice money. But the real day-to-day cash was in little deals like this one. Every month the BIL drops you a thousand here or there from the positions they've got that don't require any real work.

And while the IRS would go after somebody like Pirate Bill because he didn't report a two-hundred-dollar sale in his Etsy shop, woe betide the IRS auditor who asked some US senator about the ten thousand in cash she dropped in the bank. And those nice clothes? Oh, they're paid for by the campaign. You've got to look good to be a senator.

"Selling an estate valued at five hundred million dollars for one and a quarter is hardly a paperwork error," Ahuvit replied. "An estate, I might add, that was in the Follett Family's possession from the *foundation of Palm Beach!*"

"That's no reason to sue *my* client!" one of the attorneys down the table shouted.

"The purpose of trustees is to watch the actions of the managers," Counselor Wilder said. "There is a great deal of value missing from the Trust. It was *your* client's job to ensure that value did not flee. They therefore failed in their job and are therefore liable for that missing money..."

Mike wasn't paying any attention to the arguments. Ahuvit had assigned a partner to each of the trustees to handle the back-and-forth.

He was sitting across from Conn, wearing the best suit he could get tailored in time for the meeting, signature cravat in place. Gone was the façade of being some ignorant kid from the ghetto. He wasn't saying anything in this meeting, either. But he also wasn't playing on his phone. He was staring at Conn like a scientist examining a bug under a microscope.

This time, in a delightful swtich, Conn was actively avoiding making eye contact with Mike. He was also holding his tongue and letting his legal counsel do all the talking.

"What, kid, you don't think you inherited enough money?!" Maryann Cummins, one of the trustees, yelled furiously. "You grew up in a ghetto! A bunch of nice houses not enough for you? You want to take food from the mouths of my children!"

Mike put his hand on Ahuvit's arm.

"When my mother was murdered, she had stretch marks, Ms. Cummins," Mike replied, calmly, continuing to look at Conn. "My grandmother was sure there was an heir. Part of the bylaws of the Trust was a requirement to search for an heir. Are you aware of that, Ms. Cummins?"

"That doesn't give you the right!"

"When I was *seven*, I was in a foster home where the foster parents were deliberately starving us to *death*," Mike said, cutting her off. "The other two children in the house *died*. I spent three months mostly locked in a closet with Toby and Lavonne.

"They would scratch at the door over and over again, please, please, please. Please what? Please give us some food? Please let us out? It was just that word over and over. Please, please, please...

"I would sit at the back of the closet with my arms wrapped around my knees, just staring at the wall. I refused to give those psycho bastards an inch.

"That was in 2018," Mike said, still calmly, still staring at Conn. "During the same time period, you took the Trust's jet to a conference in Kauai on climate change, Ms. Cummins. The date was the twenty-sixth of May when you left, in case you don't recall. You returned on the thirtieth. You were accompanied by four persons who were not listed in the manifest other than as 'adult female.' The cost of the use of the jet, both ways, not including the deadhead waiting for you to be done with your conference, was one hundred and ninety-six thousand dollars.

"What, precisely, was the Trust's purpose of using *my* jet to fly to

Kauai? In what way did it *enhance* the funds in the Trust, your legal duty? In what way did it *protect* the funds in the Trust, your legal duty? In what way did it advance the *purpose* of the Trust, which was to protect and increase the funds in the Follett Trust while searching for an heir? What Trust *purpose* was there to take your gal pals to Kauai? Did you think maybe I was hiding out in a five-star resort? Under the counter in the marble bathroom, perhaps, Ms. Cummins?"

He finally turned and looked at her with dark eyes.

"If you were looking for me, Ms. Cummins, you were looking for me in the wrong place," he said. "I was in *Baltimore* locked in a *closet* being starved to *death*. Toby and Lavonne *died* of starvation. While *you* flew overhead on your way to Hawaii . . . in *my* jet . . ."

"God is building an army," Mike said.

"God has an army," Titanium replied. "She's heeere. Or rather, she's there. In New York."

"Do we have a location?" Mike asked.

"We do indeed," Titanium said. "She's at a condo in Greenwich Village."

"What about the body?" Mike said. "Another international wanted criminal turning up in New York would raise a *bunch* of questions. Especially as dead as I'll need to make her."

"Take her out and the rest is taken care of," Titanium said. "And it will be a very nice contribution to the cause. There's nearly as much on her as on you. And unlike the reward money, it's wanted dead. She's killed a bunch of people who have survivors who are pissed and have money."

"That can be arranged," Mike said. "I just need an address and a car. Oh, and I need the Vishnu to clear it. They hate it when supers fight supers."

You are sure that her purpose is to assassinate Stone Tactical?
Yes, Lord of Time. This is verified.
We do not need to lose Vishnu. The Storm is Coming. Even one such as Stormsurge might be of use. But . . . Approved.

MT: Going to dinner at one.
VV: Have a good time.

⊕ ⊕ ⊕

Mike tapped on the keys of the burner.

MT: **The mango is in town. Going to go pick it up. Okay?**
DS: **Okay.**

He didn't really *have* to ask his dad for permission to take out an assassin, but it was nice to have a dad who cared.

"Have you found him, yet?" Adina Rumapea, aka Stormsurge, said. "I was told this was going to be a quick in and out."

"He's changed his pattern. Definitely not at any of his residences. We think he's in hiding. He may know you're in town."

"If he knows I'm in town, the authorities may know as well," Adina said. "I'm not interested in taking on Super Corps."

"There's nothing on the FBI database. You're clear so far. We'll move you if that changes and we'll inform you the minute we locate him. Worse comes to worst, he'll be doing a patrol. Easy enough there."

"Okay," Adina said, sighing. "Cash ya later."

She hung up the burner and took *Real Housewives of Beverly Hills* off mute.

"What? Are you kidding me? Oh, *demi Tuhan! Tembak saja anjingnya!" Oh, for God's sake! Just shoot the dog!*

"Stop here," Mike said. He had the target locked. There were no other supers in the area, and it was definitely the right condo. Female. Bone structure of someone of Indonesian background.

She seemed agitated. He was pretty sure he was out of range. So, it shouldn't be about him.

He focused on her brain and applied Earth Move to the elements in it. She dropped immediately. Whatever had her shaking her fist at the TV was no longer an issue. Then he kept moving Earth. Supers tended to come back from the dead.

He juggled the water in her head around a little bit. Probably what she was going to do to him.

"She's down," he said. "She's not getting up as long as I've got this, but I'm not sure she's *absolutely* dead. We're hard to permanently kill."

"Got that," the driver said, sending a text.

⊕ ⊕ ⊕

Ramon keyed in the code and entered the condo. The super-assassin was on the floor with blood coming out of her ears, eyes, and nose.

He'd been informed it was going to be a clean kill, but he had the materials to handle this.

First, he very carefully removed the syringe with the overlong needle normally used for injecting adrenaline into a heart and inserted it into her eye until it stopped. Then, he injected approximately enough neo-ketamine to kill a herd of elephants. Her brain had just become a toxic waste dump.

He sent a text, laid out the plastic sheeting, and started putting on full PPE...

"We're clear," the driver said, starting the car.

"Roger," Mike said, settling back. That syringe probably *wasn't* a knockout dose of fentanyl.

MT: Dinner was short. Vodka?
VV: Bottle's on me.

"Can you drop me in Brighton Beach?" Mike asked.
"No problem."

"Introductions, Alger?"

Alger had managed to find a selection of experienced estate and house managers as well as housekeepers drawn from Vaishnava. It was time to meet the new help. They were assembled for a fairly formal meeting at the apartment.

"I'll start with Mr. Khopkar," Alger said. "Former assistant estate manager to a family in India."

"Vishnu," Mr. Khopkar said, bowing. "It is an honor to serve."

"Thank you," Mike said. He extended his aura and touched the man's forehead with light. "May this light your path upon the wheel."

Each of them was introduced with a brief résumé. It was a well-trained and experienced group.

"Please," Mike said, gesturing to a set of chairs. "Sit."

Pelton laid out a selection of drinks and offered them around.

"The first thing I need to touch upon is matters of the Vishnu," Mike said. "Unlike any other American super, I am graced by the

Vishnu with their knowledge of the Powers. Why that is, is complicated and I'm going to have to be somewhat reticent. But no other American supers—at least none that I know of—can extend their aura. Aura shape is a Vishnu practice.

"So, on that matter, one can say I am true Vishnu," Mike continued. "I practice my powers, have a Vishnu guide, a journeyman of the House of Earth, and daily prepare myself for the Storm that I might protect mortals against its rigors.

"Then there is the bit where I am not Vishnu," Mike said. "Or, rather, I am not Vaishnava. I am Christian in my beliefs. And while there is congruence in the matter of the One True Creator, there are differences and I need to touch on this lightly. I *am* an eater of unclean meats."

"Unclean meats" in Vaishnava related directly to beef. Cattle were sacred in the Vaishnava religion and their slaughter for meat was not just unclean, it was abomination.

"That is understood and recognized, sir," Mr. Khopkar said. "We were informed in advance and accepted the position knowing that. While each of us is practicing Vaishnava . . . it is different for Vishnu. The Vishnu are assured of Nirvana. They have been lifted off the wheel. You're literally a *god* in our religion, sir. What the gods do is up to *them*. It's not our place to judge the Vishnu, sir. It's the other way around."

"Okay," Mike said. "I just really do not want to offend."

"I worked for the English, sir," Eshana Jain said. She was the designated housekeeper for the town house. "It's nothing but grilled beef all day and night. I can handle it."

"Most of us have worked for non-Vaishnava, sir," Mohan Handoo added. He was going to be the house manager of the manse. His wife, Ananta, was taking the position of housekeeper for the manse. "It is truly an honor to work for Vishnu, sir. Usually only priests get to. And it is recognized that Vishnu live their lives as they please. And, as with all bosses, what goes on in the homes stays in the homes. Given that you are a Vishnu and can not only strike down our mortal bodies but cast us to the lowest place on the wheel . . . loyalty is assured, sir."

Mike could think of no good way to respond to that. He naturally had no intent to ever strike down anyone's mortal bodies and cast them to the lowest place on the wheel—except maybe Conn, of course, or an assassin like Storm Surge, or a pedophile, or . . . The point was, he would never, ever do that to a servant, even one found to be disloyal. But it really didn't seem his place to say that, so he truly had no idea what to say. The amount of power he wielded was increasing exponentially, and it was starting to frighten him.

"Okay," Mike said, nodding awkwardly. "That out of the way...My father and I are going to be staying in New York for a while, sorting some stuff out. Then we'll be going to Montana for a portion of the summer. Given that I was not accepted this year to Osseo, I'll be taking remote courses to try to get ahead of the curve. I'll also be doing business and various other activities. How much I'll be in New York, I'm unsure. So...the houses may not be in regular use.

"But they still need people to take care of them. And to ensure that nobody messes with them in my absence. I'm mostly holding onto the properties because I consider them a legacy. They've been in the family a long time."

He considered what to say, then shrugged.

"Because it doesn't translate exactly, I'm going to use Western terms," Mike said. "I am, besides being a Believer in the One True God, a believer in angels and demons and that they have effect on this world. Old homes, old estates tend to build up negative influences. These are primarily due to demonic presences. In the case of the Follett family, there were *definite* demonic presences in all the homes.

"I've had some very powerful spiritualists cleanse them all. They should be clear. If you sense or suspect anything along the lines, contact me. There should be no trace of so much as ghosts left. And as a Vishnu I've sealed all the homes against unclean influences. So, shouldn't be an issue. But if there is one, contact me directly. I need to keep these things out. They corrupt. All clear?"

"Clear, sir," Mr. Khopkar said. "And appreciated."

"Oh, could you do the same for Lord Maunton's estate, sir?" Eshana asked. "It would be *very* much appreciated."

"Given that Lord Maunton is himself a bit demonic," Mike said. "It would be difficult."

"You've *met* his lordship..."

"What do you mean she's *disappeared*?" Conn said, angrily. It was a beautiful day and he was back on his favorite golf course, but none of that could do anything to improve his horrendously sour mood.

"To be clearer, we have information she is *deceased*," Devlin said, considering his lie. "Gondola has been collecting the bounty on her. Bounties. Including half price from her Interpol notice. They are nearly as high as the price on Truesdale."

"How the *hell* do you take out a super?" Conn asked.

"Presumably with another super," Devlin said. "Our working theory is that it was Vishnu. We'd avoided using her for an attack on a super. The Vishnu don't take well to that."

"If it was the Vishnu, then why is Gondola collecting the money?" Conn asked.

"Probably acting as a go-between," Devlin said. "Or possibly the Vishnu contributed it to them." He took the swing and sliced. "Fuck! Now this little bastard is ruining *my* game. That simply won't do. The suit is bad enough. The immediate issue is what he is going to do with my stock. The quarter was off. Badly. We just need him to hold it 'til next quarter..."

"Welcome to the party everyone," Mike said over the video link.

The town house had a completely different feel, now. Gone was that feeling that made his shoulder blades itch. It just felt *lighter*. After a thorough mystic scrubbing from Sister Beulah, her prayer warriors, and a small horde of nuns and monks provided by the Church, the ghosts and demons had sought opportunities elsewhere.

On the other hand, it was still mostly unfurnished. Pretty much the entire furnishings had been moved out along with all the art pieces save two. They were both postmodernist but uncharacteristically light and kind in spirit.

An interior decorator was finding furnishings that would fit the look Mike had requested, traditional American, while an art buyer was keeping an eye out for classic pieces of art.

One thing that had made it in was another bank of screens and servers. Mr. Fulmer had been hard at work on installations even before the house was mystically cleared. Since Mike didn't drink and neither did his father, most of the wine in the wine cellar had been moved to the manse and the racks cleared out. They were replaced by server racks. It would be a cooling issue in the summer but during the winter it would reduce the need for heating in the house.

The main work area in the basement had been set up as a trading pit.

Not the sort that you saw on a trading floor but the same sort of arrangement that was used by traders in houses. It was conformable to the user and could be used for a variety of trading. In addition, there were screens for communication and others that kept up with news flow.

The news feed was from Gondola, a paid service that was available only to a select few. It was one of their sources of income and the nice thing about it was that it was as perfectly accurate as was humanly possible. Mike had worked the feed desk and knew that was the primary purpose. No propaganda, no spin. Just the best information possible. It also covered intelligence information only available to most nation-states.

The news feed cost more than the price of the servers and business trading software to support them. Because information is power, and it was worth more.

Nation-states hated it because there was no spin and frequently it uncovered things they'd prefer nobody know.

A United States Air Force B-52 on a routine training mission was, again, spotted with nuclear weapons in place of conventional cruise missiles. The plane was returned to base and the nuclear weapons removed without incident or public report.

Analysis: This is the first such incident in nine years and indicates that the USAF is again failing in accurate inventory of special versus conventional systems. No such issue has been observed with the US Navy. Anticipate relief of the regional USAF commanders involved.

The Chinese Red Army is preparing to perform training missions in the Xunxi region.

Analysis: The mountains in that region are very similar to those found in interior Taiwan. This should be viewed as an advanced preparation for invasion.

The Russian Army has moved to concentrate the 38th Division in Kamakala.

Analysis: Kamakala is closer to sources of food than their previous base in Novy Birsk. The Russian Army continues its slow degradation in logistics capability that started during the Ukraine War. At this point it can barely feed its soldiers in garrison. It should be rated at a capability comparable to North Korea.

Intercepts indicate ISIS is planning a terrorist attack in the region of Turkey. Details are sketchy and relative nation-states have been informed ...

Mike had access to it. He hadn't been allowed to pass it to his people.

"Today we begin the slow process of rebuilding my family's fortune," Mike said. "And it's going to be fun. We ready?"

"Ready as we'll ever be," Benjamin said.

"Do we drop at the opening bell?" Mike asked.

"Around ten A.M.," Rick Smallwood said. He was the designated stock trader from Asuda for Mike's account. "Dropping two million hard will depress the stock price. You're not going to get as much as you would trickling it out. But it's going to have the effect you want. And we'll make it back on the short."

"I'm looking at intel you're not," Mike said. "So, there may be times that I call a ball. My father has signed off on that. But most of it is up to you. I'll wait for the drop."

"Opening bell coming up," Benjamin said. "The options are all in place."

"Then let us begin ..."

CHAPTER 28

"Another One Bites the Dust" —Queen

"Ten o' five," Rick said. "Clear the sell."

"Cleared," Benjamin said.

"Dropping," Rick replied.

Mike was standing before the array of screens in his new command center, watching a dozen different feeds as well as several financial news shows. He could see when the two million shares of Fieldstone hit the market. The stock price immediately tanked and kept going down. He'd lost about five percent of the value by dropping it hard. He'd make that up today.

"Short Xinju Pharmaceuticals," Mike said.

"What?" Rick said.

"Sending the short order," Mike said. "It's about to drop."

"Your call," Rick said.

"Yes, it is," Mike said.

Before it was time to short Fieldstone, a fire in the primary factory of Xinju Pharmaceuticals in Taipei hit the news. The stock immediately dropped.

Mike sent an order to activate the short and move position to shorting Fieldstone.

He preferred to buy low and sell high, but right now shorts were the position to take.

He settled back in his very comfortable chair and prepared to make a *lot* of money. And, along the way, hammer some of his enemies in the shorts. Pun intended.

"Never fuck with a Folet-*T*," he muttered.

"WHAT . . . THE . . . FUUUUCK?!" Hamlin Devlin screamed. "I THOUGHT YOU SAID HE WAS GOING TO *PARCEL IT OUT*?"

"That's what he *said* he'd do!"

Smiley Garrett was not enjoying being on the receiving end of the CEO's ire.

The quarterly announcement had been a disaster. That little bastard Truesdale's dump of stock had been perfectly timed. Then a nearly billion leveraged short had hit.

The announcement, just minutes later, that Fieldstone had had a bit of an off quarter had caused the stock price to continue to drop like a meteor. Investors were dumping Fieldstone to the point that the automatic holds had kicked in. Large investors who had their money managed by Fieldstone had been calling all day long, asking if Fieldstone was going bankrupt.

"Then that's a violation of implicit contract," Devlin snarled. "We'll sue the *hell* out of him!"

"They're going to sue you, you realize?" Benjamin said, sipping champagne. Mike could hear scattered cheering in the background, as well as the *pop* of yet another bottle.

Mike was now very close to a *two* billionaire in one day of hard trading. He'd be able to keep all three houses, that's for sure. He needed to build something in Montana. Something small and homey, on the order of Versailles.

"That is what lawyers are for," Mike said. "And the SEC is going to get involved. We knew that would happen. But it was a very good day. Park all but two hundred million in T-bills. I'm going to keep going. There are markets opening in Asia."

"Sir," Mr. Khopkar said. "There is a Mr. Devlin on the video link. He requests a word."

"Oh, I'm sure he wants more than one," Mike said. "Put him through and keep Mr. Goldblatt in the loop. You do want in, don't you, Benjamin?"

"Wouldn't miss it for worlds," Benjamin said, raising his glass.

"Mr. Devlin!" Mike said as the CEO connected. "To what do I owe the honor of actually *speaking* to the *CEO* of *Fieldstone*?! Squeee! *So* honored."

"If you think I'm going to take this shit lying down, think again, you little bastard!" Devlin said. He was alone in the video with a large picture of the Wall Street bull on the wall behind him. However, muted mumbling and shadows shifting around his sides indicated there were several other people in the room with him.

"Just honest trade, Mr. Devlin," Mike said. "Honest trade."

"You engaged in a verbal contract to maintain your stock and trickle it out!" Devlin said. "*That's* a violation of contract!"

"I did no such thing," Mike said, calmly.

"I've got an executive vice president who says different!"

"Were you *in* that conversation, Mr. Devlin?" Mike asked.

"You know who I'm talking about!" Devlin snarled.

"Yes, the redoubtable Smiley Garrett," Mike said. "But you were not *present*, were you? Nor even so much as a managing director. Just an EVP for someone who was about to inherit two million shares of stock. What, you couldn't even bother with a *handshake*? Too busy schmoozing senators?

"As to Mr. Garrett's statement, it is in error. I didn't even *imply* I would trickle it out. That was stated to be *one* of a *gamut* of options, Mr. Devlin. You'd have *known* that if you were at the dinner. But you were not, were you?"

"You're saying he's lying?" Devlin said, angrily.

"I'm saying he is mistaken," Mike said. "I'm sure he thinks I said that I'd trickle it out. Wait a moment."

"I don't have a..."

Mike clicked a file on his screen and shared it to the video meeting. The picture was cut to one of Smiley Garrett sitting across from Mike at the Odeon.

> "But the issue is the stock. I have to get rid of approximately half to pay taxes. More, but it will leave me with about one million shares. I was serious about one thing, which is that you should always have a distributed portfolio. Not tied up entirely in any one thing or firm. That's simply good financial sense. That Conn et al. put all of it into one basket is terrible management. I don't care what basket that may be.

"Generally, it's advised that you only have at most twenty percent in one basket. So, at the end of the day, I'll probably only hold at most two hundred thousand shares. Ten percent of current. At most."

"So, how are you planning on disposing of them?"

"That will be up to my pater familias. I'm a minor."

"Who will be consulting financial advisors. As well as my son who has, obviously, some knowledge of this field. As do I. I have a distributed portfolio—small but I do have one. I was investing while I was in the Army."

"Note my repeated 'at most,'" Mr. Devlin.

"You recorded the whole *dinner*?" Devlin said, turning purple.

"I frequently do, Mr. Devlin," Mike said. "I'm recording *this* call. Sunshine is the best disinfectant. But you'll note that neither I nor my father expressly stated that we were going to hold *any* of your stock. That I said I would hold, at most, two hundred thousand shares. I did not *promise* to hold *any*. At most. And when asked specifically how it was to be disposed of, my father adroitly avoided the question.

"So, to the extent there was any possibility of salvaging the situation, you were the one who screwed up," Mike said. "Smiley did his best in an impossible situation."

"How did *I* screw up?" Devlin said. "Since you're such an expert in everything!"

"An EVP is someone you assign to a billionaire with two million shares of your stock for day-to-day meetings," Mike said. "You don't have them as the principal in an initial meet and greet. It was an insult and, from your reaction just now, maybe an unstudied one, which makes it worse. I'd already expressed disfavor with Fieldstone, you had been asked questions about it publicly, and you went and foisted me off on an *EVP*? For an *initial meeting*?

"Did you think I wouldn't see that as an insult, Mr. Devlin? That some hick from the sticks wouldn't realize that in this town an EVP might as well be carrying a bucket of piss? That that's all you thought of this jumped-up kid from the ghetto? Did you think I would not see the insult?

"My great-grandfather had a saying, or so I'm told: Do not fuck with a Follett," Mike said, putting an emphasis on the last *T*. "I would add don't insult them by foisting them off on one of your piss-bucket carriers. *You* were the one who fucked this up, Devlin."

"How'd it go yesterday?" Derrick said at breakfast. Sometimes it was the only time they had together anymore. The sun was bright and there wasn't a cloud in the sky. It was the first time Mike had really looked outside in several days.

"As of this morning I'm a bit more than a two billionaire," Mike said, yawning. "We're going to parcel it out into a distributed portfolio over the next few days. That's pretty much *all* my meetings. I was up late working the Asian markets. Also, Devlin called, and he was less than pleased. I showed him a clip of the video. He was even less than pleased."

"You going to do this on a regular basis?" Derrick asked.

"This and other things," Mike said. "I need to keep training my powers. And we need to head back to Montana soon. I need to establish that I'm a legal resident of Montana. The taxes in New York are *insane*. But I'll need to set up something there I can work from. But today is parceling out the money from the sale and trading and seeing where we go from here."

"Okay," Derrick said. "Don't spend it all in one place."

"Oh, I assure you, I intend to spend it in *all* the places."

"I got a call from Wilder," Derrick said. "Senator Drennen is insistent on a meeting. She feels it imperative to resolve the issue of the suit against the trustees. She's offering her services as a mediator."

"And the other shoe drops," Mike said. "Tell Wilder to set it up."

"Senator," Mike said, shaking her hand. "So good to see you again."

"And you . . . Mr. *Truesdale*, is it?" Senator Drennen said. Her lips smiled but her eyes didn't agree. She was accompanied by the redheaded female aide she'd been with when Mike had met her at The Grill.

They were meeting in Ahuvit's office, which had a cozy little conversation area by a window with a lovely view of a building across the street.

"This is . . . charming," the senator added thinly.

"We don't pay as much attention to form as some other firms, Senator," Ahuvit said. "We prefer substance. How may we be of assistance to the good senator?"

"Well, it's this latest lawsuit," Senator Drennen said. "I think we need to have what is called in diplomacy some frank discussions."

"I can handle frank," Mike said.

"That is up to you, Senator," Ahuvit said.

"Well, in that case, young man, you're getting a little too big for your britches," Senator Drennen said, the façade dropping. The aide looked overly nervous, and she drew in a deep breath to brace for the coming storm.

"How so?" Mike asked, calmly.

"First you cause a run on the stock market by shorting Fieldstone," Drennen said, her face twisted up. She jabbed a pointed finger around as she spoke. "Then you go and bring suit against a large number of totally innocent people just because you didn't get your binky! How damned much money do you want? What, inheriting a billion dollars isn't enough for you?"

She was loud enough that Mike Saw people in other offices stop what they were doing to listen in.

"Sorry," Mike said. "Confused. I was waiting for the apology."

"*What?*" Drennen said. "What the hell do *I* have to apologize for? You realize that as a super you're going to be under the control of Super Affairs for the rest of your *life*, right? And you do know who the current ranking member of the committee is, don't you? Do you really think that it's a good idea to be pissing off half of Congress, not to mention the person who decides your fate? You really think that's a good idea?"

Now, even some people farther down the hallway and one from a lower level were stealthily crowding nearby to hear the rant. The aide looked frozen in fear.

"I decide your *life*, Mike Truesdale. *If* that's the name you want to use! I can get your powers *severed*! I decide if you're in Super Corps or not! I can *ruin* you! Your life rests in *my* hands!

"So, you are going to *drop* this stupid suit! You got *enough* damned money! Be glad you get *anything*, you jumped-up *ghetto rat*!"

"That it?" Mike asked. "You done?"

The aide snapped out of it and looked at Mike in shock.

"Were you listening?" Drennen asked, tilting her head and narrowing her eyes even further.

"To every word," Mike said. "And I have an eidetic memory. I can repeat it back verbatim. But if you're done the answer is: No. So, we done? I've got to clip my toenails."

"You had BETTER be paying attention to this!" Drennen said, shaking her finger at him.

"Or what?" Mike said. "I'm still waiting for the apology, Tara."

"What did you call me?" the senator snarled. She glanced at Ahuvit as if expecting him to save her, but the counselor remained still and expressionless. "I am Senator Drennen to you!"

"Didn't Electrobolt call you Tara?" Mike asked, confused. He shifted into a falsetto. "'It's so great to see everyone who has turned out tonight to support *Tara*! We all know the difference *Tara* makes as the senator from our *great state*!' Are you saying I can't call you Tara, Tara?"

"The Electrobolt thing..." Drennen said. She looked as if someone had just knocked the air out of her lungs.

"I'm still waiting for the apology, Senator," Mike repeated. "Oh, wait, that would also be under my, yes, original name. Which you of course know, being the ranking member."

He shifted to a fair mimicry of the senator's speech patterns and shaking his finger in the air.

"'We must fight white supremacy *every day*! Michael Edwards is the very *face* of white supremacy and *racism*! He is a racist *murderer*, a murderer! *MURDERER!* The State of Maryland needs to find him *guilty* of murder and hate crimes!' Sound familiar, Senator?"

"That was..." Drennen said, getting angry again.

The aide looked away but cracked a hint of a smile.

"An eleven-year-old child who didn't want to die that day," Mike said. "The Fifth Street Kings thought I'd gotten a little too big for my britches as well. Look where it got them."

"Are you threatening me?" the senator asked.

"You know better, Tara. Don't try to change the subject. Where's my apology, Senator? For calling me a transphobe when *your* pet pedophile tried to rape me? Or for calling me, a Lakota *Lost Child*, a white supremacist and murderer for not wanting to die that day. Hell, Senator, you forgot to open with an apology for *stolen lands*. It's like you really don't believe in any of that at all, Senator."

"Look..." she said, pointing at him.

Mike leaned forward and looked at her very intently.

"I'm looking," he said. "I'm looking at a person who is implicated in stealing money from a Native American orphan."

"How am *I* implicated?" Drennen said, angrily.

"Ahuvit," Mike said, still leaning forward and looking at her.

"Your brother-in-law, Edward Alvard, took out a one-hundred-fifty-thousand-dollar loan from the Trust, which remains unpaid," Ahuvit said in a low voice, looking at a document. "According to certain sources, one week later he gave you a cashier's check for one hundred and thirty-five thousand dollars. Indicating that he had taken a ten percent cut on the transaction."

"Where did you *get* that?" Drennen said just as quietly. "That is between me and Edward!"

"Not really," Ahuvit said. "There is approximately three quarters of a billion dollars missing from the Trust, Senator, when you count up what went where improperly and interest. Conn is wealthy but not wealthy enough to recoup that. It will take tracking where the money *actually* went and going for the deep pockets. Such as yours, Senator."

"Are you saying you're going to sue *me*?" Drennen asked.

"If it turns out our little bird is correct, yes," Ahuvit said. "And since you just made an admission against interest in that matter, I would say they were correct."

"What?" Drennen said.

"'Where did you *get* that?'" Mike said, mimicking the senator again. He was still leaning forward and looking at her intently. "'That is between me and *Edward*!' That is called an admission against interest, Tara. In front of witnesses."

"You have no idea what you are dealing with, kid," Drennen said. "You think some drug gang is scary? Think again."

"I've got one hundred million euros in contracts on me right now," Mike said. "I'm pretty sure I'm aware of just how nasty it can get. And I'm still looking."

"Would you quit *doing* that?" Drennen said.

"You said 'Look!'" Mike said. "I'm still looking. What am I looking at?"

"Look, you . . ."

"I'm looking!" Mike cried. "I'm looking at a corrupt career politician who's about to get caught with her hand in the cookie jar and is panicking about it. How many of the members of the Tust who are ... close to other corrupt politicians were on there because *you* suggested it? 'It's like an endless piggy bank!' And who are now asking you how *you* screwed this up so bad? 'He's a *super*! Can't you *do* something?'"

Her jaw was hanging open and she now looked completely lost. The aide had straightened and now held a perfect, innocent poker face.

"And the answer, again, is: No," Mike said. "You can't do anything. You can put a kid who was already sexually abused into the hands of a sexual abuser, but with my community service hours complete, you can't do *anything*. I have no particular interest in your little super-cop agency. I have no particular interest in Super Affairs.

"There's an argument about how superheroes should act. Should they put themselves in the hands of corrupt politicians like yourself? Or morons like the madame secretary? 'The people elect the government! We should listen to the people!'

"Or should they act on their own? Should they disdain the orders of elected officials such as yourself and fight crime as lone vigilantes?"

He dramatically raised a noble, triumphant fist in the air, but immediately relaxed it and softened.

"Both sides are wrong, Tara," Mike said, looking her in the eye. "What superheroes should do is nothing."

"Nothing?" the senator said, confused. "Like, just ..."

"Normals do not understand superpowers," Mike said with a sigh, sitting back. "They think they're just another type of power they should wield, indirectly. That we should, in the words of the Left, be the boot of the oppressors. That is not the proper use of superpowers.

"Supers should do *nothing* until the time comes that the 'important people' such as yourself are *begging* for their help. Then and only then should they act. And when they act, it is under the agreement that they do what *they* see is the right thing to do. Not be told what to do by people who have *no* clue what they are talking about. Or have an agenda that is other than fixing the problem.

"And when they are done, they should go back to wherever they came from and disappear," Mike finished. "*That* is the proper use of superheroes. Which means I don't give a *shit* about *your* power, Tara. Because I am not going to use *my* powers until there's such a crashing emergency *you* don't *matter*. And if I don't *use* my powers, Super Affairs has no jurisdiction and therefore *you* have zero power over me."

"You really think that?" Drennen said.

"I think you're going to pull every string you can to keep from being put under the microscope," Mike said. "And eventually, you'll be under that microscope. Eventually, my forensic accountants are going to be going over your records and anything they find that's potentially probative or illegal becomes public record.

"Because I'm like that line from *Terminator*: 'I can't be bargained with! I can't be reasoned with! And I absolutely *will not stop!*'

"I am thirteen years old," Mike said. "I've got the rest of his life to make Wesley Conn's life miserable. Since you seem to be *completely* out of the loop; he raped my mother when she was eleven, passed her around to other pedos, and had her murdered when she became a liability. Means I've got some revengin' to do. *You're* not even the target, Senator. I could give a shit less about the *money* or about *you* or your corrupt little schemes.

"You're not important, Senator," he said with a shrug. "You're just in my way."

After the senator had left with her aide, Ahuvit put his hand over his mouth and made retching noises.

"'You're not important. You're just in the way,'" he said. "Are you *kidding* me? You said that to a *senator*?"

Outside, someone chuckled, followed by shushing noises.

"Ahuvit," Mike said. He stood at the window and watched the traffic on the street below. "She's just a Society *pawn*. I'm a *member* of *Gondola*. Just that, right there, makes me more important than she is. Plus, I'm a billionaire. Plus, I'm a super. You can replace a senator by throwing a rock. I mean, governors regularly replace them with whoever's the biggest crony. You can't replace any of those three easily."

"That's a point," Ahuvit said, shaking his head. "But I'm not sure if that was balls or insanity. She's going to pull out *all* the stops now. Senators do not like being called unimportant."

Mike had been focused inside during the meeting, but now he resumed his casual scan for nefarious activities in the local area with Sight. However, there wasn't much to see outside of the occasional heated argument or consenting adults fooling around. For some strange reason, petty crime had completely ceased in the surrounding square blocks over the last few weeks.

"So, next, FBI white collar takes over," Mike said. "Because there's actual embezzlement found. So, the suit gets put on hold while the DOJ investigates. Which will take some time, as much time as they can possibly take to just hope things go away, and we'll have to turn over everything. And we've made copies of everything, right? 'Cause they are notorious for losing evidence that make Democrats look bad."

"Yes," Ahuvit said. "You take all this so calmly. Most of my clients would freak out if the FBI got involved."

"I'm aware of the process from seeing the inside in Gondola," Mike said. "So, that gives them time. But the suit will be on hold until after the FBI gets done. It might not be a whitewash. It can't be *too* blatant. Conn and the comptroller at the least are going to get charged. Conn will probably disappear, be tried in absentia, convicted, stay on the run in non-extradition countries and eventually get pardoned by a Democrat president on his way out the door.

"But they'll find all sorts of ways for people like the good senator to escape. Then, when they're done, we take up the suit *again* and *keep* digging. And digging. And there are appeals and counter appeals and injunctions and stays and eventually we'll get our hands on all the records if we have to take it to the Supreme Court.

"Then highly paid accountants and attorneys will dig and dig and dig and let the sunshine in.

"The real job of a superhero is to fight evil, Ahuvit," Mike said, "so that *all* of humanity can have a better life. And the best way to fight evil like this is to let the sunshine in. It kills parasitic vampires like Conn and the good senator. Since I can't actually tear open some deep cave, I've got attorneys to do that *for* me."

CHAPTER 29

"Street Life"
—The Crusaders, featuring Randy Crawford

"Okay," Mike said. "Welcome, everyone."

They were holding the meeting on how to parcel out the money at the town house. Since it was going to be a matter of broad strokes *and* details, there were experts on everything from stocks to cattle stock. It took the *big* table at Asuda Financial and was planned to run for three days.

The two hundred million he'd kept out to trade overnight was three hundred by morning. Benjamin was suitably impressed with his knowledge of the HKEX and Hang Seng.

That portion had been kept in trading and Mike intended to have it trade continuously. Keep it moving.

Mike had chosen to wear a suit but, as with the rest, he took off his coat and hung it on his chair, then took off his ascot and rolled up his sleeves.

"General outline as previously discussed and agreed upon by my father," Mike said. "He's letting me run the financial to the greatest extent, within certain parameters, while he handles, essentially, corporate counsel.

"I intend for the Follett Corporation to be a growth property. While we have to be careful about risk, it's intended to be aggressive. As such, the general layout will be as follows:

"Forty percent will be in a range from medium to high risk. Forty percent will be in medium risk to low. Twenty percent will be low risk.

"I'm interested in keeping the money moving. While sunk investments like land are great, it's not working the money. I want most of this money moving and I'm interested in the portion of the portfolio that's in stocks and commodities to keep working twenty-four/seven. There are markets all over the world and off-hours trading.

"Keep the money moving and grow it as you do.

"So, let's get down to details..."

"Okay," Mike said, looking over the list of Asuda's preferred investment banks. "I've got the same list. Probably from the same source. Approved. Any specific preferences?"

"Carmichael," Benjamin said. "*Every* investment bank and insurance company in the *world* with the exception of Chinese is essentially controlled by the Society. They've made a campaign of it. It's impossible to avoid doing business with them entirely. If you don't get taken over by them, you get destroyed. And you don't want to try to use Chinese banks. They are, if anything, worse. But Carmichael is the least Society oriented. No C-suites are made members. Which puts it in a very precarious position."

"We'll see if we can get it less precarious," Mike said. "We're about to be taking quite a few loans."

"You were talking about buying land in the area of the Fisher River in Montana," Perla said.

"Yes," Mike said.

They were on day two and closing in on final details. The aides had done their best to collect empty food containers and continuously clean the table off, but a mess was accumulating, nonetheless. A general funk of stale air filled the room. Everyone looked worn out, with bags under their eyes, droopy eyelids, and general lethargy. Coffee flowed like water, but it wasn't helping much anymore.

"The properties aren't owned by East River Colonial anymore," Perla Krauz said. "They were sold to a Chinese development company. They'd planned on developing residential properties in the area and there wasn't enough interest plus all the ongoing Chinese banking issues. They just declared insolvency, so the properties are going on the block."

"Are they being parceled out?" Mike asked.

"The judge has indicated that they'd prefer to sell it as a block," Perla said. "But there's not much known value to the area. Probably mineral resources but the timber is going to take at minimum twenty years in some areas to regrow and up to fifty in others. So . . . it's probably going to go cheap."

"How many acres?" Mike asked.

"Two hundred and twenty-five thousand," Perla said. He held out an empty coffee mug for an aide to fill. "It's a good chunk of the area from Kalispell to the Washington border. Show you?"

"Sure," Mike said, staring at the plasma screen.

The area encompassed not all but most of the area from the Kalispell flatlands on the east to near Whitehall on the west with the mountainous areas of the Flathead Reservation bounding it on the south. The northern limit was where it reached the Kootenai National Forest and the Kootenai Reservation. It was the area Derrick and he had been exploring, though they'd only explored a fraction of it.

"That's . . . a lot of land," Mike said. "How much do you think it's going to go for?"

"It'll be at auction for the entire piece," Perla said. "If they can't sell it, whole, they'll have to parcel it out. It went for three hundred million to the developer. It's clearly not worth that much. So . . . you can probably get it for somewhere around two hundred and thirty to three hundred million? But it could go as high as five. There's a lot of interest in the area for residential properties."

"That's doable," Mike said. "Even with current interest rates. Put in a bid. Maximum is . . . Morry?"

"Four hundred million," Morry Schecter said, not looking up from his laptop. "We'll do it as a loan, obviously, but we still have to have the money for taxes. Since it comes out of commercial properties, it will have to come out of that portion of the portfolio. That reduces the farmland you'll be able to buy."

"Roger," Mike said. "Maximum bid is four hundred million. Let someone else put in an initial bid. Hopefully, it will be low."

He rubbed his eyes and took a sip of water.

"I'm told by my father that there is a mine or mines up in that area," Mike said. "The only name I have is Helonic and whatever marketing think tank came up with that name needs to be shot."

"I know Helonic," Rick Smallwood said. "Nice rate of return, depending on your stomach, but not a company to hold. They're the definition of big evil mining. Emphasis on evil."

"So, I've heard," Mike said. "Check into the status of those mines. I hear they are nearly played out. It's possible there may be worthwhile ores nearby they haven't found. The area is rife with ore. I Sensed plenty of it just driving up into the area. There's definitely money to be made there but I don't want to make it through strip-mining the entire area. On the other hand, an underground mine can go for miles. So . . .

"I need to check it out, quietly. Don't put in a bid until I see if there's anything worth buying.

"In the case that we go for it, try not to let them know I'm the interested party," Mike said. "An Earther buying a mine is fairly obvious and I'd like to get it for as little as possible."

"We can set that up," Aviden said, stifling a yawn. "Set up an offshore company. Move the money through outside banks. Hong Kong possibly. We'll need a cover for why we're buying a played-out mine, though."

"Don't lie about it," Mike said. "That can be seen as a violation of contract. But it's an underground mine. Hint that the company is considering building a remote shelter for rich people in the event of the Storm?"

"That could work," Aviden said.

"Next item is farmland," Mike said. "When you buy a farm as an absentee landowner, what you're actually buying is a field that is worked by someone local to the area. Absent buying a large local farming corporation and those rarely go up for sale. Generally correct?"

"Yes," Perla said.

"Which is fine," Mike said. "But there's a strategic purpose to my interest in farmland besides that it's a good, stable long-term investment. We don't know what the Storm is going to be, but we do know I'm supposed to fight it and I intend to."

Mention of the Storm got everyone's attention, and even a few people who'd been nodding off jerked upright and blinked the exhaustion away.

"In the event that the federal government is an active force, and depending on the severity of the Storm that is not necessarily a guarantee, and in the event I have good relations with the federal government, also not a guarantee, I should be able to fall on the Feds for logistics support in fighting the Storm. Should.

"In the event that they are *not* an active force—see movies where the disaster essentially takes them out and the US in a failed state condition—or in the event I'm somewhat at odds with them, for various reasons, I need somewhere to lay my head in some degree of safety and fall in on support. Food, clothing, shelter, repair of whatever vehicles I may be using.

"So, each farm should be in a remote area. Each farm should have a house on it or land that is potentially usable for a house either on the farm or contiguous to it. If there's no house, I'll have my side handle that. I'm going to have to have someone to manage that and I've got various people to draw upon.

"But that's the primary purpose of the farmland purchases, in my eyes. So, look for farmland that while being productive and long-term valuable has those features to it. Relatively remote. Good place to put in a 'country place.' If there is more than one patch in a particular area, I'll choose which one to put in a house. Also, from there keep an eye out for more local farmland. Clear enough?"

"Clear enough," Perla said, nodding. "I hadn't considered that aspect."

"I may be young, but I think long term," Mike said. "That the Storm hasn't come yet doesn't mean it never will. It will and I intend to be prepared..."

"Hey, Poppa," Mike said.

"So, you got the money," Jacob Sterrenhunt said over the video link. "The white man actually gave it up."

Jacob Eagle Beak Sterrenhunt had a stocky body, long black hair in a ponytail, and nearly black eyes. Despite the last name, his grandfather was the quintessential paragon of the Lakota people.

"He did, yes, Poppa," Mike said. "After a long struggle. And I think it means I'm going to be a very lazy Injun. We need to get the family out here to see some of the stuff. It's really mind-boggling. The estate would make a pretty good small farm."

"Eh," Jacob said. "You can't make any money with a small farm anymore. So, why does the big-shot grandson call his country poppa?"

"Because he loves him?" Mike said. "And because I need to pick your brain."

John Ringo with Casey Moores

"Thought so," Poppa said.

"I'm going to be investing in farmland," Mike said. He went into his thoughts on the Storm and having the land scattered in various parts of the country. "So, I'm going to be an absentee landowner."

"I run six fields for three different rich people in California," Jacob said. "I know the game."

"While I can get my investment company to look at where to buy, I need someone to run the overall operation," Mike said. "To keep an eye on the farms for me, to handle ensuring the houses are prepared and there's someone trustworthy in the area keeping an eye on them. Generally, manage those type of lands. And I've got an entire family involved in farming. Who would you suggest, if anyone, in the family to handle that?"

"David," Poppa said. "Reynolds. Sarah's son. He's gotten his bachelor's in ag and he's been helping out, but he doesn't have a real job yet. And he's not married yet. So, he's available to fly around."

"Thank you, Poppa," Mike said. "That's one decision off my plate."

"You coming back out here?" Poppa asked. "Or are you going to stay a city mouse?"

"We're headed back once most of the city mouse stuff is put away, Poppa," Mike said. "Probably early summer. Though I'm thinking of asking the family if they want to come visit out here. I'd sort of like to show them some of this stuff. It's insane."

"We could make the trip," Poppa said. "As long as it's after planting time..."

"Mr. Vaughn," Mike said, shaking his hand. "Good to meet you."

Mike was having his first working golf game at the Nassau Country Club, in Glen Cove. Mike and his father were there as guests of one Terrence Vaughn, the CEO of Carmichael Capital.

"You as well, Mr. Truesdale," Vaughn said.

"I'm going to go with Mike here," Mike said. "My father, counselor Derrick Sterrenhunt."

"Counselor Sterrenhunt," Vaughn said. He motioned to the man beside him. "My associate, Ric Kolseth."

"Mr. Kolseth," Mike said.

"Ric, please," Kolseth said.

"Derrick is a mouthful," Derrick said. "I usually go by Hunter."

"Hunter it is," Vaughn said.

"How'd you get a slot at Nassau County?" Mike asked.

"I'm a member," Vaughn said, chuckling. "Unless it's an event, that's pretty much the only way to get a tee time. Ready to go?"

"Absolutely," Mike said. "But I'm not going to bet on my score. I'm a newbie at golf."

"But you've got some extra abilities, as I understand," Vaughn said.

"Doesn't fix my slice," Mike replied.

"MOTHERFU...!" Mike said, watching his ball sail for the trees to the left of the fairway. "If I don't slice it, I *hook it*..."

He reached out, connected with the very little earth material in the ball, and adjusted the trajectory ever so slightly so it hit one of the outer trees and bounced back into the rough.

"Whooo," he said walking over to the waiting foursome. "I was afraid I was going to have to go hunt it."

Derrick, standing behind the other golfers gave him a Look.

Mike looked back with a "why would you suspect anything?" expression.

"Glad you contacted Carmichael Capital about doing some business with us," Vaughn said as they started out to chase down their balls. "We're interested in both providing and as a bond holder."

"I'm interested both ways as well," Mike said. "The low-risk portion of the portfolio is going to include farmland. Which parcels exactly are still up for discussion. There's always workable farmland going for sale somewhere."

"Agreed, and agree it's a low-risk investment," Vaughn said.

"One large buy that I'm looking at, though, is some currently unusable land up near where my father's from, Kalispell, Montana."

"Unusable?" Vaughn said.

"It's just mountainsides," Mike said. "Which were formerly tree-covered until they got logged off. It will be a while before it can be logged again. I'm looking at it as family land rather than for economic purposes. My accountant assures me I can afford it."

"At the level of an investment bank?" Vaughn asked as he stopped the golf cart by his lie.

"Two hundred and twenty-five thousand acres?" Mike said. "It's going up for bid. I've put the max on it as four hundred million. Could go as low as two twenty-five. But that would be dumb luck."

"Yeah," Vaughn said, nodding as he lined up his shot. "That's in our range."

The ball went up and corkscrewed slightly to land in a sand trap.

"This course is an absolute bugger," Vaughn said.

"What doesn't kill you makes you stronger."

Derrick's driver hit the ball perfectly. It went up and up and up and down right onto the third green.

"Jesus," Kolseth muttered.

"Did you ever consider going pro?" Vaughn asked as they were walking to the golf carts.

"I was recruited to the Fort Drum Golf Team," Derrick said. "Turned them down. I'd already decided to try for Combat Activities Group."

"Ah," Vaughn said, nodding.

As they were chasing balls, Mike chuckled.

"You don't know what Combat Activities Group is, do you?"

"Not a clue," Vaughn said. "He said try. Did he make it?"

"Combat Activities Group is part of the US Army Special Warfare Squadron," Mike lectured. "The Squadron consists of Headquarters and Headquarters Troop; Administrative Activities Group Alpha; Support and Logistics Group Bravo; Operations and Intelligence Group Charlie; and *Combat* Activities Group *Delta*. CAG is what you probably know as Delta Force."

"Oh," Vaughn said. "That was part of the information package. That Hunter had been in Delta Force."

"Which was where he got the handle 'Hunter,'" Mike said. He lined up his shot and managed to drop it square in the water trap. "Well, there goes my score. I'll take the five-shot penalty and a drop."

"I'll give you a mulligan," Vaughn said. "You're new at this."

"I'll take the penalty," Mike said. "My dad would swim in and try to chip it out."

On his second try he just chipped it short of the water. He wasn't going to try for the green from here.

"Here's the thing about military handles," Mike said. "Some military handles sound fantastic. There was one guy called Thunderblast."

"That's a pretty good nickname," Vaughn said.

"The reason he got the handle was he got raging diarrhea on an operation," Mike said. "He was blowing out huge sharts. Thunderous blasts of feces."

"Oh!" Vaughn said, grimacing.

"My father's handle is because he never did *anything* that anyone could hang a crap handle on him," Mike said, chuckling. "Sterrenhunt means 'Star Hunter.' It was the term for someone who would hunt or fight at night, which the Plains Indians essentially never did. It was considered very weird. So, with nothing they could hang on him, he ended up with Hunter. Because he never screwed up even slightly. You've got to be pretty damned perfect to even get *into* CAG. He was more perfect. Yes, I am *very* proud of my father, thank you very much."

". . . and nobody wants to provide money for coal plants!" Mike said, lining up his shot. He looked up and shrugged. "It's insane."

He took the shot and was happy to see it did nothing weird. Just went more or less where he'd hoped.

"They're very unpopular," Vaughn said. "There's major issues with carbon."

"No economy can get past a hydrocarbon phase," Mike said getting back in the golf cart. "We *all* went through it. You have to get *rich* enough to get past it. Hydrocarbon is how you *get* rich. See every Western nation and China."

"The smog in China is why most investors are against it," Vaughn said. "Have you seen how soot covered some of those cities are?"

"So, you want them to just *stay* poor?" Mike asked. "China sure does. They don't want India having their GDP. India has three percent of China's GDP *and* more people. There is no way that they can just jump from essentially zero to wind and solar, even if wind and solar *can* power an industrial economy and I'd argue they cannot . . ."

". . . yeah, the jet came with the inheritance," Mike said, then waited as Vaughn took his shot.

The ball hit the green and bounced off.

"Oooh," Mike said, grimacing. "The real question is, why did the Trust have a jet?"

"Because it was a billion-dollar Trust?" Vaughn said as he put away his club.

"There were only three physical properties left, all in the New York area," Mike said then gestured to the northeast. "One of them right over there."

"Right," Vaughn said, grinning. "The Dosoris Estate. I hear it's pretty nice."

"Now that I got a lot of the crap cleared out," Mike said. "All the capital was in Fieldstone...which is based in New York."

"Yes," Vaughn said.

"The Trust was based in New York," Mike asked as they pulled up on his lie. "The properties were in New York. The company they had all the cash in was in New York. So...*where* were they flying and for *what* reason? For business purposes. What *business* did they have elsewhere?"

"That's a good question," Vaughn said.

"Apparently, it was a business expense to fly members of the Trust to various destinations," Mike said, lining up his shot. He put it square in the sand trap. "Mother..."

He took a deep breath through his nose.

"This really *is* a good walk ruined," he said, putting away his club. "Apparently, it was very important for them to regularly go trout fishing in various places. Attend important meetings in Davos and so on. Kauai was a frequent destination.

"Records indicate that the heaviest user was Amos Young, who was a fairly minor trustee. It was, apparently, once used for his father's congressional campaign, though the campaign paid for Congressman Young's travels. Just Congressman Young, though. Not his son. He traveled in it as a trustee."

"That...sounds a bit dicey," Vaughn said.

"Especially since Monsieur Young the Younger was being paid by the campaign at the same time," Mike said. "It's one of those things that I'm sort of thin-lipped angry about. I'm going fairly aggressive in terms of growth. The Trust was all about 'we need to keep the money safe.' But apparently, they never heard the adage 'If you're going to make money, don't spend it.' They spent money like it was going out of style..."

CHAPTER 30

"I'm Alright" —Kenny Loggins

"...You understand that everything involving bond issue, I've got to get people to check the horse's teeth," Mike said as Vaughn was lining up his shot.

"Absolutely," Vaughn said then took his swing.

"Well, you're still on the fairway," Mike said.

His own lie was right nearby so he walked over to it.

"Asuda had a recommended bond issue in Vietnam," Mike said as he considered his skill versus the distance to the green. "I contacted a friend I knew from one of my classes whose family was Vietnamese big business. He recommended against it. The guy who was actually behind it is either sort of a crook or just very bad at business."

Mike considered the distance to the green and the obstacles in between. They looked hard to pick through.

"Oh, well. He fears his fate too much..."

Mike took his mightiest swing and watched the ball sail in perfect line with the putting green...and go over it.

"Son of a..."

"That was a very nice drive, though," Vaughn said.

Mike got out his sand wedge, again, and headed for the sand trap.

"So...it's lunchtime. I'm eating leftover lo mein at the foster house since I was suspended. And the back door of the town house kicks in and three dudes completely covered in tattoos walk in. Two of them are holding machetes and one's got a pistol.

"So, I'm like *'Olé! Cuomo eesta?'* Now, I speak perfect Spanish. But I *want* them to treat me as an imbecile..."

He chipped the ball and covered himself in sand to have it hit the edge and roll back.

"I hate this game..."

Vaughn was leaning on his club as Mike made another attempt to get out of the edge of the water obstacle.

"...Oh-That-Poor-Bastard is getting more and more agitated. 'This has to be the wrong guy! This is supposed to be some bad ass and this guy is a moron!' Skullface is telling him to keep an eye on me, but he's so pissed about being sent to kill some mentally retarded thirteen-year-old that he's just arguing. He'd moved the gun away from pointed right at me. So, I casually stick one of the chopsticks in me teeth, take the other one in a tight grip, and start STABBING HIM IN THE FUCKING NECK...!"

"And that's why I call him 'Oh-That-Poor-Bastard,'" Mike said as they got back in the cart.

"That's...yeah," Vaughn said, looking slightly nauseated.

"...So, you're one of the good people of Baltimore, going about your lunchtime business in the downtown sort of safe area. And you suddenly hear gunshots and screaming coming from this beat-up brown sedan. I told them there'd be a lot of screaming and blood. You can't say I didn't warn them..."

"...I open up Skullface's burner, wipe some of the blood out of my eyes, and call 9-1-1," Mike leaned his club against his stomach and made a phone gesture at his ear. "'Nine-one-one,'" he said in a falsetto. "'What is your emergency?'

"'Yeah, you gotta double and a half homicide at...'" He made motions like wiping his eyes and looked up. "'Uh, Twelve-fourteen Spring Street.' 'Double and a half?'"

He leaned over as if looking in a car.

"'Yeah, two 'um daid, third one...'" He made motions of waving in front of his neck and choking sounds. "'I don' think he's gonna make it...'"

"Oh, my God," Vaughn said, laughing and holding his hand over his mouth. "I should *not* be laughing at this."

"At least you ain't laughin' at my golf game," Mike said, looking at his shot. "Foooore!"

"Fucking poh-leese comin' from evywhere," Mike said. His ghetto accent got heavier whenever he told his Baltimore stories. "They was comin' from out the zone, from out the precinct. And you *don't* go out the precinct. Don' see what the big deal. Bodies dropping evyday in Baltimore.

"An' evyone walk over, squat down, look at the dude, look at me standin' there all covered in blood, point, and go... 'Is that a *chopstick*?'"

Vaughn was howling.

"I can't believe I'm *laughing at this...*!"

Mike was lining up a putt and he wasn't sure he was going to make it.

"Frank always smoke a cheap, smelly cigar at scenes 'cause of the smell of the bodies, ya dig? So, he lights up a cigar and stayin' back so he don't mess up the scene, he walks over and pulls up his pants a bit and squats down to look at Skullface. And he looks at Skullface back and forth, looks at me, points at it, and goes... 'Is that a *chopstick*?'

He hit the ball and it rolled right past the hole and to the other side of the green.

"God DAMNIT!"

"Probably should concentrate on your putt and not your story," Derrick said.

"Stories are *important*!"

"So, Frank, first responding officer, and Garson all line up by the cah," Mike said as Vaughn was preparing his shot. "And I'm gonna give them the *low down*.

"'So, we gots this fella, Skullface. He gots a chopstick in his eye. Then we gots the driver. *He* gots a chopstick in his *ear*. Fella in the back seat all shot up and cut *but* he got holes in his neck consistent wif a small penetrating weapon. *Could* be a icepick... but base on all the ev'dence, prob'ly a *chopstick*. And, most *important of all*, we gots that Chinese food container in tha back. That's the *sure* sign who done this here homicidin'."

"Homicidin'?" Vaughn said, laughing.

"Homicidin'. So ... they all three cross their arms and look at me standing there ..."

"Covered in blood," Vaughn said, laughing and shaking his head.

"From head to *toe*," Mike said, making a top-to-bottom gesture. "And Frank goes, 'Okay, Boogie, hit us. *Who's* the culprit?' 'It *obvious*, Frank! Cain't you *see* it? The chopsticks? The Chinese delivery container? It's obvious! The perpetrator of this dastardly deed was ... a Chinese ... *ninja* ... !'"

Mike stuck out his lips in a duck expression, crossed his arms, and nodded knowingly while waggling a finger.

Vaughn was laughing so much he hooked it into the woods.

"Damnit!"

"He was telling his Chinese Ninja story, wasn't he?" Derrick said as they headed back to the clubhouse.

"I'm embarrassed to be laughing at it," Vaughn said, shaking his head. "Jesus."

"Chinese Ninja?" Kolseth asked. "Ninjas are Japanese."

Vaughn and Mike both cracked up at that.

"Chief Stone Face did not crack a smile when I told him that story," Mike said, as they finished laughing.

"He didn't?" Vaughn asked.

"Not damned one."

"I had my sense of humor surgically removed," Derrick said.

"What's so funny about a Chinese ninja? Ninjas are *Japanese* ..."

Mike pulled off his sweat-soaked shirt in the locker and heard the usual gasps.

"Wow," Vaughn said. "I'd heard you'd been injured a few times in the past. I mean ... that story alone."

"If what don't kill you makes you stronger, I be diamond," Mike said, pulling off his pants. "And with most of this the other guy looks worse. *If* he's still alive."

⊕ ⊕ ⊕

"I think I'm gonna let you do most of my golfin' for me," Mike said as they were headed to the estate in the limousine. "That game sucks."

The Nassau Country Club smelled like money and sulfur. Glen Cove was where most of the old wealth of New York City was centered. Which meant the country club was wall-to-wall Society. Mike had been introduced to a series of people who he ticked off as either Society members or closely affiliated.

At least there weren't any bodies buried in the basement. He'd checked.

It was suggested that he consider applying for membership. He told people he'd consider it, what with his estate being right around the corner.

"*I believe my great-grandfather was a member,*" Mike had said more than once.

The Folletts had been one of the *founders*. He was pretty sure that some of the Society types giving him a fulsome welcome were aware of that. They were also aware that he'd had prayer warriors come in and scrub the estate clean. That meant he was definitely not on their side. Besides, his Society file had a notation that he was ineligible due to his "filthy Red Indian blood."

Gotta love these guys. Ripping the hearts out of children and burying them under Satanic altars was okay, but not "filthy Red Indian blood."

The Society was patient at one level. They'd wait for a later generation to corrupt. One where the filthy Red Indian blood had presumably been diluted. Preferably by some fine Aryan stock.

Okay, so the Allen girls met the definition. But still.

Supers were certain to be long-lived and might just be immortal. The oldest males still looked to be in their thirties and older female supers looked younger. California Girl was pushing sixty and looked twenty-five.

He fully intended to read his kids in on everything when they were about sixteen. Old enough emotionally to handle it. Since he might just outlive his children, he intended to keep the Society away from his family for a *very* long time.

Assuming he and Gondola didn't find a way to expose and destroy them sooner.

Or the Society managed to kill him. There was still a hundred million euros on his head. He was taking a small touch of everything he ate and drank on his lips just to see if there was any funny reaction before eating or drinking.

The problem was, he already knew how to get past that way of testing for poison. Damn Gondola training.

"If you're planning on doing business, golf is part of business," Derrick said, looking out the window as the rolling green hills of the golf course disappeared from view.

"True," Mike said. "And there are reasons. He never asked for a mulligan and as far as I could tell, he never cheated. Which says good things about Carmichael."

"Yes," Derrick said. "Same with Kolseth."

"Though a couple of times they were sandbagging so my game didn't look as bad," Mike said.

"They were trying to sell to you," Derrick said. "That's normal. Though it's not normal to direct the ball with your Powers. Cheater."

Their driver deftly threaded the limo through a series of narrow streets in the heavily built up area on the way to the estate.

"I only did that a little," Mike said. "Couple of times. Three, to be exact. We need to fly out to Montana to take a look at that property. I know you already probably know it like the back of your hand..."

"Your cousins Robert or William probably know it better," Derrick said. "Certainly of late. The area is very popular with locals. You're going to have to adjust to them using it as if was public land."

"Oh, understood," Mike said. "But this will be the kind of 'look at the property' that will involve a helicopter. And on people using it like public land, we'll have to sort out the liability issues with the state. Just when we were driving through it, I was picking up on ores."

"I recall," Derrick said.

They were passing through a quaint little town lined with small shops. He hadn't realized places like that still existed.

"But I don't want to ruin the place," Mike continued. "I really do see it as an annuity to the family in the future. I'd prefer to keep it more or less as is. There are some things I'm considering experimenting with, mind you."

"Oh," Derrick said.

"I'm probably going to cut off some areas as much as is reasonable and do some studies," Mike said. "Just ask people, politely, to stay out or if they go in do as little damage as possible. I'm a nerd. There are things I'm interested in."

"Okay," Derrick said then frowned. "Though many, if not most, of the people in the area are the type that if you tell them to not do something will do it just because you said not to."

"Then I'll have to find the right psychology," Mike said. "Say it's fine to go in there but while they are there do some specific work. Signs that say 'If you're in this area please take random tree bole measurements and send them to this website. Thanks!' One thing I'm thinking about is a beaver reintroduction program."

"You're serious," Derrick said. "Your *cousins* will hunt those out. Everybody hates beaver. Plus, it's bred into Indians. Beaver pelts were the biggest economy around for centuries."

"They're good for flood prevention, ground-water retention, and general water quality improvement," Mike argued. "Choose two areas that are very similar, introduce beaver in one and leave the other be. I'll get people to go around to schools and talk about their importance, and the importance of the experiment.

"Yes, it's logging country. Recognized and the land will eventually be logged again. But there are arguments that beaver improve forestry by retaining surface waters. I'd think that would be particularly important in Montana with the relative lack of rainfall in summer. Beavers kill trees immediately around their ponds, the ponds soak some out, but the spread of surface waters into the ground should reduce heat stress on the trees around them. That creates thicker fatter trees. They also reduce loss of soil."

The tightly packed buildings had given way to the trees and lawns of larger properties as they reached the relatively open Danas Highway.

"Trees need light, air, water, and soil to grow. Light and air, there's nothing to be done. But the more water and soil you retain, the better overall the forest should be. Beavers retain water and soil ergo they're going to be a net positive for forests. At least, that's the theory. No one has ever run the experiment for long enough or large enough with enough data points to get a solid statistical answer one way or the other. I've got time."

"You buy it, it's yours to use as you wish," Derrick said, shrugging. "And it will placate the environmental crazies. But if you think Indians *aren't* going to trap beaver if they're available, think again."

"We'll just try to explain," Mike said, shrugging. "And if that doesn't work, we'll hire some of them to hunt the other ones. Not literally, mind you..."

"Most dangerous game?"

"Go to the Rez," Mike said. "'You have this x-thousand-acre patch to patrol. You've got your own house on it. Small, but solid and livable. You get paid y amount per month. If there are no beaver missing after z time, you get a bonus. You get...v amount off for each beaver lost and at w number of beaver lost you're cutting into your income. At a certain point we find someone else to do it. Or you get a house in the middle of nowhere and an income just to make sure the beaver don't get trapped. Can do? Also, no actual hunting of poachers. Unless you're sure you can hide the body.'"

"Speaking as your counselor," Derrick said. "Stop at 'no actual hunting of poachers.'"

"You are *such* a buzzkill, Counselor."

"How are your powers coming along?" Derrick asked at breakfast the next morning. They were dining in the Green Parlor, whose view out the back overlooked the Long Island Sound. The choices were the Parlor, breakfast in bed, or the main dining room which was just too much.

The problem with the manse was that it was *too* large. The thing was enormous and neither he nor Derrick was the type to eat breakfast in bed. He'd been up as usual early morning to do yoga, pray and then go out for a run.

"I'm gaining something like two meters of Sight per day," Mike said. "I'm up to about five hundred meters. Not sure how much power I'm gaining since testing it is sort of awkward. I'm not supposed to train at all. And I'm pretty sure at this point I'd need a serious setup to test it. So, I'll just see if I've got enough when I need it."

Even as much as he'd stretched the limits of his Sight, he still couldn't See the periphery of the estate. He'd gotten used to being able to see beyond the edges of every other property he'd been in, either as owner or guest. It was a little nerve-racking that he couldn't See all of the estate's boundaries at once.

"Topic of the lawsuit against the Corps," Mike said, changing the subject. "I think negotiations have gone on long enough. We need to close it."

"I'll talk to that firm," Derrick said.

"Try to set up a meeting with the Secretary," Mike said. "Let us hash it out. I'm going to make the point I intend to donate all the money to charity. But we need to put that to bed."

"Agreed," Derrick said. "The firm is definitely dragging its feet."

"On the property in Montana," Mike said. "We need to bring in your firm in Kalispell on handling most of the Montana side. Negotiations with the state over liability, et cetera. That will give it a more local feel than if we brought in a bunch of fast-talking New York lawyers. Assuming we get it."

"Agreed," Derrick said. "As soon as I've got the few remaining things I've got on my plate put to bed, I'll be tendering my resignation. Which will be more or less next week."

"We need to use this thing for something other than storing stuff," Mike said, gesturing around at the Manse. "Memorial Day Weekend is the traditional start of the summer season. I'd like to invite my friends over for a party at Richie Rich's place. Also, even though we're going back to Kalispell for most of the summer, what would you think about bringing some of the family out here for a few days? There's plenty of room even for the Sterrenhunt army. And I'd like to invite the Allens as well. And Jane."

"That's ... doable ... ?" Derrick said, clearly considering the logistics.

"You're thinking of how much fun it is to get here from Kalispell," Mike said. "I'd charter a plane from Glacier Park Airport. Try to get them out here for Memorial Day weekend possibly. Then, shortly thereafter, head to Montana. By then we may have had the auction and I can check out the property. I'm not going to mention that 'til it's a done deal. And I need to, quietly, recheck the area around the mine so I can see if there's anything worth buying it. You want to check with the family or me?"

"I'll handle it," Derrick said. "You probably should invite people over who are not just family. You're going to be in business with the people around here for a long time. They probably want to meet the new kid."

"That too," Mike said with a sigh. "I'm not sure combining the two would work. We'll set something for after Memorial Day weekend. Among other things, I'm pretty sure that most of the *nomenklatura* have something going that weekend already. We're late to be putting out invites. I'm going to toss that at Alger."

"I think that's part of his job," Derrick said, nodding.

"In a week the first new classes open for the summer semester," Mike said. "I'm going to sign up for all the introductory stuff that will transfer to Osseo, assuming I get in next year. If I can't, it's okay. I can get a finance degree through Libertatem University. So, a good bit of my concentration is going to be on those. And huzzah! I'm even going to get *credit* for them!"

"Congratulations," Derrick said, drily. "After church I'd put one of two things on the agenda. Either work on your golf swing or skeet. There's a trap range."

"I'm going with skeet . . . ?"

"David, hi!" Mike said over the video link. "How's it going?"

"Planting time," David Reynolds said, tiredly. "I'm on a tractor all day long. What's up, cuz?"

"This inheritance is insane," Mike said. "Just the houses are insane. I've got a town house that's a castle."

"I saw that," David said, chuckling. "Grandma's been all about Mike lately."

"I hope that hasn't been an issue," Mike said. "I'm not planning on being a grinch."

"You didn't seem like the type," David said. "So, what's with the call?"

"I called Poppa," Mike said, "to ask for some advice. As part of the reinvestment strategy, I'm going to be buying some farmland. But it has another purpose . . ."

He repeated the general idea of having farms to support him in the Storm.

"So, the land is going to be scattered," Mike said. "Field with a house here, field with a house there. I'm going to be going around looking at some prospective farms soon. I'll have sort of a—*gag*—entourage. But I need someone who knows farms and farming. Any interest in coming along? It's a paid gig. You'd be paid as a consultant."

"I could get into that," David said, cautiously. "I'm not super experienced, though."

"I could hire some professor of agronomy," Mike said, "but might as well throw it at a member of the family. It would be shortly after planting is done. Poppa said he'd be okay if it was right at the tail end. Also, I asked Grandma if she could arrange the family coming out to see the crazy out here. We'd be ending up back here about then."

"That's . . . doable," David said. "I could do with a trip."

"I'm going to have Alger and Asuda get into the details, then," Mike said. "Just wanted to make sure you were onboard. In the meantime, I've got another meeting."

"I'll let you go," David said, grinning. "Richie Rich."

"You have no idea," Mike said. "Out, here."

"Pearl," Mike said over the phone. "Do we have good news?"

His days had been taken up over the last week with financials, legal, and classes. It was like being an adult except everything had to be cosigned by his father.

"As soon as all the paperwork is complete, you are the proud owner of two hundred and twenty-five thousand acres and change of, honestly, pretty close to wilderness," Ms. Krauz said. "Congratulations."

"Great," Mike said. "How much did it hurt?"

"We got lucky there," Perla said. "Two seventy-five, which for the amount of land was very reasonable."

"That *is* reasonable," Mike said. "Carmichael okay with it?"

"They are onboard," she said. "You're going to have to sign a bunch of paper again."

"I'm getting used to it," Mike said, shaking his hand to loosen up his fingers. "Now I just have to figure out where to put in a compound . . ."

"Monsignor," Mike said, shaking the prelate's hand at the front door. "Welcome to Riverside House."

"Thank you for inviting me."

Monsignor Brandon Moore was a senior prelate with Catholic Relief Services who primarily worked on projects in Latin America. He'd been recommended by Father Constanza, who accompanied him, as well as being seconded and approved by Gondola.

"Drink?" Mike asked. "Whatever you'd like."

"I'll take a glass of red wine, then," Moore said.

They settled in the study and Mike took a breath.

"I'm going to be generally contributing to philanthropy," he said, "which is good and right and all that. But I'd like to create a specific fund with a specific purpose."

"Which is?" Monsignor Moore asked.

"Orphanages in the Americas," Mike said. "Notably in Latin America. You've worked with a certain group that supports orphanages throughout the region."

"If you mean the people who rescue them from traffickers, yes," the monsignor said.

"You work with *them*?" Father Constanza said. "What part of father confessor is unclear, Michael?"

"The part where I know you're read in," Mike said. "What part of the Oath is unclear, Father?"

"Alright," Father Constanza said.

"The general idea is to found an orphanage or take over an existing orphanage and improve it," Mike said. "Make sure that the kids stay in long enough they can get a job. Teach English and computers. A sixteen-year-old in Brazil who knows English and computers can get a job. Also, buy local farms to support the orphanage and hopefully make a little profit that will go back into the fund.

"It will have to start small," Mike said. "But whenever somebody wants me to invest in something, I'll sort of mention my pet charity and they can decide if they want a tax deduction or not. And as my income increases, I'll have more to put in the fund. Does that sound doable?"

"That sounds doable, Michael," Monsignor Moore said. "And you are a good young man for it."

CHAPTER 31

"Godzilla" —Blue Öyster Cult

"Madame Secretary," Mike said, standing up as Katherine Harris walked in the room.

The meeting to resolve the suit against Super Corps was taking place in the Federal Building in the DOJ section. The conference room, despite having a window, was not nearly as nice as Briefing Room Four. It had a very sterile feel and, from his angle, the view was all sky.

Mike had his father with him as well as Jonathan Woodley, the lead attorney in the suit.

"Stone," Katherine said, sitting down. She was joined by a single counselor representing the Super Corps, a gaunt, solemn man in a suit.

"We need to put this to bed, Madame Secretary," Mike said. "I'll go ahead and state for the record that any proceeds from this suit I'm going to donate to charity. I'm setting up a foundation to assist with orphanages in developing nations, specifically Latin America, and I'll just dump it all in that."

"That's good of you," Katherine said.

"It's not like I need the money at this point," Mike said. "The rest of them can make their own choices. Jorge took the reward money and put it into his mom's restaurant. He's well on his way to being quite the little Honduran businessman."

"Was that a short joke?" Katherine said.

"Little bit?" Mike said, making a tiny gesture with his fingers. "As I said in our previous, rather contentious, meeting, you're not going anywhere any time soon and *we're* not going anywhere any time soon."

He stopped and chuckled slightly.

"Something funny to you about this?" Katherine said, a touch angrily.

"Something Bonfire said," Mike replied. "We were having another argument before going out on patrol and he could tell when we walked out. He just laughed at it. 'I was in JSC. Every patrol it's something!' He made the point that we're going to be around each other for a very long time, and we needed to realize that we were also going to have to get along.

"That is the situation we find ourselves in, Madame Secretary," Mike said. "We are going to be dealing with each other for who knows how long. We may be functionally immortal. Do you know the Vishnu believe that the Storm, when it comes, may last for a thousand years?"

"I've heard that," Katherine said. "I'm not what you call a believer."

"But it may," Mike said. "Certainly, if we cannot throw whatever it is off. Or if it just keeps coming back. So, we may have to work together five hundred years from now.

"Madame Secretary, I've forgiven you for putting me in the hands of a pedophile," Mike said. "Can we, at this point, admit, possibly, that Bolt was such?"

"That hasn't been proven in a court of law," the Corps counsel pointed out.

"Okay," Mike said, holding up his hand. "The point is, I forgive that. You are...addicted to whatever is the hot new thing in Liberal Left Land."

"I wouldn't say that," Katherine said.

"Really?" Mike said, amused. "So, you're willing to question Madeleine Cromarty's—Electrobolt's—position as being trans? That she might not be a *real* woman?"

"Well..."

"My point is that you are you, Katherine," Mike said. "And I am me. And *we* are going to have to work together in the future. I don't blame you. I blame normals like Senator Drennen."

"Can I ask what exactly you said to her?" Katherine said. "Because whatever it was has her seeing red."

"I told her she wasn't important," Mike said.

"Oh, my God, Stone!" Katherine said, rolling her eyes. "Do you *like* making powerful enemies?"

"She was part of a large number of people who decided to grab as much of my family fortune as they could," Mike said. "I don't like people who rob me. And she's *not* important. Not in comparison to me. Not in comparison to you. Not in comparison to . . . Jorge."

"I think that . . . uh . . ." the Secretary said, trying to figure out how to put it.

"Katherine," Mike said. "If the good senator dies of a heart attack today, what happens? The governor appoints a replacement. If you die, today, what happens? We lose California Girl. If we lose Bonfire, we lose an adult trained super. There may be some young kid who Acquires, but they're new. We are one in a million so there are more of us than senators. But we are *very* hard to replace. You can throw a rock and replace a senator."

"You need to try not to say that to senators," Katherine said.

"Oh, I won't in general," Mike said. "And I'll add that all sorts of senators certainly want to talk to me. The word 'billionaire' has them all excited."

"So I've heard," Katherine said, drily. "They all have access to the Supers List and would like an introduction. I pointed out that we were currently in contention on some issues."

"Which we need to get past," Mike said. "So, the question is just how much the Corps is going to pay for handing us over to a person who, at the very least, was an aggressive sexual harasser."

He turned to the Corps counsel.

"Has the Corps accepted in general that if we come to an agreement, despite the contingency fee on the part of the plaintiff's attorney, they will cover all regular and standard legal fees in addition?"

"We are in agreement on that," the Corps counsel said. "The question is more how much each plaintiff is going to receive. There are the two primary plaintiffs: yourself, the named plaintiff, and Jorge Camejo, Hombre de Poder. We feel that one million dollars apiece, with one hundred thousand to each of the other plaintiffs, is a fair number without accepting any fault."

"Got it," Mike said, turning to his attorney. "And we're at more or less two point five times that, correct?"

"Correct," the counselor said.

"So that's six million dollars versus two point four," Mike said. "So, six versus two point four. Just a bunch of zeros after that."

"Zeros matter," Katherine said.

"But they're the same zeros so not really," Mike said. "Let me point out that we started at *sixty* million dollars. So, we've already come way down. Does this come straight out of budget?"

"No," Katherine said. "It comes out of an insurance fund."

"But then your rates go up a bit," Mike said, "and that comes out of budget. You're really not going to go for the six?"

"And you're not willing to go for getting a million?" Katherine said.

"I'm planning on putting it into orphanages," Mike said. "Baby needs shoes. And I'm arguing for my teammates. They need it. Laura probably doesn't *need* more shoes, but she *wants* them."

"Fresh Breeze?" Katherine asked.

"Yes," Mike said. "You'd like her. You two would get along. Six. You can do it, Madame Secretary. Come on."

"Agreed," Katherine said, nodding. "It was a mistake. And it was my mistake."

"Ah, don't take it all on you," Mike said. "You're surrounded by people who were egging you on to support Bolt no matter what. That's your crowd. Frankly, you were just responding to peer pressure."

"Peer pressure is a high school thing, Michael," Katherine said.

"And high school never ends, Katherine," Mike replied. "I, the named plaintiff, hereby agree to this settlement. We good?" he asked his attorney.

"We're good," Woodley said, trying not to wince.

"Can I have a moment with the Madame Secretary, please, now that the legal is out of the way?" Mike asked.

Katherine looked at her counselor. Mike expected her to gesture for the man to leave, but instead it looked more as if she was waiting for permission.

"We're done," the Corps counsel said. "Just a matter of getting the paperwork completed."

"So, about those senators . . ." Mike said after the others had left.

Rather than tensing up in anticipation of a fight, the Secretary seemed relieved.

"Please try not to cause too much trouble," Katherine said with a sigh. "Your lawsuit against the Trust has half the House and Senate stirred up for some reason. They're asking if I can get you to settle or drop the suit."

"That's because it's less about getting my money back than kicking over rocks," Mike said.

"What rocks?" Katherine said.

Mike walked her through the one-hundred-fifty-thousand-dollar loan to Drennen's cousin which was transferred to the senator.

"There could be any number of reasons for that, Michael," Katherine said.

"Pull the other one," Mike said. "And it is not, by far, the only such example. They are legion. Madame Secretary, what's your net worth, approximately?"

"That's kind of a private question, Stone," Katherine said.

"Tara Drennen, famously, was a teacher before running for a school-board seat, then a congressional seat, then being appointed senator," Mike said. "So, you wanna tell me how she now has a hundred-million-dollar net worth? On a teacher's salary, then a congresswoman's salary, then a senator's? Senators get paid fairly well compared to a congresswoman but not *that* sort of money."

"She's written three books as well," Katherine said. "I've read them."

"She's never written a book in her life, Katherine," Mike said. "She sort of gave some ideas to a ghost writer. And those books sold like lead cakes. You might have read them, but bestsellers they were not. She got huge advances, but they did not earn out. And, curiously, the publishers never asked for their money back. Okay, a combined twelve million dollars from the book advances. Where'd the other eighty-eight million come from?

"Doesn't really matter, but the answer is little scams like that one," Mike said. "Plus, a bunch of legit and non-legit insider trading. The reason that it's stirring up the left side of the aisle, Madame Secretary, is that the left side of the aisle was using my Trust as an unlimited piggy bank."

"That's a very serious accusation, Mike," Katherine said. "You'd better be able to back that up."

"Which is what they are afraid of," Mike said. "That I'll be able to back up that assertion. And, eventually, I will. But there will be many back-and-forths along the way. Push me, pull you, so to speak. Law is slow. The fact that I inherited as fast as I did is the surprising part. It will take years to pull it all apart. And each revelation will lead to another and another. They are *not* going to like the experience."

"You're saying it's just the Democrats?" Katherine said. "The Republicans are worse."

"I never said Democrats, though it's telling that you assumed as much," Mike said, shrugging. "I have no brief for R versus D. I'm a classic Western philosophical liberal. The Rs are too far to the right and the left is out in la-la land. But the people who were raiding my piggy bank were all Democrats. Thus, we get to the senators. What I am *not* is a Democrat. I might have been once upon a time. But not in this day and age and not given that they were using my trust fund as a piggy bank. Ergo, I'm going to have to come out of the closet and align with the Right side of the aisle."

"Republicans?" Katherine said, grimacing. "And I thought we were getting along."

"You *want* me to do so, Madame Secretary," Mike said. "You are not popular on the right side of the aisle. And despite our clashes, here and otherwise, I'm actually in support of you remaining Secretary."

"Really?" Katherine said. "I hate to ask why but . . . why?"

"Eh," Mike said, shrugging. "I've got you broken in."

"Oh, you think so," the Secretary said, leaning back with a sly, disbelieving grin.

"We're not friends," Mike said. "Probably never will be. Too many differences. But we are both supers who have to face the reality that we are not normals and never will be. We can try not to be enemies. And we are frequently going to have to work together and sometimes be allies. I'd rather work with *you* than some of your potential replacements.

"This Electrobolt thing was, to a great degree, not your fault," Mike reiterated. "You were listening to bad advice and were pressured by not only your peers but by people like Tara Drennen. But it caused you an enormous amount of flak from the Republicans who don't like you because, frankly, you treat them like something on the bottom of your shoe."

"I don't . . ." She straightened, dropped the grin, and shook her head defensively.

"Yes, Katherine, you do," Mike said. "You see Republicans, even Republican senators, as unimportant representatives of toothless boofers from flyover country. Because that's what you've been raised and trained to believe. You're surrounded by that attitude in Washington, ninety-eight percent registered Democrats, and it's just the *truth* to you. And I assure you they have noticed.

"I'm going to make your case," Mike said. "I'm going to be in your corner with the people you treat like crap. And there is a reason for that. I've got you broken in. And that has a very specific meaning to me."

"Which is?" Katherine said, relaxing once again and looking curious.

"Let us imagine a scenario," Mike said. "All the older supers say that you only worry about the Storm when you're young. Perhaps. But I'm going to be continuing to make preparations. I agree with the Vishnu: We shouldn't be doing *anything* else. Just preparing ourselves for the Storm. And when the Storm comes, I'll be all-in in fighting it. That is our sine qua non."

Her eyes drifted off and Mike could swear he read embarrassment. In fact, she appeared to float through an entire roller coaster of emotions while he spoke. In her first meeting, she'd recounted having to fight Colonel James King, aka Major Freedom and then the Nebraska Killer. As a young woman, she'd watched her friends die in the fight, and she'd had to come to terms with killing another super.

Killing her fiancé, in point of fact.

But she'd also had decades to ponder the nature of the Storm, and there weren't too many other conclusions to come to. Major Freedom had once been the nation's best hope for dealing with the Storm. She had to know that, after his death, that role had fallen to her and the others. Mike could only assume she agreed with his conclusions and had, possibly, made the same arguments herself but lost to the political machine.

"Which means I will need to have good relations with the federal government, which means I need to have professionally adequate relations with you."

"'Professionally adequate,'" Katherine said, still looking a bit distant. "Nice phrasing."

"Thank you," Mike said. "I worked on it. But imagine for a moment that there is a time-limited period to do something to fight the Storm and you give me an order and I say, 'Oh, hell no!' What do you do?"

"That's one of the problems," Katherine said. "When you're in a situation like that, Mike, you *have* to just follow the order. For one thing, you're not looking at the whole picture. You have to trust the chain of command."

"Madame Secretary, let me give you an example from a monster movie, if I may?"

"A monster movie?" Katherine said, snapping back to the present.

"There was a scene in one of the giant monster movies," Mike said. "A kaiju was heading for San Francisco. The authorities were going to set off a nuclear weapon to kill the giant monster. The nuke was to be set off offshore.

"The same giant monster had previously attacked Honolulu because they always come ashore at picturesque major cities instead of, I dunno, Garibaldi, Oregon, or something. And when it attacked Honolulu, it killed a *hundred thousand* people! It was going to kill at least *two* hundred thousand in San Francisco!"

"So, they were going to blow it up by setting off a nuke, offshore of San Francisco. You with me, Madame Secretary?"

"Yes," Katherine said.

"If I was the person who was actually in charge of arming the nuke, someone who was a technical expert, I would have said, 'Oh, hey-yell no!' And I would have been pulled out and someone else would have set it off. In which case, to save, say, a hundred thousand people they would have killed four million. Including the two hundred thousand."

"Wait, what?" Katherine said. She hadn't really been paying attention until then. "Why?"

"How much do you know about radioactive fallout, Madame Secretary?" Mike asked.

"Oh...yeah..." Katherine said, nodding. "And saltwater fallout is the *worst*."

"That..." Mike said. "Yes. DHS briefing?"

"I...learned that a long time ago," Katherine said, her gaze drifting off in haunted thought again. This time, there was zero emotion, as if she'd disconnected into robot mode. "Before DHS existed. Used to have a really good teacher."

Lieutenant Colonel James King, perhaps?

"The fallout certainly would have landed on San Francisco," Mike said.

"And you have to have shelter for two days while it's deadly," Katherine said, raising a finger and looking at the ceiling in thought. "Forty-nine hours. Rule of sevens. Every seven hours the radiation decreases by a factor of ten, right?"

"I should not be surprised that the Secretary of Super Affairs is so familiar with bad things," Mike said. "And, yes, you are correct."

"I've been at this a long time," Katherine said. "You pick up a few things."

"Standard winds in the area are to the southeast," Mike said. "Which means it would have hit Frisco and Oakland, possibly San Jose. But it would have carried on into the Central Valley and possibly hit Stockton as well. Total casualties depend on the winds but should have been at minimum four million people. With me so far?"

"Yes," Katherine said. She blinked and completely returned. "Are you saying that in the event of something like the Storm you're going to refuse orders if it's going to kill a bunch of people? Because sometimes that's unavoidable, Mike. You try to avoid it but…"

"No," Mike said. "But what they were doing was like a Satanic trolley dilemma. 'Let's kill four million people to *not* save a hundred thousand.' Put another way, when you throw the switch on the trolley, you save one person to kill forty. Does that make sense?"

"No," Katherine said. "And I'm pretty sure we won't do that."

"Really?" Mike said.

"There are forty orphans over there that need saving," he said, gesturing to his right. "And Senator Drennen is over there to my left. And you give me the order to save the good senator. Or pick any important person. Which do I save? I'd save the forty orphans. They are forty children for one adult who is replaceable in their position.

"I might save a president, any president, even one I don't like, if the situation is such that the blow would be emotionally devastating to the nation. That, too, is important.

"But, guaranteed, when the Storm comes there will come a time when you are given a very stupid order," Mike said. "You might not even realize it's stupid. Some idiot will, with great reluctance, make Satan's choice of a trolley problem. Kill forty to save none.

"And the reason I would prefer you to be the one who transmits that order is that when I say 'No,' you *might* understand that even if it's an instant, I've thought it through and there is a *reason*, Katherine, that I've said no. Are we clear there?"

"Yes," Katherine said, nodding. "I'm starting to realize that your crazier parts aren't always that crazy. Infuriating, but not necessarily wrong."

"That, right there, Madame Secretary, is the reason I will support you *remaining* Secretary when I speak to Republican politicians with their hand out," Mike said.

"I've got you broken in."

CHAPTER 32

"Carry On Wayward Son" —Kansas

"How are your classes going?" Rick Smallwood asked as they were taking a break. His video feed was top left of four tiles on one of six screens in Mike's command center. "And what are you taking?"

They'd been going over the plan for the upcoming Canadian quarterly yield. Mike had convinced his father that since all the data pointed to his prediction scheme being on track, and since it pointed to a yield that was far lower than the market prediction, they could and should go in heavy. Essentially, by shorting Fieldstone and the arbitrage off of that they'd picked up about a half a billion dollars. In the month since the short that had increased marginally because Asuda really knew what they were doing.

He intended to bet all of it on the yield announcement. Which wasn't exactly Montrose's Toast—"He either fears his fate too much / Or his desserts are small / Who dares not put it to the touch / To win or lose it all!"—but it was going to be dicey. If his brilliant idea didn't pan out—it went south one time out of five—he wasn't going to be busted, but it was going to clip his wings a bit.

"I took what most people could call a full load," Mike said. "Twenty credit hours. All the basic introductory classes that I'd have taken at Osseo but at other universities."

"That's got to be taking up some time," Lee Miles said, smiling from the bottom right tile.

"I'm done with all the lectures," Mike said. "I've read the books. I'm done with all the required papers and I'm just basically waiting for the tests."

"Oh," Lee said, chuckling. "Okay."

"I probably should just stay with Libertatem," Mike said. "I can get either a finance or economics degree through them. But I'd like to attend Osseo. I want to get to know the people and the students. If I'm going to network, I'd rather do it through Osseo's than Harvard's. The problem being that if I do this for a year, I'll probably go in as a senior, which would sort of defeat the purpose."

"We probably should get back to it," Benjamin Goldblatt said. "But, yeah, impressive."

"Eh," Mike said, shrugging. "It's easier than astrophysics . . ."

"Based upon gathered data, the predicted yield is . . ."

Mike was sitting on the edge of his seat waiting for the results. The previous year the Ontario quarterly yield prediction had been sixty-four bushels per acre and the harvest had been sixty-five. Close.

The market was predicting a higher yield this year. He thought they were nuts.

Mike's prediction was for about sixty-one. His analysis was that the period had been cooler than last year. Much cooler. And it showed up in the meteorology sensors. Sort of. The problem was, so many of those had been overtaken by development, they showed a skewed result. Developed areas created a "heat island." That didn't accurately reflect the amount of heat that got to the grain. Sunspots were a better barometer in his opinion.

The quants in Asuda, the smart guys who could do the *complicated* math, had looked over his predictive system and agreed it looked good. They'd put it mostly into options to buy—"going long," the term used in commodities—and he wasn't going to touch the actual trading. That was for professionals.

But he had half a billion dollars riding on the next words.

"Sixty bushels per acre . . ."

That was it. Yield was down. *More* than he'd predicted. Now it was up to the traders at Asuda to decide when to activate the options.

An option was taking a position where you could optionally buy a grain unit at a fixed price. You paid someone who had a grain unit some money to hold that grain if you wanted to buy it at certain point later. You could therefore get it for slightly below market since they now had your money and could use it for other trading. There was interest on the money if nothing else.

And you could lay out a lot of options to buy. It wasn't paying the full price; it was putting some money down like if you were interested in buying a house. Usually, ten percent of the full value. If you bought the unit, the option was rolled into the sale. And options in commodities had a buy-by date and time. In this case, the options were strictly for after the announcement and by the end of the trading day.

If the price of grain stayed the same as the option price or dropped, you lost the money. It wasn't worth taking the grain and selling it since you'd take even more of a loss. The money just went away.

But if it went up, that was a different story. It meant some trader had a unit of grain they could not sell, and they got to watch the price go up and up over what you were eventually going to take it for.

At that point you could either sell the option for more than you paid for it, or you could borrow money, leverage, to buy the units and then sell them at a profit.

By putting in half a billion in options, they'd marked out over five billion dollars in wheat.

As soon as the Canadian official said, "Sixty," the price of wheat futures started to climb.

Mike really didn't have anything to do. He was leaving it to the traders. But while they had planned this carefully, there might be questions as time went on. The plan was a leveraged arbitrage.

As soon as the money from the grain trade started turning up, other actions were planned. Buy this stock, short these bonds. The necessity was to get ahead of other traders who were doing the same thing.

So, the commodities traders couldn't wait long to activate the options. It was a balance of making the most money on the wheat even if they had to not take positions elsewhere.

"Deere window is closing," Benjamin said.

Mike was linked in with the team at Asuda on this, and his father had left him final decision-making.

"Skip," Mike said.

Because there would be less wheat produced this year, more ground would be broken. If more ground was to be broken, that meant tractors. Which is why every time the price of wheat futures jumped, so did shares in John Deere tractors. But others had already jumped on that, and Deere was going up. No point in buying it. They were going to make more money on the wheat options at this rate.

As the commodities team came to the conclusion that the climb was petering out, they started activating options. Cash started flowing in. Lots of cash.

He was looking at the effect the wheat prices were having on other positions they'd planned, and too many of them were already moving. Not good.

"Recommend concentrate then go to Four Alpha," Mike said. "Marseilles."

Commercial Bank of Marseilles was heavy with loans to companies that bought wheat. While the likelihood that the price of wheat would cause those companies to go bankrupt was low, they would be squeezed. That squeeze would affect the bonds held by Marseilles, driving their value down. By shorting the bonds before others figured that out, they would be in position to make money when the value of the bonds fell.

"Confirm," Benjamin said.

Once all the options were moved and the capital was concentrated, Asuda shorts started hitting Marseilles Bank bonds. Coming off the wheat options, it was close to three quarters of a billion dollars in capital. But they'd taken leverage on the shorts, backed by Mike's redoubtable available capital. So, it was closer to three billion dollars that hit the bank's bonds. As other traders realized why, the value of the bonds started to fall, then free-fall.

Then the shorts started being taken. More capital flowed back.

"Recommend Six Delta," Mike said. "Buy TAFE..."

It was going to be a long day. But a fun one.

"How was your day, Father?" Mike asked over shrimp.

They were back in Riverside House for the time being. Mike liked Indian food, but the one thing he'd insisted on was a cook who could make shrimp tacos. So, the chef was Mexican.

Dinner, though, wasn't Mexican food. It was a shrimp course followed by rack of lamb.

It was considerably better than being starved nearly to death.

"I'm up to my eyeballs in the paperwork for your land buy in Montana," Derrick said. The table was so huge that if they'd sat at opposite ends, they would've had to shout at each other. Mike insisted his father take the head of the table while Derrick insisted the owner take it. Since they were both too stubborn to concede, they sat across from each other beside the head.

"Sorry to overwork you," Mike said, taking a bite of grilled shrimp. He tasted a touch of Latin flavorings. It was really good.

"I like the work, or I wouldn't be doing it," Derrick said. "How'd the commodities thing work out?"

"We closed up by about three quarters of a billion," Mike said. "So, the fungibles portion of the portfolio is at about a billion and a half. At this rate, I can already pay the death taxes out of what we've made. Including taking the taxes on *that*. Though maybe not if we have to pay New York taxes on it all. Gah."

"You going out to see the prospective farms?" Derrick asked.

"Yes," Mike said. "I mean, we've got a plane we haven't even seen yet. Speaking of sight unseen. You want to go along? Or do I go by myself?"

"Fun as that sounds, I have too much to do here," Derrick said. "So, who's going along?"

"David Reynolds," Mike said, ticking off the group on his fingers. "Alger. Carl as a driver and general gopher. Matt Doughty from Asuda. He's a farmland acquisition specialist. That should be all we need."

"Can you do your classes on the road?" Derrick asked.

"As long as I've got internet," Mike said. "Which I assume wherever I'm staying will have internet. I hear they even have it in South Dakota. And the plane's got it if nothing else . . ."

"David, welcome," Mike said.

He had hardly dealt with David Reynolds in Montana. He'd met him but they hadn't really talked. The son of Sarah Reynolds née Sterrenhunt was tall, six foot four, with broad shoulders, brown eyes, blond hair and fair, weathered skin. He also had calloused hands like a side of ham.

Carl had picked him up at the airport after a flight out in the Gulfstream, and they were meeting at the town house.

"Hey, David," Derrick said, nodding.

"Hey," David replied. He was mostly gawking at the main foyer of the town house. "This is something, cuz. When you said this thing was a castle, I thought you were joking."

"And you haven't seen the manse, yet," Mike said. "Come on in."

"At least I don't have to worry about if there's enough room to stay," David said at dinner, staring down the length of the dining room. Still at a standoff, Mike and Derrick had offered their cousin the head of the table, and he'd politely accepted. "Or where to get a meal. Do you eat like this all the time?"

Dinner was lobster diavolo.

"It's the definition of wretched excess," Mike said. "I keep thinking I need to just turn them into orphanages or homeless shelters or something. But I also keep thinking they're a legacy handed down from my family and I should probably preserve them to hand down to *my* kids. I'm going with legacy right now."

"So, that gets to the larger legacy," Mike said. "You got the briefing from Asuda?"

"I did," David said. "Read it on the plane out. I'd looked at it before, but planting time is busy-busy."

"Right," Mike said. "Some of the properties we're looking at on this round aren't exactly what I'm looking for as country redoubts. But the right piece will come up at some point. Summer isn't the time to buy farmland, anyway."

"Winter's better, depending," David said. "Down south there are multiple growing seasons so it's pretty much any time. But winter in the north."

"And we're going to be back in Montana to check out the Colonial properties *just before the family comes out here.*"

"Nobody can believe you bought that," David said. "You're planning on leaving it open for recreational use, still, right? 'Cause everybody in town uses it."

"I am," Mike said. "We're working out an agreement with the state similar to the previous owners. There are some areas I'm considering restricting access for some reasons…"

He covered his idea of a long-term beaver reintroduction and management program and why.

"Yeah, *that's* gonna be fun," David said, looking at Derrick.

"I warned him," Derrick said, shaking his head.

"It's gonna be that much trouble," Mike said.

"The Flathead made money for a long time off of beaver pelts," David said, shrugging. "They're less worried about the health of trees, even if you're right. So, yeah, expect poaching."

"We'll handle it," Mike said with a sigh. "Get the population up enough and breeding and limit the poaching and you get ahead of the curve..."

"So, I didn't want to ask with, uh, *Ivory Wing* around, but are you two a thing now?" Jorge asked.

The junior supers were back on patrol. It was Stone Tactical's last patrol for the foreseeable future. Katherine had signed the completion of his mandated community service time with the juniors. Bonfire had briefed the others at the outset of the patrol. It wasn't goodbye, as he assured them all he'd stay in close touch and return for the odd patrol when he could.

But it still felt like goodbye.

Josh had taken control at the outset of this patrol and greatly limited their picture and autograph time. Surprisingly, Laura hadn't fussed too much about it. Josh was now leading them toward the Ramble, where they hadn't gone since Mike's very first patrol with the group. As the oldest member, Josh had always been the notional leader, but he seemed to be taking the role a lot more seriously than he ever had.

"No, I'm sorry to say, we are very much not a thing," Mike said.

"Oh no," Laura said, trying and failing to sound disappointed. She gave him a side-eye wink. "Looking for someone a little more, shall we say, experienced?"

"Sure, something like that." Mike dramatically rolled his eyes and shook his head. Laura chuckled.

"Okay, but you definitely made out in the limo, right?" Jorge asked. "I mean, otherwise, it's a waste of a good limo ride."

"Cut it out, Hombre de Poder," Josh said. He stopped and looked around the trees. "Stone, let's not dwell on the fact that I know why you can answer this, but is there anyone within hearing distance that I might not be seeing?"

Mike drew in a breath and looked around with his eyes as much as he did with Sight. To his credit, Josh had chosen a spot with good visibility, but also enough foliage that their conversation would be muted. They did have a pair of homeless watchers who'd been stealthily shadowing them to either side, but they were well beyond hearing range.

"No, we're good," Mike said. "You chose a good spot."

Josh straightened a little at the praise. "Okay. I know I don't have to say this, but keep an eye out."

"Does that mean you brought us here for a reason?" Jorge asked.

"Are we going to look for drugs, robbers, rapists?" Laura asked.

"No, Fresh Breeze, not this time." Okay, truth be told, Josh was wandering dangerously close to cheesy superhero voice. "It's Stone Tactical's last patrol with us for a while."

A gust of wind rolled through, but it dispersed before hitting Laura. Mike had never seen her do that before.

"Stone, your first time out with us, you brought up the Storm," Josh said. "We'd never really talked about it before. Because talking about the Storm forces us to realize we need to get ready for it, and the first thing they taught all of us was not to train. Because training led to the other thing we never talk about."

"The Nebraska Killer," Jorge said, nodding.

"No," Josh said with closed eyes. "Colonel James King. Major Freedom. Like you said, Stone, he was once the best of us. Once upon a time, this whole nation slept soundly with the knowledge that if or when the Storm came, he would be the one to keep them safe from it. After he—I mean, when he was gone, people just stopped talking about it. Sure, it's still debated in small internet chat rooms and crazy History Channel shows, but it's completely out of the mainstream."

"But what's the point in keeping everyone afraid?" Laura said. She shivered, even though she was still actively keeping the wind away. "Fearmongering gets us nowhere."

Josh dipped his chin and tensed up. "But ignoring it is worse. My whole point of saying what I'm saying is that you're right, Stone. The Storm is Coming. We all heard it, we all know it. And we all know that's the entire point of these powers. It's not to get a million followers on each of a dozen social media apps. It's not to be on the cover of *GQ* or *Seventeen* or the *New York Post* or the *Gotham Herald*. It's to fight the Storm, whatever that's going to be."

"What does all that mean?" Laura asked, hugging her arms tight to herself.

"It means we need to prepare ourselves, in whatever way we can get away with," Josh said. "Like learning to fly, but way more than that."

"Hell, yeah," Jorge said. "It's about time."

Laura shook her head and backed away a step. "But that's what drove the Neb—*Major Freedom*—crazy. We can't do that. What's to stop that from happening to us?"

"*We* are," Josh said, spreading his arms to the group. "He started off on his own, and even when other supers started showing up, he was still the greatest, and that had to be isolating. Even in love with, engaged to, California Girl, she'd barely learned to fly. He was a god among them and that's got to screw with a person."

I mean, you'd probably freak the hell out if you learned the full extent of my powers. And King had the benefit of a government-sponsored torture campaign to warp his mind. But yeah, let's go with "Power corrupts." It's true enough in concept, and I should probably watch out for that.

Now Josh was in full cheese mode, as much as he was actually making some excellent points. "We can look out for each other, keep each other based. But we have to get better at what we do. Everything depends on it. We all know it."

Jorge grimaced a little and *gently* tapped Mike's shoulder with a fist. "If that's what we're doing now—and let me state for the record I completely agree—I kinda wish you'd be here to help us."

"He will be," Josh said. Then, directly to Mike, he added, "You will, won't you? I mean, don't tell me you haven't already dreamed up a million ways that all of us can use our powers in ways none of us has even considered, and don't tell me you don't have a million suggestions on how each of us can train and improve our powers. More than any of that, I bet you've got a billion ideas on how we can be real superheroes, doing real good, like you keep showing us how to do. Am I right?"

Mike glanced at the others, trying not to look suspicious. After a moment, he shrugged in mild embarrassment. "Guilty."

"Then," Josh continued, "I propose we don't just 'keep in touch.' I propose we stay in just about constant contact. You helping us train and learn new ways to use our powers, and we'll help keep you grounded, based, keep you a part of the group so we can keep each other from letting it all get to us."

Josh thrust his hand out.

"Is it a deal?"

Mike smiled and shook his hand.

Holy Leadership, Metalstorm!

"Deal."

CHAPTER 33

"Rocky Mountain High" —John Denver

"Well, this is a different way to return," Mike said as the Gulfstream circled the Flathead Valley to line up with Kalispell City Airport.

Mike had just finished traveling the country with David and the rest looking at properties. He'd enjoyed it. He could spend all his time doing just that.

There was more important work to do.

"Ready to get your head out of the clouds?" Derrick said.

"No," Mike replied. "But I assure you my feet are still firmly planted on the ground."

"I'm pretty sure your grandfather can get them out," Derrick said.

"You forget I'm the grandson," Mike said.

"True."

"Welcome back!" Grandma Maddie Sterrenhunt said, throwing her arms around Mike. She gave him a hug, then leaned back. "You've grown!"

"I have, yes," Mike said. "Hello, Poppa."

"What, no fancy scarf?" Poppa asked.

Mike was dressed in jeans and a flannel shirt.

"That's for New York, Poppa," Mike said. "This is Kalispell."

"Home sweet home," Mike said, rolling his bags into Derrick's house.

The simple home had seemed like all he'd ever desired when he'd stayed there before. Of course, it had been the first time he'd ever lived in a home with someone he could truly call family. But it seemed different now. Smaller for sure than what he'd gotten used to, though still very cozy, and it had the added bonus of not requiring a spiritual cleansing.

"Think you can handle it?" Derrick asked.

"I want to be the person that this is all I want," Mike said. "That this is sufficient and it's all that I truly desire. I'm honest enough to say that I'm not sure I'm that person. That I'm not sure that I don't prefer Riverside House with servants and a cook. I *want* to be this person. But I'm not sure that I *am* this person. And if you're not sure you're this person than you probably are not."

"You vastly overthink everything, Mike," Derrick said. "Just put your clothes away. We're going to be here a while."

"Mr. Handley," Mike said, shaking the man's hand. "Good to finally meet you."

The five-foot-ten, blue-eyed Adam Handley had been the property manager who was left behind when Mike purchased great, huuuuge...tracts of land that could barely be described as "around the Fisher River." That was just a small part of the entire parcel.

The timber and property management offices were in Kalispell. Which made things convenient.

The offices were in a two-story building built in the seventies off of US 2. They had been well maintained and were nicely decorated, so nothing to work on there. The sign above the door had been removed and a new one had yet to be hung.

"Good to meet you, Mr. Truesdale," Handley said, looking at Mike's father. "Counselor. Welcome back."

"Glad to be back," Derrick said, shaking his hand.

"Why don't you introduce me?" Mike said.

Running a property the size of the one Mike had bought was not a one-man operation. The Kalispell office for what had become the Lonely Mountain Timber and Land Company employed fifty people and worked with dozens of contractors. It wasn't a small office.

He was led through the offices, meeting the various employees. He kept in mind that he now had the responsibility for keeping them in their jobs. On the other hand, he also had to keep in mind that not every employee was the right fit.

"Okay," Mike said. "I'll get to know everybody over time. But I'd like to meet with you personally."

They went back to Handley's second-floor office and sat down at the conversation area.

"Can I get you anything?" Handley's raven-haired female executive assistant asked.

"I'm okay," Mike said, pulling a sports drink out of his backpack. "But, since I'm going to be around from time to time, might want to keep a few of these handy."

"I'll be sure to," the EA said. "Counselor?"

"Coffee," Derrick said. "Black."

"Coming right up."

"Okay," Mike said, taking a breath. "This is a big thing for a kid who was living in a ghetto six months ago."

"It is," Handley said. "How are you handling it?"

"One item at a time," Mike said. "There are certain things I'm not going to touch. For the employees, I don't foresee any layoffs. That's the first and most important news."

"That's good to hear," Handley said.

"One thing I'm pretty sure you know but not absolutely," Mike said, lifting up a piece of rock. "I'm an Earther. Were you aware?"

"I was, yes," Handley said.

His EA entered about then and Mike paused.

"I'm sorry, we weren't introduced," Mike said. "Mike Truesdale."

"Yes, sir," the EA said, smiling and setting down a coffee service. "I'm Rebecca McPeters."

"Nice to meet you, Rebecca," Mike said.

He waited again until she'd left.

"I'm going to be in and out of this office quite a bit until I get my own. That one will be the Follett Corporation, and this will be a subsidiary. Doesn't mean I won't be in and out anyway. Do you have a spare office? I could use one."

"We do," Handley said, nodding. "Right next to this one, if that works."

"Works for me," Mike said. "Can you handle getting it set up? I'm heavy on IT so it will be a tech office."

"We can handle that," Handley said. "We're pretty high tech around here."

"For everyone, this should be the last transfer," Mike said. "From here on out, the property is going to be owned by my family. And absent me going tits up financially, which I'm fighting hard to avoid, it will be owned in perpetuity. Once we put the new sign on the door, with only minor changes in name, it should run the same way by the same people for the rest of their lives. And absent there being a reason to fire people, or having to do a layoff due to a huge economic downturn, I don't have an issue with people working here the rest of their lives—as long as they've got a reason to be here and they want to keep working here. All clear?"

"Clear," Handley said.

"Okay," Mike said. "So, no layoffs.

"Changes. There will be no changes in relation to the recreational activities that people use the land for. My family has used it to go hiking, hunting, fishing. I'm not going to close it off. We're still in negotiations with the state on how to handle liability, but for right now it's the same."

"I heard you were planning on closing off some parts," Handley said.

"That's where we get to changes," Mike said. "And there are going to be a few. But I'm not going to introduce those right away. You just need to know for planning. We've got all winter to talk people into it being a good idea.

"The first item is beaver," Mike said, then explained his plans for a beaver reintroduction and why.

"Ooookay," Handley said, looking over at Derrick and taking a sip of coffee.

"Yeah, yeah, yeah," Mike said, grinning. "*Everybody* looks the same way when I bring it up. I'll get somebody to handle that. They'll work for you, and they'll take your orders. But they'll also be working direct since it's my project. We'll set up a field office somewhere closer to the action. We're going to have to choose the most remote part of the property. Choose a section that's been clear-cut and another that hasn't. The point is to gather as much data as possible and it's going to be a long-term research project.

"Just generally," Mike said, "you should know I've been taking college courses since I was eight."

"Really?" Handley said, looking again at Derrick.

"I'm published in the field of astrophysics," Mike said.

"Seriously?"

"Seriously," Derrick replied.

"So, I'm into information," Mike said. "I'm into science and I'm into research. I'm not a lefty environmentalist but I see some value in the field. One thing that I noticed on the table of organization is that we have one environmental position that is for filings, but we don't have a forest ecology person or department."

"No, we don't," Handley said, his brow furrowing.

"You're a lumber guy," Mike said. "You came into this from the timber-cutting side, right?"

"I did," Handley said. "Is that an issue?"

"Forests are living systems," Mike said, trying to figure out how to get through to the guy. "When you plant crops, you're not completely supplanting the ecology, but you are mostly doing so. A form of terraforming. These forests depend on regrowth. We don't completely clear them and replant as you would with a tree farm in Mississippi. So, the ecology of the forest is important.

"The financial bottom line from the point of view of the business is getting the most money out of the timber," Mike said. "Are your trees skinny and poorly growing? Or are they big fat boles with lots of board feet? The difference depends on how well your timber has grown over the course of the time from cut to cut. Some of that is out of our control. Too many and severe droughts and you don't get as many board feet. But if you can improve the living conditions of the timber, you will get more board feet.

"Most people don't have to worry about the next cut with the trees around here. Even a corporation is not going to hold the property that long. I'm planning on it. So, I have to worry about the property for this cut and the next.

"Let's talk about how I view it with the beaver thing for a second," Mike said. "Okay?"

"Okay," Handley said.

"Trees need a few things to grow," Mike said. "They need air. That's free so far. They need sunlight. How much they get can't be controlled. They need water. The amount of snow and rainfall can't be controlled. Out of our hands.

"But they also need soil.

"You look at the streams around here after a cut," Mike said, "and while there are a lot of things that people do to keep from having erosion, you still get silt in the streams. Sometimes a lot.

"Now, the conservationist side of me sees that and goes 'Oh, that's terrible for the streams.' It's bad for the fish. It's bad for the stream in general. And that's sad but that's it. It's sad. The silt will settle, and it will be okay. Little ugly but so what?

"The businessman side of me is *furious*," Mike said. "There's a voice in my head going 'God damnit! That's *my* motherfucking soil! Should be on *my* hillside, not in that *God damn stream!*'"

"Okay," Handley said. "Interesting take."

"I'm serious, sir," Mike said. "These mountains don't have much soil as it is. Soil loss is board feet loss in the next cut. I want *my* soil on *my* mountains, Mr. Handley. That's not a point of humor. Be very clear about that."

"Alright," Handley said, nodding.

"So, how do you reduce soil loss?" Mike asked. "One way is beaver. They trap the soil in their ponds. Those ponds aren't useful, now, for timber. But they will be at a certain point.

"The other way you reduce soil loss is you reduce the cut area by doing partial patch-cut."

"Ooooh," Handley said, trying not to make a face.

The way the property was currently being cut was clear-cutting of one-square-mile, 640-acre sections. Some mature trees were left as singletons. They contributed seeds to the area and were supposed to support regrowth of the timber.

Mike had already seen that almost all of those singleton trees were dead, which meant they weren't contributing and they were fire hazards.

Partial patch cut was a system where one-hundred-acre sections were mostly but not entirely clear-cut. *Trios* of mature trees, more or less twenty-five percent inward from the edges, were left. It was one of those places where "a bit random is better." The mature trees contributed to bringing in seeds to the surrounding areas and they survived better as trios than as single trees.

The corner trios of the surrounding areas were cut away to get an equal number of trees from the area and to create gaps to prevent wildfires.

"The new kid has all the answers going through your head," Mike said. "I'm not going to introduce any of this this cut year. We're going to take the whole winter to discuss it with the timber concessions. But I'm serious about both projects."

"Partial patch cut has..." Handley said, frowning. "There are lots of costs born by the owner, you realize, sir?"

"Like the additional surveying?" Mike said. "You can do ninety percent of that through satellite. More, probably. You already use satellite survey and GPS location to assign the cut areas. I'm giving you credit for leaving tree buffers along the streams, by the way."

"We do leave mature trees," Handley said.

"Every single one of which is dead as far as I've seen," Mike said. "I've been up in this property and seen the cuts with my father over the winter. Every dead tree is a potential forest fire, Mr. Handley. And every mature tree that was left is dead. That's a lot of potential wildfires. You might as well cut them all out. I don't know if they'll survive better as trios or not. If they don't, we might as well clear-cut. But with one-hundred-acre areas, you get less dynamic forcing of the water running off the hill. That cuts down on erosion and keeps more soil on the hills.

"Then there's the issue of seed bank," Mike said. "The soil already contains seeds. When there's dynamic forcing and it's mostly stripped, you don't just lose soil, you lose the seed bank. That means slower regrowth, so you don't have as thick of boles when you do your next cut. I'm looking at this long term not short, Mr. Handley.

"Then there's the issue of forest ecology. By creating open areas, you have feed areas and cover areas. Mile square open areas are not good for the various small and large animals. There's too much open area and not enough cover. And those are part of the ecology.

"Everybody around here guides, right?" Mike said. "My father was a hunting guide when he was in high school. The lumberjacks, the sons of the contractors, all guide.

"More broken-up timber means higher game levels. Again, open area, cover area.

"The contractors aren't going to like it," Mike said, shrugging. "I'm not going to force it down their throats. Certainly not this season. I've got the whole winter to meet with them. But most of the companies are family operations. They've got kids and grandkids they hope will one day take over the operation. And that will be my pitch. It's better for my kids, when I have them. It's better for your grandkids."

Handley looked over at Derrick.

"The beaver thing..." Derrick said and shrugged. "What I've mostly told him is that it's practically *genetic* for Indians to trap beaver. Keeping people from trapping them out is going to be the tough part.

"The cutting part? I'm in *his* corner. Adam, I've watched the cuts and they're *nightmares*. It's not just that it's unsightly. Every spring the streams are *filled* with silt. And he's right, that's coming from the hills that don't have much in the way of soil. So, it's not good for the trees. I've hated watching it. You can see the erosion gullies even in winter.

"And he's right that the whole area is covered in dead mature trees, Adam. You might as well cut them all out as leave them. Each one is standing out above the rest of the trees so they're lightning targets. So, I'm in agreement. Either cut them out or find a way that they'll survive. Trios are more likely to survive.

"And last but not least... I may have to sign off, but it's *his* land. He bought it with *his* money, and *he* negotiated the deal with the bank. In four and a half years, I *won't* be signing off anymore. So, you might as well get used to him."

"Alright," Handley said, the uncertainty clear in his voice.

"None of this happens this season," Mike said. "I'd like to introduce it, but it will take lots of planning and preparation. Changes this season are bringing in at least one forest ecologist to start working on that. They'll also be in charge of the beaver reintroduction program, which will *not* be in your budget. That's an experiment and I'll work through academia on it, probably University of Montana, and it will all be tax deductible.

"And there's one upside to the whole thing," Mike said.

"Which is?" Handley said. "Not that I'm saying there's a downside."

"You clearly think I'm a nut," Mike said, grinning. "Which I am, but I'm going to go with what we talked about absent it being clear and apparent I'm wrong. The upside is I'm an Earther. Which means that if we have a fire, I can probably snuff it faster than you'd believe. Montana *never* gets Super Corps support. They only go to California because *California Girl*! But my land and the surrounding areas that can affect it now have a powerful Earther to help out. And while everyone sees the flyers on TV, it's the Earthers that do the most good.

"Which brings up the next point," Mike said. "I know a lot of stuff. What I don't know is the first damned thing about fighting forest fires. So, I need a guy. Almost assuredly a guy. He's probably in his forties or fifties, has burn scars, and is real comfortable wearing a hard hat and one of those yellow shirts. The kind of guy they use to qualify wilderness firefighter teams. I'm not going to try to become an expert. I've got too many other things I need to become expert at. But with the right guy, I can kill a forest fire faster than you'd believe."

"That would be good," Handley said, nodding. "Can you . . . uh . . ."

"I'll go out with the guy—your choice, choose well—and test things out," Mike said. "We'll see what I can do. And again, I'd prefer to keep that out of sight and out of mind. The Super Corps is really picky about who uses their powers and when and where. Do we have a helo?"

"We generally lease them," Handley said.

"I'm going to have to get a helo," Mike said. "That's got to go on the to-do list. This thing is waaaay too big to try to get around in a truck. It's huuuuge . . . tracts of land!"

"How well do you know Handley?" Mike asked on the drive home.

"Not very well," Derrick said. "And I'm not the right guy to ask about him. My previous experience with him was representing someone in a case against the company. I will say he has a problem with sexual harassment."

"I noticed he rarely bothered to introduce the women," Mike said. "Even his executive assistant."

"He'd call her a secretary," Derrick said.

"I don't like firing people," Mike said. "And he has relationships with all the timber contractors. That can be good and can be bad. I need to meet more people. I definitely need to meet the timber people. Is there a club or something?"

"No," Derrick said. "But I do know where you can meet the power locals in an informal setting. At least on a Wednesday night."

"Wait," Mike said, thinking. "VFW poker?"

"American Legion, but yes," Derrick said.

"Well, I know where I'm going to be spending Wednesdays," Mike said.

CHAPTER 34

"The Gambler" —Kenny Rogers

"Oh, it's truly insane," Mike said, nodding. "The freaking *apartment* is bigger than Grandma and Poppa's house!"

It was mandatory fun day again and the pool at Gramma and Poppa's was reopened. Mike had jumped in as soon as they arrived and was now fielding questions from everyone about, well, everything. Everyone included quite a few people. When Mike had first met the entire extended family, Derrick had quipped that, aside from himself and his sister Abigail, his many other brothers and sisters had been trying to repopulate the Sioux Nation. He hadn't really been kidding, either.

Kids of all ages and a dozen various floats filled the pool. Parents filled tables and chairs all around in numbers that would've rivaled a public pool. A group of older men clustered around a row of grills, but beers and alcoholic beverages were conspicuously absent.

"I wanna see it," his cousin Madeleine said. She was the same age as Mike and had what he'd come to call the Sterrenhunt look, with distinctly Native American features, black hair, and dark eyes. "In fact, I need to see all your places."

"We were going to bring everybody out to visit," Mike said, "but we just ran out of time. We needed to get back here."

"Why?" Tiffany asked. The honey-blonde fourth of six Allen girls was the smartest, which was saying quite a lot. She and Mike had debated the origins of the universe on his previous visit.

"Taxes?" Mike said. "I need to spend as much time in Montana this year as possible, or at least outside the State of New York, to convince them I'm not a resident of New York. New York taxes are insane. So... we'll probably schedule a visit there sometime this summer. And anybody who happens to be there can use any of the houses. But I need to stay as far away as possible."

"That's crazy," Marlene said, giggling. At fourteen, she was the third oldest Allen girl. Even for him, it was a little dizzying keeping track of the Allen girls. "You're running away to avoid taxes."

"It's called being a tax refugee," Mike said with a sigh. "You have *no idea* what the taxes are going to be. Besides, I bought half of Montana. I probably should visit it."

"Did you *really* buy all the Colonial land?" Marlene asked. "I heard that, but..."

"I did, yes," Mike said. "Well, me and an investment bank. And it's not half of Montana but it's a big chunk of Flathead and Lincoln counties."

"That's just insane," Rob Sterrenhunt said, shaking his head. He was seventeen and worked as a ranch hand while waiting to join the military. "We're still gonna be able to use it, though, right?"

"Most of it," Mike said. "Some of it I may ask that people steer clear. I want to do some studies. But we'll see how it goes. Not much of it will be cut off, if any. Most of it will stay the same as when Colonial owned it."

"Are you going to log it?" Tiffany asked. "That's a big part of the economy around here. I mean..."

"Yes," Mike said. He'd answered all these questions a half a dozen times from the family alone. "But we may change some of the practices. One of the meetings we're going to have is with the lumber companies. I'm not big on their cutting practices. And we may be doing replanting in some areas. But, generally, except for it being privately owned there won't be big changes..."

Mike walked into Pirate Bill's Rock Emporium and looked around in surprise. There were *other people* in the place. There was a clerk and actual real customers.

Retired geologist "Pirate Bill" Harrison had a *very* large rock shop in Columbia Falls. Mike had spent a good deal of his time in Montana at the place, studying all the minerals. They'd quickly bonded over Mike's OCD need to properly re-sort minerals that customers had carelessly left in the wrong places.

He could See Pirate Bill in the back room, probably avoiding the current batch of customers. Mike shaped a chunk of not particularly interesting granite into an arrow, lifted it up into Bill's sight, and pointed to the front of the store.

"Hail, hail the conquering hero," Bill said, walking up and shaking his hand. "Welcome back. That's a meteoric rise from ghetto rat to billionaire."

"Heh," Mike said. "The *Journal* wanted to profile me after the Fieldstone short. I've already made more than I inherited on arbitrage. I just stopped by to say hello and check in on my favorite rock collection. You have actual real customers, Bill!"

"I told you it was different in the summer," Bill said. "Did I hear that the Follett Family Corporation bought the Colonial properties?"

"You did, yes," Mike said. "And, yes, I'll be looking at it for minerals. But I'm not going to mine it out. It's actually just because I wanted somewhere remote. And that's about as remote as it gets."

"You should take a look around the Helonic mines," Bill whispered. "There's probably more bodies that could be accessed."

"No idea what you're talking about," Mike whispered. "Besides, I hear that they're negotiating with some Chinese development company that's going to be putting in a Storm bunker for rich Californians."

"Seriously?" Bill said.

"How close are you to Helonic?"

"I worked for a *Chinese* mining company," Bill said. "Working with Chinese Super Force who kill you as soon as look at you. And even *I* don't have the stomach to work for Helonic."

"That's the word on the Street," Mike said. "It's definitely *not* the Follett Corporation behind some sort of shell that goes through Liechtenstein. I have nothing whatsoever to do with it."

"I know nothing," Bill said, chuckling. "How was New York? Can you handle the letdown?"

"It's not a letdown," Mike said. "I've actually eaten Wagyu beef at this point."

"Like it?" Bill said.

"Yes," Mike admitted. "But it's super rich. If you had to eat it every day, at a certain point you'd go 'Can I just have a hot dog?' That's what New York was like. The houses are too big—at least for the uber wealthy. I mean, most people are spending a fortune to live in a closet. But at the high end, the freaking Fifth Avenue apartment is the size of this place! Exaggeration, but only slightly. And I got tired of it pretty quick. I was ready for some simple lifestyle."

"Well, you certainly get that in Montana," Bill said.

"Got a question for you," Mike said.

"Shoot," Bill said then shook his head. "Knowing you, I have to add . . ."

"'Not literally'?" Mike said, snorting. "I have people for that these days. Query: You ever go to the Kalispell poker night . . . ?"

"Counselor?" the doorman said to Derrick while eyeballing Mike.

"Look, it's already an illegal endeavor," Mike said, grinning. "And whether the local power structure likes it or not, the thirteen-year-old is now part of the local power structure. And I can afford to lose the money."

"Okay," the doorman said, doubtfully. "I'm Sam. Sam I am."

"And you do not like green eggs and ham," Mike said.

"It's a thousand-dollar cash buy in," Sam said. "And there's an ATM if you run out. And in your case, I'm pretty sure that George will give you a marker."

"I'm good for it," Mike said, grinning.

The American Legion hall was about half full when they arrived. From the outside, it had looked like a run-down building from the sixties or seventies. On the inside, however, it was pretty nice and well maintained. Maybe not so much by New York standards, but definitely swanky for Montana. The saloon-style, polished wooden bar to one side was in full swing.

Mike picked up a thousand dollars in chips and started to sort out the tables.

"Over here," Derrick said, carrying his own pile of chips.

He led Mike over to a table toward the rear.

"Gentleman," Derrick said. "Mind if we sit in?"

"Not at all, Counselor," an older gentleman said. "I should be very down on you as a parent for this trip but given what I saw of your son's file, not that I can say much, a trip to the Legion to play poker isn't going to corrupt him any more than he came corrupted."

Mike had dressed for the occasion in a sports coat of primarily plum alpaca wool shot with threads of silk in gold and copper. It was, if not the best-looking coat in the room, than in the top end. Which fitted the local billionaire.

"You must be the judge that did *not* allow me to be sent back to New York," Mike said, grinning and sitting down. "Thank you for that. I almost hate to take your money. Judge Watkins, yes?"

"Yes," Judge Watkins said, grinning. The judge was in his sixties at a guess, with a shock of white hair and a ruddy complexion. "And I'm glad it all worked out."

"You're correct that a spot of poker is nothing compared to my background," Mike said. "The last time I played poker was with some of the guys in a drug gang. I was careful to not win too much as I did not want to be involved in a gunfight."

"Well, we'll try not to get into one tonight," one of the men said. "You're Mike Truesdale, obviously. I'm Lester Scoggins. I run the Century 21 franchise here in town. If you're looking for a house..."

"Pleasure to meet you, Mr. Scoggins," Mike said. "And I may not be, but I'm going to be bringing in some people, hopefully, and I'll keep that in mind."

The other two at the six-top were Jack Gardner, another local attorney, and Corey Stiefel, who was a medical equipment salesman.

"So, how'd you get in a poker game with a drug gang?" Stiefel asked after the hand was dealt.

"Problem with that being I don't talk much when I have cards in my hand," Mike said, then looked at his cards. "Which is not an issue. Fold.

"So, when I was eleven, a drug gang decided it was going to kill me," Mike said. "I objected strenuously, they lost, fair's fair."

"They lost?" Judge Watkins said.

"Ahem," Mike said. "My identity was changed by the US Marshals, Your Honor, because of a later problem with MS-13. My original name is Michael Edwards."

"I *remember* that," Gardner said. "Holy shit. The kid who killed, like...was it fifteen black dudes?"

"It was not due to white supremacy, I assure you," Mike said. "Okay, so there was this kid named Trayvon. Trayvon was always starting stuff. And he was all mouth, no trousers. The full story takes about two hours to tell properly. But if His Honor will allow some language, I'll give you the opening, which I prefer to start in the middle of action. But there is language."

"Language permitted," the judge said. "*If* you are quoting someone."

"I am, Your Honor," Mike said. "Myself.

"So, I'm eleven years old behind the wheels of a black Cadillac Escalade doing ninety down a residential street marked for thirty," Mike said, miming holding onto a steering wheel that was above his line of sight. "There's a bullet hole in the windshield that's still dripping blood and brains."

"Ugh," Scoggins said, grimacing.

"My social worker is in the passenger seat holding onto the grab bar," Mike said, "'cause she didn't put on her seat belt like I told her. She's screaming, 'WHAT ARE YOU DOING? WHAT ARE YOU DOING?'

"To which I reply: 'Bitch, you ever heard of "drive it like you stole it"? This is "drive it like you just kilt two motherfuckers and stole it"!'"

"Oh, wow," Gardner said as the whole group chuckled.

"Funky music here," Mike said, making a "bow-wow-wow" sound. "Michael and the Fifth Street Kings! Like I said, tellin' the whole story proper takes about two hours. But when you single-handedly wipe out one of the worst gangs in Baltimore's history of notorious killers, it gives you some street rep.

"So, by the time I got into it with MS-13, I'd deal with the heads of drug gangs as an equal. The two main gangs in Baltimore when I left were the Gangland Mobsters and the Port Street Posse. And they were both recruiting me as a shooter 'cause they were getting ready to get into it with each other. I was avoiding both."

About then it was time for another hand, and he studied his cards.

"I'm in," Mike said. "Raise ten."

"Could you avoid street gangs?" Stiefel asked.

"With respect, sir," Mike said, "I don't talk much when I have cards in my hand."

"Wise move," the judge declared.

Mike continued to hold until it was just him and Stiefel.

"Full house," Mike said, laying down his cards.

"Got me beat," Stiefel said.

"To answer the question," Mike said. "It's generally hard to avoid being in a gang when you're raised in a ghetto. I'd actually been a runner and a tout for the Fifth Street Kings, which was one of many reasons I was pissed that they'd tried to take me out. But I spent most of my time away from the ghetto studying somewhere safe. Library. Coffee shops. Even on the Johns Hopkins campus, not that that was entirely safe."

"What were you studying?" Gardner asked.

"Lots of stuff," Mike said. "But my main interest is astrophysics."

"I suppose you don't mind if I mention one of the reasons I was impressed by your file?" Judge Watkins said.

"The college courses?" Mike said. "I don't mind if you mention the whole file, Judge. But I doubt most would have the stomach for it."

"College courses?" Gardner said.

"He'd been auditing college courses since he was...eight, I believe?" the Judge said.

"Yes, sir," Mike said.

"Including doctoral level courses in, yes, astrophysics as well as business and economics," Judge Watkins said. "He had published papers in multiple fields."

"Really?" Scoggins said. "That's impressive."

The cards were dealt again, and Mike folded.

"You fold a lot," Scoggins said.

"It's the only sure move in poker," Mike replied. "Folding is almost always the right move. When MS-13 decided to put a stake in me, unsuccessfully, I was doing business consulting."

"Business consulting?" Gardner said.

"Small business," Mike said. "Lots of people know their field but they don't know business. And business is business. I'd always planned on getting out of the ghetto. If I survived. But I'd go around to small mom-and-pop operations and offer to go over their business practices and books. Look for ways to improve their profitability. If they thought it was worth it, they'd kick me some money, how much depended on their sales, paid out over a few weeks. Twenty bucks a week for five weeks was pretty normal.

"I'd go over their books, look at their practices, explain depreciation to them," Mike said. "Had a pair of comfortable shoes, dress slacks, and this natty little sports coat. God, I loved that thing. First decent clothes I ever had. Got shot to hell by MS-13, the bastards."

"Did they just shoot the coat?" Stiefel asked.

"Oh, no," Mike said, chuckling. "I was *wearing* it at the time. What? Were they going to steal my favorite coat and *shoot* it? But it got freaking shredded. Pissed me off. I really loved that sports coat."

"That's a pretty nice one you're wearing tonight," Scoggins said.

"Picked it up at a Goodwill in New York," Mike said, holding up a sleeve. "It *is* nice. But I liked the other one more. I bought it with money I'd taken off the Fifth Street Kings and squirreled away. There's a special feel to something you buy with money you looted off the dead bodies of your enemies."

"Oh, my God," Judge Watkins said, laughing. "Counselor, I'm not sure Kalispell is ready for your son."

"Neither am I, Your Honor," Derrick replied.

"So, I heard a rumor about you," Gardner said, cautiously.

"Most rumors about me do not equal the reality," Mike said.

"That you're a super?" Gardner said.

"Oh, that," Mike said with a scoff. "Yeah. Duh."

"Seriously?" Scoggins said, his eyes wide.

"I'm hoping there isn't anyone who's anti-super at the table," Mike said, shrugging. "If so, they can get in the long line of people who want me dead. But, yes, Stone Tactical, at your service, sir. Just don't put it on anything electronic, please. It would be *ce qui n'est pas fait* to update your Facebook."

"Ce . . . what?" Stiefel said.

"'That which is not to be done,'" Judge Watkins said.

"That was my Acquisition Event," Mike said. "Having my favorite sports coat shot to hell. I know that a lot of people are still freaked about NK. I am on the other side of the street on that one."

"Right," Gardner said. "That's . . . cool. I'm not freaked by it."

"And you bought the Colonial properties," Scoggins said. "Planning on developing them?"

"I don't really see the market, right now," Mike said. "I know there was a big movement to Kalispell with COVID but that's died down. The home prices are way up but it's not really something to fill up the mountains. If that changes I might do so in a few areas, near Kalispell. But not everywhere."

"You planning on letting people up there?" Stiefel asked.

"I don't plan on changing much vice Colonial," Mike said. "I'm going to be doing some experiments—large-scale forestry and ecological studies. Those areas I won't even cut off, but I'll ask people to use them gently. No taking in general. But that's going to be some of the area that most people don't go there anyway. The popular spots, no change."

"That's good to hear," Stiefel said. "People had been worried about that."

"My family's been using that area for a generation," Mike said. "I'm not going to kick people out. Unless they're being assholes, and that's just for being assholes."

"Stone Tactical," Gardner said. "Weren't you part of that junior team that captured that MS-13 guy?"

"I was, yes," Mike said. "El Cannibale. Who was in New York to hunt me down. Then the hunter became the hunted."

"Why was he hunting you down?" Stiefel asked.

"I'd sort of killed his grand-nephew," Mike said, shrugging. "Look, he tried to kill me, I objected strenuously . . ."

"You deliberately held onto that two pair to lose, didn't you?" Derrick said as they were walking out to the car. The dirt parking lot was full of a strange blend of trucks ranging from muddy and rusted to shiny and new, with a few expensive sedans or SUVs sprinkled throughout.

"I was *not* going to be the billionaire who takes everybody's money, Counselor," Mike said. "I could arguably make my living as a professional poker player. People think that poker is a game of chance. It's not. It's about *math*. And I was doing calculus when I was six."

"You've got a tell," Derrick said.

"You mean the ear-tug thing?" Mike said, pulling at his earlobe. "I've built that in as a tell. It's controllable."

"Okay," Derrick said, snorting.

"I was *not* playing full speed," Mike said as they got in the car. "I wasn't going to take money off the judge who did not send me back to New York. But it gave me an intro feel for some of the local movers and shakers. I did *not* like the DA. He stinks of Society. Criminal justice reform, my ass. Throw them in prison and throw away the key."

"He's not my favorite, either," Derrick said. "I wouldn't say he's popular with most of the long-term residents in the area that pay attention. Both your grandparents hate him. He was promoted by a lot of the California transplants. They basically swamped the race with California money."

"Wanna be DA?" Mike asked.

"Absolutely not," Derrick said. "I've got enough on my plate being your primary counsel."

"Who's a good choice?" Mike asked.

"You planning on buying the DA?" Derrick asked.

"I'm not just planning on buying this one," Mike said. "Seriously. Who's a good choice?"

"The previous DA," Derrick said. "Arthur Woodward. Wasn't there tonight. He's a partner in Schribner. Good guy."

"Firm but fair?" Mike asked. "Tough on crime but got a heart?"

"Yes," Derrick said.

"We need to meet," Mike said. "Elections are coming up. I wonder what the max contribution you can give to a DA in Montana is? And then there are all the other races."

"You're going to need someone to handle that," Derrick said. "Among other things, the legal aspects."

"Agreed," Mike said. "It's on my to-do list. I've just got other things to do first."

CHAPTER 35

"Just some people out camping..." Mike hummed. "And, yes, the mosquitoes *are* a pain."

The Helonic Wolf Creek Mine was off what was now Montana 114 and *had* been a dirt-and-gravel national forest road. When the mine was opened, Montana took over the ownership of the road and, with money from the company, widened it to two lanes and otherwise improved it. It now ran from Kalispell to near Libby, where it joined US Highway 2.

The road was less important than the railroad that paralleled it. The mine loaded separated ore into railcars then shipped it to various destinations. There was no local smelter.

It was estimated to have about two years of ore left. There had been various prospects in the area, drilling to check out the possibility of new bodies. It was unlikely they'd missed one.

But it was worth checking out. Which was why Mike and David were up sort of near the mine, camping out. Not on the company's land. In fact, they were on *Mike's* land since his purchase surrounded the mine.

At the moment they were *in* Wolf Creek, fly-fishing.

"Mosquitoes come with the territory," his cousin David said, flicking his fly out into a passable pool.

Mike cheated, again, dropping a dry fly onto a spot where there was a trout. It didn't take the fly. So, he tried another spot he could See trout. Got one that time.

"How the hell are you doing that?" David asked.

"Just got to set your hat right, David," Mike said, slapping a mosquito.

"You did pretty well for a beginner, Mike," David said, frying the trout over a fire.

"I have to confess," Mike said, chuckling. "If I can see a deer on the other side of a hill and I can see ores, you really think I *can't* see where the trout are?"

"That's *so* cheating," David said, shaking his head.

"I'll handle the dishes," Mike said, contritely.

"You suck, cuz," David said, chuckling.

Mike was washing the frying pan with dirt, holding the pan up and scrubbing it using powers while twiddling his thumbs and whistling.

"Think that's bad, watch this."

He held the pan out over the nearby stream and hit it with a blast of water.

"How the *hell* did you do *that*?" David asked.

"I found the chakra of water," Mike said, bringing a globule over to the camp. "And unless I'm much mistaken, it's *pure* water. Just in case, I also hit it with something that kills everything in it. So...potable water. And I can heat it up or cool it."

"You suck," David repeated.

"I have worked *hard* on this, David," Mike said. "It was skull sweat but it was still hours and hours and days and days of trying.

"When I told my Vishnu mentor, he said there was no way. Now I'm up to metallic iron, metallic aluminum, oxygen, and water. I'm trying hard for carbon but that's not really working. All of those elements are common in earth and carbon is fairly rare. But it took a lot of work and even surprised the Vishnu. And they've been at this seriously for a long time."

"Well," David said, shrugging, "I appreciate skull sweat. God knows I sweated enough at college. How are your classes going...?"

It seemed like the sun in Montana never rose in winter and never set in summer seemed like.

It was past eleven when it was dark enough for Mike to start his foray. He didn't intend to enter the area of the mine company's property. They would have thoroughly surveyed that zone. He was just on his property. But he still didn't want them to know he was looking.

He walked out of the light of the campfire as if going to take a whizz, then took off flying through the trees. He was carrying a hand-held GPS in part to mark anything he might find and in part to find his way back.

Helonic owned a five-thousand-acre patch that was bordered on the north side by the railroad bed. On the east, west, and south it was just a line on a map. Mike had purchased everything around that and made sure to include the mineral rights. It was surprising how often those *weren't* part of a land acquisition.

So, he kept to his land, marked on the GPS, and started circling the Helonic properties.

He was directly opposite the mine on the north side of the railroad when he Sensed something. He only had five hundred meters of Sight range, so he started to feel around for it, flying under the branches of trees. It was dark but he could See trees faintly by the earth matter in them. He'd avoided the branches so far.

He headed up the hill opposite the mine and the Sense got stronger. Then he could begin to See the ore body. It was deep beneath the hill. Right at the limit of his range. None of it came anywhere near the surface. And it was large enough he wasn't sure how far it went. He could only See the upper portion. But what he could See was probably enough to run the mine for another five years, at least, and close enough that it should be worth extending it. He was no expert at this.

He pulled up a sample, marked it on the map, and kept going . . .

"Yer back," David said, rubbing his eyes as he climbed out of the tent. "I went to bed. You were gone for a while."

It was right after dawn of the short Montana night. And it was cool enough the mosquitoes were still sleeping in.

"I just got back," Mike said. He was cooking bacon over a fire. "Didn't sleep."

"How'd it go?" David said.

Mike just gestured at a pile of what looked like marbles.

"You found something," David said, picking up one of the samples. "Chalcocite?"

"Yep," Mike said. "Mixed with other stuff. Mostly chalcocite and argentite."

"Where'd it come from?"

"Everywhere," Mike said, pulling out the bacon and pouring out the grease. He dumped pre-scrambled eggs in and started stirring them.

"What do you mean, 'everywhere'?" David asked. "I'm not going to talk about it..."

"That's not the issue, David," Mike said. "I trust you on that. But that's the answer."

He stirred the eggs for a few seconds and sighed.

"I almost feel sorry for Helonic," Mike said. "Big evil mining corporation, yes. But still. You understand crustal faulting, right? Do I need to explain that to someone from Montana much less a Sterrenhunt/Reynolds?"

"No," David said.

"So, with Sight I can see the underground topography," Mike said. "Only down five hundred meters but that's far enough for most stuff. And I think what happened was there was this big ore body and it got cracked along a fault. And the stuff on one side of the fault ended up getting slid up high enough it showed. The stuff on the other side of the fault, it didn't. It actually slid *down*. And slightly sideways."

"The railroad runs along a fault," David said.

"Correct," Mike said. "The Wolf Creek bed is a fault line. So, this little chunk of ore got slid off the main ore body and ended up...*south* of Wolf Creek."

"So..."

"*The hillllls are alive with the smell of copppper,*" Mike sang, shaking his head. "And other stuff. I hit ore body after ore body after ore body every time there was an uplift, and it was in range. And I'm thinking that most of them are contiguous. Not only that..."

He pulled up one of the samples with Move, then handed it to David.

"Unless I'm much mistaken, that's a mix of copper, silver, platinum, *and* gold sulfide ores," Mike said, shaking his head. "Low sulfide, high metallic. You can practically toss it in a fire and get copper, gold, and silver alloy. And that's the majority of the ore that I found."

"Oh, shit," David said.

"What I specifically located was all individual bodies, but I think they're essentially contiguous. Most of the ore is chalcocite and argentite with very little in the way of chalcopyrite. Any of them, though, are large enough to extend the mine. And I think that the Helonic bodies were the upper bodies and thus lower concentration. Also, just a tiny chunk off of the main ore body. I'm going to have to have those assayed and there will need to be drilling but, yeah, this was all worth it. And all of it was on land I bought just 'cause I wanted to own a big chunk of Montana.

"David . . . I think I just—no shit—became, like, richer than Gates, richer than Bezos. If that's as big as it looks and as high grade . . . I might just be the richest man on *Earth*."

"Holy . . . shit," David said, sitting down. "I'm not sure I'm prepared for that before coffee."

"This is insane," Mike said, tipping out the scrambled eggs. "I nearly starved to death when I was seven. This is insane."

"The only place I could see it was in the folds," Mike said.

He'd had a small section of a US 7,500 quadrangle blown up to poster size and was laying out the marbles. Each had the waypoints he'd marked drawn on them. As he laid them down, he shaped them to match the ore body he'd found, including the area, more or less in three dimensions underground and more or less to scale.

"But if you think of how each of these looks," he continued, "I'm thinking there's a nearly contiguous belt of copper ore that runs along the track of the Wolf Creek fault. But the majority of it is on the *north* side of the creek, not the south."

"Yeah, I can see that," Derrick said.

"This one directly across from the mine entrance is one of the larger ones," Mike continued. "Just with what I saw I'd rough estimate it would be worth mining over to. Just what I saw was enough to extend the mine for probably five years and make a profit. Start a new mine, probably not. But it's worth extending. And like I said, beyond my Sight it's just fog. But Sense extends farther, and I could Sense ore all along the curve. There's a shit ton of copper in them thar hills."

He looked at his father and shook his head.

"I'm not going to ruin the area, Dad," Mike said. "I'm going to keep it small footprint. Smaller than it currently is, if I can do it."

"Part of what I was thinking, yeah," Derrick said.

"Then there's the hydrology question," Derrick continued. "What forms are going to have to be filed. It's on the same watershed. We may be able to get by with the current hydrology profile."

"That's one thing I'm going to change," Mike said. "Helonic is pumping out into a catchment and letting it settle. I'm going to filter. I'll still make money and it's going to keep the river from getting contaminated. Also, I don't think much of their loading area. There's contamination all over the railhead. Environmental schmental. That's lost ore."

"What are you going to do about it?" Derrick asked.

"May have to ship out some water," Mike said. "Slurry will keep the dust down, which means less contamination and less ore loss. Which means we'll need permissions from the Montana Water Board. I'm also going to need a good mine manager. Somebody who is more into the modern thought process. Keep the damage down. I'll check with Asuda. But for right now, I've got to send them the code to start the process of seeing if we can buy it. Quietly. Without my name being involved."

"I'm also thinking about the legal aspects," Derrick said. "When it turns out you were the one buying the mine, Helonic is going to flip out."

"That will be fun," Mike said. "I can add them to the long list of lawsuits in which I am involved."

"Mr. Brauer," his secretary said over the intercom. "There's FBI here to see you."

"And what can we do for the Bureau this afternoon," Ahuvit said, looking at the credentials, "Special Agent Blatt?"

"Yes, Counselor," Blatt said. "Financial crimes. We're going to need all original evidence related to the Follett Trust. There have been numerous reported issues that may rise to the level of criminality. The US Attorney for the Southern District of New York has opened an investigation and may be summoning a grand jury."

"That's going to make our suit rather difficult to proceed, Agent," Ahuvit said, drily.

"We understand that, Counselor," Blatt said. "Sorry. But criminal takes precedence over civil."

"We will, of course, cooperate fully," Ahuvit said.

⊕ ⊕ ⊕

"...We already filed a plea for continuance," Wilder said over the video link. "I'm seriously pissed."

"Only to be expected with all the rocks we'd been turning over," Mike said, shrugging. "We knew this was going to take years. This just adds some."

"You're very calm about this," Wilder said. "I'm pissed off. Do you think they'll...actually do anything?"

"Yes," Mike said. "Look, Conn's on the hook for the most charges, right?"

"Yes," Wilder said. "We were preparing to hang him out to dry."

"So, he runs to a non-extradition country," Mike said. "Then he waits 'til there's a friendly Democrat president, like the current one, who is on his way out of office to give him a pardon. And he's back in business. If he faces jail time, it will be a few years of Club Fed and that's sort of become something with a cachet in certain circles.

"But none of that protects him from *us*," Mike continued. "*We* can pursue him and his money to the ends of the earth. We just have to let the FBI and DOJ finish their kabuki theater. I'm young. I'm patient. I have all the time in the world to torment Mr. Conn. In some ways, it's better that it drags out. Revenge is a dish best served cold..."

EPILOGUE

"My Demons" —Starset

"I'm still on!" Mike said as they pulled up at the river.

The gang had taken a bunch of horses and trailers up to the Fisher River country and gone riding. For only having done this a few times, Mike was starting to get the hang of it. He hardly ever fell off anymore. He could even keep up when they galloped. Mostly.

"You're becoming quite the rider," Marlene said, rearing her Appaloosa and holding a mare in the rear. The mare crow-hopped a few steps, then landed back on all fours.

"I'm just getting started at this, okay?" Mike said, laughing. "I didn't grow up on a horse like all you *Lakota*."

"You're doing okay, Mike," Rob said, dismounting and starting to remove his saddle. "But you've got to curry your own horse."

"There's a metaphor in there somewhere," Mike said. He threw a leg over and dropped to the ground, carefully ensuring he had the reins held tightly. His horse tended to want to go off on her own.

Mike tied the horse to the picket line they'd set up and pulled off his saddle and blanket. Those went over to the campsite. Then he got out the hoof pick and curry brush and headed back.

He stopped as he was starting to curry the mare and looked off into the distance.

"You okay, Mike?" Tiffany asked. She managed to put her gelding next to his mare.

"Yeah," he said, getting back to combing out the knots in the horse's coat. "I'm good. Never better..."

"You've got that expression again," Tiffany said as they were riding back to camp.

"What expression?" Mike said.

"The sad one," Tiffany said. "Aren't you having fun?"

"Lots," Mike said. "That's why I'm sad, Tiff. Not too long ago, I'd never have imagined in a million years this would be my life."

"What's up?" Derrick said as they were having dinner the next night. The small, round table was so much cozier than the massive dining room of the apartment. And they didn't have to fight over who sat at the head.

The group had stayed overnight and done more riding the next day through the area that Mike had bought. You couldn't cover a small patch of it on horseback in a day. It would take years for him to get to truly know it.

Unless the Storm arrived, he had them.

There were several groups camping in the area around Lost Lake and Mike made a point to visit with each of them and talk. Everyone was worried about the area being restricted. He placated fears on that and talked about beaver reintroduction. That met with mixed reactions.

But after a day they'd headed back to Kalispell. There was plenty of time to explore the vast wilderness that was now owned by a former ghetto rat.

Jane had been called out on a CPS case, so the bachelors had the house to themselves.

"Hmmm..." Mike said.

"You've been unusually quiet," Derrick said. "And you've got a different expression than your 'Mike scheming' expression or your 'Mike thinking about science' expression."

His father was the most relaxed Mike had ever seen, both physically and emotionally. He expressed genuine interest, in contrast to the quiet judgment he usually showed.

"Yeah," Mike said. "I've got the 'Mike is thinking about how much his mother would enjoy this' expression. It's coupled with the 'Mike still hasn't tortured Wesley Conn to death' expression. There's also the 'Mike is wondering what is going to come along to ruin all of this amazing joy' expression, which is along the lines of 'Mike wondering what the Storm is going to be' expression. But mostly it's the first one. The 'Mike thinking about his dead mother' expression. She loved horses. When she stopped riding it should have been obvious something was off."

Mike looked at his father's growing look of concern and shrugged.

"If you don't want to know the answer, don't ask the question, Counselor," Mike said.

"The Vengeful One" —Disturbed

"No, I wanted to know the answer," Derrick said. "So. I'm driving along this back country road coming back from a range that ISA runs out in the hills of Virginia and there's this chick walking along, carrying a pair of stripper heels, dressed like she really should have been on Fourteenth Street. Coming around a curve. Nearly hit her. But I stopped. Don't really know why. But I did."

They sat on the front deck, watching the stars and enjoying the warm weather.

"She got in, not even a flinch about it. I could have been a serial killer and I'm not sure she would have cared. Asked her where she was going. She said if I'd give her a ride to, yes, Fourteenth she'd give me a blowjob. I told her it wasn't really on my way but if she could handle a place to hole up that night, I'd give her a ride in the morning.

"Never did take her over to Fourteenth. She asked if she could hang out. I said sure. Figured she'd rip something off from the apartment at some point. Didn't really mind. It's not the sort of thing I worry about too much. The sex was easy, and it was good. She couldn't cook worth a damn.

"I knew she was worried about something. She didn't like to go out. We ate a lot of takeout or what I'd cook. She liked to stay in. Sometimes I'd catch her looking out the window, peeking from behind the curtains. Figured it was an ex-boyfriend or pimp or both. She would clean, though, and she was neat. That was good enough. It was nice to come home to folded laundry."

His father stared wistfully into the endless sky. He seemed almost euphoric, clearly remembering one of the best times of his life.

"Got her to a doc-in-the-box and got everything cleaned up. She didn't have anything permanent. Another surprise. And she cleaned up nice. I'd slip her some cash from time to time, but she never shopped if she could avoid it. I ended up picking up some stuff for her. Clothes. Women's products. That sort of thing doesn't embarrass me.

"We went out a couple of times, but she was always skittish. Looking around. Hiding behind her hair. I thought agoraphobia was weird in a street hooker. But it wasn't that. She was specifically afraid of something or someone seeing her.

"Then I asked her to go to the ball. That did involve a trip to buy a dress; she suggested Goodwill, and she made it look like a million dollars.

"But when we were there, she was really skittish. She kept pulling me away in different directions. I asked her what was going on. 'I didn't realize there would be so many congressmen and senators here.' So, she had problems in that region. Okay. Maybe former johns?

"We got our picture taken and left early.

"Couple of weeks after that I came home, and she was gone. Left me a note. 'You're a good guy. You don't deserve my problems. Take care, Anna.'"

He paused in thought, then shrugged. The walls came back up and the stone face returned.

"I was at a weird point in my career," Derrick said. "There I am going to Georgetown. That's generally a ticket to higher things. And...I could see, we all could see, we weren't winning. Not the GWOT, definitely not in Afghanistan, none of it. There wasn't any endgame. Nothing we could do about that. We weren't in charge of overall strategy and I'm not sure there was one that would or could work. But we could service as many targets as they asked, there were always more. Servicing targets wasn't going to win the war. It was just...servicing targets, then servicing more targets.

"So, I'd kind of been thinking about giving up on servicing targets and getting, you know, a job that didn't involve killing people. Like, an attorney maybe?

"If you're an attorney, you need to build clients. Go golfing at the country club. And it's useful to have someone to go with you. Play tennis. Hang out with the ladies. Back channel. Preferably someone who knows the moves. Anna definitely knew the moves. Though she was skittish at the ball, she knew the moves. 'Why, Mrs. Congressman, what a pleasure to meet you! Oh, what a lovely brooch, wherever did you get it?' I asked her about it, and she admitted to 'hundreds of hours of Miss Manners classes.'

"I'd spotted before that she wasn't trailer park or street. I'd pegged her as upper middle class, slipped down the ladder.

"But she wasn't on drugs. And she cleaned up nice. That's what was in my head when I thought about maybe asking her if she was interested in more of a relationship. Just . . . the sex was easy, she was easy on the eyes, and she cleaned up nice. She'd do well at a country club. I convinced myself that was all it was.

"Then she disappeared."

Derrick blinked rapidly clear up the tears in his eyes. He fought to remain stoic, but kept softening in small increments.

"And I missed class for most of the rest of the week. Ever heard that song 'Kentucky Rain' by Elvis? That was me. I was out on the street with that one picture I had, asking every hooker and drug addict and, hell, the pimps if they'd seen her. Of course, none of them would talk to me. I knew that going in.

"Couple admitted they had no clue where she was or what had happened to her after some time in an alleyway. Really hadn't seen her in months. The whole time she'd been with me. Since that night she hadn't been seen on the street. And she hadn't been back. Not in D.C.

"I finally gave up. Anna was gone and I finished Georgetown, put on my war face, worked back up to perfection, and went overseas to service more targets.

"'Cause it was the only thing I knew to do."

He shifted to work out some muscles, straightened, and glanced at Mike.

"You were never on my side of my desk here at the office. Were you?"

"No," Mike said.

"If you had been you'd have seen my background," Derrick said. "It was that picture that you showed me. If for that reason and that reason only I was willing to see if you were, in fact, my son. Mine and Anna's. I knew who you were, son, the moment I saw your eyes. And when you told me she was dead, a little part of me died.

"Because, yes, she was a prostitute and yes, she was all those things,"

Derrick said. "But there was something special about Anna. I miss her, too. Every *single* day. And every single day when I see your eyes it reminds me that I was crazy in love once. But the one good thing that came of it was you, son. And I wish she could see what you've become."

"Thank you," Mike said, softly. "*Dad.*"

All at once, sorrow transformed into seething rage.

"Which means we need to do something *really* bad to Wesley Conn," Derrick said. "I have dreams."

"That will be taken care of by others," Mike said grimly. "The matter of Wesley Conn has been *delegated.*"

"Oh?"

"We need to keep our hands clean on Conn," Mike said. "For now. We're too close to him. Anything that overtly happens to him, we're the obvious suspects and the Society will use that.

"But ... things *are* going to happen and they're going to start happening very soon. Remember that night I said I had some Gondola skullduggery to do? The skullduggery was breaking into his apartment ..."

Conn opened his personal safe and started taking out valuables. The cash and jewels were less important than the files, ledgers, and hard drive.

He put them all in a security briefcase, took one look out the windows of his apartment, and headed for the door.

The limo took him to an airport where he boarded a chartered Gulfstream G650. In less than an hour since he found out an arrest warrant was being issued, he was in international airspace on a non-US aircraft that *wasn't* going to turn around.

He opened up the security briefcase and pulled out the hard drive. With the *kompromat* on that alone he was going to be able to arrange a pardon. All he'd need is a reasonable president on his way out ...

When he checked it, the software simply stated: NO FILES FOUND.

"What the *fuck* ...?"

"... so, when he checks it, if he's not in New York it will show 'no files found,'" Mike said, taking a bite of steak. "They erase automatically when he opens it outside of the continental US ..."

⊕ ⊕ ⊕

Conn started to worry and pulled up his offshore accounts . . .

". . . which we drained as soon as he ran," Mike said, taking a bite of broccoli. "We'd just been waiting . . ."

"WHAT THE FUCK?"

". . . and we leaked that we had copies of his membership list to the Society as well as Initiation Ritual videos. They managed to 'hack,'" Mike said with air quotes, "one of our servers . . ."

Wesley Conn looked at the text message from his Society contact in Switzerland and blanched.
"Tell the pilot we need to divert," he said. "We can't go to Switzerland."
"To where, sir?" the attendant asked.
"Uh . . ."

"The best way to get people to believe something is to let them steal it," Mike said, finishing off his potatoes. "Bottom line is, we'll let him run for a while. His *kompromat* insurance policy is gone, his accounts in the US are frozen. We stole all his offshore black accounts, which is mostly my money anyway, but I just donated it to Gondola. Baby needs shoes. And he'll keep running until his money and contacts run out."
"Then bring him back to the US?" Derrick said.
"Oh, no," Mike said, shaking his head. "No, no, no. Perish the thought. First, some Democrat president will just pardon him if we do that. He's still a full member of the Society. They'll forgive him for losing the membership list. He's actually capable and they have the same problem with membership that we have. So, they'll arrange a pardon and won't kill him.
"Second, American prisons are just too *nice*. All the DOJ has on him is financial crimes. That's Club Fed. Not good enough. Otherwise, I'd just let the Society take care of him . . ."

When Dion Bafundo entered his condo, it was apparent something was wrong. The air felt . . . off.
Walking in through the marble-floored foyer, he saw the doors to the balcony were open.

Stupid housekeeper.

He walked over to close them, and two very large men closed in on either side. A third man, the well-dressed but rough-looking Thomas Leeth, strolled up behind them. Dion had never formally met the man but knew him well by reputation. A visit from Leeth only meant one thing.

"Sorry about this, Dion," Mr. Leeth said. "But you're facing disbarment and prison, and you just know too much."

"Leeth, no!" Dion said as the men dragged him to the railing. "I'm not going to talk!"

"So sad," Mr. Leeth said, turning away.

The lawyer's feet did *not* touch the edge as he hurtled into thin air.

"Don't get comfortable, gentleman," Leeth said as he walked to the door. "We still have Mr. Spoon to deal with tonight..."

"We have something *better* planned for Mr. Conn," Mike said, wiping up his plate. "Remember, Bratva doesn't like him, either. Eventually, when we've run him for a while seeing who he meets, picking up additional members, we'll give him to Bratva. And *they* won't kill him, either. They'll *disappear* him. Into the Russian prison system."

"Ouch," Derrick said, nodding. "That is..."

"The gulag archipelago never went away," Mike said. "There will be orders to ensure that he lives. You don't just *murder* someone like Conn. The burn ward isn't good enough for him. You keep him wallowing in freakish misery, doing manual labor, cutting trees in a pine forest in Siberia, being beaten not *quite* to death by the Bratva prisoners on a more or less daily basis, for the rest of his *life*. And you make sure that life is a long one. Why kill someone when you can torture them for simply *years*? And just... delegate it."

"I love you, son," Derrick said, mock sniffing and wiping his eyes. "You make me so proud! The best I was coming up with was waterboarding or possibly an ant mound and some honey!"

"It's in my blood," Mike said, a touch sadly. "I'm what you get when you cross Sioux and Follett: two bad, motherfuckin' lines of blood..."

"Line of Blood" —Ty Stone